THE BIG SIX

THE BIG SIX

ARTHUR RANSOME

"But who are the Big Six?" asked Pete.

"It's the Big Five really," said Dorothea. "They are the greatest detectives in the world. They sit in their cubby-holes in Scotland Yard and solve one mystery after another."

"But why Six?"

"There are only five of them and there are six of us," said Dorothea.

RED FOX

A Red Fox Book

Published by Random House Children's Books
20 Vauxhall Bridge Road, London SW1V 2SA

A division of Random House UK Ltd
London Melbourne Sydney Auckland
Johannesburg and agencies throughout the world

First published by Jonathan Cape 1940
Puffin edition 1970

Red Fox edition 1993
Copyright © Arthur Ransome 1940

3 5 7 9 10 8 6 4 2

Set in Linotype Century Schoolbook by
Falcon Graphic Art Ltd, Wallington, Surrey

Printed and bound in Great Britain by
Cox & Wyman Ltd, Reading, Berkshire

RANDOM HOUSE UK Limited Reg. No. 954009

Papers used by Random House UK Limited
are natural, recyclable products made from wood grown in
sustainable forests. The manufacturing processes conform to
the environmental regulations of the country of origin

ISBN 0 09 996370 1

TO
MARGARET AND CHARLES RENOLD

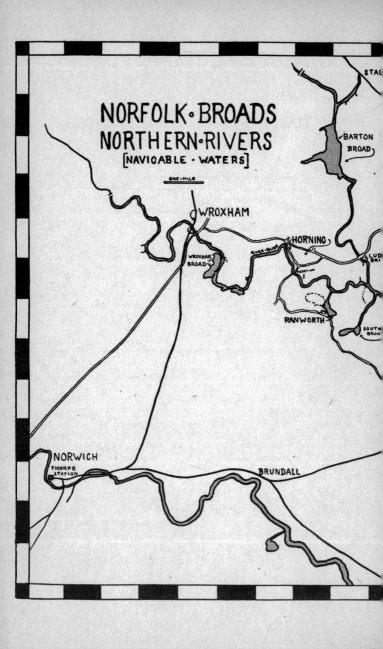

NORFOLK · BROADS
NORTHERN · RIVERS
[NAVIGABLE · WATERS]

ONE · MILE

STAL

BARTON
BROAD

WROXHAM

HORNING

LUDE
BRI

WROXHAM
BROAD

RIVER · BURE

FERRY · INN

RANWORTH

SOUTH
BROAD

NORWICH

THORPE
STATION

BRUNDALL

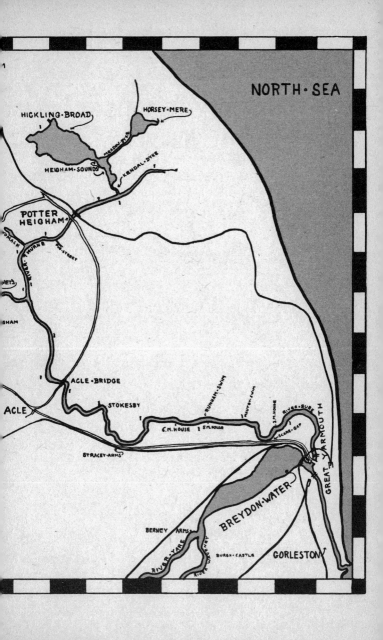

CONTENTS

ILLUSTRATIONS

AT THE STAITHE

CHAPTER I

OUT OF THE DENTIST'S WINDOW

PETE had a loose tooth, and could not keep his tongue from jiggling it.

The day had been warm and sunny, one of those pleasant days that so often come towards the end of the summer holidays. The season for hiring boats on the Norfolk Broads was nearly over and there were only two vessels moored beside the staithe. The staithe? Everyone knows the staithe, where boats tie up when calling at Horning. Everyone knows the inn at the bend of the river above it, and the boatbuilders' sheds below it, and the bit of green grass beside it, and the pump by the old brick wall, and the road with the shops on the further side of it. The staithe is the centre of that riverside world. In midsummer it is a crowded place, what with boats coming and boats going and visitors from up and down the river stepping ashore there as if in a foreign port. But on this September day there were two boats only. One of them was a motor cruiser that had done its season's work and was waiting to be hauled up into Jonnatt's shed for the winter. The other was the *Death and Glory*, which belonged to Joe, Bill and Pete, who were all the sons of boatbuilders and had spent the last few weeks being boatbuilders themselves.

The *Death and Glory* was unlike any other boat on the river. In the spring she had been no more

than an old ship's boat. Then she had been given
a new mast and sail and an awning, so that Joe,
Bill and Pete and Joe's white rat could camp in
her at night. But now they had built a cabin-top
on her, and decked her forrard, and Joe's father
had made a tabernacle for their mast so that they
could lower it for going under bridges. They had
made three bunks for themselves inside. They had
even got hold of a rusty old stove and cleaned it up
and fixed it inside the cabin with a pipe coming out
through a hole in the roof. They had had trouble
over getting the stove to draw but had got over it
in the end by fitting a tall earthenware chimney
pot over the pipe. Even then they had found the
smoke blowing back into the cabin, so Joe had
made a conical tin cap with three legs to it to
hold it off the top of the chimney. This worked very
well, and if the *Death and Glory* was the only ship
on the river with an earthenware chimney with a
mushroom top to it, her owners did not care. They
would be able to sit over a fire in their snug cabin
even in the winter, and all through this warm day
they had been looking forward to lighting up in the
cool of the evening. In old days at the masthead
there had been a black flag, but this summer
they had given up piracy, and they now flew a
white flag with a coot on it to show that they
were members of the Coot Club started by Tom
Dudgeon, the doctor's son. On the cabin-top was
a narrow board fixed up on edge with "SALVAGE
COMPANY" painted on each side of it. There was
a small flagstaff at her bows with a white three
cornered flag with the letters "B.P.S." to show
that the *Death and Glory* was a patrol boat of

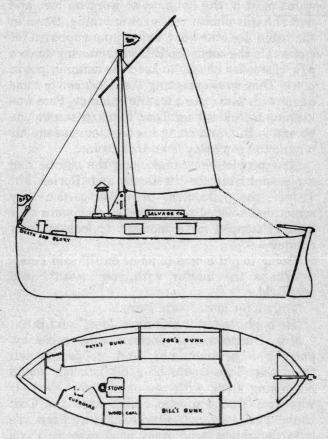

THE *DEATH AND GLORY* INSIDE AND OUT

the Bird Protection Society, which was really the most important part of the Coot Club. They had spent most of the holidays at work on her, and now she was almost ready for anything. Down in the cabin Joe was busy fixing up a cupboard for stores. On the cabin-top Bill was screwing down a pair of wooden chocks to keep the chimney pot in place. They were expecting Tom Dudgeon to come along with some paint for the chimney. Pete was keeping a look out for Tom, handing screws one by one to Bill, and doing his best to persuade his tongue to keep away from that tooth.

Most people who came along the staithe had a pleasant word for the Death and Glories. Mr. Tedder, the policeman, in whose garden they sometimes weeded when Pete wanted worms for fishing, stopped for a moment to look at their chimney.

"Going to put a coat of paint on it," said Pete.

"What's the matter with your tooth?" said Mr. Tedder.

"Only a bit loose," said Pete.

"He ought to out it and have done," said Bill.

Mrs. Dudgeon, the doctor's wife, came by, pushing a perambulator, and stopped to tell them that Tom would be a bit late but would be coming along with the paint before dark. It was Tom Dudgeon who had started the Coot Club, with Port and Starboard, Mr. Farland's twin daughters, who were now away in Paris instead of crewing in their father's little racing boat. It was Tom Dudgeon who had set them all bird protecting. It was Tom Dudgeon who had had to cast off the moorings of the *Margoletta*, a big motor cruiser, because her crew of noisy Hullabaloos had moored her over No. 7 nest, the nest of a coot with a white feather, and so had cut her off from her chicks. After that he had been chased all over the Broads, and the Death and Glories had had a share in saving him from his enemies.

"My word," said Mrs. Dudgeon. "She does look fine now you've got the cabin painted."

"We'll be going a voyage soon," said Pete.

"Why, Pete," said Mrs. Dudgeon. "What have you done to your teeth?"

"Bit loose, one of 'em," said Pete uncomfortably.

"Don't swallow it," said Mrs. Dudgeon, and passed on to say a word to Mrs. Barrable, who had taken a bungalow in the village and was busy at the moment making a painting of Horning Reach, sitting at her easel on the staithe, while her plump pug-dog, William, snored at her feet. She too was a friend of the Death and Glories, and, as Admiral of the *Teasel*, had had a share in the adventures of the spring.

The only passers by who did not have a friendly word for the Death and Glories were a couple of larger boys who strolled along the staithe, stood for a moment in front of Mrs. Barrable's easel so that she had to stop her painting till they moved on, and raised their voices so that Bill and Pete, busy on the cabin-top, could not help hearing them.

"Interfering young pups," said one of the two larger boys.

"What business is it of theirs?" said the other.

Pete, sitting on the cabin-top, looked over his shoulder.

"Hear that George Owdon?" he whispered.

"I hear him," said Bill.

"What's that other?" said Pete.

"Same sort," said Bill. "He's visiting at George's uncle's."

"Lucky it's not the nesting season," said Pete and gently jiggled his loose tooth with the tip of his tongue.

"If you jiggle that tooth again I'll put you overboard," said Bill fiercely.

"Sorry," said Pete.

"George Owdon won't have much of a chance at beardies' eggs next year, nor yet at buttles',"[1] said Bill. "Now we've got her so we can sleep in her, come nesting, we'll be watching all the time."

Late in the afternoon, when the sun had swung round and the shadows were lengthening, Mrs. Barrable packed up her painting things and stopped a moment by the *Death and Glory* to say "Good-bye".

"Dick and Dot won't know her when they see her," she said.

"When are they coming?" asked Bill.

"Four days from now."

"We'll be ready before that," said Pete. "There's only them cupboard doors to do and the chimbley to paint."

"If you were to give that tooth a little bit of a jerk," said Mrs. Barrable, "I don't believe you'd really feel it coming out."

---

[1]Bearded tits and bitterns.

"We been telling him all day," said Bill. He banged on the cabin-top, leaned over and shouted, "Come up, Joe, the Admiral's just off."

The noise of hammering stopped and Joe crawled out into the cockpit.

"D's here in another four days," said Bill.

"Good luck," said Joe. "That bring the Coot Club here in Horning up to six. We been short with Port and Starboard away."

William, the pug-dog, was sniffing noisily along the boat, and put his forepaws on the gunwale as if to come aboard.

"How's Ratty?" said Mrs. Barrable.

"He's all right," said Joe. "PETE!"

"Sorry," said Peter, closing his lips in a hurry.

"Well, good night," said Mrs. Barrable. "I hope that tooth falls out before you swallow it, Pete."

"It's not all that loose."

"It doesn't look to me very solid," said Mrs. Barrable. "But I expect you know best. Good night. Come along, William."

They watched her out of sight, with the stout William walking beside her.

"That Tom's later'n he said," said Bill. "If he don't look out, it fare to be too late for paint. Rightly it's too late already. No use putting good paint to be dewed."

"What about grub?" said Joe. "It's that dark below you can't hit a nail more'n once in three and get your thumb the other two."

"I'm going to light up that stove," said Bill. "We'll do no painting now."

They tidied up on deck and went into the cabin. Bill lit a fire in the stove, Joe put a kettle on, and, after admiring the way the chimney drew and the fire roared up with a single match, they went out again to admire the smoke blowing away from the top of the chimney.

It was slow work boiling a kettle on the stove, but it saved paraffin, and when the stove was burning it was better sense to use it instead of lighting a primus in the ordinary way. They sat on the cabin roof watching the sun go down and taking turns to go below to see what was happening to the kettle. When at last the singing of the kettle turned to a brisk bubbling and then quietened while a steady jet of steam poured from the spout they went down into the cabin, made tea, lit their hurricane lantern, hung it from a hook in the roof, and settled down to a solid supper of bread, cheese, butter, marmalade (a present from Mrs. Barrable) and apples. Joe let his white rat out of its box and it sat on his knee on its hind legs, eating bread soaked in milk and nibbling at a nut which it held in its forepaws like a squirrel.

"She's snugger'n a wherry," said Joe, sitting on his bunk by the stove and looking into the forepart of the old boat at the cupboard on which he had been working.

"Fit to cruise anywheres," said Bill. "Pete! Do leave that tooth alone."

"That fare to drive anybody mad," said Joe, "seeing you sitting there goggling at us and jiggling that tooth like it were on a hinge. Bill, we're short of screws for that cupboard door. Can't make do with nails for that."

Pete sucked his tooth into place. "I got some," he said. "Three. And I'll get some more tomorrow.

My Mum promise me threepence when I out that tooth."

The others turned on him. "If you'd have said that before," said Joe, "we'd have had it out in two twos. Too late now with the shops shut. But if it ain't out before morning we'll take pincers to it."

"It's getting looser all the time," said Pete.

"Well, you out it," said Bill.

The sun had gone down and it was nearly dark outside before running steps sounded on the staithe and there was a tap on the roof of the cabin.

"Who go?" said Joe.

"Coots for ever," said Tom Dudgeon coming aboard.

"And ever," answered Joe, Bill and, after a moment's pause, Pete.

"Mind your head," said Joe, as Tom stooped in the cockpit to come in through the cabin door. He was too late. Tom was several inches taller than the tallest of the Death and Glories.

"I'll never get in without bumping if I live to be a hundred," said Tom, dropping down on Bill's bunk and feeling carefully to make sure there was room to spare between his head and the beams. "Sorry I'm so awfully late. Too late for painting, but I've brought the paint. I've shoved it under the after deck. Hullo! What's the matter with Pete?"

"Loose tooth," said Pete.

"He's been jiggling, jiggling it all day till we want to knock it down his throat," said Bill.

"And threepence coming to him when he out it, the young turmot," said Joe.

"I'm going to out it," said Pete warily.

"Well, you out it now," said Joe. "We won't look."

Pete turned his back to the others and there was a long silence.

"Outed?" said Joe at last.

"It won't come," said Pete.

"Let's have a look at it," said Tom. "Why, it's as loose as anything. Just give it a pull."

"Don't touch it," said Pete.

"Pull it out or stop jiggling," said Joe.

Pete did not answer.

For some time the others sat there talking in the flickering light of the lantern watching the red glow of the stove. They were talking of what they would do when Dick and Dorothea came. Of course it was a pity that Mrs. Barrable was living in a bungalow now instead of in a boat. But, after all, Tom had his *Titmouse* for sailing, and the *Death and Glory* was ready to voyage once more. They would be able to do a good deal.

"He's at it again," said Joe suddenly.

All three of them looked at the unlucky Pete who hurriedly withdrew his tongue and let the tooth drop back into its place.

Tom laughed. "Upper tooth," he said. "And just hanging. I say, if you don't pull it out you'll go and swallow it in the night. . . . And what about your threepence then? My mother never gave me a farthing for the two I swallowed. Get it out and have done with it. I read in a book once . . . I say, Pete, I know a way of getting it out so that you'll never feel it go."

"I'll out it myself," said Pete.

"Oh come on, Pete," said Bill.

"Don't waste it," said Joe.

"It won't hurt him at all," said Tom. He spoke privately to Joe.

"We got some fishing line," said Joe.

"That'll do," said Tom.

"No that won't," said Pete. He turned his back on them and fingered his tooth again.

"Come on," said Tom. "You get that line and we'll want . . . I say, Bill. . . . "

"Easy," said Bill. "I'll slip across and get one. Come on, old Pete."

They went out into the cockpit and Tom bumped his head again in getting through the door. It was very dark outside, but the short stumpy mast of the *Death and Glory* showed against the sky.

"It's not high enough," said Tom.

"She wouldn't carry more sail," said Joe.

"Even if he climbed to the top it wouldn't be high enough," said Tom.

"I don't want to do no climbing," said Pete.

"What we really want's a house," said Tom. "Come on. Have you got torches?"

"Gone pretty dim," said Joe.

"Mine's all right," said Tom. "I'll go first. The loft over Jonnatt's boatshed'll do. Where's Bill?"

Bill came hurrying out of the darkness. "I got it," he whispered to Tom.

"I'm going home," said Pete.

"And you a Coot," said Joe. "Tom won't hurt you."

They went along the staithe and in at the open doors of the big boatshed, moving carefully because of the rails that ran down from the shed

into the river. Tom went first lighting the way
with his torch. They climbed up the ladder into the
sail loft. Pete was still jiggling his tooth in the hope
that it would come out of itself. The others knew
he was jiggling it because every time they spoke
to him there was a pause before he answered.

Tom, avoiding piles of boat gear, stored spars
and spread-out sails, went to the window which
looked out over the slipway and river. Joe gave
him a coil of fine fishing line. Bill gave him a
brick which he had taken from the loose top
of the wall between the staithe and the road.
Pete sat by himself on a bundle of sail close by
the top of the ladder, jiggling his tooth in the
dark.

It was very dark in the loft. By the light of
Tom's torch Joe and Bill made one end of the
fishing line fast to the brick. At the other end
of the line Tom made a small slip-noose.

"Come along, Pete," said Joe, and Pete came,
wondering why he didn't bolt for it.

"You hold the torch, Bill," said Tom, and Bill
lit up Pete's mouth and that dangling upper tooth
while Tom carefully fitted the noose round it and
pulled it tight, with a finger against the tooth so
as not to jerk it.

Pete squeaked.

"That didn't hurt, did it?" said Tom. "I'm awfully
sorry."

"No, not bad," said Pete.

"Come along now and lean out of the window
and look down."

Pete knelt by the low window and put his
head out.

THE DENTISTS

"Can't hardly see the ground," he said. "It's too dark."

"Have another look," said Tom. "And mind you keep your mouth open. Just as wide as you can. . . . Wider. . . . " And then he just reached over Pete's head and dropped the brick out of the window.

"Oo," squeaked Pete. "You're hurting my tooth."

"What tooth?" said Tom. "It's gone."

"Why that's a rum 'un," said Pete. "It's outed."

"Hullo! What's that down below?" said Tom suddenly.

The next second there was a crash of breaking glass. Something heavy fell on the floor of the loft and Tom put his hand to his cheek where a splinter of glass had hit it. He felt wet blood on a finger.

Bill switched the torch about.

"It's that brick," he said, "and there it was, with the line still fast to it, and Pete's tooth still at the end of the line.

"Gosh!" said Tom. "There must have been someone down there on the slip. Hi! Hullo!"

There was no answer.

"There's nobody there," said Joe. "They all gone home long since."

"Well, that brick didn't bounce," said Tom. "Somebody threw it back. Luckily I didn't kill him, dropping it on his head."

"He cut your cheek proper," said Bill, throwing the light on Tom's face. "And don't you spit blood on Jonnatt's sails, young Pete."

"Come on down and see who's about," said Tom. "And we ought to put that brick back."

"Keep the bit of line," said Joe. "That's a good line."

"Let's have my tooth," said Pete, and put it in his pocket.

They went carefully down the ladder into the shed and threw the light into every corner of it. Nobody was lurking there among the stored boats.

"Whoever it was must have cleared out when he heard the glass smash," said Tom. "Well, it's my fault. I'll have to pay for it anyway. It can't be helped."

"Your face is still bleeding," said Bill.

"Bother it," said Tom. "I hope to goodness we haven't got any blood on those sails."

"It's outed," said Pete joyfully. "That's worth threepence in the morning when I see my Mum. If I'd have known it were as easy as that."

They walked along to the end of the staithe where that cruiser was moored ready to be taken into the boatshed for the winter. No. There was nobody about. They went back to the *Death and Glory*. They told Pete that even if his tooth had left a gap he needn't keep his tongue in it. They sat there, wondering who it could have been who had so nearly had a brick on his head. At last Tom went home to look for iodine, and the crew of the *Death and Glory* settled down for the night.

CHAPTER II

FIRST SIGN OF TROUBLE

"Somebody's been up early," said Bill, sputtering and blowing after dipping his head in a bucket of water. "Never heard 'em shift that cruiser."

Joe and Pete crawled out into the cockpit, and rubbed the sleep from their eyes. The *Death and Glory* was alone at the staithe. The motor cruiser, their neighbour of the night before, that had been tied up ready to be dismantled and taken into Jonnatt's shed, was gone.

"Quiet about it, they was," said Joe. "Getting her into the shed too. Why, that old capstan squeak like billyo. Somebody must have give her a drop of oil, or we'd have heard her. Come on, Bill. You done with that bucket?"

"Can I light the stove?" said Pete.

"We don't want that," said Bill, who was sitting on the top of the cabin rubbing his head with a towel. "Keep the chimney cool for painting. We'll use the primus. You slip across and fill the kettle at the pump. . . . And keep your tongue out of where that tooth was."

Pete ran across the staithe and filled the kettle, passed it below to Bill who was lighting the primus and took his turn at the bucket when Joe had done with it and gone into the cabin to make sandwiches of bread and dripping. Then, when he had tied the towel in the rigging to dry, he went ashore once more but came running back to the ship when Joe shouted that breakfast was ready.

For some minutes they were too busy to talk. Pete found that the gap left by his tooth could be used for blowing on his tea to make it cool enough to drink. He was the first to speak.

"Wonder where they've shifted that cruiser," he said. "She's not in the shed. I just see."

"You haven't looked," said Bill with a full mouth. "They'll have haul her up inside."

"There's nothing in the shed more than was there last night," said Pete.

"Put that tooth away or you'll lose it," said Joe.

Pete hurriedly put his tooth back in his pocket.

"Worth threepence, that tooth," he said.

"Don't you lose it," said Bill.

"I'll take it home as soon as we done washing up," said Pete.

But the mugs and spoons were still being joggled overboard in a bucket when the *Death and Glory* was hailed by Tom Dudgeon.

"Letter from the D's this morning," he called. "I'll be back in a minute, as soon as I've been into Jonnatt's to tell them about that pane of glass."

Tom had scarcely gone into the shed before Pete sighted a motor cruiser coming slowly up the river.

"There you are," he said. "I tell you she weren't in the shed. Trying her engines, likely."

The others turned to look at her.

"We was sleeping hard not to hear 'em start up," said Bill.

The cruiser came up the river, stopped just below the *Death and Glory* and turned in towards the boatshed to come to rest on a wooden cradle that was waiting for her on the slip. Two of Mr. Jonnatt's boatmen were aboard her and a rowing dinghy was towing astern. One of the men shook his fist at the Death and Glories.

"Don't you boys know enough to leave boats alone?" he shouted.

"We haven't touched her," said Bill.

"Fiddling about with other boats' ropes," shouted the man. "Nice time we've had looking for her. Right down by the Ferry she bring up. Might have done herself a power of damage. Not your fault she haven't. And I know she were moored proper. I tie her up myself."

"She was here last night," said Joe.

"I know that," said the man. "What I want to know is why did you cast her off?"

The next moment he had jumped ashore from her foredeck and he and his mate were busy, making ready to haul her up into the shed.

The crew of the *Death and Glory* looked at each other and then at the empty space beside the staithe where the cruiser had lain the night before. The same thought was in all their minds.

"Tom'd never cast her off for nothing," said Joe.

"With them Hullabaloos there was a reason," said Bill. "Mooring on the top of No. 7 nest."

"But there's no nests on the staithe," said Pete.

"Nor likely this time of year," said Bill. "Birds don't nest in September."

They waited for Tom to come back from seeing Mr. Jonnatt. Tom would explain. Whatever Tom did was right. But when it came to casting off moored boats Bill, Joe and Pete, all sons of boatbuilders, felt that whatever the reason might be it must be a very good one.

They waited, minute after minute. It seemed as if Tom was never coming back.

He came at last, not on the run, but slowly, with a serious face.

"I say," he said, as he stood beside the *Death and Glory*, "what on earth made you do it? I couldn't help doing it to the *Margoletta* when there was no other way of saving our coot's chicks. But that boat wasn't doing anybody any harm."

"Well, we never touch her," said Joe. "We was thinking it must have been you."

"It jolly well wasn't," said Tom. "Mr. Jonnatt thought it was me. He was quite beastly when I went in and told him about the broken window. He said, 'So you *were* here last night. There's other things to talk about besides broken windows.' I said I didn't think we'd done anything else, and we didn't break the window really, only it got broken because we were there. Then I said there might be a drop of blood on one of the sails but I didn't think there was, and if there was much on the floor I'd clean it up. And he looked hard at me and asked if I was telling him I didn't do it. And I asked what. And he said, 'If it wasn't you it must have been those young friends of yours,' meaning you. And then he told me you'd cast loose the cruiser that was lying at the staithe and his men had gone down the river to find her. And he said 'This sort of thing has got to stop. I'll have to say a word to their fathers. . . .' "

"But we never touch her," said Bill.

"We never would," said Pete.

"We thought it was you," said Joe. "And we know you must have had a reason for it."

Tom looked at them. "Well," he said. "I didn't and you didn't, but everybody'll think we did because of what I had to do to those Hullabaloos at nesting time. Mr. Jonnatt said there was nobody else who could have done it. He said there wasn't anybody else about here after dark."

"But there were," said Pete. "There were someone who bung that brick back with my tooth."

"I told him about that," said Tom, "but he only laughed. He was very decent about the pane of glass. He said he had a spare bit handy and there was no need to pay for it, and then he said there was no need for fairy stories about bricks with wings either. He said it was an accident, and let it go at that."

"But that were no fairy story," said Pete. "Somebody bung back that brick." Once more he took the tooth out of his pocket and not without pride let his tongue feel the space where it had been.

"I told him so," said Tom, "but he just went on talking about not being able to leave a boat alone."

"Pete," said Bill. "You'll lose that tooth."

"I'll take it home now," said Pete.

"Whoever done it had a reason," said Joe. "Let's go and have a look."

Tom, Joe, Bill and Pete walked along the staithe to look at the place where the cruiser had been lying. There was nothing there to suggest why anybody should want to cast off her moorings and send her drifting down the stream.

" 'Tisn't like summer with the river full of boats when somebody might shift her wanting room to tie up," said Bill.

"And who'd send her adrift even then unless by accident?" said Tom.

"Middle of the night, too," said Bill. "She were here when we go to bed."

"Come on," said Joe at last. "Let's get that chimbley painted. Where's that Pete?"

"Run off home with his old tooth," said Bill. "Looking for his threepence."

They went back to the *Death and Glory*, rubbed down the old chimney pot and put on a first coat of Tom's green paint.

"That look a sight better," said Joe.

"Nobody'd guess it were a pot one," said Bill.

They sat about in the cockpit watching it dry, listening to the creak of the capstan in the boatshed and seeing the cruiser slowly leave the water and move inch by inch up the slip. Presently Pete came back carrying a big pie dish in both hands.

"Look out," he said, handing it over. "Keep it steady. Mum said not to spill. . . . And I got a pennorth of screws," he added, "and two pennorth of humbugs. I tell how we outed that tooth and she say it was worth another threepence if she had 'em but she hadn't." He passed over the bag, and took a paper of screws from his pocket. "Somebody's took and told my Mum we cast off that cruiser. I tell her we didn't and she say, anything like that and we'd have to come off the river."

"It were a silly thing whoever done it," said Joe. "And we don't want it patched on us."

But, as the day went on, it became clear that the news was all along the waterside, and that even the best friends of the Coot Club were ready to believe them guilty. After all, everybody knew by now the whole story of the Easter holidays, when Tom had indeed cast off a motor cruiser and been chased all over the Broads by the Hullabaloos who, in the end, had been rescued by the *Death and Glory* after ramming a post and nearly sinking on Breydon Water. Thanks to that glorious bit of salvage, no one had thought the worse of the Coot Club at the time, but now it seemed to be in everybody's mind that if the Coots had cast a boat off once they were the likeliest of all people to do it again.

Yesterday, and for many days before, everybody who came to the staithe had had a kindly word for them and a friendly question to ask about how they were getting on with the work of turning their old boat into something better. Today all talk was on the same subject.

George Owdon and his friend strolled past, smoking cigarettes. They did not talk to the Death and Glories but talked at them.

"At their old tricks again," said George loudly. "Casting off boats."

"Is that the sort they are?" asked his friend, and stared at them as if they were some ugly sort of animals behind bars in a zoo.

"You've heard of Yarmouth sharks?" said George. "They wreck boats and then get the credit for salving them. No better than common thieves."

Tom got hot about the collar. Joe clenched

his fists. Pete was on the point of saying "We didn't," but caught Bill's eye in time. The four members of the Coot Club said not a word and pretended they had not heard. But, out of the corners of their eyes, they saw George and his friend stroll up the staithe, look at the mooring rings to which the cruiser had been tied and look back at the *Death and Glory*.

"Talking about us," said Joe between his teeth.

It was bad enough to be suspected by their enemies, but it was much worse to find that even their best friends were ready to think they had had a hand in that kind of mischief.

Mrs. Barrable, taking William for his morning walk, stopped by the *Death and Glory*. Pete offered her a humbug and she took it and thanked him. He offered one to William, but she said that William did not really care for humbugs but could do with a lump of sugar if they had one to spare. Then she asked if she might come aboard and Tom sat on the cabin roof to make room for her in the cockpit. And then, sitting in the cockpit in the friendliest way, she said, "What's this I hear?"

"It's all lies," said Joe.

She looked at him. "Well I'm glad to hear that," she said. "You people must remember Dick and Dorothea are coming and I don't want them mixed up in any trouble. I don't want them to be turned into outlaws and hunted all over the Broads. Not that I don't think you were right that time, Tom. Those Hullabaloos were most unpleasant people. William thought so too."

"I didn't cast this boat off," said Tom. "And the Death and Glories didn't either."

"Good," said Mrs. Barrable. "I was a bit afraid you might have done. Your ship's nearly finished, isn't she?"

"Cupboard doors to do," said Joe.

"We'll be going a voyage in a day or two," said Pete.

"What are you looking at, Tom?" said Mrs. Barrable.

"Watching for the eelman," said Tom. "I've got leave to go and see him lift the nets."

"Think he'll let us come too?" said Pete.

And for a few moments, talking of eels, they forgot what people were thinking of them.

But Mrs. Barrable had hardly been gone ten minutes before Mr. Tedder, the policeman, came along and stood beside the boat, looking severely at her crew.

"Casting off boats again?" he said.

"No," said Tom. "And they didn't cast the *Margoletta* off either."

"I know that," said Mr. Tedder. "Weeding in my garden they was when you put her adrift. But weeding that time's no sort of evidence now."

"We didn't do it," said Bill.

"Your Dad won't be too pleased if it was you," said Mr. Tedder, looking at Tom.

"But it wasn't," said Tom.

"Well, don't you go casting off no more," said Mr. Tedder and walked away.

"They all think we done it," said Joe angrily.

Not all, however. Twelve o'clock came, and the three boatbuilders, fathers of Joe, Bill and Pete, walked by the staithe as usual with a group of their friends, on the way to have their midday pints at the inn. They too stopped by the *Death and Glory*.

"You cast off that boat?" said Bill's father to his son.

"No," said Bill. "We didn't. None of us."

"You hear that," said Bill's father, turning to his friends. "Bill never tell me a lie in his life."

"What about young Tom Dudgeon?" said one of the other men.

"I didn't," said Tom.

"You was here last night."

"I went home as soon as we'd got Pete's tooth out," said Tom.

"Pete's tooth?" said Pete's father.

Pete told the story of how his tooth had been pulled out by dropping a brick out of the window of the sail loft. The men laughed.

"Mum say it was worth an extra threepence but she hadn't the money," said Pete.

"Up to you, Peter," laughed one of the men.

"I'll be going short of beer," said Pete's father, digging in his trouser pocket. "But here you are. He's a good plucked lad is my Pete and know too much to cast a boat adrift. Didn't I tell you?"

"Well, if none of 'em did it, who did? We tie her up all right. The boat couldn't have cast herself adrift. . . . "

The men moved off towards the inn.

George Owdon and his friend came sauntering back and sat on the wall by the pump as if they had nothing better to do than to stare at the Death and Glories. But, now that they knew that their fathers at least did not think they had had anything to do with the loosing of that cruiser, the members of the Coot Club did not care what George Owdon and his friend might be thinking of saying.

"That make sixpence for one tooth," said Pete.

"Better loosen another," said Joe.

"What about getting at that pie?" said Bill. "Come on in, Tom. We've enough for four."

"I've got to be home by one o'clock," said Tom, looking anxiously up the river. "Good. Here he is, coming down now."

A small black tarred boat, wide in the beam and pointed at both ends, was rounding the bend by the inn, rowed by an old man with a mane of grey hair that hung down on his shoulders from under an old black hat.

The old man came rowing up to the staithe and brought his old boat in close astern of the *Death and Glory.*

Tom took a flying leap to the staithe to meet him.

"How go?" said the old man.

"Fine," said Tom. "What about tonight?"

"Bit late for you," said the old man. "Tide'll be working up till after twelve and eels won't be running till tide turn."

"That's all right," said Tom. "I've got leave. Can we all come?"

"We'll lend a hand," said Joe.

The old eelman laughed. "Come if you like," he said. "But come quiet. Midnight. Not after. But who's to wake you? Sleeping you'll be when old Harry draw his setts."

"We won't," said Tom.

"Not us," said Bill.

"Midnight then," said the old man, "for them as wakes."

He stumped off across the staithe to do his bit of shipping.

"Who'll come and dig me out?" said Tom.

"I'll do that," said Joe.

"I'll put the string out," said Tom. "But you'll have to be jolly quiet. We've our baby sleeping in the next room."

"Bat quiet," said Joe. "And you can't beat bats for that."

"And now I've simply got to bolt," said Tom, and was gone.

"What about that Pete?" said Bill. "We promise his Mum . . ."

"Get a bit of sleep in early," said Joe.

For a long time they had wanted to spend a night at the eel setts when the eels were working down the river. They had often visited the eelman by day, in the derelict old hulk in which he lived beside his nets, but they had never before had a chance of seeing him at work. When you sleep in houses people are not too pleased if you slip out at midnight, but now that they were living in the *Death and Glory*, Joe, Bill and Pete could for the first time make their hours fit their business.

False suspicions about the casting adrift of their neighbour of last night bothered them no more. They had something else to think of as they sat in their cabin eating their meat pie. They were talking not of boats but of eels as they finished up the doors of the cupboards and fastened on the home-made leather hinges.

They forgot about the bother over the cruiser

until late in the afternoon when a stranger, coming from somewhere down the river, sailed up to the staithe and moored his boat, a tall white-sailed cutter, just where the cruiser had been. The first coat of paint on the chimney had dried and Joe and Bill were standing by while Pete put on the second. All three of them turned to watch. The stranger tied up his yacht, stowed her sails, called out to ask when was the next bus to Wroxham, and was strolling off the staithe when he met George Owdon and his friend who just then rode up on their bicycles. The stranger half turned and looked back at his yacht and then at the Death and Glories. They could not hear what he said.

"Well, don't say we haven't warned you." George Owdon's rather high voice sounded across the staithe.

The stranger nodded and walked off.

George Owdon and his friend came nearer.

"You're to leave that boat alone," said George.

"We haven't touched her, have we?" said Joe.

"You'd better not," said George.

"Patching everything on us," said Bill.

George and his friend got on their bicycles and rode away.

A little later, the old eelman came back to the staithe laden with his parcels. He got into his boat and pushed off. Beside the *Death and Glory* he rested on his oars.

"Who's been pushing off boats?" he said.

"Don't know," said Pete. "But it weren't us."

"I tell 'em so," said the old man. "I tell 'em so. Well, see you midnight if so be you ain't sleeping. Mind you come quiet. When eels run they're like

other folk, want to have the river to themselves.
You can fright eels easy, same as other fish."

After an early supper they turned into their
bunks. Joe wound up the old alarm clock that
was still working as a clock though not as an
alarm. "Anybody who wake after eleven wake
the ship," he said.

"Better leave the lantern burning," said Pete.

CHAPTER III

EEL SETT AT NIGHT

"CLOSE on twelve," said Joe. "I'm off to fetch Tom."
He opened the door and let the cool, night air into
the cabin, where, for the last hour, the Death and
Glories had been stewing round their stove. Joe
wiped the sweat from his face as he came out into
the cockpit.

"Phew! That's cold," he said. He shone his dimming torch over the side. "Tide's still flooding,"
he said. "Plenty of time, if Tom don't sleep too
hard." He shut the others in with the warmth,
stepped ashore and, as soon as his eyes grew
accustomed to the darkness, set off at a steady
jog trot through the sleeping village. He slowed
up at Dr. Dudgeon's gate and, on his toes, crept
round the house till he stood by the Coot Club
shed close under Tom's window.

He felt for a dangling string and could not find
it. Had Tom forgotten? He switched on his torch
and by its faint red glow saw the end of the string
swinging just above his head. He took firm hold of
it and gave it a hearty tug. Nothing happened. He
tugged again. He picked up a handful of gravel
and threw it up against the window. Some of it
came down again on his upturned face. He spat a
bit of gravel from his mouth. Drat that Tom! And
then a whisper came from above him.

"Who's there?"
"Coots for ever!"

"And ever!"

"String must be stuck," said Joe. "Thought I'd break it if I tug harder."

"Sh!" whispered Tom. "You tugged hard enough. Nearly had my leg off, but I couldn't shout. I'll be down in half a minute. Stand clear. . . . "

A sea-boot dropped and then another. They seemed to make a dreadful noise as they landed on the path in the quiet of the night. Tom waited, listening. Then an oilskin coat floated down, slipping sideways like a huge bat. Then came the two ends of a doubled rope.

"Got them?" whispered Tom. "Give them a pull. Both ends at once."

Joe tugged.

"Hold them steady," came a whisper from above. "I'm coming."

The ropes jerked. Joe held on till a pair of feet were kicking near his head. A moment later the President of the Coot Club was standing on the ground beside him.

"Where are those boots?"

"I got one," said Joe. "And the oily."

"Here's the other," said Tom, pushing his stockinged feet into them. "I'll just get rid of the rope. They'll be awake before I come back." He pulled on one end of the rope and went on pulling, hand over hand while the other end climbed up into the darkness and presently dropped at his feet. Nothing was left to show that the President of the Coot Club had chosen that way of coming out instead of using the stairs and the front door. Tom coiled the rope and put it in the shed. "Let's have that oily," he said, and bundled it up to carry under his arm.

They went quietly round the house and into the road.

"Come on," said Joe, and began to trot.

"We're not late are we?" said Tom, trotting beside him.

"Tide's not turned yet," said Joe, "but we want to get up there before it do."

"I wonder if it's a good night for them," said Tom.

"You never know with eels," said Joe.

They kept up a steady, easy trot along the deserted road. There was no moon, but it was not inky dark and they could see the shapes of the houses against the sky.

"Weren't you scarey coming along here alone?" said Tom.

"I ain't young Pete," said Joe, and suddenly stopped short.

"What's the matter?"

"What's that light?" said Joe. "Somebody's up late."

"Where?"

"In there. It's gone. . . . Listen. . . . "

They had come as far as the first of the big boatsheds that lay between the road and the river. At this time of year, with the season ending, boat after boat was being hauled up into it to lie under cover through the winter. They knew that men had been working late there. But this was midnight and all the village ought to be asleep, except for Tom and Joe, the other two who were waiting for them at the staithe and the old eelman who was going to let them see him lift his nets.

"There can't be anyone in there," said Tom.

"What's the light for then?"

"It was a star shining in the window."

"Stars not bright enough tonight," said Joe. "More like a bike lamp or one of our torches. It flash off sharp while I look."

"Nobody's got any business in there anyway," said Tom.

On tip toe they crossed the road and looked into the shed through an open door. All was black dark.

"Listen," said Joe.

"Only an old rat," said Tom. "Come on, Joe. He'll have all the eels out of the river before we get there."

"Not with the tide still coming up," said Joe.

"Come on," said Tom.

"Run quiet," said Joe.

They ran on, as quietly as seaboots would let them, past dark, sleeping houses, past one after another of the boathouses looming huge between the road and the river, past Mr. Tedder's and came at last round the corner of Jonnatt's big shed to see two cabin windows glowing brightly by the staithe.

Joe slapped the cabin roof.

The door opened, a puff of hot air came out and with it the heads of Bill and Pete.

"You been a long time coming," said Bill.

"We're here now," said Tom.

Joe was already casting off the *Death and Glory*'s mooring ropes.

"All clear," he said. "Stand by for engines."

Pete and Bill took the oars from the cabin roof. Joe pushed off and came aboard.

"See she don't touch that yacht," he said. "Go

astern on port engine. I'll fend her off. Now then. Ahead both engines. Keep her in the middle of the river. Look out, Tom. Let's go in the cabin. No room for four in the cockpit when she's under power."

He dived into the cabin. Pete and Bill were standing in the cockpit, facing forward to work their oars. One nudge from an oar was enough for Tom. Bumping his head as he went in, he crawled after Joe.

"Gosh! You've got it warm in here," he said, blinking in the light of the hurricane lantern and looking at the glowing stove.

"Just snug," said Joe.

"Let's have a bit of air in," said Tom, opening the door which Joe had carefully closed, and sitting as near it as he could.

"Tell you what," said Joe, lamenting the hot air pouring out, "we'll sit on the cabin-top. Then we can shut her up to keep warm while we're with old Harry. We'll be there in a minute. He say not to come too near."

"Good," said Tom.

"Hi!" called Joe through the door. "Half speed with engines. Don't crack us on the head while we get out."

Pete and Bill lifted their oars from the water and held them steady for a moment while Tom and Joe came out and crawled forward out of their way. Then they set to work again. *The Death and Glory* was moving up the short reach above the inn, past dim, lightless bungalows. Tom and Joe, sitting on the top of the cabin, peered forward into the darkness.

"We must be pretty near the bend now," said Tom.

"There's his light," called Joe. "Easy with starboard engine. Full ahead port engine. . . . "

The *Death and Glory* swung slowly round the bend of the river. A distant glimmer light, reflected from the water, showed where the old eelman had his houseboat and his nets.

"Don't go too near," said Tom.

"I know that," said Joe, straining his eyes. "But we got to hit the right place. . . . Easy both . . . . " The *Death and Glory* slid silently on. "Half speed. . . . Easy. . . . " Joe stood on the foredeck holding to the mast and peering at the wall of reeds that showed a little darker than the sky. "Port engine ahead. . . . Easy. . . . "

There was a brushing sound as the *Death and Glory* nosed her way into the reeds. She stopped as her stem cut gently into the soft mud, and there was a sudden loud squelch as Joe jumped ashore with rond anchor and mooring rope.

"Gone in?" asked Tom.

"Not over my boots," came Joe's voice out of the darkness. "She'll be all right here." The dim glow of a torch showed where he was stamping the rond anchor into the mud.

"Bring our lantern," called Joe. "We'll dowse it before we get too near."

"I'm going to put some more on the fire," said Pete.

"Buck up," said Tom.

The four of them, one behind the other, led by Bill with the lantern, squelched their way through the reeds. The ground quivered as they put their

feet down. Every now and then a splash told
where a foot had gone into the water. Suddenly
the eelman's light showed close ahead of them.

"Dowse that lantern," said Joe, and Bill blew
it out.

"Who go?" A hoarse deep voice spoke out of
the dark.

"Us," called Tom.

"Made sure you'd be sleeping," said the voice.
"But tide's not turned. You're on your time. We'll
not be lifting yet awhile. Mind your step now. Give
me your hand. . . . "

They were on slippery mud almost touching the
black tarred side of the eelman's old hulk. Once
upon a time it had been a boat, but it would never
swim again unless in a flood. It had been turned
into a hut years ago, with a couple of windows,
and a stove and a chimney almost as simple as
those of the *Death and Glory*. In this old ark the
eelman lived and mended his nets and watched
the river, and baited his eel lines, and made his
babs, when the weather was right for that kind
of fishing. But the eel sett, a net stretching from
one side of the river to other, lowered to the bottom
when boats were going by and lifted when the eels
were running, was his serious business, and the
members of the Coot Club had long been waiting
for a chance to watch him at it.

"There's a step on the side," he said. "Come
in now, and better bump heads than stamp feet.
Eels don't fare to run with elephants stamping
round."

The old eelman's cabin was higher than the
Death and Glory's. Even Tom could stand upright

in it except in the low doorway. There was a bunk along one side, with a patchwork bedspread over it. There was a table under one of the windows. There was a bench beside it. An old Jack Tar stove was in the middle of the floor, nearly red hot, with a big black kettle singing on the top of it. A long-barrelled, ancient gun hung from a couple of nails on the wall over the bunk. There were shelves with all kinds of gear, weights for nets, coiled eel-lines with their twenty or thirty hooks stuck in a cork that rested in the middle of the coil. On the table was a big pair of steel-rimmed spectacles, with all the metal work painted white to keep off the rust. The walls were covered with pictures of Queen Victoria's Jubilee, pictures cut out of newspapers, brown and smoky with age, pictures of soldiers off to South Africa, and pictures of the Coronation of Edward the Seventh. The old man's interest in history seemed to have stopped about then, for there were no pictures of anything that happened later.

The four Coots stowed themselves where they could, Tom and Joe on the bench, Bill and Pete on the eelman's bunk. The old man himself poured water from the kettle into a huge enamel teapot. He stirred it with a spoon and put it on the stove beside the kettle.

"How soon will you be lifting the pod?" said Tom.

"Lifting?" said the old man. "Tide's only turning now. Got to raise the sett first. Give the ebb time to run and eels with it and we'll see." He took three mugs from nails on the wall of the cabin, filled each mug nearly up with tea as black as stout, slopped some milk in and added a big spoonful of sugar. "Two to a mug now, and one for me," he said. "Take a drink of that now. Why young Pete's gaping. Take a drink of that and keep awake and I'll nip out and haul up."

The hot, bitter tea scalded their throats, but after a drink of it, even Pete no longer wanted to yawn or rub his eyes. The old man looked out into the dark. "I'll haul now," he said. "Tide's going down. No. You stay here. Don't want you slipping all over."

He was gone. The four Coots came out of the cabin. At first they could see nothing. But they heard the creak of an old windlass. Then, dimly, they saw that the eelman was crossing the river in his boat. They heard creaking from the other side. Then they saw that he was coming back, though they could not hear the noise of oars. Presently, he was with them again, went into the cabin, told them to shut the door behind them, poured himself out another mug of tea, blew the steam from it and drank.

"You ain't never seen pods lifted?" he said. "Seventy year tomorrow I see 'em first."

"Seventy years," said Tom.

"My birthday tomorrow," said the old man.

"Today or tomorrow?" said Tom.

"You're right. Gone midnight. Seventy year today."

"Many happy returns," said Tom.

"Many of 'em," said Joe, Bill and Pete.

The old man chuckled. "Live to ninety we do," he said. "Another twelve year anyways. On my birthday seventy year gone my old uncle let me sit along of him by the eel sett same as you're sitting along of me. Above Potter was his old setts. . . . Drink up. There's plenty more." He filled up the teapot from the kettle. "You know Potter, you do? But there been changes since then. There weren't no houses at Potter then, saving the wind pumps. And there weren't no yachts, hardly. Reed-boats and such, and the wherries loading by the bridge. And there were plenty of netting then, and liggering for pike, and plenty of fowl. . . ."

"Did anybody look after the birds?" said Tom, thinking of the Coot Club.

The old man laughed. "Gunners," he said.

"What about buttles?" said Pete.

"Shot many a score of 'em I have," said the old man.

"Oh I say. . . . Not bitterns," said Tom.

"Many a score. There was plenty of 'em then, and then they get fewer till there ain't none. Coming back, they tell me, they are now. If I was up Hickling way with my old gun. . . ."

"But you can't shoot bitterns," said Pete, horrified.

"And why not?" asked the old man. "In old days we shoot a plenty and there were a plenty for all to shoot."

"But that's why they disappeared," said Tom.

"Don't you believe it," said the old man. "They go what with the reed cutting and all they pleasure boats. . . ."

Tom looked at the faces of the other Coots, to see how they were taking these awful heresies.

"But they're coming back," said Joe. "And no one's allowed to shoot 'em. And there'll be more every year. We found two nests last spring."

"Who buy the eggs?" asked the old man.

"Nobody," said Joe. "We didn't sell 'em. We didn't take 'em. But they would have been taken if we hadn't have watched."

"Some folk are rare fools," said the old man. "Now if I'd have knowed where them nests was, it'd have been money in my pocket and tobacco in my old pipe."

The Coots looked at each other. It was no good arguing with old Harry, but, after all, it was one thing for an old Broadsman to talk about taking bitterns' eggs and quite another for somebody like George Owdon who had plenty of pocket money already without robbing birds.

The old man caught the look on Pete's face.

"Old thief. Old Harry Bangate," he said. "That's what you think. And I say, No. What was them birds put there for? Why, for shooting."

"But if you shoot 'em, they won't be there," said Joe.

"When we was shooting them there were always a plenty."

It was clear that the old man would never understand why the members of the Coot Club spent their days and nights in the spring guarding nests and watching birds, and Tom was wise enough to change the subject.

"Tell us some more about what it used to be like," asked Tom, and the old man talked of ancient times, of the hundreds of wherries there used to be (he had been a wherryman himself in his youth), of regattas on Barton, of punt-gunning and smelt-catching on Breydon Water, of the great flood of fifty years ago, and of the fights over the chaining up of the entrances to some of the smaller Broads. No one noticed how the time went till at last, looking at a huge old watch hung on a nail, the old man got to his feet, opened the door of his cabin and let in a great rush of cool, night air.

"We'll have a look at them old eels," he said.

He lit their lantern for them, and took his own from its hook. "You'll want that in here," he said. "Two'll stop here and two with me. Can't have more in the boat."

"Who'll go first?" said Tom.

But there was no argument about it. The eelman's boat was afloat close by the stern of his old hulk, and he just took hold in the dark of the two nearest to him, who happened to be Tom and Bill, and told them to hop in and hop in quiet. A moment later he had pushed off.

Tom and Bill sat at one end of the boat, with the lantern at their feet. Before them a huge flat box went from one side of the boat to the other instead of a rowing thwart. They could see that the old man was leaning over the bows.

"How's she moving?" whispered Tom.

"Has he got a hold of the rope?" whispered Bill.

It was quite dark, except for the lantern at their feet and that other lantern in the eelman's hulk, which shone through the open door and showed them Pete and Joe standing in the stern of the hulk as if they had been cut out of cardboard.

The boat stopped, and the old man reached down with a pole that had a hook on the end of it.

"Here that come," he said. "One of you hold the light and t'other give me a hand."

Up it came, a long tube of netting, keeping its shape because of rings of osier fastened inside it.

Bill and the old eelman lifted the end of it aboard. Tom thought it was empty, but then, suddenly he saw that the narrow tip of it was swollen and shining and white, and he knew that the light of the lantern was reflected from the glistening bellies of the eels.

"Ope the keep," said the old man and Tom, holding the lantern in one hand, pulled open the lid of the flat box in the middle of the boat. The old man brought the pointed end of the net over the box, untied a knot and let loose a shining stream of eels. Then he pulled tight the lacing that closed the narrow end, retied it, and dropped the net over the side.

"Tremendous lot," said Tom.

"They're working. They're working," said the old man.

The boat was moving slowly back across the river.

"Have you got any?" They heard Pete's voice from the hulk.

"Dozens," said Bill. He and Tom were trying to count the eels by the light of the lantern. But it was not easy, for the keep was half full of water, and the eels were swimming with their dark backs uppermost and no longer showing their white bellies.

"My turn next time," said Pete as they climbed back into the hulk.

"If you ain't asleep," said the old man.

More tea was drunk, blacker than ever, for

LIFTING THE POD

the teapot had been standing on the stove all this time. The old man talked of eels. "Where are they all going?" Pete had asked, and Tom had told him about their spawning grounds in the far Atlantic and how the little eels on their way to England meet the big eels on their way back, and how the big eels live comfortably on the stream of little ones. "Cannibals," Pete had said. But the old man would have none of such a tale. Eels, for him, were born in the mud and went down the rivers to get a taste of salt water. "Smell the tide, they do and follow that down."

"What's the biggest eel you've ever caught?" said Tom.

"I didn't catch him," said the old man. "Not to keep him. But he were a big 'un, that warmint. I dart for him with my old spear and catch his tail, and he shake his tail and throw my old spear into the reeds, and he near upset my boat before he go off fierce downstream with a wash after him bringing the banks down like them motor cruisers. Did you never hear tell of the old eel that come up through Breydon Water to Reedham to swop crowns with the king? That were a rare old eel. And did you never hear tell of the sea-serpent that very near stick between banks going down between Yarmouth and Gorleston? Sea-serpent? That weren't no sea-serpent. Great old eel. That's what he were."

An hour and more went by, and again the old man looked at the big watch hung on its nail. Again he opened the door to the night air, but this time Pete and Joe went with him in the boat and Tom and Bill watched from the hulk as the boat moved slowly out along the net, the lantern glowing in the dark.

"They've stop now," said Bill.

The lantern was lifted up and they saw its reflections dancing in the stirred water as the eelman brought up the pod.

They heard Pete's voice, "Whoppers."

They heard the splash of the eels pouring from the end of the pod into the keep. "Gosh! He's got a lot that time," said Tom.

Presently the lantern was coming nearer. They were coming back.

"Hundreds," said Joe, shaking the water from his hands.

"Working nicely, the warmints!" said the old man.

"He's going to give us some of 'em," said Pete.

And again there was tea to drink, and the door of the cabin shut out the night and the lantern hanging from the roof shone more and more dimly in the steam from wet clothes and the smoke from the old man's pipe.

"How are we going to cook 'em?" said Bill. "Stew 'em?"

"There's stewing," said the old man, "and souping, and frying and smoking. But you won't try smoking. You want a close fire for that and to hang 'em in the chimney."

"We got a stove," said Joe.

"And what about our chimney?" said Bill.

"Let's smoke 'em," said Pete. "We ain't never tried smoking. And with our stove. . . . "

"What do you have to do?" asked Bill.

"Skin 'em and clean 'em and hang 'em in the

smoke," said the old man.

It sounded simple enough, and since the *Death and Glory* had a stove and a chimney it seemed a pity not to try it.

"We'll smoke 'em," said Bill.

"And you take a couple to your Mum," said the old man, turning to Tom. "Don't you go smoking 'em. Mrs. Dudgeon she like 'em stewed."

"I'd like to try smoked," said Tom.

"You can come and share ours," said Joe, and so it was agreed.

But by now not even the black tea could keep Pete awake after coming in from the night to the steaming cabin of the hulk. The old man talked on to the others and to himself but the questions came less often and presently stopped altogether. He looked from one to another of his visitors, chuckled to himself, refilled his pipe and poured himself another mug. And when the light began to show in the sky, and he thought it was time to lift the eel pod for the last time, he looked at his visitors again and went quietly out without waking them.

CHAPTER IV

MISLEADING APPEARANCES

BILL woke first. The eelman's lantern was burning palely. A window of the cabin was a bright square in the dark wall. Pete had slipped sideways against Tom as he fell asleep, and Tom had let him lie and had fallen asleep himself. Joe, with his mouth open, was snoring, not loudly, but evenly, as if for ever. Old Harry the eelman was gone, and gone without a lantern. There was the lantern of the *Death and Glory* on the floor in the corner. Bill moved to that brighter window and looked out. There was a glow in the eastern sky. Down river the water shone silver with splashes of green. The dawn was climbing, putting out the last of the stars.

The door opened and the eelman came in.

"Time you was in your beds," said he. "And I'm for mine. Eels won't work no more."

Joe stopped snoring and sat up suddenly, with blinking eyes.

"Gosh!" said Tom. "Have I been asleep?"

"I haven't," said Pete. "The last thing you was saying was . . ."

"More'n a hour since," laughed the old man. "Fare to be a fine morning, but I don't reckon to see much of it. Fish by night. Sleep by day." He poured himself out a mug of tea, sloshed some milk in, emptied some sugar after the milk, cut himself a round of bread, put a thick slice of

bacon on the bread, and settled to his breakfast. "Cold bacon afore you goes to sleep and you
won't wake with empty belly. Go on, now. Help
yourselves."

But not one of the Coots felt like eating. What
they wanted was sleep.

"Come on," said Tom. "It's daylight already."

"Wake up, Pete," said Bill. "Sleep in your bunk.
Joe and me'll work her down to the staithe."

"No wind," said Joe. "Engines."

"Tom'll steer," said Bill. "Hi, Pete! Don't you
drop off again."

The old man came out with them, munching
his bread and bacon. "How are you going to carry
them old eels?" he said.

"I'll run for our bucket," said Bill.

"I'll lend you a bucket," said the old man. "I'll
be coming down for a pint later on, and pick it
up." He went down to his boat. "When are you
going to cook 'em?" he said.

"When we've had a bit of sleep," said Bill.

"I'll fix 'em for you," said the old man. He
opened the keep and looked in. His gnarled old
hand darted down among the eels like a heron's
beak. Up it came again with a wriggling eel. Bang.
He had stunned the eel with a blow on its tail. The
next moment he had picked up his knife, jabbed it
into the eel's backbone close behind its head and
dropped it into a bucket. Again his hand shot down
into the keep. One after another he brought up
half a dozen good eels, stunned them and killed
them and dropped them in the bucket as easily
and quietly as if he were thinking of something
else. The Coots, remembering gory struggles with

eels they had caught themselves, cut fingers, tangled fishing tackle thick with slime, watched with awe.

"However do you do it?" said Tom.

The old man looked up. "Scotching the warmints?" he asked. "Practice," he said. "Practice. Seventy year of it."

He gave them the bucket, said they could come again some time if they would like another night, and climbed back into his hulk. They thanked him, and splashed off along the reedy bank to get back to the *Death and Glory*. The cool fresh air of the September morning made their cheeks tingle after coming out of that hot cabin, and by the time they got aboard the *Death and Glory* and pushed off into the smooth river, even Pete was thoroughly awake.

"You go below and have your sleep out, young Pete," said Bill.

"You go below yourself," said Pete.

Bill and Joe, each with an oar, worked their ship into the middle of the stream. Tom, though there was no need, perched on the gunwale right aft, and took the tiller. Pete, with a hand on the mast, stood on the cabin-top. Somewhere in Horning a cock crowed and was answered far away by another. A bream turned with a splash sending widening rings over the smooth water ahead.

"Gosh," said Tom. "That was fine. Let's do it again when the D's come."

"Wonder if the Admiral like eels," said Joe.

"That's only one of the things we'll do," said Bill. "We can take the old ship anywheres."

The affair of the cast off boat of the day before

had gone clean out of their minds. Someone had
cast off a boat. People had for a moment thought
they were to blame. But they were not and after
their night at the eel sett they were thinking of
quite other things. They rowed steadily down the
river, rounded the bend below old Harry's and
were half way down the short reach above the
staithe when Pete gave a sudden shout.

"What boat's that?" he said.

"Funny place to lie," said Bill.

"Must be a foreigner," said Tom.

There is just one place in that short reach,
just before the river bends round under the inn,
where the trees hang out over the water. It is a
place that skippers of yachts, even if strangers,
usually have the sense to avoid. And just here,
close to the trees, was a yacht.

"Starboard your hellum," said Joe. "We'll go
and have a look at her."

"Something wrong with that yacht," said Bill.
"Look how she lie."

As they came nearer, they saw that things
were very wrong indeed. The yacht was neither
anchored in the river, nor yet made fast fore and
aft along the bank, but lay askew to the stream,
held where she was by the top of her mast and by
nothing else.

"Hullo," said Bill. "She's that yacht was tied
up ahead of us."

"Salvage job," said Joe. "Get that rope ready,
Pete."

"How on earth did she get there?" said Tom.

"Drift up with the flood and catch in them
trees. Didn't, she'd be away down river. Must

have come adrift just before high water."

"Tide were still flooding when we came up, and it turn soon after," said Bill.

"She were all right when we leave," said Joe. "I see her. Remember, I stand by for fear we touch."

They were close to her now, and, looking up at the masthead of the yacht, the salvage company could see that a bough had worked itself in between the mast and the forestay.

"What are you going to do?" said Tom.

"Take her back to the staithe and make her fast," said Joe. "Can't leave her like that."

"Look at her warps hanging," said Pete.

"That chap must have moored her pretty careless," said Joe. "Gently now. Fenders out. Now then, Pete. Don't let her touch there forrard. Unship your oar, Bill." He unshipped his own as he spoke, leaving the *Death and Glory* with just enough way on her for Tom to turn her and bring her alongside. He was aboard her before the two boats touched. Pete followed.

"You haul in that bow warp," said Joe, hauling in the rope that hung over the yacht's stern. Both ropes came up with rond anchors on their ends.

"That's a rum 'un," said Bill. "However'd she get away?"

"Got to shift her sideways, same as she come on," said Joe, squinting up at the leafy twigs between the mast and the stay. "Let's have that tow-rope, Tom. Under where you're sitting. Keep a hold of one end."

He made the other end of the rope fast to the yacht's mast and told Bill to take the *Death and*

Glory to the middle of the river. "We don't want to bump her if she come sudden. Never mind the rudder, Tom. Better with the oars." The Death and Glories, boatbuilders' sons all three of them, were in their element. This was work for the salvage company. Tom, older though he was, waited for orders and did what he was told. There was no argument. Joe was in command.

The *Death and Glory* moved away. The tow-rope tautened. A flutter of leaves dropped from the masthead. Joe, watching, lifted a hand. Bill and Tom let the salvage tug drop back, and then took her forward again, as Joe pointed in a new direction. There was a scraping noise overhead. Twigs and leaves fell on deck and in the water, and the yacht shook herself free.

"Good work," said Tom.

"Tiller, Pete," said Joe. "Half ahead there, in the tug. Go steady."

The salvage tug moved slowly on towards the staithe, followed by the rescued yacht with Pete steering, while Joe coiled the mooring ropes at bow and stern, with anchors on the top of the coils, ready to take ashore.

"Slow ahead," he called as they swung round the bend under the inn.

A window was suddenly flung up in the inn, and a maid leaned out of it, shaking a duster. Horning was waking up.

"I'm casting off now," called Joe. "Stand by to haul in the tow-rope. All gone!" He ran aft. "Now then, young Pete. You go forrard ready to hop ashore. I'll bring her in."

The yacht slid slowly alongside the staithe.

Tom and Bill were bringing the *Death and Glory* back to her old berth a few yards lower down. Pete and Joe hopped ashore from the yacht, each with an anchor and warp. They were just making her fast to the rings on the staithe when two larger boys, on bicycles, came round the corner of the boatshed, rode along the staithe, jumped off and stood watching them.

"At it again," said one of them. "Well. There are two witnesses this time. Now then. Just you leave those warps alone. Lucky we were passing. You leave those warps alone. . . . Casting boats off and then telling people you didn't."

"Well, we didn't," said Pete. "So there. You can see we didn't. We're tying her up, not casting her off."

"Likely story. Why, we caught you at it, with the warps already loose. Come on, George, let's go and report them to that policeman right away."

"When we get back from Norwich," said George Owdon. "No time to waste now. Caught them in the act. And young Tom Dudgeon in it too."

Tom jumped furiously ashore.

"We didn't cast her off. We found her adrift, with her warps hanging loose. Her mast was caught in a tree. Look at the leaves on the deck. Anything might have happened if we hadn't come along."

"Salvage job," said Joe.

"Casting off the *Margoletta* was salvage, too, I suppose," said George Owdon. "You make those ropes fast again at once, and don't think you can cast her off after we've gone. We've seen you at it."

"We're making 'em fast anyway," said Joe. "You see we was."

"We saw you with the warps loose, casting her off," said George Owdon. "And I suppose you'll say you had nothing to do with all the others. I suppose you'll say you didn't touch the Towzers' rowing boat, or the green houseboat, or the *Shooting Star*?"

"What?" exclaimed Tom. "Nobody's gone and touched the *Shooting Star*?"

"Haven't they? You ought to know. I suppose she got away by herself, and the rowing boat, and the houseboat. Likely, isn't it? And this time you're caught with the warps in your hands. Come on, Ralph. You others'll be hearing about this."

George Owdon and his friend mounted their bicycles and rode away.

"Nasty beasts," said Pete.

"It doesn't matter a bit," said Tom. "We all know where we found her."

Bill was not so sure. "Who's to prove it?" he said. "They all thought it was us with that cruiser yesterday and we know we never touch her."

"What about them other boats?" said Joe.

"Harry Bangate knows we were with him all night," said Tom. "We couldn't be casting off boats and lifting eel pods at the same time."

"Lucky for us," said Joe.

They went back to the *Death and Glory*.

"You take your pick of them eels," said Joe.

Tom took a couple out of the bucket. "These'll do for me," he said. "Are you going to do yours now?"

"Going to have a sleep first," said Joe. "Pete's near yawning his head off again. Have to keep the fire going too, and who's to stay awake to keep stoking."

"I'm off now," said Tom. He too was yawning. "I'll be back later, when I've had a bit of sleep. Where's that oilskin?"

He went off, with the oilskin bundled under one arm and an eel in each hand.

"I'm going to sleep till next week," said Pete.

The milkboy rattled past the staithe on his tricycle. When he saw the Death and Glories he stared, hopped off, and wheeled his tricycle up to the boat.

"Hullo," he said. "Why ain't you down at the Ferry?"

"What for?" said Bill sleepily.

"Salving boats. There's half a dozen gone adrift and brought up there."

"We got to get some sleep," said Joe.

"Did you push 'em off?" said the milkboy.

"No," said Joe.

"Some of 'em think you done it," said the boy.

"Let 'em think," said Bill. "We been eeling all night along of old Harry Bangate at the eel setts."

"Get any?"

"Lots."

"And you didn't cast off no boats?"

"Get out," said Bill. "You leave us alone. We're going to sleep."

"Can't a chap ask a question?" said the milkboy and rode away on his tricycle.

Bill went down into the cabin and came out again with a board on which he had pencilled in big letters, "ASLEEP. DON'T DISTURB". "That's what my Dad put up when my Mum was sick," he said.

"Fine," said Joe.

They fixed the board up on the roof of the

cabin. Then, almost too sleepy to know what they were doing, they went below, kicked off their boots, turned in on their bunks without undressing, rolled to and fro to get their blankets round them, and began to make up for lost time.

CHAPTER V

DARKENING CLOUDS

"ASLEEP. Don't disturb." Someone was reading Bill's notice.

"What cheek!" said someone else.

"I'll disturb 'em," said a third voice.

For some time Joe, Bill and Pete, lying on their bunks in the *Death and Glory* feeling better after a few hours' sleep but in no hurry to get up, had heard people talking close by. Now a hearty bang on the roof of the cabin brought them to their feet. They came out into the cockpit to find the staithe crowded. The stranger whose boat they had rescued was looking at her mooring ropes and talking to George Owdon. The owner of the green houseboat was telling people how he had waked in the night to find himself drifting down the river. The two Towzer boys were telling how they had found their rowing skiff caught in the chains of the ferry. The owners of the *Shooting Star* were explaining that only luck had saved their little racing cutter from being wrecked against some piling, though they had tied her up themselves after sailing in her the day before. Mr. Tedder, the policeman, who had banged on the roof of the cabin, was looking at his note-book and sucking the end of his pencil. Everybody seemed to be talking at once but, as the Death and Glories came out into their cockpit, the angry chatter died to a sudden silence.

"So you're at it again," said Mr. Tedder. "What are you doing it for? Up late last night you were. I see a light in your windows. And now this morning you were seen casting off that yacht. . . . "

"Tying it up," said Joe.

"Why did you want to send my houseboat adrift?"

"What about our rowing boat?"

"You might have done fifty pounds' worth of damage sending *Shooting Star* down the river."

"We ain't touched any of 'em," said Joe. "Ask Tom Dudgeon."

"Tom Dudgeon," somebody laughed. " 'Ask Tom Dudgeon' they say. Why, it was Tom started this game."

"Where were you last night after twelve o'clock?" said Mr. Tedder. "Where were you? Casting off moorings and sending boats adrift all down the reach. That's what you were doing."

"We wasn't," said Joe.

"There'll be no peace on the river till they're off it," said a voice.

"What's ado here?"

"Dad," called Pete, as his father pushed his way through the crowd.

Mr. Tedder turned round. "Your Pete'll be in trouble over this," he said. "And it'll be you to pay the fine. Why don't you look after him?"

"What have you been up to, Pete?" said his father.

"Nothing," said Pete.

"Haven't they?" Again half a dozen people began talking at once.

Pete's father listened.

"Shurrup," he said suddenly. "Pete. You tell me. Have you touch any of them boats?"

"No," said Pete.

"Hear that," said Pete's father.

Mr. Tedder silenced everybody. "I'm making this inquiry," he said. "Where was this boat last night after twelve o'clock?"

"Up river," said Joe.

"Down river, you mean," said somebody.

"Up river," said Joe.

"What were you doing in her?"

"We wasn't in her."

"Ar." Mr. Tedder wrote busily in his book.

"They were ashore casting loose my houseboat."

Mr. Tedder waved his pencil to quiet the old man.

"What were you doing?"

"Catching eels."

"Eels! A likely story. Let's see 'em."

Bill said not a word but held out the bucket. Mr. Tedder looked solemnly at the eels in the bottom of it.

"We was with Harry Bangate at the eel sett," said Joe.

"I bet that's a lie," said George Owdon.

"Soon settle that," said Pete's father. "Here's old Harry now coming down the river."

The eelman was rowing steadily downstream. Everybody knew him, with his grey mane hanging over his shoulders from under his tattered black hat. They shouted. He looked round as if to see what they were shouting at, and rowed on silently till he brought his old boat in beside the stern of the *Death and Glory*.

"Done with that bucket?" he said.

Bill emptied eels, blood and slime from the eelman's bucket into their own and began sluicing the borrowed bucket over the side.

"Harry Bangate," said Mr. Tedder. "These boys say they was with you at the eel sett last night."

"And so they was," said the old man. "Eels run well, the warmints."

"How long was these boys with you?"

"They come before turn of tide," said the old man. "Twelve o'clock, likely, and they stay with me till daylight when the warmints stop running. Anything amiss?"

"I tell you so," said Pete's father. "They never touch your boats."

People on the staithe looked almost disappointed. Bill gave his bucket back to the eelman, who put it in the bottom of his boat, stepped ashore, and stumped off towards the inn. Mr. Tedder shut up his note-book, and looked first at one and then at another.

"Rum thing," he said.

"They managed it somehow," said one of the boat owners. "There's nobody else to do it."

"Two nights running," said Mr. Tedder, scratching his head. "There was that cruiser of Jonnatt's yesterday, and now all these."

"Well if it wasn't them," said the owner of the green houseboat, "it's up to the police to find out who it was. And to stop it. A pretty pass we've come to if I can't sleep in this reach without having to get up at all hours to see that no rogue's casting off my mooring ropes."

"It's all very well," said George Owdon. "But

we caught them at it when they were turning
this yacht adrift."

"And I tied her up all right last night," said
her owner.

"We find her with her mast in that tree,"
said Joe. "There's leaves on her deck yet. If you'd
been a bit sooner you'd have seen us getting of
her clear."

"You hear that," said Pete's father.

"It certainly looked as if they were casting
her off," said George.

Half a dozen people at once were trying to
talk to Mr. Tedder.

"Something's got to be done."

"Don't you keep an eye on things at all?"

"Police can't be up all night and all day,"
said Mr. Tedder.

"We'll háve to go turn about in keeping watch."

"We will if you will."

The crowd drifted away, the owners of the
boats that had been cast loose, George Owdon
and his friend, still talking to Mr. Tedder and
telling him what ought to be done as he walked
slowly off the staithe.

"Tom was right," said Joe. "They couldn't prove
nothing."

"Drat 'em," said Bill. "What about smoking
them eels?"

"What about breakfast?" said Pete.

"Breakfast!" exclaimed Joe. "We oversleep
breakfast. What about dinner?"

*

"Shove that kettle on the primus," said Bill.

"No need for anybody to go home. We got bread. We got cheese. We got apples. We got a tin of milk. And we got tea. Where are them sacks? Joe and me'll be getting wood for the stove and we'll be back, come that kettle on the boil."

Twenty minutes later they had breakfast and dinner all in one. Two sacks full of waste scraps of wood and shavings lay in the cockpit. Joe and Bill had taken the empty sacks to Jonnatt's boatshed as usual, but had been angrily told to clear out by the boatmen who were still sure they were to blame for the trouble of the day before. They had been luckier at the boatsheds down the river and had got a good lot of pitchpine, which always burns well, cedar which burns still better and mahogany shavings which they thought ought to make plenty of smoke.

"Chimbley's good and wide, that's one thing," said Joe. "We'll take the cap off. That's easy. Put a stick across and they'll hang beautiful."

"I'll bend up some wire hooks," said Bill. "There's that bit of telephone wire I save. I know that'd come handy for something."

Then came the skinning of the eels. This was done by Joe and Bill together. Joe cut the skin round the neck of an eel. Bill held its head in a bit of cloth to stop it from slipping through his fingers. Joe worked round with his knife till he had loosened half an inch of skin. Then, with another bit of cloth, he got hold of that and pulled. After a few slips, pull devil, pull baker, pull Bill, pull Joe, the skin peeled off inside out like a glove. Then the skinned eel was handed over to Pete, who did the cleaning, getting rid of the insides of the eel and the black blood along the backbone, while Joe and Bill were getting the skin off another.

"Mucketty truck," said Pete, scraping away with his knife.

"You get it all out," said Bill. "Poison a chap, that would, if you left it in."

The next job was to get the eels into the chimney. They took off the tin smoke cap they had made to prevent the smoke blowing down their chimney instead of drawing up it. Bill bent four bits of wire into S-shaped hooks. Joe held a stout stick while he hung the eels on it, and then, carefully, they lowered the eels down the chimney till the ends of the stick rested on the edges of the chimney pot. Meanwhile, Pete had lit the fire and come up on the cabin-top again to see how things were going.

"There's not much smoke coming up," said Joe. "You go down and stoke a bit."

Pete went below and came out again in a hurry.

"It smoke into the cabin something awful," he said.

"Bound to," said Joe.

"Can't help that," said Bill.

"What about putting the cap back?" said Joe.

"Could do," said Pete. "That'd stop it blowing back."

"That don't want to draw too well," said Bill. "There's plenty smoke coming out atop."

"There's plenty more in the cabin," said Pete.

All three went below.

Pete choked. Joe coughed. Bill wiped his smarting eyes.

"That'll smoke us right out," said Pete.

"You can't smoke eels without smoke," said Bill.

"They ain't half bad stewed," said Pete.

"We'll smoke 'em now we've started," said Joe.

"Try shutting the door," said Bill.

"Put the cap on the chimbley quick," said Joe. "We'll have the fire out if that go on blowing back."

Bill fixed the tin cap on the chimney. That helped a little but not much. At least as much smoke found its way out into the cabin as found its way up past the eels. But, as Bill pointed out, if the fire drew too well the eels would be broiled instead of being smoked.

Pete started choking and could not stop.

"You'd better get out, young Pete," said Bill, and Pete struggled out into the cockpit.

"Shut that door," said Joe, and Pete shut the door behind him. In a few minutes his choking stopped and he opened the door again. A red face showed through the smoke in the cabin and told him to shut it and keep it shut. He could hear that they were putting more wood on the fire. Clouds of smoke blew from the chimney. Presently the door suddenly opened and Joe put his head out and took deep breaths of air. "It's when the grease drop on the fire," panted Joe, and disappeared again.

Then Bill put his head out. Tears ran down his cheeks, but he grinned cheerfully.

"I'm going to fish," said Pete.

"Fish away," said Bill. "We could do with some perch. Joe and me's going to smoke them eels or bust."

"Shut that door," shouted Joe out of the smoke

in the cabin, and Bill took one more breath, and
shut the door behind him.

*

An hour went by and then another. Pete
sat fishing on the cabin roof. The eel-smokers
coughed and choked below, putting their heads
out now and again to save their lives. They had
long stopped saying anything. First one head
showed in the smoke that poured from the door
the moment it was opened, and then the other,
and then for as long as they could bear it, they
shut themselves with the smoke.

There is always a chance of a perch by the
staithe, and Pete was fishing with small red
worms that had spent a week in moss and were
at their very best. They were grand worms, red,
bright and lively, but for some reason the perch
that usually hang about the wooden piling and
camp-shedding were not on the feed. One after
another Pete kept catching small roach. Big roach
are not bad when you have nothing better, but
little ones are no good to a cook, and Pete put
them back in the water as fast as he caught them,
hoping every moment to see the two dips and the
steady plunge of the float that would mean that a
perch had taken his worm. But none of the bites
were like that. Now the float would slip sideways,
now it would sink a quarter of an inch deeper in
the water, now it would do no more than steady
itself in the stream. At each of these signals, Pete
struck. Each one of them meant, if he was quick
enough, another roach to be unhooked and dropped back into the river. It was disappointing, but

anything was better than being smoked like the eels.

"Forty-seven," he said to himself. "Or is it fifty-seven? Come on old perch!" But no perch took his worm. He began to fish not quite so keenly, and presently missed a bite because instead of watching his float he was looking at a small motor cruiser coming up the reach.

He knew at once that she was not a local boat. Like all the motor cruisers she carried her official number, and the letter in front of the figures was not B, meaning Bure, but W, meaning Waveney. She must have come up through Yarmouth from the south.

The cruiser was coming very slowly and the man at the wheel slowed her down still more when he saw that Pete was fishing. He even put his engine out of gear and the little cruiser slipped along almost silently. Pete had a good look at her, and saw that she was not an ordinary cruiser but a boat specially built for fishing. He saw rods lying in rests along the cabin-top, and other rod-rests fixed to the cockpit coamings.

"Wonder if he's had any luck," thought Pete.

He read the name on her bows, *Cachalot*, and remembered that was some kind of whale. He looked at his float just in time to catch a roach. He unhooked it, dropped it back, and almost instantly caught another.

"Hi!" called the man in the cruiser.

Pete looked up and down, saw nobody about, and realized that the man was calling to him. He lifted a hand as the wherrymen do, to show that he had heard. The cruiser was turning slowly round.

ANOTHER ONE TO PUT BACK

"Like to catch me some bait for tomorrow?" called the man.

"Could do," said Pete.

"Have you got a keep-net to put them in?"

"No," said Pete. "But we got a bucket."

"Best put them in a keep-net. I'll come round and leave you mine. I want a dozen or so good pike baits about the size of that one you just put back."

Pete took in his rod and laid it along the cabin-top. The *Cachalot* swung round, went downstream and came up again even slower than before and slid close by the *Death and Glory*. The fisherman reached out and swung a keep-net to Pete.

"Penny a bait," he said. "Twopence for really good ones. No tiddlers. You be here tomorrow afternoon. I'm going up to Wroxham for the night and I'll call for them on the way down."

"Waveney boat?" asked Pete, looking with interest at the little cruiser.

"Built in Beccles," said her owner. "This is her first season."

"Fine for fishing," said Pete.

"That's what she's for," said her owner.

He put the engine into gear and the slight wash stirred up by the propeller moved the *Death and Glory* where she lay. The cabin door flew open, and Bill's face appeared. He was very red, his eyes were streaming and smoke poured past him out of the cabin.

"What's up," he said.

"Money for nothing," said Pete, and pointed to the *Cachalot* which was moving off round the bend. "He want bait for pike-fishing and I'm to catch 'em. Penny each, and twopence for big 'uns. And there's a shoal right handy. I been putting 'em back one after another. How's them eels?"

"Getting smoked," said Bill. "And Joe and me's pretty near kippered." He came up into the cockpit to have a better look at the *Cachalot* before she disappeared.

Joe also came up for a breath of air, and stood in the cockpit wiping the sweat off his face. "This is the last lot we smoke," he said. "That want bigger chimbleys than what ours is."

"Pete's going to earn a bit of money," said Bill. "Is he coming for them baits tonight?"

"Tomorrow afternoon," said Pete.

"That mean we can't be off early."

"Off?" said Pete.

"Out of here," said Joe. "Bill and me's been talking, and we're going to go down river tomorrow just for the night."

"Can't go far," said Bill. "But she's all ready. Just a trial trip and to get away out of here. We got to get a bit of money before we go voyaging proper so as not to have to keep running home for grub. How many baits do you reckon to catch, young Pete?"

"There's plenty about," said Pete.

"You get him a dozen big 'uns," said Bill. "That's two bob. We could stock up well with that."

This was a heartening idea and Pete settled down to fishing for roach while the two firemen shut themselves up in the cabin to go on with the job of smoking themselves and the eels.

Now that roach were wanted, they were not so willing to be caught. The bites were further and further apart and towards evening stopped altogether. Only four were swimming in the keep-net, hung over the side of the *Death and Glory* and Pete was thinking regretfully of the dozens he had put back before he had known they would be wanted.

At last Tom Dudgeon, who had had his sleep out, came rowing up to the staithe in his little *Titmouse*. On the way up he had been stopped by the Towzer boys who had asked him what the Coot Club was playing at, sending their rowing boat adrift. Bill and Joe decided that the eels must be pretty well done and that they need stoke no more, but let the smoke blow out of the cabin. They came up and joined Tom and Pete on the cabin roof. They told him how Mr. Tedder and all the others had been at them about what had happened in the night.

"But you told them you were at the eel sett?" said Tom.

"We tell 'em so, and Harry Bangate come along himself and tell 'em too."

"They was still saying it was us," said Bill.

"They're going to watch the staithe and all this reach," said Joe.

"We're going down river a bit tomorrow," said Bill. "And if we get a bit of money we'll go voyaging, so if anything more happen they can't patch it where it don't belong."

Just then, the old eelman came down to the staithe, unfastened his boat, and made ready to row away. He looked gravely at the four sitting on the roof of the *Death and Glory*.

"You didn't play havoc with them boats *before*

you come up to mine?" he asked cunningly.

"Of course we didn't," said Tom.

"There's some of 'em think you did," said the old man. "Now that sort of thing you didn't ought to do."

"But we didn't," said Tom.

The old man said not a word, but dipped his oars and rowed steadily away up the river.

"You hear that," said Bill. "If everybody think that, we'd best be somewheres else."

"But Dick and Dorothea'll be here the day after tomorrow," said Tom.

"We won't go all that far," said Bill.

"What about those eels?" said Tom.

"Ought to be done by now," said Joe.

"Smoke's well blowed away," said Bill. "Let's have supper."

"They smell jolly good," said Tom.

Joe, not without burning his fingers, got the cap off the chimney while Bill lifted the stick with the four eels shining black with grease and soot.

"I got a handkerchief," said Pete.

"We better wash that before you take it back to your Mum," said Bill a few minutes later.

"They look all right now," said Tom.

"One apiece," said Joe. "You cut the bread, Pete." He held up his hands to show why. "Bill, look what you done to that kettle."

"That'll come off after," said Bill.

They settled down in the cabin to eat their eel supper.

"It's been an awful job," said Joe.

"Worth it," said Bill, smacking his lips, before taking his first mouthful.

"For some minutes there was silence.

"Not bad," said Bill hopefully.

"Bit sooty," said Joe.

"Try with plenty of salt," said Tom.

"Go on, Pete," said Bill. "Ain't you hungry?"

"Not clammed," said Pete.

"It's their not being hot and not exactly cold," said Tom.

"Some eels ain't as good as others," said Bill. "This ain't a very good one, that's all."

Presently they gave up and emptied their plates into the river.

"It'll bring the fish," said Pete.

They made up their suppers with bread and cheese.

"Worth trying anything once," said Joe.

"We say we smoke 'em and we done it," said Bill.

After supper Joe and Bill put up their rods and fished for a while with Pete. Tom watched. Not one of the three had a bite.

"Too many at it," said Pete.

"Pete's the fisher," said Bill.

"I'll get up early tomorrow," said Pete, "and catch 'em at their brekfusses."

Across the staithe they saw Mr. Tedder, George Owdon, his friend, and the two Towzers in earnest talk.

"They aren't really going to keep watch all night?" said Tom.

"That's what they say," said Joe.

"Let's get to bed," said Bill. "And we'll wake young Pete early."

Tom went off.

"I say, Tom," said Bill as Tom rowed away,

"you tell your Mum not to try smoking them eels."

"Stew 'em," said Joe. "Less work and better eating."

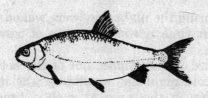

CHAPTER VI

TOW OUT OF TROUBLE

TWICE during the night they were waked.

The first time it was the noise of oars, long after dark.

Joe heard it and slipped out of the hot cabin into the cold night air, wondering who it could be, moving on the river at such a time. The rowers had gone by, upstream, but he could hear the regular drip drip of their oars and the creak of rowlocks, which, he thought, needed a bit of greasing. Presently the noise grew louder again. The boat had turned and was coming back. Dimly, in the dark, he thought he could see something moving on the water.

"Who's there?" he called.

"River patrol."

"What?"

"Watching to see no more boats get cast adrift. So don't think you can do it without being caught."

"We didn't. . . ," began Joe.

"What are you waiting up for?" said the voice.

The boat drifted by. Someone struck a match to light a cigarette and Joe caught a glimpse of a face.

"I know you, Jim Towzer," said Joe. "I can see you."

"No need to see you to know you," come the voice out of the dark. "Just try casting our boat off again and see what you'll get. What's the time, Jack?"

Another voice answered him.

"Half an hour after midnight, and they're up, watching for a chance. We'll report that. Come on, Jim."

The oars dipped again and the boat slipped away into the night.

Joe crawled back into his bunk.

"What was it?" said Bill.

"Them Towzers watching the river," said Joe.

"Good luck to 'em," said Bill sleepily. "Hope they catch the chap whoever done it and then we'll be let alone."

"They think it's us," said Joe.

"Good night," said Bill. "Lucky you ain't waked that Pete."

*

Two hours later they were waked again, this time by a gentle lurch of the *Death and Glory*.

"Chimney's cold," said a voice Joe knew well.

"They'll be asleep likely."

"Better make sure, Mr. Tedder," said the first voice. "They may be ashore and casting somebody's boat off this minute."

There was a bang on the roof of the cabin.

"What's that?" Pete started up and bumped his head.

"Tedder and George Owdon," said Joe in a whisper.

"All right, Joe," said Bill. "I'll see to 'em. You went out last time." But Joe was already out of his bunk and feeling his way into the cockpit. A torch flashed in his face.

"Only one of them," said George Owdon.

"Pete and Bill in there too?" asked Mr. Tedder.

"What's wrong?" asked Bill. "Have you caught somebody?"

"Not likely if you're all three here," said George Owdon. "Unless it's Tom Dudgeon."

"Tom never . . . "

"Shut up," said George. "Everybody knows Tom did. Is Pete in there?"

"I'm here," said Pete coming out and blinking in the light of the torch.

"Better go to bed again," said Mr. Tedder. "Just had to make sure where you was. This casting adrift's got to stop."

"Look here," said Joe, "we was asleep, we was."

"Go to sleep again," said George.

"No harm done," said Mr. Tedder. "But I tell your Dads and I tell you, you'd be better in your beds at home."

"Well, there's one thing," said Joe, settling angrily into his bunk. "There won't nobody come waking us tomorrow night. Wind come west and we'll be away down the river."

"Dead calm now," said Bill.

"There'll be wind in the morning."

"We can't start till that fisherman come for his baits," said Pete.

"You go to sleep," said Bill, "if you count to be up early. Good night."

"Good night!" grunted Joe. "Good morning."

*

As is often the way in fishing, getting up early was waste of good time that might have been spent in bed. Pete began fishing soon after seven. It was a still day, without a breath of wind, and until the sun grew hot you might have thought that there was not a fish in the river. After breakfast Bill and Joe went to their homes to collect stores, milk, cheese, bread and bacon. They also went to Pete's home to tell his mother, too, that they were going to take the *Death and Glory* a little way down the river. On their way back they went to Mr. Tedder's garden to pull a few weeds and collect some worms, for fear Pete should run short. Mr. Tedder came out to them.

"You?" he said. "Sorry I had to wake you last night. My Missus say I didn't have no call to. But we can't take chances not with police work. And see here. If there's any more boats cast off I can't have you coming and digging worms in police headquarters."

"Shall I put 'em back?" said Joe.

"You can keep 'em," said Mr. Tedder hurriedly, looking in the tin. "But we don't want no more boats messed about. Owners mad, and natural too, and it all come on the police."

"We never touch a boat," said Bill.

"Don't you touch 'em no more," said Mr. Tedder.

"Wish Tom'd never cast that *Margoletta* adrift," said Bill as they went back to the staithe.

"There was nothing else he could do that time," said Joe.

"Nobody forget it," said Bill. "Don't seem nobody never can forget a thing like that."

"Drat 'em!" said Joe. "Anyways we'll be out of this tonight."

"Come a bit of wind," said Bill.

*

All that morning Pete fished, more and more desperately, while the others tinkered in the cabin (doing no hammering for fear of scaring the fish) or watched from the staithe for the coming of the *Cachalot*, dreading to see her before Pete had caught his dozen.

Pete looked at nothing but his float. "A penny a bait and twopence for good 'uns." If only they had been biting as they had been biting yesterday when he was putting them back as fast as he caught them. At nine o'clock he caught his first fish, a good one. At half-past ten he caught another, not so good. Then came a long string of little ones not worth taking. Every penny earned would help in buying stores for the *Death and Glory* so that they would be able to go to distant places and not have to run home every other day for supplies. He spoke never a word, dropping the little ones sadly back into the river, welcoming the rare twopennies with a slow grin. He never even looked round, though once or twice he was too late in striking because of things said about casting boats adrift by people who stopped on the staithe behind him and watched, as people always do watch a fisherman, to see whether he was catching anything or not.

Dinner time came and he had five possible twopennies in the keep-net and three others that he thought might almost do. There was happily no sign of the *Cachalot*. The water was as smooth as glass, there was not a cloud in the sky, and the smoke from Horning chimneys trickled straight up in the still air.

"It'll be engines, not sailing," said Joe, wetting a finger and holding it up to see if he could feel a breath of wind.

"Come on in for grub, Pete," said Bill from the cabin.

"Gimme mine out here," said Pete. "That old float bob just now."

All afternoon he fished on, and did better. But now the other two were no longer hoping the *Cachalot* was not in sight but were wishing she would hurry up. The day was going, there was still no wind, and even if the engines were doing their very best, the *Death and Glory* was a slow old boat.

"We'll never get nowhere if he don't come soon," said Joe.

Towards five o'clock Joe suggested that they had better start without waiting for him.

"Perhaps he ain't coming at all," said Bill.

"He say to wait for him here," said Pete.

"We can tell someone to tell him we've gone on down river."

"If we tow them baits in the keep-net we'll drown the lot," said Pete.

"How many've you got?" asked Bill.

"I put in one since you count," said Pete. "And there was sixteen then. Seventeen there'll be. And a dozen of 'em good twopennies."

"How many he want?"

"Dozen or so, he say. But he may not want the little 'uns."

Nobody wanted to lose all the money that was swimming about in the keep-net.

"Tell you what," said Joe. "We'll have all ready

for shifting so we can be off as soon as he come
for 'em."

"What if he don't come at all?" said Bill.

"There he is," shouted Joe. "Go on, Bill, get
them ropes aslip. Put your rod up, Pete. Shift that
keep-net, so he won't mash it coming alongside.
I'll hang our fenders over."

The little fishing cruiser was rounding the
bend above the staithe.

"We got 'em," shouted Pete.

The owner of the *Cachalot* waved his hand.
He took his little cruiser below the *Death and
Glory*, turned her and brought her creeping up
alongside with his engine ticking over. Bill took
his bow warp, Joe hauled in on a rope the fisherman threw him from the stern, while Pete, lifting
the keep-net in the water, showed it half full of
silver, splashing roach.

"Well done you," said the owner of the *Cachalot*.
"How many have you got?"

"Seventeen," said Pete, "but there ain't but
twelve big 'uns."

"They look just what I wanted. Let's have
the net and I'll empty them into the bait-can."

In another moment a stream of fish was pouring into an enormous bait-can in the *Cachalot*'s
cockpit.

"Seventeen, you said?"

"Only twelve big 'uns," said Pete.

"Twopence each for the big ones. That's two
shillings. And five at a penny. . . . I'll take them
too. Call it half a crown. All right?"

"Rather," said Pete.

The fisherman of the *Cachalot* handed over

a sixpence and two shillings to the fisherman of the *Death and Glory*.

"All ready to slip?" said Joe. "We'll be off right away."

"Hullo," said the owner of the *Cachalot*. "Are you off on a voyage too?"

"We was only waiting till you come," said Joe. "No wind, worse luck, so we got to get going."

"Where do you want to go?"

"Down river."

"I'm going to Potter Heigham. I'll give you a tow if you want one."

"Gee whizz!" said Joe.

"Wouldn't we?" said Bill.

"All the way to Potter?" said Pete.

"Why not?" said the fisherman. "It'll be too late for me to fish tonight. So there's no hurry. Have you got a tow-rope? No. Better use mine. Here you are. Don't make fast till she's taken the pull. . . . "

"We know about towing," said Joe.

"Pete," said Bill, who was holding the bow warp of the *Cachalot*. "There's your Mum by the Post Office. Tell her where we're going and she can tell ours. We say we was only going a little way down. . . . "

Pete leapt ashore and raced from the staithe to the street. He ran full tilt into somebody coming round the corner of Jonnatt's boatshed.

"Sorry," he said, and dashed across the road.

"You look where you're going," said George Owdon.

Pete took no notice, but shouted to his mother, "Mum! We're off to Potter. Tell Joe's Mum and Bill's."

"Potter?" said his mother. "You'll never get there today."

"Got a tow," said Pete.

"You'll go to bed in proper time," said his mother. "Bill and Joe promised me that. Have you got plenty of food?"

"It's only for one night," said Pete, who saw himself being stopped and loaded up with stores while the *Death and Glory* went off without him. "We've got lots enough for that. We got to be back tomorrow. Coot Club meeting. That Dot and Dick are coming."

"Don't you do nothing foolish," said his mother.

"Hi! PETE!"

The shout came from the *Death and Glory*, and Pete raced back and jumped aboard just as the *Cachalot* moved out into the stream. Bill was easing the tow-rope round the little bollard on the foredeck of the *Death and Glory*. Joe was at the tiller. The *Death and Glory* stirred and slipped away from the staithe. Bill made fast. In the wide bend by the inn the *Cachalot* swung round with her tow. The *Death and Glory* was on her way, water rippling under her bows, the tow-rope taut, chug, chug, chug sounding from the *Cachalot*'s engine, and the well-known banks of the home reach slipping by on either side.

"Nobody's going to come waking us tonight," said Bill.

It was as if in leaving Horning they were leaving their troubles behind them.

"Remember when the *Come Along* tow us up to Acle from Breydon Water?" said Pete, and stopped suddenly. He remembered very well that long and

glorious tow, but that had been after the salvaging
of the *Margoletta*, and it was just because of that
old story of the *Margoletta* that people were so
ready to think that if a boat was cast adrift the
Coot Club must have something to do with it.

No need now to remember things like that.

Down the long reach they went, past Dr.
Dudgeon's house with its golden bream for a
wind vane high above the roof. There was Tom
hard at work with the lawn-mower.

"Hey, Tom," shouted Joe. "We're going to Potter."

Tom looked up and saw them.

"Going to Potter," shouted Joe.

"Potter?" shouted Tom. "I say, Joe. Dick and
Dot are coming tomorrow."

"We'll be back," shouted Joe. There was no
time for more. Already the *Cachalot*, with the
Death and Glory close astern of her, was passing
Mr. Farland's. On they went past the Wilderness,
on and on, past the old windmill, past the ferry,
past the inn. They came to the notice on the bank,
telling boats not to move at more than five miles
an hour through Horning. The fisherman looked
over his shoulder, saw they were all right and
waved a hand. The noise of the *Cachalot*'s engine
changed to a rapid brrrrrr.

"Full steam ahead!" said Joe gleefully, and
Bill laughed, moving his arms backwards and
forwards, as much as to say he was glad that
for once he wasn't an engine.

On they went, past the vicarage with the
water-hens and the black sheep on the lawns by
the waterside, past the dyke leading to Ranworth,

past Horning Old Hall, past the mouth of the Ant, past the old ruins of St. Benet's Abbey, on and on, recognising place after place, wind-pump after wind-pump, straight reach, sharp bend, one land-mark after another.

"How's this for her first voyage?" said Joe.

"There'll have to be an east wind tomorrow," said Bill, thinking that the farther they went the farther they would have to get home.

"Fare to be," said Joe. "Calm like this and a clear sky."

"Isn't, we'll be rowing all day," said Bill.

"Shurrup," said Joe. "Easterly wind tomorrow and we'll make it easy. Come on, Pete. You steer for a bit. But keep her nose close on him or you'll have her sheering anywheres."

Pete took the tiller, set his feet wide apart and settled to his job. Plumb on the stern of the *Cachalot* he must keep the *Death and Glory*'s little flagstaff with the three-cornered flag of the B.P.S. He could do it, just as well as Bill or Joe. Um! Perhaps not quite as well as Joe. Ouch! She was off a bit then. Starboard an inch . . . Now port . . . Now steady. This was something like steering, going at such a lick.

They met or passed a few sailing yachts and small cruisers, not many, for the letting season was nearly over and most of the holiday-makers were back in the towns from which they came. The sailing yachts were being slowly quanted along, for there was no wind to fill their sails.

"Lot of hard work tomorrow if there don't come an easterly," said Bill as they met one of the unfortunates grimly poling up against the stream.

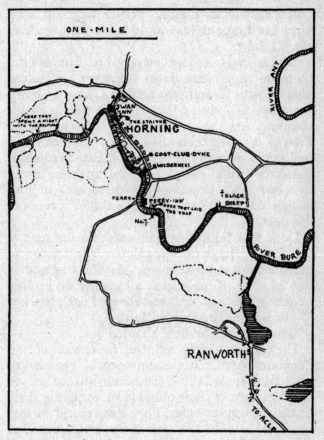

MAP

"Got an easterly in my pockut," said Joe.

"Don't you go saying tomorrow you've let it get away," said Bill.

Joe patted his pocket. "Never fear. I'll keep him. Let him out just when we want him. You see if I don't."

The sun was already low, shining from behind them as they came down the river to Thurne Mouth, with its signpost pointing the way, down the Bure to Acle and up the Thurne to Potter Heigham. As they turned left and went up the Thurne it threw their shadows on the reeds. Bill had taken over the steering and Pete pointed at the shadows that seemed to be racing them, trying to keep his pointing finger on the shadow of himself as it skipped from one high clump of reeds to the next.

Dusk was falling as they came to the first of the Potter Heigham bungalows. The master of the *Cachalot* reduced speed. Just for a second or two he shut off his engine altogether, to be able to hear what they said, and shouted back to them to ask where they wanted to stop.

"This side the bridge," shouted Joe.

They went slowly on, the fisherman of the *Cachalot* putting his engine out of gear every time they passed other fishermen sitting on the bank in front of their bungalows, watching their floats in the quiet water. They came round the last bend and saw the low arch of the bridge ahead of them, and the big boatsheds, and on both sides of the river a line of moored yachts, one or two with awnings up, but most of them with bare masts and no sails on their booms, waiting to be laid up. One look at the crowded staithe was enough for Joe.

"We'll never get a place along there," he said.
"We better go through. Hey!" he shouted.

The master of the *Cachalot* may have heard
him or may not, because of the noise of the engine.
Anyhow, he looked back and pointed at the row of
moored boats.

"Through the bridges," shouted Joe, pointing
upstream. "Give us time to lower. You take her
Pete. Bill and I'll have the mast down in two ticks."

The fisherman waved a hand to show he understood, and kept the *Cachalot* hardly moving while
Bill and Joe ran forward over the cabin-top, cast
off the forestay and slowly let the stumpy mast
fall aft, Joe keeping his weight on the stay while
Bill, moving along the cabin-top, eased the mast
gently down.

The fisherman was watching, and when Joe
signalled "Ready", headed the *Cachalot* for the
low, narrow stone arch of the bridge.

"You take her, Joe," said Pete.

But there was no time to change helmsman.
The *Cachalot* was already nosing in under the
arch. The *Death and Glory* followed her.

"Keep her straight," said Joe. "She'll clear."

"Look out for the chimbley," yelled Pete.

"If the mast clear, that do," said Bill.

Joe, crouching on the foredeck and Bill, back
in the cockpit, were ready to fend off. They put
out their hands and touched the old stones of the
arch as they went through.

"Phew!" said Pete with relief when they were
out again, and he glanced back over his shoulder.
"It never do look as if there'd be room."

A minute later they had passed under the railway bridge. They were looking for a place to moor. The *Cachalot* began to work towards the bank. They passed one possible place and then another. The fisherman pointed ahead. Joe, who was standing on the foredeck with rond anchor ready in his hand, pointed to the right. The two boats were hardly moving. Just before they touched, Joe and the fisherman jumped ashore.

"All right here?" asked the fisherman.

"Thank you very much," said the Death and Glories.

"Going to fish here?" asked Pete.

"Higher up," said the fisherman. "A bit below that dyke that goes to the Roaring Donkey. I was up there last week and lost a good one. Come along in the morning and see what your baits are worth."

"We'll come," said Joe.

"Well, good night to you," said the fisherman, pushed the *Cachalot*'s nose from the bank, stepped aboard and went slowly up the river.

They watched him out of sight.

"Let's hurry up and go into Potter," said Pete.

"What for?" said Bill.

"We got half a crown to spend. And we might see Bob Curten."

"Shops closed," said Bill. "No. Let's light up and get our grub and have all snug. Young Bob'll be home with his Mum."

They planted their rond anchors, stood for a moment on the bank, admiring the *Death and Glory* safely moored at the end of her first long voyage as a cabin boat, set the mast up again, and then settled down for a quiet night in a new place.

"Wonder if he catch anything," said Pete.

"Have to get up early if we're going to see," said Joe.

They lit the stove and made the cabin as hot as they could bear it. Joe let his white rat out for a run, and played tunes on his mouth organ while the others were watching the kettle and cutting bread and cheese. They had supper and, last thing before going to bed, went out into the cockpit for a breath of cool air.

"No wind yet," said Bill.

"In my pockut for tomorrow," said Joe.

"That Tedder's waking someone else tonight," said Pete.

CHAPTER VII

THE WORLD'S WHOPPER

THE morning mist was heavy on the river and on the sodden fields that lay on either side of it. The fields were below the level of the river and the Death and Glories, marching along the rond that kept the river from overflowing, looked down on feeding cattle and horses whose thick coats were pale with moisture.

Joe walking in front along the narrow path startled a great carthorse which went suddenly thundering away, its shaggy hoofs splashing as they struck the wet ground.

"There she go," he said, as if he were speaking of a wherry.

They disturbed a heron at his morning fishing, and heard his sudden, hoarse "Fraaaaank!" and the steady beat of his wings as he flew off into the mist.

Up at dawn, they had made a hurried breakfast, left the sleeping bungalows of Potter Heigham behind them and were getting near Kendal Dyke, hoping every minute to see the moored *Cachalot* and their friend of the day before.

"There she is," cried Joe. "He's got her moored snug."

The squat, lumpy little *Cachalot* showed through the mist ahead of them. They broke into a run.

"Hullo, you! Steady on with that galloping."

A little further along the bank they saw the fisherman, who had turned and was standing there in the mist, with a milk-can in one hand and an empty sack in the other. He beckoned to them and came back to meet them, and they went on, trying to walk like cats instead of like elephants.

"I've got one of your baits out now," he said. "There'll be nothing much doing till this fog lifts off the water, but there's no point in scaring the fish. I'm just going along to the Roaring Donkey. They promised last night to keep some milk for me in the morning. You keep an eye on the ship for me. Keep quiet if you go aboard. See that nobody touches the rod. I'll be back in a minute or two."

"Right O," said Joe.

"If anyone else comes monkeying along, don't drown them right here. It would put the pike off. If anybody comes stamping round, like you did, take him upstream a bit and kill him quietly."

"Drop him dead," said Pete.

The fisherman waved his empty sack at them and went off into the mist along the reedy bank.

The *Cachalot* was moored against a bit of firm bank, so that it was easy to step ashore from her or go aboard. They stood, admiring her. A thin cloud of blue smoke hung about a glittering plated cowl on the top of a short chimney that came through the cabin-top.

"See that?" said Bill. "He's got a stove."

"Built for fishing," said Pete. "He tell me so. She'll be out all winter same as us."

Ropes were out ahead and astern, and they had a critical look at the rond anchors.

"Got 'em in proper," said Joe. "Not like some."

"Look at his rod," said Pete. "Not that one." (Joe, by the bows of the *Cachalot*, was looking at a roach-rod on the roof.) "The one he's fishing with."

They looked at the big pike-rod, lying in a rest on the cockpit coaming. They looked at its big porcelain rings, its dark varnish, its enormous reel. Six feet of the rod were poking out over the river and from the end of it a thin green line was pulled out straight by the tug of the stream.

"Where's his float?"

"Gone," said Joe. "No. There it is. Away down by them reeds. That's a likely holt for a big 'un."

"He say we could go aboard," said Pete.

Joe climbed aboard and stood in the cockpit. Bill followed.

"Aa, you," said Joe. "Step easy. You'd scare every fish in the river." He pointed to the ripples running across the water after Bill had got into the cockpit. "Now then, Pete."

"Wonder if the bait's died on him," said Bill.

Twenty yards downstream, two small pilot floats and a big white-topped pike float swung gently on the top of the moving water, tethered by the thin green line that ran from the tip of the rod. They lay so still that it was hard to believe that anything but a dead bait hung beneath them. Pete watched them as keenly as if he were fishing himself.

Joe was fingering the reel. He gave a gentle tug at the line above it and heard the reel click as it turned. He looked at the back of the reel and touched the brass catch.

"That makes it run free," he said.

"It's not like the ones on our reels," said Bill.

Joe pressed the catch, gently at first and then harder. Suddenly it slid back and the reel began to turn, faster and faster as the line ran out.

"He say not to touch the rod," said Pete.

"He'll have the liver and lungs out of you," said Bill.

For a moment Joe could not get the catch to move back. He managed it and the tip of the rod dipped and straightened. Far away down the river the floats that had been moving with the current stopped dead.

"Gosh!" said Joe. "I thought that were going to run right out."

"Don't you touch it again," said Bill.

"The bait's waked up," said Pete suddenly.

The big white-topped float bobbed sideways, twice, and then swung back into line with the pilots above it.

"Will it be an old pike after him?" said Bill.

"Fare to be," said Joe. "See if that bob again."

For some minutes they stood silent in the cockpit, looking away downstream at the two little floats and the big one rippling the water a yard or two out from the reeds. Joe and Bill soon tired of that.

"Let's scout along the rond," said Bill.

"Come on," said Joe. "He say to keep anybody off."

"Float bobbed again," said Pete.

The other two, who were just going to jump ashore, thought better of it. The floats certainly did look as if something might be going to happen.

"What do we do if an old pike take him under?" said Bill.

"Yell like billyo," said Joe. "Nothing else we can do." He stopped short. "He'll have a horn, being a motor cruiser. Here you are. Press that button and it'll wake the dead."

"That's the starter," said Bill.

"It might be," said Joe. "Well, he's bound to have a foghorn. You keep your eye on them floats, Pete."

Doubtfully, he opened the cabin door that the fisherman had shut to keep the mist out of the cabin. He saw the glow in the neat enamelled stove. He saw a comfortable bunk, not yet made up after the night, and breakfast things ready on the table. Then he saw what he wanted. There it hung, just inside the door, so as to be within easy reach of the steersman, a smallish brass foghorn. Joe took it from its hook and put it to his mouth.

"Don't you do that," said Bill anxiously. "He'll think something's up."

Joe blew gently into the horn. Nothing happened. He blew a little harder and a sudden "yawp" started them all.

"Float's bobbed," said Pete.

"Don't jump like that," said Joe. "Look at the wave you make." He put the horn carefully back on its hook and closed the cabin door.

For some minutes he stood still, looking now at the floats and now upstream along the reedy bank, half expecting to see the fisherman coming on the run. But the floats did not stir again. It was they had gone to sleep. And the fisherman ot come. Joe decided that it was all right. It had sounded pretty loud in the cockpit but, after all, it had been the very shortest of "yawps".

"Who's coming scouting?" he said at last.

"I'm coming," said Bill.

They stepped ashore as quietly as they could.

Pete, his eyes still on the distant floats, said, "I'm coming too."

"Come on then," said Joe.

Pete had one more look. Was that float stirring? No. The others were already moving off along the rond. Pete had another last look at the floats and joined them.

"Knives in your teeth," said Joe.

"We needn't open them," said Bill.

Scout knives are awkward things to hold in the teeth on a cool misty morning and it was as well that these had been well warmed in their owners' pockets. Stooping low, and muzzled by their knives, the three set off along the bank. The reeds already hid the boat from them when Joe, the leader, stopped short and took his knife from his mouth.

"Password's 'Death and Glory'," he whispered, and then, startled, "What's that?"

A harsh "Krrrrrrrrr", like the cry of a corncrake, sounded from behind them. Pete's knife dropped from his teeth. He fumbled for it on the ground. Bill, his knife in his hand, listened, gaping.

"Krrrrrr . . . Krrrrrrrrrr . . . Krrrrrrrrrr. . . . "

"Out of the way, Pete," shouted Joe. "Look out, Bill. It's that reel. . . . It's a pike. . . . " He rushed back the way they had come, followed by the others.

"Krrrrrrrr . . . Krrrrrr . . . Krrrrrrrrrrrr. . . . "

The rod was jerking. The reel spun . . . stopped . . . and spun again.

"Krrrrrrrrrr . . . Krrrrrrrrrr. . . . "

The rod straightened. The reel stopped spinning, as Joe climbed aboard.

"Quiet," he whispered as the others dropped into the cockpit beside him.

"Floats have gone," said Peter.

"All three of 'em," said Bill.

"He's off with the lot," said Joe.

"Look where the line is," said Pete.

The line no longer stretched straight down the river. It disappeared into the water a little above the *Cachalot* and about half way across. There could be no doubt that a pike had taken the bait, gone downstream pulling at the rod and had then turned and swum up.

"He's weeded it," said Joe. "Weeded it and gone."

"No, he ain't," said Pete. "Line's moving."

The line, though still slack, was pointing further and further upstream.

"He's still on," said Bill.

"There's a pilot," cried Pete.

One of the small pilot floats showed well above the *Cachalot*, moving slowly along the surface of the water. Another showed ahead of it. The big white-topped pike float came to the surface.

"He's thrown it out," groaned Joe.

"We ought to have struck him," said Pete.

"Better wind in, I reckon," said Joe.

And then, suddenly, the floats dived again, the

THE BIG FISH

line pulled taut, the reel screamed and Joe, grabbing the line and rod together as the rod jerked, struck with all his might.

The rod bent nearly double. The top of it slammed down into the water. The line raced out, cutting Joe's fingers.

"He's on," shouted Joe, getting the point of the rod up. "He's on. Hi! ... Hey! ... Let go with that foghorn, somebody. Go on. Quick.... Keep at it.... Hey!"

Bill had the cabin door open in a moment, seized the horn, blew and kept on blowing.

"Gee whizz, he is a big 'un," said Joe, hanging on to the bent rod, and bruising his fingers on the handles of the spinning reel.

"Wind in," said Pete. "He'll have all the line out if you don't stop him."

"Keep on with that horn," panted Joe. "No. Stop it. No good. He's gone after all."

"Wind in," said Pete.

The line had gone suddenly slack. Joe, finding it very difficult to hold the heavy rod and wind in at the same time, rested the rod on the cockpit coaming. He wound and wound and still the line was slack and came in as if there was nothing on the end of it.

"Shut up," said Joe. "No good hooting now.... We lost him.... And that was a big old pike too."

"There's a float," cried Pete. "There.... Under water.... It's moving. Coming downstream. Wind in.... Wind in.... He's still on if he ain't broke the line."

Joe wound and wound. The curve of the line slowly straightened. It was cutting the water

almost opposite the *Cachalot*. Suddenly the rod
dipped, the reel screamed, and the spinning handles nearly broke Joe's fingers. He let them spin
and held the rod up.

"Give him the horn again, Bill. He's still on.
Up on the cabin-top, Pete, and see if he's coming.
Hey! Hey! . . . Hey!"

Twenty yards down the river it was as if
there had been an explosion under water. Just
for a moment they saw an enormous head, a
broad dark back and a wide threshing tail, as
the big fish broke the surface and dived again.

Bill was blowing the horn. Joe, holding up the
rod and feeling the heavy tugs of the fish, was
shouting at the top of his voice. But still there
was no sign of the owner of the *Cachalot*. The
big fish turned and came upstream again. Joe,
desperately winding in, saw the line cutting the
water only a few yards from the boat. Again the
pike rushed away upstream. The reel screamed.
Joe tried to brake it with his thumb and nearly
had the skin taken off.

"Hang on to him," said Pete.

"Ain't I?" panted Joe. "Why don't that chap
come. Hey! Hey! Hey!"

The reel stopped spinning. Joe began winding
in again, getting a few yards, and then having
to get his fingers out of the way of the spinning
handles when the pike made another rush. And
then again the great fish came downstream, this
time deep in the water, so that they did not see
the floats as he passed. The line tautened again.
There was another sudden, long rush, on and
on, as if the pike were making for Yarmouth.

It stopped. The floats showed on the surface far downstream opposite a big clump of reeds, in the place where they had been lying before the pike had taken the bait. They rested there a moment, bobbed, and came up again close to the reeds.

"He's going back to his holt," shouted Pete. "Stop him! Stop him! There he go. . . . " The floats shot suddenly sideways into the reeds.

Joe pulled. It was as if he were pulling at a haystack. He wound at the reel till the rod top was on the water. He tried to lift. The line rose, quivering and dripping. Joe let the reel spin to ease it. It was no good. Deep in the reeds the pike lay still and, for the moment, the battle was at an end.

"Lemme have a go," said Bill.

"You can't shift him," said Joe. "No good breaking the line. We'll lose him if you do. Gosh, I wish that chap'd come."

Bill tried to wind in, while Joe blew frantically on the horn. Suddenly he stopped. "We can't let him lie there chewing and chewing till he throw the hooks. We got to get him out of that. Where's Pete?"

From behind the reeds, far downstream, came Pete's voice. "Where is he? This is the place?"

The tops of the reeds waved violently.

"Further down," shouted Joe. "That's it. Hang on there whiles I bring the boathook. Here, Bill. No good winding till he come out. You keep blowing. I'll be back as soon as we shift him."

Joe took the long boathook from the *Cachalot* and ran to join Pete behind the reeds. Just there the reeds were very thick and they could see little of the water. Joe poked this way and that with the boathook. The foghorn from the *Cachalot* sounded in long gasps. Suddenly there was a clang as it dropped on the floor of the cockpit.

"He's moved," shouted Bill. "He give a tug just now. . . . No. He's stopped again."

Once more the foghorn sounded its desperate call for help.

"May be right in under the bank," said Joe. "Come on, Pete. We got to drive him out. Make all the row you can."

He stabbed away with the boathook, while Pete, standing on the very edge of the solid bank, kicked at the water sending wild splashes through the reeds.

"Touched him!" shouted Joe. "Gosh, he is a whopper." There was a tremendous flurry in the water. Waves ran through the stems of the reeds.

"He's close in," shouted Joe. "Go on, Pete. Splash! Splash!"

Pete, in his seaboots, took a further step, stamped in the water, slipped, tried to recover himself and fell headlong. His struggles made a bigger splash than ever he had made with his boots. Reeds swayed this way and that as he fought for foothold in the soft mud, for handhold among the slimy roots.

"You all right?" said Joe. "Take a grip of the boathook."

"All right," spluttered Pete, spitting river water from his mouth. "Ouch!" he yelled suddenly, and came splashing out of the water on all fours. "Joe," he said. "I trod on him."

"He's out. Joe! Joe!" Bill yelled from the boat. Joe raced back with Pete after him.

"What's all this row about?"

The fisherman, hurrying not at all, with a full milk-can in one hand and a full sack in the other, was coming back along the path. He saw Pete, muddy and dripping, on the bank beside the *Cachalot.*

"Hullo," said the fisherman. "Fallen in?"

The foghorn sounded again. "Hey! Hey!" shouted Joe.

"They've a pike on," yelled Pete. "We just chase him out of the reeds."

The fisherman darted forward.

Joe, in the cockpit, had grabbed the rod from Bill's trembling hands. Far away, out in the middle of the river, a great tuft of reeds showed above the surface, moving slowly across the stream. Joe wound in, and the reeds came upstream, jerking now and then, as if something were tugging angrily at their roots. Bill blew and blew.

The fisherman spoke from the bank behind them.

"Ever caught a pike before?"

"No," said Bill.

"You take him," said Joe, looking over his shoulder.

"How long have you had him on?" asked the fisherman.

"Year or two," said Joe shortly.

"Carry on for another month then," said the fisherman. "You're doing very well."

"He's a big 'un," said Joe.

"Been all over the place," said Bill. "Most up

to Kendal Dyke and back and then he go into the reeds."

"How did you get him out? He seems to have taken a good bunch with him."

"Chase him out," said Joe. "Pete tread on him."

The fisherman turned to look at Pete, who was standing dripping on the bank, thinking of nothing but the fish. "Look here, you," he said. "We don't want to have you dying. Kick those boots off and get out of your clothes. Go into the cabin and . . . don't let that line go slack! Wind in, man! Wind in!"

The pike had turned and was coming back towards the *Cachalot*. Joe was winding for all he was worth. "You take it," he said. "You take it."

The fisherman, who had come quietly aboard, put out his hand to take the rod, but changed his mind. "Not I," he said. "You've hooked him. You've held him. You've played him. I'm not going to take the rod now. Hullo. He's a beauty. . . . Go on, Pete, get into the cabin. Never mind the wet. It'll drain into the bilge."

"Lemme see him caught," said Pete.

"He's coming now," said the fisherman and reached for the long gaff that lay on the top of the cabin. "Wind in a bit more, you with the rod. Now, lift him. . . . Gently. . . . "

For the first time, they could see how big the pike was. A huge fish, mottled light green and olive, rose slowly to the top of the water. He had shaken free of the reeds, which were drifting away. He opened a wide, white mouth, shook a head as big as a man's and plunged again to the bottom of the river, making the reel whizz.

"He's all of twenty pounds," said the fisherman quietly. "I was sure there was a good one about. Don't lose him now. Bring him in again. That's the way. . . . "

"There's the float," said Pete. "He's coming. There he is."

"Keep still."

The fisherman leaned from the cockpit with a long gaff deep in the water. The big fish was coming to the top once more. The fisherman suddenly lifted.

"Look out now," he shouted, and in another moment the big fish was in the cockpit, threshing its great tail among their feet.

"How are you going to kill him?" said Bill.

The fisherman lifted a seat in the cockpit, took a short weighted club from the locker beneath it and brought it down heavily, once, twice, on the pike's head. The great fish lay still.

"He's swallowed his last roach," he said. "By gum, he must have been the terror of the river, that fish. Twenty pounds? He's twenty-five if he's an ounce."

Joe stood, holding the rod and feeling shaky at the knees.

"Going to weigh him?" said Bill.

The fisherman took a spring balance from the locker. "I doubt if this is much good," he said. "It only weighs up to twenty-four."

He put the hook of the balance carefully under the pike's jaw and lifted it. "Twenty-four anyhow," he said. "The balance can't go down any further. We shan't know what he weighs till I take him to the Roaring Donkey." He laid the fish down again on the cockpit floor. "Best fish I've ever seen," he said. Then he remembered Pete. "Into the cabin with you, all of you. Go on. Take the clothes off him and roll him up in a blanket while we get them dry. We don't want his mother to say we've murdered him."

"Come on, Pete," said Joe. "What did he feel like when you tread on him?"

Pete grinned, with chattering teeth.

Five minutes later Pete, wrapped up in a red blanket, was sitting by the fisherman on the bunk at one side of the *Cachalot*'s cabin, while the other two sat on the settee opposite. The fisherman had stoked up the fire, which was roaring up the chimney. Pete's clothes were hanging round it. The fisherman had taken four bottles of ginger beer from the sack he had brought from the inn. Four mugs, now only half full, were on the table, a saucepan full of pea soup was warming on the top of the stove, and the whole story of the catching of the pike was being told from the beginning.

"There was nothing we could do but try," said Joe.

"I near bust that horn hooting," said Bill.

"And then he go into them reeds, and he'd have been there yet if young Pete hadn't jumped on him," said Joe.

Pete, of whom nothing was to be seen but his head, grinned from his red blanket. "Might have been a crocodile," he said.

Twice the fisherman opened the cabin door to look out into the cockpit at the huge fish, as if to make sure that it was really there. In the end he left the door open, perhaps to let out the steam from Pete's drying clothes, perhaps to be able to go on looking at the fish.

"Are you taking him to the Roaring Donkey to weigh him?" asked Bill.

"I've another reason for that," said the fisherman. "You'll hear all about it if you like to come too. I've a little bet with the landlord. I was trying for that fish all last week. He'll open his eyes when he sees him."

CHAPTER VIII

AT THE ROARING DONKEY

PETE's clothes took a long time drying. The fisherman turned them inside out and all but cooked them and hung his boots close under the roof beside the hot chimney. The crew of the *Death and Glory* settled down in the *Cachalot* and heard all about her building, and how her owner meant to use her all through the winter season when the pike fishing was at its best. They heard how he had been trying again and again for the big fish, coming all the way round from Norwich because of the better fishing in the northern waters. He gave them an enormous meal of pea soup and cold roast beef and chip potatoes and jam tart. At last soon after midday he let Pete get into his clothes again, though patches of mud on his knickerbockers were still too damp to brush. They washed up, after the meal, while the fisherman sat smoking, looking at the huge pike.

"And now for the Roaring Donkey," he said at last.

The mist had been lifted and driven away by a light easterly wind that was shivering the willow leaves and rustling the tall reeds, to Bill's great relief, for he had been afraid they would have to row all the way home. "Didn't I say I had it in my pockut?" said Joe.

"Ain't you going to do no more fishing?" asked Pete.

"Never get another fish like that," said the
fisherman. "No. We must get him weighed at
the Donkey, and then, if we're quick about it, I'll
go down through Yarmouth. That fish is too big
to post, and I'll have to take him up to Norwich
to have him stuffed. I'll give you a tow as far as
Thurne Mouth and you'll blow home all right if
this wind keeps up."

He disappeared into the *Cachalot*'s fo'c'sle and
came back with a long plank taken from the
fo'c'sle floor. "How's this for a stretcher?" he said.

Bill and Joe laid the plank on the path beside
the *Cachalot*. The fisherman brought the big fish
ashore and laid it on the plank.

"Better cover him up," he said. "I don't want
anybody to see him at the Donkey till I've had
a word with the landlord." He went back into the
Cachalot and brought ashore a couple of empty
coke sacks, with which he reverently draped the
corpse.

Joe took one end of the plank. Bill and Pete,
one each side, took the other.

"Ready?" said the fisherman.

"Right," said Joe.

"On with the funeral," said the fisherman, and
the procession set out along the path beside the
river until they turned off to the right along the
narrow dyke that led to the Roaring Donkey.

The little inn did not look prosperous. The dyke
that led to it from the river was only big enough for
rowing boats, so most of the yachts and cruisers
passed it by. Even at the height of summer there
were seldom more than one or two odd visitors
sitting on the benches outside its latticed windows.

FUNERAL PROCESSION

Today there was nobody. The roof looked as if it badly needed some new thatching. The flagstaff from which hung a tattered green flag with the letters "ALL ARE WELCOME" was needing new paint, and so was the signboard where a white donkey stood roaring its heart out on a field the green of which had blistered away in patches.

"He'll be crowded out," said the fisherman, "when he has that fish on his mantelshelf."

"Doctor Dudgeon's got one," said Pete, "in the room where he look at my tongue. But that ain't nowheres near as big as this 'un."

"People will be coming from all over the place to see it. A fish that size and caught only a few yards from the house."

"Seems more'n that," said Joe, who was finding it awkward walking while holding the end of the stretcher.

"When he's got that fish in his parlour, they'll be coming all the season through to try to catch another like him."

"There's one in the Swan," said Joe.

"This is bigger," said the fisherman. "Now look here, you three. Licensed premises. Can't take you in. Round you go into the yard and wait there. Don't let anybody see what you've got." He waved a cheerful hand towards the big gate into the yard behind the inn and himself went in at the low doorway, stooping so as not to bump his head.

The stretcher-bearers went round into the yard.

"Best go under the shed," said Joe. "Don't want anybody coming out and asking questions."

They went into an open shed at one side of

the yard and rested the bier between a pile of faggots and a chopping block. Pete lifted a sack to have another look at the corpse.

"Wouldn't like to have my hand in his mouth," said Bill. "He's got teeth in him big as a harrow's."

"Someone coming," said Joe, and Pete let the sacking fall back. A girl came out of the back door of the inn, crossed the yard with a bucket, filled it at a pump and went away again, never knowing that three watchers were wondering what to say to her if she should happen to ask what they were doing.

Something moved in a box at the back of the shed. A pale, long, arched body stirred in some straw and put up a clawed foot against the wire netting that covered the front of the box.

"Ferrets," said Joe.

They went nearer to have a look.

"Now then, Pete, you keep your fingers out of that wire," said Bill. "Remember the old keeper that time he show his. Old bitch ferret he had and four young ones. 'Don't be afeard of 'em', he say. 'They'll never touch you if you show 'em the back of your hand', and he shove his hand in, close fist, and the next minute he were yelling blue murder with all them ferrets fanging his knuckles and the blood spawling out."

The back door of the inn opened again, and they heard the fisherman's voice.

"A shilling a pound for any fish over twenty pounds, you said?"

"That's right, Jemmy, we hear you say it," laughed someone else.

"That's all right. If he's a real big 'un he's

well worth it. But, see here, Mister, this isn't
the first of April." The landlord, a stout, red-faced
man in corduroy breeches, was looking rather as
if he thought that someone was playing a trick on
him. Two or three labourers came out behind him
to see if it was indeed true that the fisherman had
caught a monster and the landlord had lost his bet.

"The corpse is somewhere here," said the fisherman. "I told the bearers to carry it into the yard.
Hi, you! Oh, there you are."

Pete, Bill and Joe lifted the bier and carried
it out of the shed.

"What do you think of that?" said the fisherman,
whisking the sacks off, and showing the great pike
with the tackle still hanging from the corner of his
jaw.

The men stared at the fish.

"Biggest I've seen in twenty year," said one.

"Fork out, Jemmy," said another.

"He's a big 'un all right," said the landlord,
pressing his thumb against the firm, shiny body.
"He's put away some fish in his time."

"Water-fowl too," said one of the men, whom
the boys knew as a reed-cutter. "A fish like that
make nothing of a young coot or a duckling."

The landlord went into the shed, took a steelyard from the wall and hung it from a beam.

"Put it at twenty-four pounds to begin with,"
said the fisherman. "We know he weighs that."
He had lifted the pike from the stretcher and
brought it into the shed.

With the help of one of the men he hung it
from the hook at one end of the steelyard and
held it up to keep its tail from the dust and chaff

on the floor while the landlord put a stone weight and half a stone and a four-pound weight into the scale. The tail of the fish dropped nearly to the ground.

"Twenty-five pound," said the landlord and added another pound. It seemed to make no difference.

"Twenty-six pound," said someone in a tone full of awe.

The landlord added another pound. Then he took off all the smaller weights and added another stone weight to the first.

"Twenty-eight," he murmured, and added a pound.

"Twenty-nine."

He added another pound and the fish rose slowly and dipped again.

"He'll go more than thirty pounds," said the fisherman.

Another pound put the balance on the wrong side. The landlord took it off and slid a smaller weight along the steelyard. The fish on one side and the weights on the other swayed slightly up and down, and came to rest.

"Thirty pound and a half," said the landlord, almost as if he were in church. "Thirty pound and a half . . . " and then he slapped his knee. "Pay!" he almost shouted. "I'll pay and welcome. And it'll cost me the best part of a fiver to have him set up and I'll pay that too. Mary! Come out here. If that fish don't make the fortune of the Roaring Donkey I'll give up innkeeping and take to poultry farming. Come on out, Mary, and have a look at this."

The landlord's wife came running.

"Make our fortunes, that fish will," said the landlord. "With that in a glass case we'll have all the fishermen we can do with. Once they know about that they'll be coming from London and Manchester, and where not. We'll have the spare beds full from June to March."

"Maybe you'll be wanting a bigger inn," laughed his wife.

"You never know," said the landlord.

"I don't care what you do to it," said the fisherman, "so long as you don't call it an hotel."

The landlord chuckled. "It's got a good enough name," he said. "Custom's what it wants . . . and when we can show a fish like that. . . . Come on, chaps. Drinks on the house. . . . And see here, Mary. . . . Pop for the young 'uns."

They had only just finished an enormous dinner aboard the *Cachalot*, but when the landlord's wife came out with three glasses of ginger beer and three hunks of fruit cake, they found a little more room and filled it. They had hardly done when they saw the landlord and the fisherman coming out again into the yard.

"All the same to you," the fisherman was saying, "if you let me have two ten shilling notes for this pound?"

The landlord pulled out his wallet, put away the pound note and gave the fisherman two ten shilling notes in exchange.

"Come on now, you stretcher-bearers," said the fisherman. "We've got to hurry. Pick him up and away. I want to get down through Yarmouth as quick as I can." He turned to the landlord. "All right. I'll give him full instructions and you shall have the fish as soon as he's ready."

They carried the great fish, laid out once more on the plank, back along the dyke and down the river bank to the *Cachalot*, while the fisherman was telling them what the man in Norwich would be doing, taking a mould of the fish, skinning him, letting the skin dry on the mould, varnishing and painting and setting him up with sand on the bottom of the glass case and a blue back to it and weeds arranged here and there so that the great pike would look as if he were resting in the water ready any moment to dart out at a passing roach.

"Are you all ready to start?" he asked, as he went aboard the *Cachalot* and took the fish from them.

"Have to lower the mast," said Joe. "That don't take a minute."

"Skip along then as fast as you can. I'll be coming down right away, and I'll give you a tow if you're ready for it. . . . And now. . . . Just half a minute. . . . " He pulled three ten shilling notes from his pocket. "Thirty and a half pounds your fish weighed and the landlord paid up like an honest man. Thirty shillings and sixpence. That's ten and twopence apiece. No need to go telling everybody you've got it, or you'll be snowed under with begging letters. And don't go putting it in the savings bank. There it is. Money to spend and well earned."

They stared.

"For us?" said Pete.

"Ten bob," said Joe. "Ten blessed blooming bob!"

"And twopence," said the fisherman.

"There's not a boy in Horning as rich as that," said Joe.

"There's not a boy in Horning who's caught such a fish," said the fisherman. "And there'll never be another. It's quite all right. Your fish. Your money. . . . "

"But it were your rod," said Joe, "and your bait, and you put the bait out and the old pike hook himself. We didn't do nothing, only hang on till you come and pull him out."

"I saw what you did," said the fisherman. "He'd be in the river yet, but for you, and I'd have lost line and tackle and maybe my best rod as well. Why, no matter who had the rod, no one could have caught him if Pete hadn't gone into the water after him like a spaniel, chasing him out of the reeds. Go on. Put the money in your pockets and keep your mouths shut till the fish comes back from Norwich. Then we'll all go over to the Roaring Donkey and everybody'll get a bit of a surprise. And now, skip along and be ready before I come."

He went into the cabin, leaving the Death and Glories staring at each other and at the notes in their hands.

"Come on," said Bill, and they set off at a run to get back to the *Death and Glory*.

"Ten bob apiece. . . . Gee whizz!" said Joe as they ran. "New ropes. . . . A proper iron chimney. . . . "

"And stock up," panted Bill. "We can go cruising for a month. . . . "

"Gee whillikins!" said Pete. "That's something to tell Tom Dudgeon."

"Can't tell him yet," said Bill. "How long do it take to stuff a fish the way he said? Gosh! I'd like Tom to see when we go to the Roaring Donkey to look at that old pike in a glass case."

They climbed aboard the *Death and Glory* and had her mast down just as they heard a quiet rumble from up the river. The *Cachalot* was coming down.

"Put the forrard anchor aboard Bill," shouted Joe. "Pete and I'll hang on to the stern warp and let her swing round. We'll have her heading the right way.... That's right.... Push her head out.... Round she go."

There was a short toot from the horn they had blown so furiously during the fight with the pike. A moment later, the *Cachalot* was in sight. Her skipper put his engine into reverse and stopped her. She drifted slowly past them. A coiled rope flew to Bill. He caught it and took a turn round the bollard on the foredeck.

"Get aboard, Pete," cried Joe, hurriedly coiling the stern warp, putting it aboard with its anchor and clambering aboard to take the tiller as the tow-rope began to tauten.

"All clear," he shouted.

The fisherman threw up his hand to show that he had understood. In another moment there was a flurry of water round the bows of the *Death and Glory*, and they were off.

Just above the railway bridge they passed an old man sitting on a chair on the bank, watching a pike float a few yards below him. The *Cachalot*'s skipper put his engine out of gear to slip by quietly. The old man lifted a hand by way of saying thank you, and called out, "Nothing doing today. Not a touch since breakfast."

"We've had one," said the *Cachalot*'s skipper.

"Any size?"

"Not bad."

He put on speed again.

"Like to know what he'd call good," said Joe.

"If you keep looking at that note you'll lose it," said Bill.

Pete pushed his note deep into his pocket.

They passed under the railway bridge. They shot the stone bridge with care, but there was plenty of room though, as before, there was a moment when they felt sure they were going to touch. They were already well below the bridge when they saw a small boy run out on the staithe.

"There's young Bob," said Bill. "What's up with him?"

The small boy was waving wildly.

"Something he want to tell us," said Pete.

"Well, he can't," said Joe shortly, busy with his steering as the *Cachalot* swerved to the right to avoid a yacht that was being towed up to the staithe by a couple of men in a dinghy.

Bill and Pete waved cheerfully to the small outpost of the Coot Club, who was still signalling when a bend of the river below the staithe shut him out of sight behind a bungalow.

"Semaphore," said Pete. "That stuff Dick and Dorothea show us at Easter."

"Did you read it?"

"Couldn't," said Pete. "I've forgot it. But that's what he were doing."

"Probably he want to come too," said Joe. "But the *Cachalot*'s in a hurry and we can't make him stop."

"Course we can't," said Bill. "We're in a hurry same as he is. Wonder if that Dick and Dorothea get to Horning yet." He pulled his ten shilling note from his pocket to make sure it was there. He caught Pete's eye and pushed it back again.

"Thirty bob," he said. "There's almost nothing we couldn't do."

They left the bungalows behind and the hum of the *Cachalot*'s engine changed its note. It was higher, more urgent.

"Moving now," said Pete, looking at the banks flying by. It seemed almost no time before the entrance to Womack was in sight and Thurne Dyke beyond it.

"Gosh!" said Joe. "We got that mast to get up. You take her, Pete."

Pete steered. Joe and Bill got the mast up, and made all ready for hoisting sail. They were nearing the mouth of the Thurne. The fisherman aboard the *Cachalot* slackened speed, and waved to the right.

"All ready," shouted Joe from the foredeck of the *Death and Glory*.

The *Cachalot* swung out into the wide meeting place of the Bure and the Thurne. She swung for a moment up the Bure, so that the *Death and Glory* was heading for home.

"Now then, Bill," said Joe.

"Up she go," said Bill.

The little lugsail on its yard staggered up the mast, steadied and filled. Bill joined Pete in the cockpit.

"Ready to cast off?" shouted the fisherman.

"Ready."

"Cast off!" shouted the fisherman and, as Joe let the tow-rope slip, they saw him hauling it in hand over hand and coiling it at his feet. Already the *Death and Glory* was sailing. The *Cachalot* circled round her. The fisherman lifted the huge pike. The Death and Glories gave a cheer.

"See you again," shouted the fisherman. "And keep your mouths shut." He headed away down river. Just before he went out of sight at the corner they saw him turn and face them, standing in his cockpit, and stretching out his arms as wide as he possibly could.

CHAPTER IX

MONEY TO BURN

Joe's easterly wind filled the sail of the *Death and Glory* and drove her fast up the river, with a pleasant bubbling of water under her bows. The three took turns in steering. Pete had brought out the big telescope, but hardly looked through it. Joe, when not steering, sat in the cockpit with his back to the cabin and played his mouth organ. All three knew they were later than they had meant to be, but nothing seemed to matter beside the money in their pockets. It was not always in their pockets. They kept fingering it and turning it over so often that anybody might have thought they were seeing the new moon for the first time every other minute. From being ordinary hard-up boys, they had become capitalists overnight. Ten shillings and twopence each, as well as the half-crown Pete had earned by catching baits.

From time to time they passed fishermen, in moored boats out in the river, or sitting on the bank. They looked at them with new eyes. If those chaps only knew. . . .

"Any luck?" Bill would sing out in something like the manner of the fisherman of the *Cachalot*.

"Nothing much," would come the reply, and each time the Death and Glories heard it, they looked at each other and simmered with a secret joy.

"We're not to say nothing about it," Joe reminded them. "Not till that old pike come back in a glass case."

"Wonder what that chap at the Roaring Donkey'll say when he know."

"None too pleased he won't be," said Joe. "Why, if he'd have known we caught it, he'd have given us half a crown and we'd have thought we done well. But thirty bob and a tanner. Thirty bob and a tanner! There's many a man don't earn that in a week."

It was late in the afternoon before they drove round the bend by the ferry and came roaring up the home reach.

"Wonder if they've come," said Pete as they were nearing the doctor's house, with the golden bream high above its thatched roof.

"There's Tom anyways," said Joe. "Hullo!"

Tom was waving from the lawn. "Pull in and tie up," he shouted. "They're here."

A smallish boy with large black-rimmed spectacles and a girl with straw-coloured plaits flying in the wind raced across the lawn to join Tom at the water's edge.

Joe steered to pass close by.

"Meeting in the Coot Club shed," said Tom.

"Can't stop," said Joe. "Got to get up to the staithe before the shop shut." Such is the effect of having a pocket full of money. He turned to Bill. "Give 'em a feast," he whispered.

"Good idea," said Bill.

"Coot Club meeting in our cabin," said Pete.

"Come on to the staithe all three," shouted Joe. "Supper in the *Death and Glory*."

"In our cabin," shouted Pete.

There was hurried talk among the three on the bank. Something about telling Mrs. Barrable was heard aboard the *Death and Glory* as she swept by.

"All right," shouted Tom. "But they'll have to tell the Admiral first."

"Good," said Bill. "That just give us time."

"We'll show 'em," said Joe. "What about it?"

"We got all Roy's to choose from. . . . Mushroom soup. . . . That's pretty good. . . . And what about a steak and kidney. . . . Tom give us that once in the shed. . . . "

"Christmas pudding," said Pete.

"Why not?" said Bill. "Gee whillikins, we'll do it really proper."

The *Death and Glory* came foaming up towards the staithe.

"Hullo," said Joe, who was steering. "There's *Sir Garnet* in our place. We'll have to tie up ahead of her. Stand by to lower sail. No. . . . Never mind. Lower after we bring up. Tide's flooding and we'll better swing round and head this way."

Sir Garnet was the fastest trading wherry on the river. Her skipper, Jim Wooddall, and her mate, old Simon, were old friends of the Death and Glories, and of Tom Dudgeon, and indeed of all the members of the Coot Club who were scattered up and down the rivers at all the different villages at which *Sir Garnet* used to call. Jim Wooddall was just closing the door of his cabin, and had a small bag in his hand. Old Simon was coiling down a brand-new grass rope that they had been towing astern of them to get the viciousness out of it. Both men lifted hands in greeting, and the Death and Glories waved back.

They brought the *Death and Glory* up to the staithe and made fast close by *Sir Garnet*. Jim Wooddall was already walking off.

"Gone to catch the bus to Wroxham," said old Simon. "Not sailing till the morning."

"Where are you going?" asked Bill.

"Yarmouth."

"That's grand rope," said Joe.

"Wicked when it's new," said old Simon, coiling down the last of it on the top of the hatches. "Well, I'm off, too. You'll keep an eye on her? Don't want nobody larking about."

"Nobody shan't touch her," said Joe, and old Simon strolled off to his cottage.

"Come on, Pete," said Bill. "We got to hurry before the shops shut. Come on, Joe."

Joe took a last look at the *Death and Glory*'s mooring ropes, slackened her stern warp, tightened the one at the bows, and ran after the other two.

They were crossing the road to the shops when George Owdon and his friend rode up on their bicycles and jumped off beside them.

"So you're here again?" said George.

"Any more boats cast off?" asked Bill.

"Nobody to cast them off with you away unless it's young Tom," said George Owdon.

"Not likely with us watching," said his friend.

They mounted their bicycles and rode off.

"You didn't ought to have said nothing," said Joe.

"Oh, it don't matter," said Bill. "Come on.

George Owdon's nothing. Where do we go first?"

"Roy's," said Pete. "We want to get all stocked up before they come."

They walked, as millionaires, into Roy's shop. Always before, when they had had money to spend, there had been so little of it that they had spent an hour or so outside the window, calculating just how far it would go, and deciding to go without chocolate for the sake of getting bananas, or to do without bananas because it was a long time since they had had tinned fruit. Today there was no need for doubt. They marched in with, first of all, the thought of the Coot Club supper in their heads.

"Mushroom soup," said Pete. "Three of them and three of us. Reckon we'll do with three tins."

"A steak and kidney," said Joe. "One of the big ones."

"And what about tins of beans?" said Bill.

"Christmas pudding," said Pete, reading aloud from this label. " 'Cover with water and boil for half an hour.' That's easy, like the steak and kidney. I say, Bill. Oughtn't we have lit the fire?"

"Burn up in two ticks," said Bill. "What about loganberries? And we want plenty of that milk chocolate they give us that time at Acle Bridge."

They walked round and round the shop, looking at the shelves that were loaded with tinned foods of all kinds to meet the needs of the summer fleets of visitors sailing the hired boats. They read the notice: "Anything bought and not used will be taken back if returned unopened." That removed the last faint touch of thrift. "Go on, Pete," said Joe. "You have it if you want it. Shove it on the counter with the rest."

The pile of tins on the counter grew and grew. Steak and kidney, stewed oxtail, corned beef, peas, beans, pears, peaches, marmalade and strawberry jam, condensed milk, cocoa, chocolate both plain and nutty, a dozen bottles of ginger beer. The shopman, who knew them well, began to think that they were joking with him.

"Who's going to pay for all this?" he said.

"We've got the money," said Joe, pulling out his ten shilling note.

"That's all right," said the shopman. "Has your ship come in?"

"We just tie her up," said Pete, and wondered why the shopman laughed.

Laden with their buyings they staggered back to the *Death and Glory*. Bill lit the stove and put a saucepan of water on to boil. Then, crouching in the fo'c'sle, he lit the primus and put a kettle on that. They filled the new cupboards with their stores, keeping out only what was wanted for the feast. Pete was sent racing back to the shop to buy new batteries, badly needed for their pocket torches. He came back to find Joe fixing up the table, an old folding table, broken and discarded by one of the hire boats, mended by Joe and now one of the prides of the ship. It almost filled the space between the bunks.

"That look all right, that do," said Joe. "Now, when they come, we'll put 'em to sit along this side, two of 'em, and one t'other side, by the door.

We'll want to be handy for the stove and things."

"Coots for ever!" The visitors were standing on the staithe.

"And ever! Come along in."

"I say," said Dorothea. "She's simply lovely. We'd never have known her. Real bunks. And a stove. I don't know how you've done it."

"That stove was the worst," said Pete. "Before we had that chimbley. One minute that'd come roaring up and us in a stew for sparks on deck, and next minute, come a change of wind, and smoke and flame start hunting us out of the cabin. Not bad now that's painted green. Nobody'd know that were a pot chimbley."

"It looks very nice," said Dorothea. "And I do like your orange curtains."

"My Mum made 'em," said Pete.

"Come on in," said Joe. "You work along that side. What do you think of our cupboards?" He flung open a door and showed the row of stored tins. "Come on in, Dick. You work in next to Dot. And Tom by the door. . . . "

"What's that?" asked Pete.

"Camera," said Dick, unslinging it.

"Better hang it on that peg," said Joe. "How long have you come for? Are you going to have the old *Teasel* again?"

"Not this time," said Dorothea. "The Admiral's too busy painting. But we're going sailing with Tom in *Titmouse*."

"We're all going to Ranworth tomorrow," said Tom. "We've just told the Admiral. And Dick and Dot are coming to breakfast at our house so that we can start early."

"Taking photographs," said Dick. "The Admiral's letting me turn the bathroom into a dark room. I say, I'll take a photograph of the *Death and Glory*. We're going to be here till the end of the holidays, and at Easter we're going to be here again and I'll take photographs of all the birds' nests."

"He's practising all the time," said Dorothea. "He can even take photographs in the dark."

"Flashlight," explained Dick. "But I'm not much good at it yet."

"Did you finish that story?" asked Pete. "About the Outlaw of the Broads?"

"It's more than half done," said Dorothea.

"Come on in, Tom, and get sitting down. Bill's ready with the soup."

Tom, who had been sitting on the floor of the cockpit with his feet inside the cabin, bumped his head getting up, and wriggled into the corner by the door. Bill was having a hard time watching two stoves at once. He poured pea soup into three mugs and three saucers. Joe dealt out six spoons, five in good condition and one that had lost part of its handle. This he kept for himself. Pete was cutting hunks of bread.

Bill burnt his tongue hurrying with his soup, and tackled the tin of steak and kidney pudding, burning his fingers in getting it out of the hot water. It was one of those tins that open with the twisting of a key, but the key twisted off and Bill had to use a tin-opener.

"Ouch!" said Bill, wringing his fingers.

"Dip them in butter," said Tom.

Joe got out three plates which, with the three

saucers, were used for the steak and kidney. Bill, more successfully this time, opened two tins of beans.

"I say," said Tom, who knew well that the Death and Glories mostly lived on bread and cheese. "You must have spent an awful lot of money. Somebody had a birthday?"

"Ah!" said Joe.

"We got plenty," said Pete. "Earned it." He caught Joe's eye and said no more.

"There's been a lot of fuss about all those boats that got adrift," said Tom. "People were watching the river again last night. Mr. Tedder's been bothering Dad about it all. All because of that beast George telling everybody he'd caught us casting her off when we were tying up the one we found loose."

"Well there's been no more" said Joe.

Bill, who wanted darkness for reasons of his own, was watching the dimming light. The sun had gone down. Dusk was falling, but even in the cabin it was not as dark as he thought it ought to be.

"Don't bolt your grub, Pete," he said. "There ain't no hurry."

Everybody took the hint, and ate in stately slowness, while the saucepan bubbled on the stove. They talked of the wild chase of Tom by the Hullabaloos back in the Easter holidays. They talked of what could be done, with the *Titmouse* and the *Death and Glory* sailing in company. They talked of the foolishness of people tying up boats so that they could go adrift and bring blame on the heads of the innocent. They talked of the twins,

Port and Starboard, who had been sent away to school in Paris. They talked of the gorgeous time that would be coming next year when the birds would be nesting and the Coot Club, thanks to Dick and his camera, would be able to make a collection of photographs as well as the usual catalogue of all the nests on the river.

It grew darker and darker.

"What about a lantern?" said Pete.

"In a minute," said Bill, who was holding a big tin in a damp rag that kept slipping and letting the heat get at his fingers while he was trying to use the tin-opener.

"You can't see what you're doing," said Tom.

"Joe, you get the grease off them plates," said Bill. He got his tin open and emptied its contents, black and shiny, out on a frying pan.

"Shall I lend you a torch?" said Dick.

"No, thanks," said Bill and turned his back on the party, taking the frying pan with him into the fo'c'sle.

They heard the striking of a match, which lit up the little fo'c'sle, though Bill's body was in the way and they could not see what he was doing. They heard him strike another, and yet another.

"What's gone wrong, Bill?" said Joe.

"Drat it, there ain't nothing go wrong," said Bill. "You wait, can't you."

Another match flared in the fo'c'sle and went out. Then after a dark pause, they heard the gobble, gobble of liquid pouring from a bottle.

Another match was lit, and the next moment Bill was coming backwards into the cabin, bearing the Christmas pudding in a sea of blue flames.

"What about that?" said Bill.

"I say," said Dick.

"It's lovely," said Dorothea. "Oughtn't you to slop the flames all over it and get some of it burning on each plate?"

Bill hesitated a moment.

"Better not," he said. "Wait till that die down."

He put the frying pan with the flaming pudding on the table and turned to the lighting of the lantern. The lantern, burning brightly, was hanging from its hook under the cabin roof by the time the sea of flame round the pudding had shrunk, died away, flamed up again and gone out. There was a most decided smell of methylated spirits.

Bill carved his pudding and served it out, a helping each on three plates, and a helping each on the three saucers. He watched anxiously the faces of the visitors.

"That want a lot of sugar," he said.

People helped themselves to sugar again and again and in the end the helpings of pudding disappeared.

"It did burn beautifully," said Dorothea.

"That's the way to make it," said Bill, much relieved. "That don't fare to light without you have a drop of spirit."

They washed it down with ginger beer, and finished up with oranges, the juice of which took away the last traces of the methylated, which had hung about in people's mouths in spite of all the sugar. Everybody agreed that it had been a first class feast.

Bill was just passing round a bag of humbugs and everybody was talking at once when there was a sudden bang on the roof of the cabin.

"Who's there?" called Joe.

Tom, sitting close to the door, put his head out into the dark evening.

"No, it's not you I want to see," said Mr. Tedder, the policeman. "It's that young Joe and the others."

Not one of the crew of the *Death and Glory* could get out while their visitors were in the way. Dick and Dorothea joined Tom in the cockpit.

"No, it's not you neither," said Mr. Tedder. "Glad to see you back."

Joe crawled along one bunk and Bill along the other. Pete was already in the doorway.

"Now, young Joe," said Mr. Tedder, "you wasn't here last night."

"No," said Joe. "But there hasn't been any more boats cast off. George Owdon say so."

"Not here there hasn't," said Mr. Tedder. "Where was you last night?"

"Above the bridge at Potter Heigham."

"Ar," said Mr. Tedder. "I heard you was there. And how many boats did you cast off? Word just came through there was half a dozen boats sent adrift below Potter Bridge last night."

"We never touch no boats," said Joe.

"You was there," said Mr. Tedder. "I'll ring through to Potter and see you in the morning."

He left them and went off along the stage. They heard his slow voice booming in the dusk. "They was there right enough. Thank you for telling me."

"Who's that with him?" said Bill.

"Only George Owdon," said Tom.

"Him again," said Bill.

"But they can't patch that on us," said Pete. "We never go below bridges. We never touch no boats at Potter."

"Nor anywheres else," said Joe. "But if Mr. Tedder think we do."

The cheerful party came to a gloomy end.

"It's just bad luck," said Tom.

"It's jolly unfair," said Dick.

"Our Dads'll stop us off the river," said Bill.

"Oh they can't," said Dorothea. "Not for something you didn't do."

"That makes no difference," said Tom. He, like Joe, Bill and Pete, knew what the boatbuilders were thinking, and not only Mr. Tedder and George Owdon but all the people who were used to tie their boats along the river banks and leave them in confidence that nobody would interfere with them. Why even Mrs. Barrable had thought for a moment that they were to blame. And Tom's own father.

"They'll have to emigrate," said Dorothea.

"What's that?" asked Bill.

"It's what the pilgrims did when they were persecuted. They just went off in the *Mayflower* and founded America. We'll all go to Ranworth and you can lie hid there just like Tom did when he was an outlaw."

"We could do," said Pete doubtfully.

"We will tomorrow anyway," said Tom. "We'll be waiting for you in *Titmouse* as soon as we've done breakfast."

"I say," said Dorothea. "We ought to go home. We only got here today and the Admiral's letting us go off before breakfast tomorrow."

*

The Death and Glories tidied up after the feast. It was a grim tidying.

"Wish I never catch them baits," said Pete. "If I never catch them baits, that *Cachalot* wouldn't have give us a tow, and we'd never have been at Potter when them fools cast their boats off."

They shut up the table and put it away and made ready to settle in for the night.

Last thing, a thought struck Joe.

"Come on," he said. "We don't want *Sir Garnet* going off. Let's have a look at her warps."

"Nobody'd touch a wherry," said Bill.

The three of them clambered out on the staithe and felt in the darkness along the mooring ropes of the big vessel lying below them. Each one was well made fast to a mooring ring, each one made fast as it should be, with a fisherman's bend.

"She's all right," said Joe. "You don't catch Jim Wooddall making slip knots by mistake. I just want to make sure no one been monkeying round since he leave her."

Dimly, in the dusk, they could see the great mast of *Sir Garnet* towering into the sky. Dimly they could see the long low bulk of her beside the staithe. They felt better. She was the finest, the most famous wherry on the Broads, and whatever other people might be thinking of them, her skipper, Jim Wooddall, was still their friend, and her mate, old Simon, had asked them to keep an eye on her.

"She's all right," said Joe again. "Come on,

young Pete. We promise your Mum to see you get to bed."

In the middle of the night, Pete started up in his bunk in the fo'c'sle and hit his head under the deck.

"What's up?" said Bill sleepily.

"Dream," said Pete, talking fast. "You and me we moor up that old pike stem and stern, and he start flapping his tail. He knock me down with his tail and he shift his head and I see he were coming unmoored and I try to get to him and I got the cramp and can't stir, and he shift, and he shift, and I see the rope slipping. . . . "

"Shurrup," said Bill. "You eat too much of that pudding."

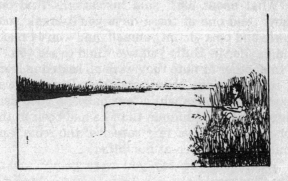

CHAPTER X

BREAKFAST AT DR. DUDGEON'S

Dᴉᴄᴋ and Dorothea came round the corner of the house just as the gong was ringing for breakfast. Tom, coming downstairs eight steps at a time, met them in the hall.

"Tom!" exclaimed his mother, from the dining-room, as he reached the ground floor with a final bump.

"All right, Mother. No victims to hear me." The doctor's patients were not in the habit of calling before breakfast.

"What about me?" said his father. "And our baby? And one of these days you'll break your ankle and be a victim yourself, and won't I make you pay for it. Hullo you two. Glad to see you."

In another minute they were all seated in front of their porridge bowls, and Mrs. Dudgeon was pouring out coffee while "our baby", a good deal bigger and more human than he had been in the spring, lay in a cot in a corner of the room, and smiled and bubbled at his father.

"Where did you say you were going?" asked Mrs. Dudgeon.

"Ranworth," said Tom. "Coot Club expedition. The *Death and Glory*'s coming toc."

"Keep an eye on those young Coots of yours," said Dr. Dudgeon. "Tedder looked in last night after you'd gone to bed. He'd been talking on the telephone with Mr. Sonning at Potter Heigham."

"But they hadn't done anything," said Tom. "It's all a mistake. They just moored above the bridges, spent the night there and came back yesterday. They never touched another boat."

"Mr. Sonning tells quite another story," said his father. "He says they were seen going up through Potter Heigham Bridge. That's all right. But then, after dark, when there was no one about, they came down and cast off half a dozen boats moored by his sheds. All his men were busy getting hold of the boats next morning and your three had disappeared. And then, it seems, they came down through Potter astern of a motor boat and were away before anybody could stop them."

"I'm dead sure they didn't touch any boats," said Tom.

"They were as surprised as anything when the policeman came and told them about it," said Dorothea.

"I don't think they're that kind of lad," said Mrs. Dudgeon.

"No more did I," said Dr. Dudgeon. "But you must admit it looks rather funny. One coincidence is likely enough ... But three! ... "

"Oh, but look here, Dad," said Tom. "I'm sure they didn't cast off that cruiser, and that other boat at the staithe ... why I was with them when they found her, and nobody would have thought we'd had anything to do with it if only George Owdon hadn't seen us bringing her back to the staithe and tying her up."

"Yes, I know," said his father. "But what about the other boats cast off that night? They've been about each time boats have been cast off here, and when they go to Potter the same thing happens there. And you know, Tom, at the back of my mind I can't help remembering that cruiser you cast off yourself, and I can't help thinking they've been acting on the principle that what was right for you is right for them."

"Oh, but I say," said Tom. "You said yourself you didn't see what else I could have done. The *Margoletta* was moored right on the top of our coot's nest. Her chicks. . . . "

"It's no good going into old history," said Dr. Dudgeon. "But you just keep your eye on those lads and give them a hint that casting off boats isn't cricket as a general thing."

Mrs. Dudgeon changed the subject by asking what they were going to do at Ranworth, and Dick, who had hung his camera over the back of his chair while at breakfast, told her they were going to take photographs of some of the old nests, just for practice so as to be sure they made no mistakes later on when they were going to photograph the birds actually sitting.

They had finished their porridge and were busy with bacon and eggs when Dr. Dudgeon, who was, as usual, eating his breakfast and reading the newspaper at the same time, suddenly laughed.

"Your Coots again," he said. "Listen to this. Somebody must be pretty angry to be writing a letter about them to the paper."

He read aloud:

"Sir,
Hitherto this district has had a good reputation, with the exception of one seaport town which I

need not name and which, thanks to its excellent
and public-spirited corporation, has done much to
remove the blot on its scutcheon (Browning) made
by the behaviour of certain longshore pickers up of
unconsidered trifles (Shakespeare). Latterly however I understand that I am only one of many
sufferers from an outbreak of hooliganism that is
afflicting a district once well known for its civilized
amenities to the benefit of the boating public. Boat
after boat properly moored in places legitimately
set aside for that purpose has been sent adrift to
the risk of its own damage and that of others. I
am informed that it is well known that this is
the work of a regular gang of boys masquerading
under other auspices. Their names are known.
That they are allowed to continue their activities
unhindered is a poor testimonial to our so-called
police. May I suggest that they should devote more
time to their duty and less to the winning of prizes
at agricultural shows.

I am, Sir,

Yours, etc.,

Indignant."

"That's a hit at poor old Tedder," said Dr. Dudgeon. "It was his marrow won the silver medal,
wasn't it? I don't think 'Indignant' means that
the gang of boys are successful gardeners, though
that is what he actually says."

"I wonder who 'Indignant' is," said Mrs.
Dudgeon.

"He can't be one of the Potter Heigham people,"
said Tom, "because that was only yesterday morning. He might be the owner of that boat we

salvaged when she was adrift with her mast in the trees. He ought to be jolly grateful instead of calling the Coots a gang."

"Well," said Dr. Dudgeon. "He's certainly gone the right way about making things hot for them. That touch about Tedder's prize-winning will stir him to the marrow."

"Dad!" exclaimed Tom.

Mrs. Dudgeon smiled. Dorothea laughed aloud. Dr. Dudgeon said he was sorry. He had not meant it for a pun.

"It was an awfully good one," said Dorothea.

"Thank you," said Dr. Dudgeon. "Now, if I'd been able to put '(Shakespeare)' after it, in brackets, like Indignant, it would perhaps have been appreciated even by my own family. Have some toast, Dorothea, and will you have marmalade, or honey? 'Our so-called police' is another shrewd touch. I think you'll find Mr. Tedder coming round to take out summonses. . . . "

"Oh no, Dad," exclaimed Tom. "He can't. You mustn't let him. They've not done a single thing. It was just bad luck, their happening to be somewhere about when someone else was casting boats off, or leaving them not properly tied up or something."

"Mr. Tedder won't get his summonses unless he can produce his evidence," said Dr. Dudgeon. "You can be sure of that. But I am not quite so sure as you are that he won't be able to get it. And it isn't only Tedder who'll be after them. If they've. . . "

"They haven't," said Tom.

"If anyone's been casting off Sonning's boats

at Potter, he won't stand it, and you know who his solicitors are."

"Not Uncle Frank?" said Tom.

"Well, he's in the firm, and if Mr. Sonning stirs up Farland, Farland & Farland you'll have Uncle Frank after whoever it is and pretty determined to get them."

"But he's Port and Starboard's father, and they're Coots. He'd know it wasn't the Death and Glories anyhow," said Dorothea.

"He may not have quite the opinion of your young friends that his daughters have," said Dr. Dudgeon. "Well, let's hope they don't get into any more trouble. Where are they now?"

"At the staithe," said Tom. "Or on their way here. We're all going to Ranworth together."

"Any other boats at the staithe?" said Dr. Dudgeon.

"No," said Tom. "No small ones. Only *Sir Garnet*, and nobody'd dare to send a wherry adrift. . . . " Tom stopped suddenly. From where he sat at the breakfast table he could see out of the window across the open lawn to the river. At the side of the lawn there were bushes, and over those bushes he had seen something moving.

"She's coming down now," he said. "Bill told me old Simon said they were going down through Yarmouth today. They must be quanting. No sail up. I can see her vane above the trees. You'll see her in a minute. Here she comes. . . . I say. . . . Come on, Dad, QUICK!"

Dr. Dudgeon was out of the door almost as soon as Tom. *Sir Garnet* was coming down the river as Tom had said, but she was coming down broadside on and there was nobody aboard her. No one was at the helm. No one was walking her side decks with a long quant. Her gaff and big black sail were still stowed as they had been the night before. She was coming down the river by herself.

Tom and his father raced across the lawn. Dick and Dorothea raced after them. Mrs. Dudgeon watched them from the window.

"She's coming close in," said Tom. "She'll touch. . . . She'll . . . "

There was a sudden long scrunch as the stem of the great wherry, pointing rather upstream than down, hit the wooden piling along the edge of the lawn. As she touched, Tom jumped aboard. There was enough spring in the piling to throw her off again, and, as she drifted on, she was further and further away.

"Steady, Tom," called Dr. Dudgeon. "Don't try to jump back. Make fast lower down if you get a chance."

But Tom was not listening. His father was a fisherman but Tom was a sailor first of all. He had seen *Sir Garnet*'s mooring rope hanging over her bows and was hauling it in and coiling it on his arm just as fast as he could. Another five yards and he would be too late. . . . Another three yards. . . . "Stand clear, Dick," he shouted. "Catch, Dad." The coil of rope came spinning through the air, uncoiling as it came. Dr. Dudgeon caught it.

"Hang on, Dad, hang on. . . . Take a turn round that post. . . . Ease her. . . . Well done, Dad."

A wherry drifting with the stream is a heavy

thing to stop, and Dr. Dudgeon could not have
held her without the post to help him. But he
had got a turn round it and had only had to
ease out a foot or two of rope before the stern
of the wherry began to swing in, and her bows
came again towards the piling. Tom leapt ashore
to fend off. Dick and Dorothea were fending off too.
Between the four of them they had stopped her
and made her fast. Another minute and it would
have been too late. She would have drifted below
the Coot Club dyke and they might not have had
a second chance.

"Well," said Dr. Dudgeon. "I'm glad of one
thing. I can give evidence myself that you and
Dick and Dorothea had no hand in casting her
off. But what about those others? I wonder if she'd
have gone adrift if I'd had the whole Coot Club to
breakfast instead of only you three."

"I'm sure they didn't touch her," said Tom.
"Joe was as pleased as Punch because old Simon
had told them to keep an eye on her."

"And here she is," said Dr. Dudgeon.

"Gosh!" said Tom. "Look here. I'd better take
Titmouse straight up to the staithe to say we've
got her."

"Quicker to run," said Dr. Dudgeon. "And the
sooner the better. You find out what those Coots
of yours were doing. And get word to old Simon or
Wooddall if he's about. Put things right as quick
as ever you can."

But as Tom turned to go he glanced up the
river. A dinghy with two men in it was coming
down and by the way the oars were splashing
anybody could see that they were in a hurry.

"It's Jim Wooddall," he said, and a minute or two later the wherryman, very red, brought his dinghy alongside the lawn and jumped out, followed by his old mate.

"What's this?" said Jim angrily. "I know you cast off that *Margoletta*, but casting off *Sir Garnet*! What have we done for you to play a trick like that?"

"Steady, Wooddall," said Dr. Dudgeon. "Tom was having his breakfast and happened to see the wherry drifting down and you may thank him for jumping aboard and mooring her for you. He had nothing to do with casting her off."

"Then it's them lads," said the wherryman. "And if their Dads don't wallop the hides off 'em I'll. . . . Simon, ye old gaum, where did you leave that warp?"

"On the hatch-top I coil him," said old Simon. "You see me do that, and wicked he were too, for all our towing. . . . "

They looked this way and that over the wherry. The big coil of new rope had disappeared.

"Pushed over, likely," said Jim Wooddall. "And they sons of boatbuilders. . . . Ought to be in jail they ought. . . . Forty fathom of new coir rope."

"It'll float, won't it?" said Tom, looking downstream.

"Not two minutes longer than anyone see it," said Jim. "Why, I just bought that rope . . . " All the time he was looking round *Sir Garnet*. Old Simon had taken the dinghy's painter aboard and was looking anxiously along the other side of the wherry.

"No damage," said Dr. Dudgeon. "Bit of tar

SAVING *SIR GARNET*

perhaps, and she may have shifted some of my piling. But it's lucky it's no worse."

"She ain't hurted herself nowheres," said Old Simon coming ashore again.

"No thanks to them lads," said Jim Wooddall. "You ought to teach 'em better, young Tom. Going to the bad they are, straight as the New Cut."

"And that lie straight as a crow fly," said old Simon.

Jim glared at him. "If you'd have slep aboard," he said. "Come on now. Cast off that bow rope and we'll swing her and up sail. We got to get down to Yarmouth and maybe find that rope as we go. Going through to Norwich, we are, or I'd have something to say to them lads. There ain't never been goings on like this, and when I come back. . . . What's that Tedder doing? 'Police Station' up over his door and that close again the staithe and *Sir Garnet* cast off as if there weren't no police nearer than Kingdom Come."

He calmed suddenly.

"Well, Tom," he said. "The Doctor can speak for you, and I'm glad I were wrong. I never would have thought it till I see you with her. And thank you kindly for pulling of her up. She'd likely have been into the ferry by now and me with damage to pay out of my pocket. I 'pologise, Doctor. Ought to have knowed it weren't your son. But as for them three by the staithe. . . . Now then, Simon. . . . "

"I'm pretty sure they didn't do it," said Tom.

"I'm sure they didn't," said Dorothea.

Dick was nervously cleaning his spectacles. He put them on again. "Why should they want to do it?" he said.

"Doggone it," said Jim Wooddall. "You'll be saying next I cast her off myself. If they ain't done it, who did? And when I get back. . . . Easy now, Simon. . . . So she go. . . . "

The great wherry's bows had swung out and round with the stream. Old Simon was aboard and winding at the winch. Jim Wooddall who had taken a stern warp to the post on the lawn, now let it slip, hauled it in and took the tiller. The big black sail lifted, the gaff swinging as it went up. *Sir Garnet*, the fastest wherry on the river, was on her way.

The little group at the edge of the lawn watched her go.

"Well, Tom," said Dr. Dudgeon. "I don't wonder Jim Wooddall was a bit upset. It might have been a serious thing for him. And he's known those lads since they were born, and you see what he thinks about them."

"But he thought first it was Tom," said Dorothea, "and we know it wasn't."

"Wrong once may be wrong twice, you mean," said Dr. Dudgeon. "Well, I hope so. Your Coots ought to be above suspicion, and I'm afraid they're not. And if they've been taking Wooddall's rope. . . . Hullo. Here the culprits are, and I'll leave them to you. . . . "

"But they aren't culprits," said Tom.

"Better make sure," said Dr. Dudgeon. "I'll get to my work. I don't want to ask questions and be told lies. . . . "

"They won't tell you any," said Tom.

"I don't want to give them the chance," said his father. "But you'd better talk seriously to them and find out if they've had a hand in this or not."

He walked back to the house, leaving Tom and Dick and Dorothea at the water's edge, watching the *Death and Glory* which was coming down the river, not under sail but rowed by Bill and Joe, who were standing in the cockpit, each working an oar, while Pete sat on the forward end of the cabin top, with his head in his hands.

"They're in an awful stew," said Dorothea.

CHAPTER XI

"WE GOT TO EMIGRATE"

JOE and Bill were almost too short of breath to speak and Pete was biting his lips and trying to look as if he didn't care when the *Death and Glory* rounded up by the Doctor's lawn, and Tom and Dick took their ropes.

"What happened?" asked Tom.

"Somebody cast off *Sir Garnet* while we was asleep," said Pete.

"Pete wake first and we chivvy him out to put his head in a bucket," said Joe, "and he sing out she've gone."

"We come up and look," said Bill, "but we didn't think nothing of it, only they'd been quiet getting away. We know she weren't tied up with no slip knots or nothing, because we look at 'em after you was gone, just before we turn in."

"We didn't think nothing," said Joe. "We has our brekfuss, and we was just about finished when we hear old Simon on the staithe, singing out to know if Jim had left a message for him. And then come Jim Wooddall and he were fair out of his mind when he see she gone. And he come ranting at us thinking we done it. And there was somebody fetch Tedder. They was all shouting and saying we ought to be kept off the river. And George Owdon go telling how he catch us casting off that yacht we was tying up. And there was chaps from Jonnatt's telling about that cruiser.

And somebody say 'Fetch their Dads', and Bill
say to me we better get out, and we begin to
cast off and get our ropes, and then somebody
grab hold of the old ship and won't let go, and Jim
Wooddall were shouting to know what time of tide
we push her off, and we was telling him we didn't
push her off, and there was everybody come across
the road from the shops hearing the shouting and
yelling, and our Dads wasn't nowheres handy and
whatever we say get shouted under, and then that
young Phil come from his milk round and say he
seen her down river and not so far neither, and
Jim and old Simon they grab a dinghy and was
off after her, and Jim saying he'd settle with us
proper when he come back.

"And then we try to shove off again, but there
was half a dozen of 'em grab hold. Somebody sing
out to know where we was off to, and we tell 'em
we was only going to Ranworth with you. I will
say that for George Owdon. He were the only one
to speak for us. He say to let us go, we couldn't do
no harm in Ranworth being out of the river. And
they start arguin', and we see our chance and give
a shove off. They was still arguin' when we get
away."

"We'll get stopped off the river," said Pete bitterly. "And we ain't done nothing at all."

"We got to emigrate like you say," said Bill,
looking at Dorothea.

*

Mrs. Dudgeon came across the grass to the
waterside carrying the baby.

"Tell me all about it," she said.

ESCAPE FROM THE STAITHE

"We try all her ropes after Tom go home last night," said Joe. "Fit to hold a battleship they was. And this morning she ain't there and everybody think we done it. And we ain't done nothing."

"You don't think you could have loosened the ropes when you were trying them," asked Mrs. Dudgeon but, at the look on their faces, went on: "No, of course you couldn't have done that. I was forgetting you are shipowners yourselves. And so Jim Wooddall thought you had cast off his wherry and taken his coil of rope. You didn't touch that by any chance?"

"He ain't lost his new warp!" exclaimed Joe. "Why, it were brand new. They was towing it yesterday and we see old Simon coiling it down."

"It had gone," said Tom.

"And this ain't Yarmouth," said Joe indignantly. "My Dad always say them Yarmouth sharks'd grab the bottle from a baby, but there ain't nobody here like them chaps."

"He never think we take his warp," said Bill. "He never say nothing about that."

"He didn't know about it till he came down here to get aboard *Sir Garnet*," said Tom.

"He got her all right?" said Joe with relief.

"We just caught her drifting past," said Tom.

"When did you first see she had gone?" asked Mrs. Dudgeon.

"Pete were up first," said Joe, and between them they told her the whole story again. She listened quietly, jiggling the baby every now and then.

"And Honest Injun you had nothing to do with it?" she said when they had run out of breath describing their escape from the staithe.

"Honest Injun we ain't never touched her only last night when we make sure how she were moored," said Joe.

She looked at Bill.

"Honest Injun we didn't," said Bill.

She looked at Pete.

"Honest Injun," said Pete.

"I believe you," she said, and the eyes of the Death and Glories were like those of three grateful dogs.

"It's just a bit of bad luck," said Mrs. Dudgeon. "And it'll come right in time. What are you going to do now?"

"Coot Club cruise to Ranworth," said Tom.

"And never come back no more," said Pete. "Then they'll be sorry they try patching it all on us."

"Rubbish," said Mrs. Dudgeon.

"We'll stop the night in Ranworth," said Joe. "No good our coming back."

"We just *got* to emigrate," said Bill.

"Do your mothers know?" asked Mrs. Dudgeon.

"We didn't have time to run round," said Bill. "We was lucky just to get away. But they won't have nothing against our going. Our Dads say why not us cruising when others do."

"What about food?" said Mrs. Dudgeon.

"We got plenty of that," said Joe more cheerfully, remembering the well-stocked cupboards.

"Now, look here," said Mrs. Dudgeon. "I shall be going up the village later on, and I'll see your mothers and tell them where you are. Perhaps it's just as well for you to be away from the staithe when people seem to have got a wrong idea into their heads. But don't get into any more trouble if you can help it. Dick and Dot have got to be back at Mrs. Barrable's by dark, and Tom's got to bring them, but I dare say they'll sail down again and bring you news in the morning. Photographing old nests is the idea, isn't it?"

"Just for practice," said Dick.

"Well, off you go," said Mrs. Dudgeon. "I dare say everything'll be cleared up before Jim Wooddall gets back."

"It ain't only *Sir Garnet*," said Joe. "There was boats loosed at Potter and they're on to us about that."

"And all them other boats," said Bill gloomily.

"Forget them for the day anyhow," said Mrs. Dudgeon. "Come on, Tom, and you two, and load up the *Titmouse*. Your sandwiches are all ready."

Five minutes later Tom sculled his little *Titmouse* out of the Coot Club dyke just below the lawn. Then with Dorothea at the tiller, Tom and Dick got the sail up, and they took a short tack up the river while the Death and Glories pushed off. Presently the sails were set in both boats, the water was rippling under the bows, and the six members of the Coot Club were on their way, sailing together for the first time since their adventures in the spring.

*

The klop, klop of water under the bows of a small boat will cure most troubles in this world, and if another small boat is klop, klopping along within talking distance, and first one and then the other seems to be getting the best out of the wind, worries, however bad, simply disappear.

The wind was south-westerly so that just at the start the two boats were reaching easily along and, in spite of the *Death and Glory* being a clumsy old craft, were going at about the same speed. Then, when the river bent to meet that south-west wind they had to tack, and the *Titmouse*, nipping to and fro across the river, was soon ahead. The *Death and Glory* sailed all right with a fair wind or on a broad reach but, being an old ship's boat with a long, straight keel, one thing she could not do was to go close to the wind, and another thing she could not do was to spin on her heel and make short tacks. There was nothing for it but to ring up the engines for full steam ahead, which meant that Joe and Bill took to the oars and drove her with flapping sail straight into the wind. Pete steered, sitting on the gunwale in the stern to be out of the way of the engines who stood in the cockpit to work their oars. Even he, who had been wretcheder than any of them, cheered up.

"Half ahead, starboard engine," he shouted. "Full ahead, port engine. . . . Look out, Bill, you'll have her into the bank pulling like that. . . . Rudder won't hold her. . . . Full ahead, both engines. Go it. We're catching 'em. Tom's losing wind under them trees. Stoke up. Easy, Joe. . . . Half with the port engine. Full ahead. Hi, Tom! She ain't half bad under power. Stick to it, both engines. We'll be sailing again in a minute. Bill, Bill! Full ahead! Full ahead, or you'll catch the ferry chain with that old oar. We're up to 'em. What? What? . . . What's that? . . . "

"Steam gives way to sail," called Tom. "Look out!"

"Stop, both engines!" Pete shouted. "Full astern! Yow, that were a near thing. . . . "

The *Titmouse* slipped across their bows with an inch or two to spare.

"Full ahead now," yelled Pete. "Dig in. Dig in and she'll have to pass astern of us next tack."

"Please take her, please," begged Dorothea who was steering the *Titmouse*. Tom grabbed the tiller and did his very best, bringing her round close to the bank and off again on the other tack without losing way. But the *Death and Glory*'s engines were working fit to burst their boilers and, as the *Titmouse* shot again out towards the middle of the river, she was pointing not ahead of the *Death and Glory*'s bows but at them, then amidships, then at the panting engines, and finally clear of her stern.

"Done it," said Pete, looking gleefully over his shoulder.

As the river curved again below the ferry, the wind came clear off the shore again. The flapping sail filled and steadied. Their ship was moving faster than they could row her.

"Finished with engines," said Pete, and Bill and Joe thankfully brought their oars inboard and stowed them on the cabin-top.

"There's No. 7 nest," cried Dorothea, and for a moment their troubles came back into their minds as they remembered how in the Easter holidays Tom had cast off the Hullabaloos who had moored their *Margoletta* close over that nest and had refused to move when they were asked. They all knew that it was because of this that everybody was so ready to believe that the Coots had been casting off boats again.

Dick alone thought of something else. "What about taking a photograph?" he said. But already the two boats had swept by.

"Get it in the spring when the coot with the white feather's sitting on it," said Tom. "There'll be lots more in Ranworth."

There came another reach where the *Death and Glory* needed the help of her engines, and then a reach where the wind came dead aft, and they blew together down the middle of the river towards the lawns with the water-hens and the black sheep. Then another bit of careful steering and they came round the big bend to the entrance to Ranworth Broad, where the engines made ready to set to work in earnest to drive her through the narrow dyke into the teeth of the wind.

"That's where Port started chasing swans' feathers to keep the Hullabaloos looking the other way," said Dorothea. "And it's round the next bend that the Admiral was moored in *Teasel* and we saw the Death and Glories for the first time."

"We was pirates then," said Pete a little regretfully.

Both boats turned into the narrow dyke. The *Death and Glory* lowered sail, and after a tack or two Tom did the same. Both boats rowed slowly up the dyke together.

"That fare to rain," said Bill, looking up at the darkening sky before them.

"It does look like it," said Tom. "I say. We never brought our oilies."

"It won't rain yet," said Dick. "We'll have plenty of time to get some photographs."

"We can change when we get home," said Dorothea.

"We're all right, come wet, come fair," said Joe.

"What about your cabin when it rains?" asked Tom.

"We putty up them leaks," said Joe. "We putty 'em before that last rain, and there waren't no more come in, only that drip over Pete's bunk, and we puttied that after."

"That come down on my head like a water-spout," chuckled Pete.

Half way along the dyke they came on a couple of men loading reeds into a reed-boat, and they waited while Tom rowed *Titmouse* into a good position for Dick to take a photograph.

"Focus fifteen yards," said Dick aloud, getting his camera ready. "Exposure one fiftieth. . . . Stop six point three. . . . "

"You haven't set the shutter," said Dorothea.

"Just in time," said Dick, stood up in the boat, took his photograph, sat down hurriedly and wound on to be ready for the next photograph. "I keep on forgetting that," he said, "and then I press the button and nothing happens. The other thing is to remember to wind on after each exposure. And to remember I've wound on if I have, so as not to wind on again and waste a bit of film."

"He gets very good photographs," said Dorothea . . . . "The ones that do come out."

"What about getting a photograph of the *Death and Glory*?" said Tom.

"Wait till we're out on the Broad," said Joe. "Get her when she's sailing."

There were trees now on each side of them instead of only reeds. The dyke divided, one branch, with chains across it, leading to some private water, the other gradually widening, leading to the open Broad.

"It's the Straits," cried Dorothea. "There's the place where *Titmouse* was when Tom came back after dark, and we saw the outlaw's lonely light. Here's where we were in *Teasel*. There's the place where the Admiral painted out *Titmouse*'s name. There's Ranworth. . . . "

The Broad opened before them, trees and offlying islands of reeds to the right. Straight ahead of them on the far side of the Broad was Ranworth staithe, with the inn and the old malt houses and the little village and, away to the right, the square tower of the old church rising above the trees.

Up went the sails again and away went both boats, no banks to worry about, a steady wind and open sailing water. Dick took a photograph of the *Death and Glory* foaming along at her best speed, with Joe steering, Bill at the main sheet, and Pete peering through his big telescope as if they had just sighted land for the first time after a month of ocean voyaging. Then, none too easily, Tom brought him alongside while the Death and Glories kept their sail idly flapping, and Dick clambered across from one boat to the other, passing his camera across first. Tom sheered off again, and presently Dick, after letting Joe, Bill and Pete look at the tiny picture in the finder of the camera, took a photograph of the *Titmouse* with Dorothea steering while Tom lay in the bottom of the boat so as not to be seen. Then he took a photograph of Tom sailing *Titmouse* by himself while Dorothea lay low in the same way. Soon after that, Pete sighted a crested grebe, and Joe did his best to sail the *Death and Glory* so as to bring the photographer within camera-shot of it, but it dived every time they came near it and did not come up again till it was too far away to be of any use as a picture.

"Come nesting time, she'll wait for you," said Pete. "Sailing quiet, she'll sit her eggs till you can come near touching her."

"Not rowing, she won't," said Bill.

"Sailing," said Pete. "And the same with coots, specially if it's one what know us. No. 7, now, she'd never stir while we sail close by."

"Do you think we'll have any chance of photographing a bittern?" asked Dick.

"Got to find 'em first," said Joe. "But old buttle, he don't fly if he don't have to. He sit tight, and he straighten up his neck and he straighten up his bill atop, and you might be looking at him near as I am to you and think he were a bunch of reeds."

"Is buttle another name for a bittern?" asked Dick and pulled out his pocket-book.

Joe laughed as he watched him write down "Buttle = Bittern".

"And Harnsey's a heron," he said, "and Frank's a heron. . . ."

"Hear him go 'Fraaaank' when you stop his fishing," said Pete.

Dick took more notes.

SAILING ON RANWORTH

"We'll get photographs of all of them," he said, "and keep the whole collection in the Coot Club shed."

"What if there ain't no Coot Club?" said Joe, suddenly gloomy again. "And if we get stopped off the river who's to watch the nests? That George Owdon'll be selling bitterns' eggs and warblers' and beardies' and no one to stop him. Who's to stop him taking eggs if no one knows what nests there are and where to find 'em?"

"Hullo. Tom's coming back," said Bill.

Tom and Dorothea had taken the *Titmouse* far away to the other end of the Broad and were now foaming back towards the *Death and Glory*.

"What about grub?" he called as he came near. "Where shall we tie up?"

"Let's anchor instead," said Pete. "We got a mud-weight."

"I haven't," said Tom.

"Tie alongside," said Joe. "Anchor in the open sea. You get our weight, Bill."

He ran forward, and lowered the sail. Bill got out the heavy mud-weight. They made it fast to a rope and lowered it over the bows. Down it went into the soft mud at the bottom of the Broad, and presently the *Death and Glory* was lying quietly head to wind. Tom brought *Titmouse* alongside and tied up.

"I say," said Dorothea, "this is much better than being tied up to a bank."

Bill brought up cheese and bread out of the *Death and Glory*'s cabin. Joe got a packet of butter from under the after deck. Tom handed over Mrs. Dudgeon's sandwiches and three thermos flasks of hot coffee. Pete disappeared into the cabin and was presently passing out bottles of ginger beer from the storeplace under Joe's bunk.

"I say," said Tom. "You oughtn't to go and waste your money."

"We got plenty," said Pete.

"And fetch up two of them tins of pears," said Joe. "The tin-opener's on the nail behind the chimbley. And let's have old Ratty out on deck."

*

After a good mixed meal, during which Dick took a photograph of Joe's white rat holding a nut in its paws, they set out to look for old nests among the reeds. Many of the nests, of course, had sagged down into the water or fallen to pieces, but they found a very good coot's nest for Dick to photograph and showed him what had once been a grebe's nest but now was hardly worth photographing. Dick took two photographs of the coot's nest, carefully noting the different stops and shutter speeds in his note-book.

"I say," he said. "That's the lot. I can't take any more. Seven already."

"What have you got?"

He showed Tom his pocket-book with the list:

(1) Reed men and boat
(2) *D. & G.* sailing
(3) Dot sailing *Titmouse*
(4) Tom ditto
(5) White rat
(6) Coot's nest F.6.3 $1 = 50$ sec.
(7) Ditto F.8.1/25 sec.

"Gosh," said Tom. "I thought you were going to take nothing but nests."

"It doesn't really matter," said Dick.

"What about the last one?" asked Tom. "Aren't there eight to a film?"

"Got to keep that one for tonight," said Dick. "For photographing the Admiral."

"There won't be much light then," said Tom.

"I'm going to do it after dark," said Dick. "That's why I want to keep the last one of a roll for her, so that I can develop it before we go to bed."

"Flashlight," said Dorothea. "He's got a thing that strikes a spark and flares up a lot of powder."

"People use it for photographing wild animals," said Dick. "They fix up their cameras at a salt lick or a ford where the animals come, and wait in the dark, and then let off the flash when they know the animals are there."

"He's only going to practise with it on the Admiral," said Dorothea.

With no more films to spare, they took to sailing again until, though there was still sunshine, they were startled by the first drops of rain.

"Don't fare to be more'n a drizzle," shouted Bill from the *Death and Glory*.

"It'll blow over," called Tom. "But it's going to pelt in a minute. Look here, let's keep dry in your cabin till it's over."

The two boats made for the staithe which, with the wind bringing up the rain from the south-west, gave them good shelter. There Bill and Joe, in their oilskins, tied up both boats, while the whole crew of the *Titmouse* crowded headlong into the cabin of the *Death and Glory* just as the rain came down in earnest, beating on the cabin roof and splashing the smooth water into bubbles. The wind dropped. There was light below the clouds. Pete lit the stove, and after the violence of that first shower was over, the six Coots stewed themselves in the cabin watching through the open door a thin mizzle of rain and listening to the trickles of water running off the cabin roof.

It stopped at last, and they climbed out through the wet cockpit that shimmered in the sun which had once more come out from behind the clouds. They stood on the staithe looking down at their rain-washed boats.

"She'll do here for the night," said Joe. "But we'll have a look round first. We don't want nothing else going adrift and patched on us."

They walked along the staithe and looked at two or three boats moored in the dyke at the eastern end of it. They were all small boats, in good shelter and well made fast.

"Nothing to go wrong there," said Tom. "Let's have a look at the other side."

On the western side of the staithe there is green grass to the water's edge, and here the Ranworth people pull their fishing boats up and out of the way. There were perhaps half a dozen of these boats, some of them pulled right out of the water, some with just their bows lifted out, and all of them with anchors laid out ahead and firmly sunk into the turf.

"None of those'll get off by accident," said Tom. "You'll be all right here."

"Reckon we'll have to stay here till the end of the holidays," said Bill.

"There are lots of birds to look at," said Dick.

"But staying in one place," said Dorothea.

"Better'n being stopped off the water," said Joe.

More clouds were working up and Tom decided to make a push for home. He borrowed a towel from the *Death and Glory* to dry sitting places for the *Titmouse*'s crew.

"No good getting wet without you have to," agreed Bill. "You're coming in the morning, aren't you?" said Pete.

"We'll be here soon after breakfast," said Tom. "And I bet things'll have cleared up about *Sir Garnet*."

"We ain't going back without they have," said Bill.

Up went the sail of the *Titmouse*, dripping water as it lifted. It was Dick's turn to steer. The wind off the staithe was a fair one for the mouth of the dyke at the other side of the Broad, and the Death and Glories, watching critically, observed that his wake was straight enough, except for two slight waggles due to the sighting of grebes.

*

"Hullo!"

The Death and Glories, back in their cabin, looked out to see that they had a visitor.

"Hullo, young Rob. You're just too late. Tom Dudgeon's gone."

"Come aboard," said Pete.

"And wipe your boots," said Joe.

Young Rob was a small outpost of the Coot Club, and was very pleased to come aboard. He had never seen the *Death and Glory* since the building of her cabin. There was a lot to show him, particularly the stove on which Bill had put a kettle to boil ready for supper. They fed him with chocolate but told him nothing of the troubles they had escaped. Things were bad enough at Horning without starting people talking at Ranworth as well. He did not stay long. The rain came on again and as the first drops fell they heard a woman's voice calling for him.

"You skip along, young Rob," said Bill. "That's your Mum."

Young Rob skipped.

"You come along in the morning and we'll take you sailing," said Joe.

"Tell you what," said Bill. "You ask your Mum to keep some milk for us."

"Right O," said young Rob and fled across the staithe under the shower.

By the time they had had their supper, cocoa, pressed beef, boiled potatoes and two apples apiece, the rain had blown over. Before settling down for the night they went ashore and made a round of the staithe. All was well. Last thing before going to bed, they looked out once more. There were lights in the windows of the inn. Someone was singing and they could hear the cheerful plunk, plunk of darts finding their target.

"It's all right here," said Joe as they turned in. "Nothing can't go wrong."

Later still, waked by the noise of wind in the trees, he crawled out once more. The last of the clouds were blowing across the sky and it was a clear cold night.

"What's up?" asked Bill, as Joe got back into his bunk.

"Nothing," said Joe. "Bit more wind. Gosh, how that Pete do snore."

CHAPTER XII

WORSE AND WORSE

PETE woke slowly. Light was coming in through the windows of the cabin, but there was very little in the fo'c'sle where he had his bunk. Pete's was one of those muddled wakings, when yesterday and today seem to have run together. He woke, still half dreaming, into all the noise of yesterday's row on Horning staithe, with Jim Wooddall and Mr. Tedder and George Owdon, and everybody else all shouting together. It was a minute or two before he knew that no one was shouting at all, and that the only noise he could hear was the steady breathing of Joe and Bill and the faint creak of the *Death and Glory*'s wraps. Why, of course, they were not at Horning staithe but at Ranworth, where there were no wherries to get adrift and bring all kinds of trouble on the heads of honest Coots.

He reached out for an apple that he had put handy before going to sleep, took a good bite out of it, and lay there chewing and wondering what news Tom would bring. Perhaps by now someone had found out who had cast *Sir Garnet* adrift and everything would be all right and there would be no more shouting at the crew of the *Death and Glory* about things they had never even thought of doing . . . and wouldn't have wanted to do if they had thought of them. He bit almost fiercely at his

apple and thought of the trouble there must have
been in Horning even after the *Death and Glory*
had got away. Somebody, certainly, would have
told their Dads. Nothing would make his own
Dad believe he had had a hand in casting off a
wherry or any other boat, but he might not be
so sure about Joe and Bill. And their Dads, of
course, might think Joe and Bill could be trusted
but might have their doubts about Pete. And if the
three of them quarrelled over that, their Mums
would have something to say. And the worst of it
was that even if they all thought different things
Pete was very much afraid that the fathers and
mothers of all the Coots would agree in one thing,
that, no matter who had been casting off boats, the
simplest way of avoiding any more trouble would
be to have the Coots off the river. Just when at last
their boat had a cabin to her and a stove and they
were looking forward to being afloat to the end of
the holidays and spending week-ends aboard her
all through the winter. Just when that Dick and
Dorothea had come to join Tom and there were a
hundred things they would be able to do with the
Titmouse and the *Death and Glory* sailing about
together. And then he thought of Tom's father and
mother. Well, Mrs. Dudgeon had known they were
all right anyway.

He finished his apple and crawled through the
cabin to throw the core overboard and to have a
look at the weather.

The wind was much less than it had been
in the night, but was still blowing freshly off
the staithe towards the reeds along the further
shore. Pete, warm from his bunk, stood in the

cockpit and clinked the money in his pocket. It
was early. He knew that. But how early? He
looked back into the cabin to see what time it
was. Joe, last night, had forgotten to wind up the
old clock. Pete looked across the staithe. The sun
was well up. Everything looked extra bright after
yesterday's rain. A cat, on its way home, walked
slowly across the road by the inn. He heard a man
whistling. Why not slip along to young Rob's and
be back with the milk before the others woke? He
pulled out the milk-can from under the after deck
and scrambled ashore.

Swinging the milk-can, Pete walked to the edge
of the dyke beside the staithe and stopped with
a jerk. Surely there had been boats in that dyke
last night. Why, he remembered looking at them
with Tom before going to the other side of the
staithe to see the fishing boats pulled up on the
green turf. And now the dyke was empty. He ran
across the staithe. Half those boats had gone too.
There were still a few pulled right up out of the
water but all those that had been lying afloat or
half afloat with anchors ashore were gone. Pete
looked out across the wide Broad. What was that
by the reeds away on the further side? The next
moment he was haring back to the *Death and
Glory*.

He put the milk-can down on the staithe,
jumped into the cockpit and charged, stooping,
through the cabin to get his telescope.

Bill blinked at him from his bunk. "What's
the hurry?" he said.

"Come out and look," said Pete, hurrying back
into the cockpit with his big telescope. "Salvage

job, I reckon. That must have blowed hard in the night."

He lifted the telescope and trained it on the distant reeds. Over there was rippled water, and the reeds were waving in the wind, and the water was splashing among them, and . . . one, two, three . . . why, there must have been half a dozen boats or more blown against the reeds. Looking through the telescope he could see the water beating along their sides.

"Come on, Bill," he cried. "Quick. Come on, Joe. We got to get them boats."

Bill was first into the cockpit, Joe close behind him. Pete was already on the staithe, casting off the *Death and Glory*'s warps. He pushed off and jumped aboard.

"Quick. Quick," he cried. "We'll get 'em all back before anyone know they've gone."

But Bill and Joe thought differently.

"They'll take no harm against them reeds," said Bill.

"Up with that sail," said Joe.

"But ain't we going to get them?" said Pete. Always before, the mere sight of a boat in difficulties had been enough to bring the *Death and Glory* full speed ahead to the rescue.

"Not going to be had that way twice," said Joe. "If anybody see us with them boats they'll say we cast 'em off, same as George Owdon say when we tie up that cutter that were caught in the trees."

"Sure as eggs is eggs they'll say it's us," said Bill, who was hurriedly setting the sail.

Joe steering with one hand and hauling taut

the sheet with the other was anxiously looking
back towards the village.

"No one stirring yet," he said.

"What are we going to do?" asked Pete.

"Dig out," said Joe.

Already they were moving fast. With every
yard they got a better wind as they left the
shelter of the land and the *Death and Glory* fled
from Ranworth staithe as if pursued by ghosts.

"If we can get clear of the Broad before anybody see us," said Bill coming back into the
cockpit.

"But they see us here last night," said Pete.

"It's the worst that happen yet," said Joe.
"Who's going to believe us now?"

"Can't we do nothing about them boats?" said
Pete. It was dreadful to see them, three or four
open rowing boats, a small motor cruiser, a half-
decked sailing boat and a couple of dinghies,
splashed by the waves and tossing, tossing end-
lessly against the reeds.

"We just got to get out," said Joe. "It's the only
thing we can do, and that ain't much. Anybody
showing yet, Bill?" With the strengthening wind
he had to look to his steering.

"No. . . . At least. . . . Hullo. . . . There's chaps
on the staithe now."

A distant shout was blown after them across
the water. A man. . . . Two men and a small boy
were standing waving on the staithe.

"There's young Rob," said Bill, who had grabbed
Pete's telescope and was looking through it. "He'll
tell 'em it weren't us."

"Put your head in a bucket and boil it," said

Joe angrily. "He don't know who done it but he know who we are."

Joe at the tiller, could not look back. The other two saw one of the men take a furious kick at something on the staithe that flew into the air and landed with a splash in the water.

"They're raging mad," said Pete.

"They're pointing at us," said Bill.

"Course they are," said Joe between his teeth. "And they ask young Rob, what's that boat? and young Rob he chirp up and tell 'em that's the *Death and Glory*. He won't know no better."

"I ain't walk under a ladder," said Bill. "Not since that time I do and fall in the next day. And I ain't spilt no salt. And I ain't seen never less than two magpies together. I ain't the Jonah." He looked doubtfully at Pete.

"I ain't no Jonah," said Pete.

"Shurrup," said Joe. "Nobody ain't no Jonah. Somebody cast off them boats apurpose. Tell me all them boats could get away together and call it bad luck. Somebody push 'em off. What are them chaps doing now?"

"Getting a boat out," said Bill.

"Coming after us," said Pete.

Joe glanced over his shoulder and then looked ahead once more. In another few moments the *Death and Glory* would be out of the Broad and behind the trees in the dyke leading to the river.

"They'll not catch us now," he said. "And they won't try. They've enough to do with all them boats to tow off of the reeds. But that don't make no differ. That'll be patched on us same as everything else. Stand by to gybe. . . . "

In another moment Ranworth staithe was out of sight behind the trees, and the *Death and Glory* was blowing slowly down the dyke. They met a reed-boat with the men whom Dick had photographed. The men waved, and the three Coots waved back.

"That done it," said Joe gloomily when they were out of hearing. "Them chaps have seen us, even if young Rob don't give us away."

"But we ain't done nothing," said Pete.

"Tell that to Mr. Tedder," said Joe.

They swept out of the dyke into the main river.

"Let's go down to Acle," said Bill.

"We can't," said Joe. "There's Tom coming and that Dick and Dot. We got to stop 'em going to Ranworth. We got to go so's they'll meet us. Gybe oh!"

The sail swung across with a loud flap and the *Death and Glory* turned upstream. That way, at least, were friends as well as enemies.

Free from pursuit, they began to think of breakfast. Also, the further they got from Ranworth the nearer they came to Horning and the less they were inclined to hurry.

"Look here," said Bill. "We don't want to get back before Tom bring us the news."

"Stop anywhere now," said Joe.

They were passing the lawns with the black sheep, and coming into a reach where the wind headed them.

"Out oars," said Joe. Today, he had not the heart to talk of engines, at least until he had his breakfast inside him.

They rowed grimly up that reach and then,

getting the shelter of some high reeds, tied up a little below No. 7 nest.

"We got to use tinned milk," said Pete.

"Course we got to," said Joe.

"I were just going off with the milk-can when I see them boats adrift," said Pete.

"Where is that can?" said Bill, glancing under the seat.

"Oh gosh," said Pete. "That were our milk-can that man take a kick at. I go and leave it on the staithe."

It was the last touch.

"Cheer up, young Pete," said Joe. "That handle come off twice already. We got to get a new one anyway."

"We got money for that," said Pete, and at the thought felt better.

CHAPTER XIII

TWO WAYS OF LOOKING AT THE SAME THING

Tom had already brought the *Titmouse* out of the dyke and round to the edge of the Doctor's lawn when Dorothea arrived on the run to say she was sorry they were late and Dick would be coming in two minutes as soon as he had been able to put his photographs to wash.

"Did he get any good ones?" asked Dr. Dudgeon, who was sitting on the wooden seat by the river, smoking an after-breakfast pipe.

"One's a beauty," said Dorothea. "Two others would have been only they both came out on the same film. Joe's rat's rather blurry, but he knew it would be because of the focus. The flashlight picture of the Admiral came out all white. But the one of the *Death and Glory* is as clear as anything. You can even see Pete's telescope. He developed them last night before going to bed and printed them before breakfast. He was fixing the prints when I thought I'd better come and explain why we were a bit late."

"What's that?" asked Dr. Dudgeon, looking at the exercise book Dorothea had in her hand. "Holiday task?"

"It's part of my story," said Dorothea.

"What's it called?"

"*The Outlaw of the Broads.*"

"Outlaw or Outlaws?" said Dr. Dudgeon, rather

grimly.

Before she had time to answer someone else came round the corner of the house.

"Hullo, Uncle Frank," said Tom.

"Hullo to you," said Mr. Farland.

"You've met Dorothea," said Dr. Dudgeon.

"How do you do?" said Dorothea.

"How do you do?" said Mr. Farland. "Well, Tom, I hope we shan't be putting you in gaol."

"What for?" said Tom.

"You and your young friends. Mr. Tedder's got a list of crimes against them that looks pretty bad. That's what I wanted to see you about, Dudgeon. They seem to have been up to something worse at Potter Heigham than casting off other people's boats."

The Doctor took his pipe out of his mouth.

"By Jove, Tom, I wish you'd never touched that cruiser in the spring, even though I did tell you I didn't see what else you could have done. It's going to be a bit difficult for me if Mr. Tedder comes and asks for a summons against those three for casting boats adrift when I know my own son set them an example."

"Oh well," said Mr. Farland. "Tom doesn't go in for stealing."

"Stealing!" exclaimed Dot and Tom together.

"Old Sonning of Potter Heigham's been on the telephone to me again this morning," said Mr. Farland. "He was pretty well het up about all his boats being set adrift, but he didn't know then that those young rascals had been into his store and cleared out a lot of gear. He says there's a gross and a half of new gunmetal shackles missing."

"But I'm sure they never did," said Tom.

"Sonning's sure they did," said Mr. Farland, "and he's asked us to advertise a reward for evidence leading to conviction. He says they're bound to have sold them to someone else, and the only people who'd buy them would be other boatbuilders. He doesn't think there'll be any difficulty in getting the evidence."

"But Tom's young friends seem to get along very well without money," said Dr. Dudgeon. "I don't suppose they've ever had more than a bob or two in their pockets in all their lives."

Tom looked at Dorothea. She had turned white and for a moment looked as if she were going to be sick. Both of them were remembering the feast in the *Death and Glory* and the crammed cupboards that night when the three small Coots had come back from Potter Heigham.

Dr. Dudgeon was going on talking. "And it's all very well, Farland, but Tom isn't the only one who thinks they didn't have anything to do with the casting off of those boats. Ella had a talk with them and she's come down on their side. Tedder's been here too and he tells me there was a free fight about it yesterday among some of the men and young Pete's father got a black eye. Tedder wanted to know what he was to do about it, and I told him he couldn't serve a summons on a man for having a black eye nor yet on someone else for giving him one unless he was in at the fight, or unless one of them asked for a summons against the other. I hope that's good law."

Mr Farland laughed. "Good enough," he said. "By the way, where are they now, Tom?"

Tom looked up doubtfully. "You're not going to arrest them?" he said.

"Wish I could," said Mr. Farland. "At least, I wish we had proof enough against them to get the thing settled. I'd only like to know where they are, in case somebody else finds his boat adrift."

"They've gone to Ranworth to be out of the way," said Tom. "So if any more boats are cast off everybody'll know it isn't them."

"They may be tired of the game," said Mr. Farland. "Three times they've done it. . . . "

"But they haven't done it at all," said Dorothea.

"Put it differently," said Mr. Farland. "Three times boats have been cast adrift when they were somewhere handy to do it if they had had it in mind."

He had a few more words with Dr. Dudgeon, said goodbye, and a moment later they heard him start his car and drive off on his way to Norwich to the office of Farland, Farland & Farland.

"My goodness, Tom," said Dr. Dudgeon. "I used to think that Coot Club of yours was a very good thing, but I can't say I'm so sure about it today."

"But they haven't done a single thing," said Tom indignantly.

"Things keep happening where they are," said his father.

"Suppose," said Dorothea, "someone else likes doing those things and always manages to do them when the Coots are there to get the blame."

Dr. Dudgeon looked at her gravely. "Potter Heigham's a long way from Horning," he said.

"Well, nothing else is going to happen where

they are," said Tom. "They'll be all right at Ranworth."

"If anything were to happen there," said Dr. Dudgeon, puffing at his pipe, "I might begin to think there was something in Dorothea's brilliant theory. But I don't think anything will. Whatever else those young rascals may be, they are not half-wits, and if they've cast off boats here and at Potter they'll take good care not to do the same at Ranworth now the hue and cry is out after them. No. Nothing will happen there, but that won't stop Uncle Frank and Mr. Tedder from finding out what they can about the other things."

Mrs. Dudgeon was walking across the lawn with a parcel.

"Cook's made you a pie," she said. "Keep it this way up and give the innocents my love."

"Innocents!" exclaimed Dr. Dudgeon.

"I'm sure they are," said Mrs. Dudgeon. "And you can tell them their parents think so too. They wanted to bring them home but I told them it would be rather hard on the boys to spoil their holiday if they haven't done anything. So you're to tell them they'd better keep away from the staithe and wait till things blow over."

"You haven't heard the worst, Ella," said Dr. Dudgeon, and told her about the stolen shackles.

"It's not the sort of thing those boys would do," said Mrs. Dudgeon and got a grateful look from both Tom and Dorothea.

Dick came running with a damp photograph in his hand.

"Sorry I'm so late," he said. "I had to give it a

bit of a wash after fixing. I'll go on washing it on the way."

It was a pretty good photograph of the *Death and Glory*, with the water foaming round her forefoot, Bill and Joe sailing her, and Pete looking through the big telescope. Mrs. Dudgeon looked at it over her husband's shoulder. "They aren't that kind of boys," she said. "Don't tell me."

"I hope to goodness you're right," said Dr. Dudgeon.

*

The *Titmouse* sailed away down river to carry the news to the emigrants at Ranworth. Dick towed the photograph overboard, holding it first by one corner and then by another, to get it properly washed. Tom and Dorothea were talking over what Mr. Farland had said.

"The Admiral doesn't think they did it," said Dick.

"And we don't. And their fathers and mothers don't. And Tom's mother doesn't," said Dorothea. "But everybody else does. I say, Tom, where did they say they got the money for all those stores?"

"They said they'd earned it," said Tom.

Dorothea opened her mouth to speak, but said nothing.

The *Titmouse*, after tacking down to the Ferry, swept round the corner with a free wind.

"They'll be wondering what on earth's happened," said Tom. "I said we'd be down there soon after breakfast."

"They won't mind when they see Dick's photograph," said Dorothea.

"What went wrong with the flashlight one?" asked Tom.

"Fogged," said Dick. "It was my own fault. I had the flashlight close to the Admiral to show her knitting in her chair, and I forgot that it was in front of the camera."

And then, as they turned the next bend below No. 7 nest, they saw the *Death and Glory* moored against the reeds.

"They've come to meet us," said Dorothea.

"Young idiots," said Tom. "They ought to have stopped in Ranworth. What's the good of plans if people don't stick to them?"

The next moment he was bringing the *Titmouse* alongside and the three Coots were tumbling out into the cockpit of the *Death and Glory*.

"What's happened?" asked Tom, when he saw their worried faces.

"Someone cast off half a dozen boats," said Joe. "They was blown all across the Broad against them reeds and Pete see 'em when he turn out."

"I go and leave our milk-can on the staithe," said Pete.

"What did you do?" asked Tom. "Salvage them and take them back?"

"Not likely," said Joe. "And have everybody saying they seen us casting 'em off. We up sail and bolt for it."

"Anybody see you?"

"They come on the staithe just before we make the dyke," said Bill. "And young Rob were there. He know the *Death and Glory*, being a Coot. It's the worst yet. . . . "

"Good, oh good!" said Dorothea.

"What do you mean. . . . Good?" said Joe angrily.

"It means one more person on our side," said Dorothea.

Tom explained. "Dad said that if boats got cast off at Ranworth while you were there, he'd begin to believe someone else was doing it, because you wouldn't be such fools."

"Well, we wasn't," said Joe. "But now there's another lot'll be out after us. We may as well give up."

"Oh, no," said Dorothea.

"Mother says your people say you can stay on the river, at least at Ranworth, but better keep away from Horning staithe."

"We can't lie at Ranworth," said Bill. "Not now."

"Tell you what," said Joe. "We'll lie in the Wilderness above the Ferry."

"Well, that's off the river and handy for us," said Tom.

"Emigrating ain't no good," said Bill.

"I say," said Tom. "You know all that money you had the other night. . . . "

"We got some still," said Joe. "Are you wanting any?"

"Where did you say you got it?"

"Earned it," said Joe. "Selling fish. . . . " He caught Bill's eye, and winked. "Thirty bob and a tanner we get and another half-crown for Pete's baits. Coining money we was. . . . "

"That's all right," said Tom with relief. "I thought it was. . . . "

"Why, what about it?" said Joe.

"You know the night those boats were sent

adrift at Potter. Someone took a lot of new shackles from Sonning's store."

"Nobody don't say we was stealing?" burst out Pete indignantly, and Dorothea's heart warmed again.

"They put the two things together," said Tom, "and they're advertising to catch the thieves."

"Papering 'em, same's they did you over that cruiser?"

"Yes," said Tom a little uncomfortably. "They think the thieves'll have sold them, and they'll catch them that way."

"Hope they do and hope they skin 'em," said Joe. "Broads ain't Yarmouth."

"And that'll let us out," said Bill.

"Not about *Sir Garnet* and those other Horning boats and now this Ranworth lot," said Tom.

"Someone *must* be doing it on purpose," said Dorothea. "But everyone thinks it's the Coots so they aren't looking properly for anyone else."

"It's getting pretty serious," said Tom.

"What we want are detectives," said Dorothea.

Dick, who had been holding his print in the water, fished it up and shook the drops from it. "I say," he said. "Can I stick it flat on one of your windows while it dries?"

Just for a moment the photograph of themselves sailing wiped their troubles from the minds of the Coots. Dick came aboard and put the print to dry against the glass of one of the cabin windows. The light poured through it. Joe, Bill and Pete admired their ship. "That peak ought to be a bit higher," said Joe, "but it's a grand picture."

They went out again into the cockpit. Dorothea,

sitting in the *Titmouse*, was talking to Tom.

"Why shouldn't we find out ourselves?" she went on almost as if talking to herself alone. "I've never tried writing a detective story."

Tom heard her.

"Plenty of detectives in Horning," he said. "They're all detectives now and every single one of them's trying to prove the Coots have been casting off boats when they haven't touched a single one."

"Why shouldn't we be detectives too?" said Dorothea.

"We don't need to be detectives to know we ain't done it," said Joe. "We know that without."

"We could use my camera," said Dick. "They always have one."

The Death and Glories looked doubtfully from face to face.

"All the world believed them guilty," said Dorothea. "Their fathers' and their mothers' grey hairs went down in sorrow to their graves. . . . Were going down . . . " she corrected herself. "The evidence was black on every side. . . . And I say . . . " She suddenly changed her tone. "William'll make a splendid bloodhound."

"But William ain't a bloodhound," said Pete. "Nothing like it."

"Well, we need one anyway," said Dorothea, "and William's the best we've got."

"What's the camera for?" asked Bill.

"Photographing clues," said Dick.

"When there's a murder," said Dorothea, "they always dash in and photograph everything."

"But there ain't a murder, not yet," said Bill.

"There may be," said Dorothea excitedly. "The villain fights like a rat once he's cornered."

Bill, despairing of Dorothea, turned to Tom. "We ain't none of us villains," he said. "You know that."

"Who said we were?" said Tom. "But everyone thinks we are and with one thing and another it looks like it. Why, you yourselves thought I'd pushed off that cruiser from the staithe. And I thought you'd done it. The D's are right. If we're going to clear ourselves and save the Coot Club we've got to find out who really did do it. Someone did."

"All Horning's trying to catch him," said Joe. "There's that Tedder popping out everywhere. And George Owdon and that other watching the staithe. And them Towzers. And our Dads. And Jonnatt's chaps. And Hannam's. Everybody in the place is out to catch him. Trouble is, they all think he's us, barring our Dads."

"Well," said Tom again. "That's one up to us. We know who it isn't. And they don't."

"Them boats couldn't have got loose by accident," said Joe.

"Too many of them," said Tom.

"There may be a whole gang of villains," said Dorothea. "Can't we do what you did when Tom was being chased by the Hullabaloos and you had sentinels everywhere?"

"Put the whole Coot Club on to it?" said Joe. "We could do that. No nests to watch now. We can turn 'em all on. And tell 'em we'll drown anybody who lets a boat get cast adrift without seeing who done it. We could do that. We got members at Ranworth and Potter and Acle. . . . "

"That boy who had a stomach-ache?" said Dorothea.

"He won't have another, not in a hurry," said Joe grimly.

"Bill's got a bike," said Pete.

"We've each got one," said Dick.

"So've I," said Tom. "Let's do that. We'll turn all the Coots on everywhere to report the moment a boat gets cast adrift anywhere, and then we'll go there and find out who did it."

"From end to end of the country the net was set," said Dorothea. "Day and night patrols were out, risking their lives against a ruthless enemy. Here a chance word, there a suspicious glance was noted. The telephone bell rang continually. . . . "

"But I say," said Tom. "It mustn't. It's bad enough with victims ringing up every other minute. And it's always Dad or Mother who goes to the telephone. I can't sit by it all day."

"All right," said Dorothea. "It doesn't matter. The order had gone out that the detectives were never to telephone. The wires were tapped. The villain might be listening. So the messengers, their lives in their hands, rode through the darkling night."

"Most of 'em's got bikes," said Joe. "And you could hang the string from your window, Tom."

"We'd better begin at once," said Dick. "While the clues are fresh."

"We couldn't find out anything about Potter now," said Bill.

"But at Ranworth," said Dick. "If the villain

was casting boats off there last night he may have left clues all over the place."

"Let's go and look," said Dorothea.

"We dursn't go back to Ranworth," said Joe.

"We can," said Tom. "That's it. You get along to the Wilderness with the *Death and Glory* and we'll take *Titmouse* to Ranworth. We'll see Rob and find out something anyway. We'll come straight back. And I say. Mother sent a pie for dinner."

Dorothea handed it across.

"Don't you go and get in bad too," said Bill.

"We won't," said Tom, glad at last to have something to do instead of just waiting for worse to follow on bad. "Hop aboard, Dick."

A few minutes later the *Titmouse* with her crew of detectives was out of sight.

CHAPTER XIV

THE FIRST CLUE

THERE have been changes in the last few years along the bank of the river above the Ferry, and one or two neat bungalows have been built on what was once the Wilderness, a marshy bit of land with an old wind-pump on it, a lot of osier bushes and a narrow dyke running through it from the river to the road. The Wilderness was divided from the road by a wooden fence with a padlocked gate in it that no one used. It was also possible to get to it from Dr. Dudgeon's by going through Mr. Farland's garden and on along the river bank. The dyke was rather wider than the one in which Tom kept his *Titmouse*. There was plenty of room to bring the *Death and Glory* into it. It was not quite straight, and a boat in there was screened by the osier bushes and could not be seen from the river.

Joe, Bill and Pete brought their old ship round the bend by the Ferry, downed sail and paddled and poled her far into the Wilderness dyke. There they moored her, to the northern side of the dyke, so as to be handy when they wanted to slip along to Tom's.

"Anyone see us come in?" asked Joe.

"Not as I know," said Bill.

"Anyways," said Joe, "there ain't no boats in the Wilderness to *be* cast off."

They left the *Death and Glory* and went back to

the mouth of the dyke to watch for the return of
the detectives. Pete took his fishing rod with him,
and the worms, and caught four perch, three good
ones and a small one, which settled the question of
supper. But this success, though it cheered Pete,
did not lift the gloom from Joe and Bill who had
begun to think that if people were accusing them
of stealing boat-gear even their fathers would
think it best to make them lay up the *Death
and Glory* at once. Bill whittled away at a willow
stick, just for something to do. Joe played tunes
on his mouth organ so slowly that he turned even
cheerful ones into dirges. He played them slower
and slower till Bill said he couldn't stand it and
Joe put the mouth organ in his pocket.

At last the *Titmouse* came into sight. Dorothea
saw the waiting Coots as soon as they saw her and
eagerly waved the exercise book that was Volume
Five of *The Outlaw of the Broads*. Tom, who was
steering, waved too, and Dick seemed to be trying
to show them something, though he was much too
far away for them to see what it was.

"All right for them," said Bill. "Nobody'll turn
Tom Dudgeon off the river."

"They've found something," said Joe. "All of
'em waving like that."

Pete hurriedly took his fishing rod to pieces.
The *Titmouse* came alongside. Joe steadied her,
grabbing at her gunwale while Dorothea passed
the anchor to Bill.

Dick held out a small bit of rubber tubing.

"That's from a bike pump," said Bill.

"It's the first clue," said Dorothea.

"Jolly good thing we went there," said Tom.

"That young idiot Rob thought you'd been playing the fool with those boats."

"And he tell the others," said Joe bitterly. "I know he tell 'em when I see him there pointing. The young turmot."

"I told him you hadn't touched them," said Tom. "But they'd already sent someone off on a bicycle to tell Tedder, and the chap came back while we were there."

"He helped like anything without meaning to," said Dorothea. "He came and leant his bicycle against the fence above that green place where some of the boats were yesterday. They'd brought the boats back. Well, you know where that green bit ends by the fence and the gate into the wood. There's a bit of bare earth there and yesterday's rain had wetted it. Dick was looking about all over everywhere. He's awfully good at seeing things. Lots of people had been trampling about, pulling the boats up, and I said it wasn't any good looking for footprints when there were such lots of them. And then Dick asked the man to move his bicycle a bit, and he did, and then Dick asked if anybody else had been there with a bicycle, and nobody had. And then Dick made a drawing of the track left by the man's bicycle. I gave him a blank page out of *The Outlaw*."

"I thought he'd gone dotty," said Tom. "But he hadn't."

Dick had come ashore and was polishing his spectacles. "I couldn't have done it if it hadn't been for that rain yesterday," he said.

Dorothea went on. "Then he grovelled again ... The Admiral won't be awfully pleased ... I

"IT'S A DIFFERENT TYRE"

say, Dick, don't rub it in now. We must wait till
the mud's dry before we try to get it off ... He
grovelled again and made another drawing. And
we could see it was a different sort of tyre."

Joe jumped into the air. "Gee whillykins!" he
said. "Someone come on a bike to cast them boats
off."

"He found out much more than that," said
Dorothea. "Some of the tracks of that other bicycle
were funny and wide with hardly any pattern and
a groove each side. And some of them were narrow
and the pattern as sharp as anything. And Dick
said that someone came there on a bicycle last
night and had a puncture and pumped up his
tyre before he rode away again. And we hunted
along with our noses to the ground and we lost
the tracks and found them again on the road to
the Ferry, on a damp patch, two lots of them. ... "

"Coming and going," said Dick. "And there were
the man's tracks as well, quite different."

"Then we went back to the place by the gate,"
said Dorothea. "We started hunting again and I
found the tube from a bicycle pump. It was trodden
in the mud and I expect the villain couldn't find it
when he dropped it in the dark."

"I bet he trod on it himself," said Tom.

"Let's see them tracks," said Bill, and Dick
opened his pocket-book and took out a folded
sheet of exercise paper on which were the two
drawings.

"Dunlop, that one," said Bill. "Same as mine.
What's the other?"

"John Bull," said Dick. "But that one doesn't
matter. That's the track of the Ranworth man.

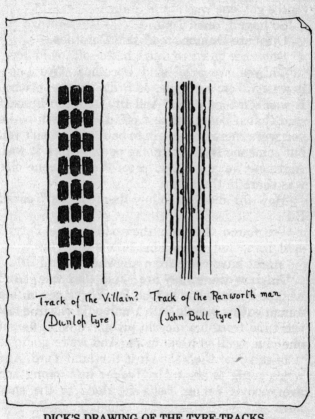

Track of the Villain?   Track of the Ranworth man
   (Dunlop tyre)   (John Bull tyre)

DICK'S DRAWING OF THE TYRE-TRACKS

It's the other that had the puncture and was there in the night and lost his pump-tube."

"There's lots of chaps got Dunlops," said Joe. "Bill's got 'em."

"So have I," said Tom.

"Ours are Dunlops too," said Dorothea.

"Don't see as we're much better off," said Joe.

"Oh yes, we are," said Dorothea. "We know it wasn't Tom's bicycle, or Bill's, or one of ours. It was someone else's. And Dr. Dudgeon himself said that if boats got cast off at Ranworth while you were there he'd begin to believe it wasn't you but someone trying to make people think it was. And now we've got real proof that someone else was there in the night."

"How far did you follow them tracks?" asked Bill.

"We found them on the road to the Ferry," said Tom, "but we couldn't follow them far."

"Might have come from anywhere," said Bill.

"Anyhow there they are," said Dorothea. "And we know now what to look for. We've got to find a man with a bicycle with Dunlop tyres who's lost the tube from his bicycle pump. Now we've got one clue we'll get lots more. And we're going to turn the Coot Club shed into Scotland Yard. And we're going to show Mr. Tedder he's wrong and everybody's wrong. Let's go along to the shed now. . . ."

"What about that pie?" said Tom. "It's long after dinner-time."

"All right," said Dorothea. "Let's have dinner and then go there."

"We got her well stowed away," said Joe. "And

there's nothing to cast off here, only her."

"Come on," said Tom.

They left the *Titmouse* moored at the mouth of the dyke and went along to the *Death and Glory*, to eat Mrs. Dudgeon's pie. Dick's photograph had dried and peeled off the window, and Dick put it in his pocket-book and sat on it during dinner to flatten it. After dinner he gave it to the Death and Glories who pinned it up on the cabin wall, between the pictures of a coot and a bearded tit that had been given them by a friend in the Norfolk and Norwich Naturalists Society. They had just agreed that they had got it straight when Dorothea asked a question.

"Does the Ferry run at night?"

Five brother detectives looked at her with admiration.

"It don't," said Joe. "But anybody who knowed it could work it for himself."

"And its chains clank," said Dorothea. "Somebody may have heard them."

"Bill's Aunt Alice work at the inn there," said Joe.

"Let's go and ask her at once," said Dorothea.

They went through the osiers to the head of the dyke and climbed over the fence into the road, and were well on their way to the Ferry Inn when Bill pulled up short.

"What is it?" said Dorothea.

"I better go ask her myself," said Bill. "Aunt Alice work there and she won't say thank you for all six of us crowding in."

Tom backed him up at once. "You go along, Bill. We'll wait for you."

They sat in a row on the fence while Bill went
on. He was back in a very few minutes. He had
walked there but came back on the run.

"It's all right," he said. "She hear them chains
rattle last night. She wake and she hear them and
she wonder who's going so late."

"Did she hear them twice?" asked Dorothea.

"Only once," said Bill. "And she don't know
which way that old ferry were going. She say if
that chap were crossing from this side she never
hear him come back, and if he were coming back
she never hear him go across."

"She must have been asleep one of the times,"
said Dorothea. "But it's good evidence anyhow. We
know now that somebody did use the ferry in the
middle of the night."

"He'd be wheeling his bicycle on the way back,"
said Dick. "His tyre had gone flat quite when he
pumped it up, and with a puncture it would soon
go flat again and the next time he wanted to pump
it he found he'd lost the tube of his pump." Dick
looked again at the little bit of tubing, but it did
not tell him any more.

"Hope he walk all the way home," said Joe.

"And a nail in his shoe," said Pete.

Tom and Joe climbed the fence into the Wilderness to fetch the *Titmouse* to the Coot Club
dyke. The others went slowly along the road past
Mr. Farland's house and in at Dr. Dudgeon's. They
found Mrs. Dudgeon in the garden just as Tom and
Joe, after tying up the *Titmouse*, came to meet
them round the corner of the house.

"What?" said Mrs. Dudgeon. "Back already? I
thought you were going to lie low at Ranworth."

"They can't," said Tom. "There were boats cast off there last night, and they had to bolt for it. But Dot and Dick and I have been there and Dick found a clue."

"Boats cast off at Ranworth?" said Mrs. Dudgeon. "Well, you wouldn't be so silly as to do that as soon as you got there."

"Even Dad will agree now that it's someone else doing it on purpose," said Tom. "And we're going to find out who. Dick's a jolly good detective. It was somebody who went there on a bicycle and had a puncture while he was there. We've got a bit of his bicycle pump."

"I'm afraid that won't take you very far," smiled Mrs. Dudgeon.

"It's only the beginning," said Dorothea. "And we know something else. It was someone from here. He was heard crossing the Ferry in the middle of the night."

"We'll get him all right," said Tom. "Coot Club shed's going to be Scotland Yard, and we're going to stir the Coots up everywhere."

Mrs. Dudgeon laughed. "Plain-clothes men in every port," she said. "Well, good luck to you. By the way, you do know they're talking of something much more serious than casting off boats?"

"I told them," said Tom.

"They can't patch stealing on us," said Joe.

"I'm sure they can't," said Mrs. Dudgeon. "And I hope they find the thief quick. It's a horrid thing to happen. But you know you are not the only detectives? Mr. Tedder was here again today."

"He think we cast off them boats," said Bill.

"I told him I thought he was wrong," said Mrs.

Dudgeon. "But if you've got any clues or get any you'd better hand them over to him."

"But they never do that in the books," said Dorothea. "We've got to find it all out for ourselves and then, just as the judge puts on his black cap . . ."

"But he don't put it on, only for murder," said Bill.

"Well, whatever he does put on," said Dorothea impatiently. "Somebody gets up in court and shows what really happened, and the judge leans out of the dock . . . no, that's where the prisoners are . . . anyway, he leans out and shakes hands with the prisoners and there are cheers and the judge gets a pair of white gloves after all."

Mrs. Dudgeon turned to go into the house. "I'll ask cook to let Scotland Yard have a jug of tea a little later on . . . And I suppose detectives can eat cake."

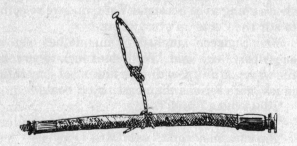

CHAPTER XV

RIVAL DETECTIVES

THE Coot Club shed did not look very much like
Scotland Yard when the six detectives trooped in.
It was a lean-to against the side of the Doctor's
house just above the dyke where Tom kept his
boats. There were oars and a spare sail with its
spars propped up in one corner of it. A couple of
fishing rods hung from nails on the walls. There
was a small table with a vice fixed to it that
served Tom as a carpenter's bench. There were
two chairs, one of which was a safe one. The
other needed care. There was also a low bench
along the wall under the window, but it was piled
with junk of all kinds. There was a big wooden
box with a primus stove on it, partly taken to
pieces for cleaning. On the walls were a lot of
pictures of birds cut out of newspapers. There
was a big map of the Broads that was really in
two parts which had been fastened together so
as to have it all in one. There was another map
on a much larger scale, made by Tom, showing
just the reaches of the river near Horning and
marking with numbers the nests the Coot Club
had found and watched over in the spring.

"Oh gosh!" said Tom, as he came in. "I never
finished cleaning that stove." He grabbed up the
burner that was lying loose and screwed it in so
that it should not get lost. "Go on. Sweep everything off that bench. Shove it into the box. All

right, Joe ... on the floor in the corner. We'll
have it all ship-shape in a minute. ... Blue pencil?
On the window sill, I think. There you are, Pete,
behind those tin tobacco boxes ... No ... You
give it to Dot. ... "

On the main wall, to the right of anyone coming in at the door there had hung a large card
with THE COOT CLUB printed on it in big blue-
pencilled capital letters. Dorothea had noticed it at
once, had taken it down, and now with the stump
of pencil Pete had found for her was printing
SCOTLAND YARD in big letters on the back
of it. She hung it again on its nail.

"Fine," said Tom.

The shed was already looking different. The
bench was clear for anybody who wanted to sit
down. Tom took the doubtful chair and gave the
loose leg a bang or two with a hammer. Pete was
stowing things away in the box, and even if there
was a huge pile of all kinds of junk in the corner
the box more or less hid it and anyhow people
need not look unless they wanted.

"I'll get that vice off the table in a minute,"
said Tom.

"Can I have the hammer?" said Dick.

"What for?"

"The clues."

He drove two nails into the wall side by side
and spiked the drawing of the tyre tracks on one,
while Joe, seeing what he wanted, took a bit of
string and with a neat arrangement of a bowline
knot and a clove hitch hung the tube from the
villain's bicycle pump on the other.

Dorothea sat herself down at the table and

suddenly jumped up again. "Oh bother," she said. "I left *The Outlaw* in the *Death and Glory*."

"But you don't want it now," said Dick.

"We want lots of paper," said Dorothea.

"I'll get some," said Tom, bolted out and was back in a moment with a pad of prescription forms.

"It's a pity they've got Dad's name on them," he said.

"Disguise," said Dorothea. "All the better, if anybody happened to see our notes. They're just what we want."

The map of the Broads caught her eye and gave her a new idea. "Pins," she said. "And, I say, Dick, you know those black envelopes your printing out paper comes in. . ."

Dick rummaged in his pocket and pulled one out.

"What for?" he asked, while the others waited to see what was coming next.

"Flags," said Dorothea. "We'll make little black flags and stick them in the map at each of the places where boats have been sent drifting."

"Good," said Tom, and rattled one small tin box after another to find the one with the thin noise of pins among all the boxes that made the noise of screws or nails. He found it at last. The pins were rather rusty, but Dorothea said that did not matter.

Joe opened a scout-knife and cut the envelope into small oblong strips of black paper. Dorothea put each pin twice through the edge of a black strip.

"Now," she said, when a dozen little flags lay in the lid of a tin. "Let's stick them in."

"Shall we take the map down?" said Tom.

"Better have it where it is," said Dick, "so that we can get a general view."

A few minutes later they stood back from the wall to look at the half of the big map that showed the Northern Broads. A cluster of black flags at Horning staithe, a few black flags along Horning Reach, black flags at Ranworth and black flags at Potter Heigham showed where the criminals had been at work.

"But them's just the places we've been," said Bill.

"How do we know boats haven't been cast off at other places too?" said Tom.

"Crumps," said Joe. "If they've been doing it in places where we wasn't things'll look a sight better."

"That's it," said Tom. "We've got to set all the Coots on the look out in case any more boats get cast off, and we've got to find out if any have been cast off already that we don't know about."

"Too late to do it today," said Bill.

"Tomorrow," said Dorothea.

"How many bikes can we get hold of?" said Joe. "There's Bill's, but it ain't here and how's he to get it without showing up on the staithe?"

"I'll slip round and bring it. We can keep it in here."

"At headquarters," said Dorothea. "And then there's Dick's and mine. That's three."

"And mine," said Tom.

"Four anyway," said Joe.

"We've an awful lot of places to go to," said Tom.

"Split up and we'll do the lot in a day," said Joe.

SCOTLAND YARD

"We ought to get that done first of all," said
Dorothea. "It's awfully important to know at once
the moment the villain does anything else. The
detectives ought to come charging in while all the
clues are fresh."

"What do we do now?" asked Pete, looking over
Dorothea's shoulder at Dr. Dudgeon's prescription
forms, on which she was ruling lines with a pencil.

"We want separate notes for each case," said
Dorothea. "Then they compare them and the truth
comes leaping out."

"Hope it do," said Bill.

"What was the first?" said Dorothea.

"That cruiser at the staithe," said Tom.

Dorothea wrote "Place" at the top of her first
column and under it "Horning staithe". "Where
was the *Death and Glory*?"

"Horning staithe," said Tom.

"We wasn't the only ones there that night,"
said Pete. "What about the bloke what bung the
brick back with my tooth?"

Dorothea wrote busily, in a column marked
"Possible clues". Then she took another prescription form. "What was the next?" she said.

"We were at the eelman's," said Tom, "and we
found that boat with her mast in the trees on our
way back in the morning."

"And there was boats cast off that night all
down the Reach," said Bill.

"Place ... " said Dorothea, "Horning staithe
and Horning Reach ... *D and G* at eelman's
... Possible clues ... I'll just have to leave that
blank."

"We never saw nobody," said Pete.

"Next," said Dorothea.

"That were *Sir Garnet*," said Bill. "And there ain't no clues neither."

"Old Simon ask us to keep an eye on her," said Joe. "And last thing I go round her ropes and then in the morning she ain't there."

"Horning staithe," wrote Dorothea. "*Sir Garnet* . . . ."

"*Sir Garnet* weren't next," said Pete. "There was that lot at Potter Heigham."

"Good thing I'm doing it on separate sheets," said Dorothea. "Now, Potter Heigham. . . . Boats cast off? . . . "

"Lot of Sonning's yachts. Half a dozen, that Tedder say."

Dorothea wrote "Six yachts". "Clues?" she asked.

"We never saw nobody there neither," said Joe. "We was up above bridges for the night and next day we come straight through. We see young Bob Curten, but that was when we was coming away being towed and couldn't stop."

"Bob Curten," wrote Dorothea.

"What about those shackles?" said Tom. "Uncle Frank said that whoever took them would probably sell them and get found out that way."

"Hope he do that quick," said Bill.

Dorothea wrote "Shackles . . . " "If we could only find out who's got them," she said, "that would clear the Death and Glories."

"That wouldn't," said Bill. "Not about the boats."

"It would help an awful lot," said Dorothea.

"And then there's Ranworth," said Tom.

"There was Rob," said Joe. "Night and morning. . . . But he wouldn't cast off them boats. Couldn't neither."

"He didn't know anything," said Tom. "He thought you'd done it."

"Silly young turmot," said Bill.

"But we do know something about Ranworth," said Dick, looking at the clues hanging on the wall.

"Possible clues," wrote Dorothea. "Someone crossed Ferry in middle of night. Bicycle with Dunlop tyres. Punctured tyre gone flat and pumped up. Bit of his pump missing and held at Scotland Yard."

"We've got a jolly good lot about Ranworth," said Tom.

"That's because the detectives were on the spot at once," said Dorothea. "If we get the plain-clothes men working everywhere so that we all get quickly to the scene of the crime we'll probably be able to grab the villain the next time he tries to do anything."

She laid the five sheets of paper in a row on the table and pored over them.

"Scientifically," began Dick and hesitated.

"What?" said Tom.

"Greatest Common Factor," said Dick. "We ought to compare all the crimes and see what was the same in each case."

"They was all different boats," said Pete.

"Yes, I know," said Dick, looking from one sheet of paper to another.

"The *Death and Glory* was there each time," he said, "but that won't be a Common Factor if we can only find some other boats have been cast off in other places. And, I say, there's one other thing. All the crimes were done at night. . . . "

"Who'd cast boats off in broad daylight?" said Bill.

"Let's make a list of things to do," said Dorothea.

By the time Mrs. Dudgeon's cook had brought them a jug of tea and a large seed-cake, their list was already a long one. Tomorrow was to be a busy day. Messengers were to go from Scotland Yard to the Coots all over the district to turn them all into plain-clothes men and to arrange for them to report at once if any boats should be cast adrift anywhere. The messengers were also to find out if any boats had been cast adrift already and if so, when and where. Then there was to be a general examination of Horning bicycles and a list made of those which had Dunlop tyres. Further, Scotland Yard was to make inquiries about anybody who had been seen mending a puncture or had taken a bicycle to the shop to have a puncture mended. With all these things to do, the detectives were in high spirits, and even Bill began to think their innocence as good as proved.

"Meet at Scotland Yard at nine tomorrow," said Tom when at last they separated and Dick and Dorothea went back to Mrs. Barrable's and Tom went off to get hold of Bill's bicycle for him, and Joe and Bill and Pete went back to their hiding place in the Wilderness to fry perch for supper in the *Death and Glory*.

"You'd never think that Dot got such a head on her," said Bill, as they climbed over the fence.

"And that Dick get things taped, don't he?"

said Pete. "Wonder if that chap mend his puncture himself or go to old Bixby's to get it done."

*

But they were not the only detectives who had been at work that day. They had skinned, fried and eaten their perch and were topping up with stewed peaches when they heard heavy steps among the osier bushes and then a heavy hand thump on their cabin roof. They came out into the cockpit to meet Mr. Tedder.

"Now, you listen to me, Joe, and Bill, and you, young Pete," said Mr. Tedder, who had been thinking just how best to surprise a confession out of the criminals. "What have you done with all them shackles you took that night you was casting off boats at Potter Heigham?"

"We ain't never touched a shackle," said Joe angrily.

"And we ain't been casting off no boats," said Bill.

"We got a lot of clues," said Pete, but shut up quickly on catching Joe's eye.

"I got all the clues I want," said Mr. Tedder solemnly. "You cast off that cruiser from the staithe and then you was seen casting off that sailing yacht. And then you go off to Potter and play old Harry. You come back and first thing you do, you cast off Jim Wooddall's wherry who ain't done you no harm. And last night. . . . Do you think I don't know what you was doing at Ranworth?"

"We tie up by the staithe there and in the morning there was a lot of boats blow across the Broad," said Joe, "but we ain't touch none of 'em."

"Why did you clear out instead of helping chaps bring 'em back?" said Mr. Tedder. "And you claiming to be salvagers."

"Bring 'em back and be told we cast 'em off!" said Joe. "That's what happen when we find that yacht with her mast in the trees."

"Listen to me," said Mr. Tedder. "I know your Dads and got nothing against 'em. I don't want to be harder on you than need be. You own up honest and hand over them shackles and I'll make things as easy as I can."

"We haven't got no shackles," said Joe.

"It'll be worse for you in the end," said Mr. Tedder. "There'll be a notice on the staithe in the morning. Printing it now, they are."

"Giving a reward?" said Joe.

"Giving a reward they are," said Mr. Tedder. "You ain't got a dog's chance."

"Maybe we have," said Joe. "We'll have a try for the reward."

Mr. Tedder grunted. He had made up his mind not to lose his temper. "There's another thing," he said. "Maybe you ain't got them shackles, not now, but you know who has. You been spending a lot of money."

"We earn it," said Joe.

"Who did you work for?" said Mr. Tedder. "They tell me you was throwing it about. And you didn't get it from your Dads. I know that."

"We earn it selling fish," said Pete.

"What fish?"

"Pike," said Pete. "We catch a whopper."

"Pike!" exclaimed Mr. Tedder. "Who'd give you a penny a pound for it to throw it away?"

"Chap fishing," said Pete.

"Where is he?"

"Gone away to Norwich," said Joe.

"So he would," said Mr. Tedder. "Now, don't you tell me lies like that. You've been good lads all of you till you take silly and start acting silly. Just you own up and make it easy for yourselves."

"We ain't got nothing to own up," said Joe.

"There's other ways of finding out," said Mr. Tedder, and went off through the bushes.

"How did you know we was in here?" Pete called after him.

"There ain't very little as the police don't know," said Mr. Tedder. "As you'll find out."

SHACKLES

CHAPTER XVI

SPREADING THE NET

At nine in the morning Joe, Bill and Pete were just turning in at Dr. Dudgeon's gate when Dick and Dorothea came into sight on their bicycles. They went through the garden together and found Tom waiting for them in Scotland Yard.

"They've done it," said Tom. "Uncle Frank told Dad."

"What?" said Dorothea.

"Put up that notice," said Tom grimly.

"Papered us," said Joe. "That Tedder tell us last night they was printing it."

"You didn't go to see him?" said Tom.

"He come to see us," said Joe, "wanting them shackles we ain't got."

"You didn't tell him about our clues?" said Dorothea.

"We tell him we ain't got no shackles," said Joe.

"Let's go and look," said Pete.

"But ought they to go to the staithe?" said Dorothea.

"Nothing to stop us now," said Bill. "That Tedder know where we are."

"We'll go in a minute," said Tom. "But there's no point in going and coming back again before we start out. Some of us'll be going that way anyhow."

"Who's going where?" said Bill.

"Four bicycles," said Tom. "I got yours last

night. Oh, and I had to tell your mother where
you were. She wanted to know if you were still
at Ranworth. She wanted to come and see you
today, but I told her not till tomorrow, because
you were going bicycling."

"Did you see my Mum too?" asked Pete.

"No," said Tom.

"Mine'll tell her," said Bill.

"Now look here," said Tom. "It's no good Dick
and Dot going. They don't know the other Coots
and the other Coots don't know them. We'll have
to borrow their bicycles. You don't mind, do you?"

Dorothea minded very much. But she knew
Tom was right. This spreading of the net was not
a job for strangers. So all she said was, "Mine's a
girl's, but if it'll do."

"Pete's smallest," said Tom. "He'll be all right
on it. Now have a look at the map. We've got
members pretty well everywhere. I'll do Potter
and then go on to Hickling. Somebody else'll
have to do Irstead and Barton and Stalham. I'll
do Ludham on the way to Potter. Then somebody's
got to do Wroxham. And then there's Ranworth,
South Walsham and Acle. Acle's a likely place. I
wish we'd thought of it yesterday while we were
at Ranworth so as not to have to go there again.
But we've got to put Rob on the watch."

"Ranworth chaps'll be looking for us," said Bill.

"Mustn't be caught," said Joe. "I'll go there."

"Yes," said Tom. "Joe goes to Ranworth and
Acle."

"I'm as good as Joe," said Bill. "They'll as likely
catch him as me."

"Toss for it," said Joe.

Tom tossed. Joe called, and won, and began to look with interest at Dick's bicycle.

"I can move Dot's saddle a bit lower," said Dick measuring Pete with his eye.

"Don't get into rows, anybody," said Dorothea. "That won't help. All we want now is information . . . and getting detectives on the look out in each place."

"Dot's right," said Tom. "No rows. Just find out if there's been trouble with any other boats and tell all Coots to report full tilt to Scotland Yard the moment they hear of a boat being cast off anywhere. Bill does Irstead and Stalham. Stalham's the likelier place. Pete'll do Wroxham. Not so far to ride. . . . Coltishall too if he likes, but we haven't got a member there."

"I can easy ask the chaps with the boats," said Pete.

"What are we to do?" asked Dorothea.

"Somebody ought to be about at the Yard," said Tom. "And keep a look out generally."

"And keep that Tedder off the *Death and Glory*," said Pete.

"We've got to have lunch with the Admiral if we're not going anywhere," said Dick.

"You see we're staying with her and we've been out nearly all the time," said Dorothea. "She was very decent, and said she wouldn't mind if we were taking our bicycles anywhere. . . . But if we're not . . . . "

"That's all right," said Tom. "So long as there's someone at the Yard to get the reports when the detectives come in. That won't be till afternoon. I say, what about grub?"

"We got ours," said Bill, patting a fat pocket.

"And I've got mine," said Tom.

"Let's start," said Pete.

The four detectives who were to spread the net of Scotland Yard all over the northern Broads wheeled their bicycles out of the Doctor's gate. The other two came with them. Dick took a spanner from the tool case that hung behind his saddle and lowered Dorothea's saddle an inch to make it easier for Pete.

"That looks about right," said Tom.

"Let's try it," said Pete. He put a foot on one pedal, pushed off and flung his other leg across. Dorothea laughed.

"That's not the way to get on," she said.

"Never mind," said Tom. "He's on all right."

Pete wobbled a little but presently steadied himself. He turned in the narrow road without falling, rode back to them and got off in the same way that he had used when getting on.

"It ride same as a boy's," he said. "It only look different."

The six of them walked together to the staithe. A couple of Jonnatt's boatmen looked at them in no very friendly way, and turned round to watch them as they went up to the notice-board.

Tom read the notice aloud. Yes, there was no doubt about it. There it was, in two parts . . . . "Damage done to private property by interference with moored craft. . . . "

"But there ain't been no damage," said Bill.

"There may have been," said Tom.

He went on reading. "STOLEN. From Sonning's boat-yard at Potter Heigham . . . one gross of two-inch gunmetal shackles . . . half a gross of inch shackles . . . information leading to conviction . . . to Messrs. Farland, Farland & Farland or to any Police Station . . . reward will be paid . . . . "

"Gosh! That do sound awful," said Pete.

"Well, it ain't us anyhow," said Joe.

"Everybody think it is," said Bill.

"But it isn't," said Dorothea. "And won't it be a sell for everybody if the Coot Club gets the reward?"

That was a better way of looking at it. But it was with serious faces that the detectives made ready to set out.

"Scotland Yard this afternoon," said Tom.

"We'll be there," said Dorothea. "Hi! Dick!"

Dick had forgotten everything but a row of swallows on the telephone wire.

"Sorry," said Dick. "I didn't hear. I was just wondering how they know when to go."

"They're going now," said Dorothea.

"I meant the swallows," said Dick, but came back to earth in time to see Pete mount Dot's bicycle, again in his own way, and ride off with Tom and Bill.

Joe watched them till they turned the corner by the inn.

"See you again," he said, and Dick and Dot standing in the road by the staithe watched him jump on Dick's bicycle and go off at a tremendous pace on his way past Dr. Dudgeon's to the Ferry.

"Hullo. Are you left behind?" Mrs. Barrable, followed by the stout pug-dog, William, came up to them carrying her painting things. "I've just

met Tom and two of his friends bicycling as if
their lives depended on it."

"Everything does," said Dorothea. "Have you
seen the notice?"

They took her to the notice-board. She read
the notice carefully through.

"Somehow I can't believe they did it," she said.

"Of course they didn't," said Dorothea. "Don't
you see, Admiral, it's like this. . . . "

"Well, I hope you're right," said Mrs. Barrable.
"But where are they off to in such a hurry?"

"Far and wide," said Dorothea. "Scotland Yard's
begun to cast its net. You see if we can only find
who did do it, everything'll be all right. And if
boats have been cast off when they weren't anywhere near people'll begin to see it wasn't them.
And if any more boats get cast off we want to
start detecting right away. There may be a clue
for William to work on. . . . "

"William!" exclaimed Mrs. Barrable.

William looked up at her and grunted.

"He's our bloodhound," said Dorothea.

"I'd never have thought it of him," said Mrs.
Barrable. "But I'm sure he'll do his best. What
are you going to do with the rest of the day?
Aren't you bicycling too?"

"It wasn't any good our going," said Dorothea.
"You see we don't know the Coots they've gone to
see. We've lent them our bicycles. We're in charge
of Scotland Yard and the *Death and Glory*."

"I wonder if they'd like a picture of their *Death
and Glory*," said Mrs. Barrable.

"They'd simply love it," said Dorothea. "They
were awfully pleased with Dick's photograph. And

DETECTIVES ON THEIR WAY

if you're going to paint I can get on with *The
Outlaw*. I left Volume Five there last night."

"What about Dick?"

"There are sure to be some birds in the Wilderness," said Dick.

The three of them strolled through the village with William. Mrs. Barrable looked in at
Dr. Dudgeon's and had a word with the Doctor's
wife while Dick and Dorothea visited Scotland
Yard and had a look at yesterday's clues and
notes. Then they crossed the Coot Club dyke by
the drawbridge (which in these days was never
raised) and went through the Farland's garden
and so along the bank of the river to the dyke
in the Wilderness where the *Death and Glory* lay
hid.

"She makes a lovely picture in there among
the willows," said Mrs. Barrable. "And if I plant
myself here those reflections give a patch of colour
just where I want it." The Admiral took her folding
stool from Dick and prepared to settle down. "But
I wish those boys were on board."

"Would it do if I sat in the cockpit?" asked
Dorothea. "I'll be keeping still anyhow writing.
I'll just slip into the cabin to get the book."

She climbed aboard, and jumped down into
the cockpit. This was just the place to write
The Outlaw, afloat in the old boat. She turned
the handle of the cabin door. It would not open.
She rattled it, and looked at the keyhole. There
was no key there, but the door was locked.

"Oh, bother!" said Dorothea.

"What's the matter?" asked Dick.

"I can't get in."

Dick came aboard and tried the door.

"What's the matter?" asked the Admiral.

"They've locked us out," said Dick.

"Oh rubbish," said the Admiral. She too came along and tried the door. She, too, failed to open it. And then, as people do when they cannot get into an empty house, they looked in through the windows. And there, on the opposite bunk, lay Volume Five of *The Outlaw of the Broads* where Pete had put it, meaning to bring it to Scotland Yard.

"What am I to do?" said Dorothea. "I can't do any detecting till the others come back, and I've got a bit of the *Outlaw* all ready to write."

"What about the book you had with you after breakfast?" asked the Admiral.

"That's for Scotland Yard," said Dorothea. "Evidence and reports from scouts and all that. And I'm in the middle of a chapter in Volume Five." She looked dolefully through the cabin window at Volume Five lying in a patch of sunlight on the bunk.

"I can give you a bit of paper," said the Admiral. "Write on that and copy it out afterwards. Lots of authors never work any other way. Like sketching, you know, before doing a picture."

"Yes, I could do that," said Dorothea. "It's a bit of dialogue and I've got to get it just right."

The morning passed peacefully away. Dorothea with pencil and paper worked in the cockpit of the *Death and Glory*, trying to keep her mind on *The Outlaw* and not to let it go wandering off after the four detectives. Dick lay in the grass and watched a water-hen. Mrs. Barrable painted.

William explored, coming back to them now and then to make sure that he was not really alone.

Once William stiffened and barked. For a moment they thought they heard someone moving in the bushes at the head of the dyke, and Dorothea started up, thinking that one of the others had come back. But, if there was anyone there, he went away and William barked no more.

Towards one o'clock they went home to Mrs. Barrable's for lunch and in the afternoon Dick and Dorothea borrowed the bloodhound and came back to Scotland Yard to wait for the return of the detectives.

CHAPTER XVII

NEWS FROM THE OUTPOSTS

"WHAT's happened to the sun?" said Dorothea. "I can look straight at it without blinking."

Dick and Dorothea were standing outside Scotland Yard. William was lying down. It is hard work training a pug-dog to be a bloodhound, hard work for everybody.

"It's like that day when we got stuck in the fog on Breydon," said Dick.

"I wish they'd hurry up," said Dorothea and as she said it they heard the ring of a bicycle bell.

"Pete!" exclaimed Dorothea. "That's my bell."

Gravel scrunched under wheels suddenly braked, and, a moment later, Pete, pushing Dorothea's bicycle, came round the corner of the house. He looked a little wobbly at the knees and was very out of breath.

"Ain't biked for a long time," he said.

"Well?" said Dorothea. "What happened? Come on. Let's go in. I ought to write down your report."

"Nothing to report," said Pete. " 'Cept we've lost a member."

"How?"

"We hadn't only one in Wroxham and that was young Tim and now he's out. His Dad come raging up when I were talking to him, and he tell me to get further and he say he won't have his Tim mix up with any gang like the Coot Club

223

and if he'd have knowed what Tom Dudgeon was up to he never would have let his Tim join us. 'Bird Protection!' he say. 'Getting into gaol more like.' "

"They'll be sorry some day," said Dorothea.

"They're all the same," said Pete. "There's Rodley's. They was friends of ours after we salve that *Margoletta* for 'em, but now they was as bad as Tim's Dad. I go along there and ask if anybody been casting off boats at Wroxham, like you said, and they start laughing at me. 'Come to the wrong place you have' say that fat foreman. 'Ain't no Coot Club at Wroxham. You better go to Horning and ask there.' "

"But didn't you find out?" said Dorothea. They had gone into Scotland Yard and Dorothea, pen in hand, was at the table looking at a page on which she had written "District Reports". She had divided the page into four columns headed "Place", "Boats cast off", "Date", and "Where D & Gs were at the time".

"None cast off at Wroxham," said Pete. "I'd got that out of Tim before his Dad came along. I only ask at Rodley's to make sure. But there ain't none been cast off. Tim'd have know if there was."

Dorothea wrote "Wroxham ... None", and said, "But, of course some may be any day."

"We won't know," said Pete. "Who's to tell us with Tim out?"

"What about higher up the river?" said Dorothea. "What's that other place?"

"Coltishall," said Dick, who was looking at the map.

"Nothing cast off there," said Pete. "But they hear about boats cast off at Horning and Potter, and about them shackles being stole. They ask me who done it, and I say we was working to find out."

"That's right," said Dorothea. "They always say that. Scotland Yard is following up a clue and an arrest is expected shortly."

"Well we got lots of clues," said Pete. "It's the following up's the job."

Dorothea wrote "Coltishall ... None". She looked regretfully at the little heap of black flags on pins that she had been hoping to stick into the map to show that boats had been cast off where the Coots could not have had a hand in it. "Oh well," she said. "The other places are much further away, and the further away the better the proof. Who'll be back next?"

"Let's go out in the road and see if anyone's in sight," said Dick.

"Let's go along to the *Death and Glory*," said Dorothea. "I've left *The Outlaw* there and I've got something to write in it. I could see it through the window, but I couldn't get in."

"You can't now neither," said Pete. "With that Tedder about, Joe he take the key."

There was nothing to be done but wait.

"Oh well," said Dorothea. "Somebody always has to do a lot of waiting while detectives are making inquiries. At the real Scotland Yard people are waiting about day and night."

*

Bill was the next detective to return.

"They know about us right away at Stalham," he said, as he leaned his dusty bicycle against the shed. "The way that talk do fly. Jimmy Pellacote at Stalham he ask me where we sell them shackles. I tell him we ain't got no shackles, nor never cast off no boats, but he say everybody know better'n that. And I go for to teach him different but he run off home and me after him and his Mum come out to me and tell me to leave him alone and there's no more bird protecting for any son of her'n if that's what it come to, and what do my Dad think of me? And how do I dare show my face, and on and on she go getting hotter while she talk."

"What did you say?" asked Dorothea, hurrying in and sitting down at the table.

"She don't give me no chance to say nothing," said Bill. "She push that Jimmy in behind her and slam her door and I come away. But there ain't no boats been cast off at Stalham. I ask a lot of chaps."

"Bother," said Dorothea, and added "Stalham . . . None" to her list.

"Did you see Tommy at Irstead?" asked Pete.

"Is he a Coot too?" asked Dorothea.

"He ain't a Coot not really," said Bill. "He ain't got a head on him no better'n a squashed frog. I see him all right but he don't know nothing. Fishing he were on the gravel reach."

"Catching anything?" asked Pete, who, detective or no detective, was still a fisherman.

"Perch," said Bill.

"Oh, never mind the fish," said Dorothea. "Had any boats been cast off?"

"He tell me to keep my shadow off the water," said Bill. "So I creep up and give him one of my sandwiches and when I ask if any boats been cast off, why Tommy he say, 'How do you know?' "

"Go on. Go on," said Dorothea, reaching out for one of the little black paper flags all ready on its pin.

"I say I don't know but I want to know and Tommy he say it weren't his fault and I say when were it and what boat and Tommy he said it were his Dad's row-boat and he give it Tommy to tie up and Tommy he tie it to a stick what broke and he have to go in swimming to catch it."

There was a groan from Dorothea. "That doesn't count," she said and wrote "Irstead . . . None".

"Nothing at Barton neither," said Bill, and Dorothea wrote again.

"Never mind, Dot," said Dick. "Tom may have found some more have been cast off at Potter Heigham. And Joe's not back yet either."

*

It was already late in the afternoon when Tom rode round the corner of the house and vaulted off his bicycle by the door of Scotland Yard.

"None at all?" said Dorothea, who knew the moment she saw his face that he was not bringing good news.

"Not a boat," said Tom. "Either at Potter or Hickling. And the boatmen at Sonning's were rather beastly. They're all dead sure the Death and Glories did it and they said if they catch one of them they'll make him sorry for it, police or no police."

"They won't catch us here," said Pete. "And if they try anything my Dad'll . . . "

"Oh yes, Tom," said Dorothea. "But . . . "

"There's never been any boats adrift at Potter except just that one night when they were there. It's awfully unlucky."

"It was done on purpose that night," said Dorothea. "I'm surer than ever."

"Well they all think it was the Death and Glories," said Tom. "And young Bob Curten ran away the moment he saw me and I had to catch him and then he said he wasn't going to be a Coot any more."

"Same as Jimmy at Stalham," said Bill.

"And young Tim at Wroxham," said Pete.

"There's going to be no Coot Club left," said Tom. "What about boats at Stalham and Wroxham?"

Dorothea showed him her melancholy list.

"None cast off anywhere," said Tom. "Joe back from Acle?"

"Not yet," said Bill.

Dick was at the door, looking up at the tops of the trees over the dyke. "I say, Tom," he said. "Does fog always come with an east wind?"

Dorothea looked anxiously at Tom. People didn't always understand the way Dick's mind wandered off. But Tom was quite glad to think for a moment of something other than the troubles of the Coots. "The sea's over there," he said. "So it usually does."

"It did that day when we were on Breydon with the Admiral," said Dick. "And it's coming up now. Look at it drifting through those trees."

Tom put his head out. "Just a sea roke," he said. "Doesn't look like a bad one. Nothing to worry Joe. Gosh, I do hope he's found something down at Acle."

"Likely enough place," said Bill. "There's always boats tied up above the bridge or below. But who'd go casting them off?"

"Well, I wish he'd hurry up," said Dorothea. *"The Outlaw*'s locked up in the *Death and Glory* and Joe's got the key, and I've got nearly half a chapter to copy in."

"Things look pretty bad," said Tom.

"It'll be all right in the end," said Dorothea. "Scotland Yard always wins."

Steps sounded outside. "Well, I'm sure it deserves to," said Mrs. Dudgeon at the door. "If you would like your tea in here, you must come and fetch it."

"We'll be having supper when Joe come back," said Pete. "We can't get aboard till he do."

"Nothing against having tea here as well," said Mrs. Dudgeon. "Come along, Bill. Can I trust you to carry the jug? And Tom can bring the tray. It's all ready."

"Thank you very much," said Bill.

"That biking do parch you," said Pete.

"Have you all been bicycling?" asked Mrs. Dudgeon.

"Four of us," said Dorothea. "Far and wide. They're all back except Joe. He's gone to Acle."

"Acle!" exclaimed Mrs. Dudgeon.

"And Tom's been to Potter Heigham and Hickling. And Bill's been to Stalham. And Pete's been to Wroxham and that other place."

"Whatever for?" said Mrs. Dudgeon.

"Looking for evidence."

"And did they get any?"

"Joe may have done," said Dorothea, but even she said it without much hope.

*

Tea in Scotland Yard turned into something very like a feast. Of tea itself there was a bedroom jug full. There were two loaves of bread, white and brown, and butter and strawberry jam and marmalade, and when Bill caught sight of the pile of sausage rolls that Mrs. Dudgeon had provided he said they were enough to sink a ship.

The detectives set to work at once, being careful to set aside one sausage roll for Joe for each round of rolls they ate, so that he should have his fair share. William, the bloodhound, liked sausage rolls better than bread and jam, but he was not allowed so many as the others, and after he had eaten three Dick and Dorothea agreed that he ought not to have any more, because Mrs. Barrable had said that he was quite fat enough, considering how little exercise he took.

"No more rolls, William," said Dorothea, "but you shall have your share of chocolate later on."

Joe's pile of sausage rolls grew and grew, but still there was no sign of him. Two or three times Pete, who could not help fearing that Joe might have got into trouble at Ranworth, went out into the road to see if he was in sight. Finally Tom went out too and came back to say that the mist was thickening into a regular roke. "Not that it'll matter to Joe . . . but I do wish he'd come."

"He's the last hope," said Dorothea. "If no boats have been cast off except the ones we know about then it's no wonder people think the Coots did it."

Time went on. The evening began to close in and Dorothea began to worry about getting home. "It doesn't matter being a wee bit late, but we've got to be back by dark, and I can't get *The Outlaw* out of the *Death and Glory* till Joe turns up with the key." She looked at Joe's pile of sausage rolls and down into the jug. "And the tea we've left for him must be stone cold," she added.

"Shall I go and get some more?" said Tom.

"Listen," exclaimed Pete. "What's that?" And the next moment Joe, hot and dusty, came round the corner of the house wheeling Dick's bicycle.

"What news?" said Bill, Tom and Pete, all together.

"None we couldn't do without," said Joe. "And I get a puncture in your bike, Dick. I get it mended in Acle. It's all right now. . . . But everything else is all wrong. And my throat's parched to nothing."

"The tea's cold," said Dorothea.

"Good," said Joe, and Dorothea poured him out a mugful and he took it down in big gulps.

"I bike about two thousand mile," said Joe.

"You never," said Bill.

"Ten thousand," said Joe. "All along of young Rob at Ranworth. I come there, going careful round by the church and I see young Rob and he see me, and then that old farmer come round the corner and he see me too, and he sing out to some others, 'Here's one of 'em,' and come running. And I round with my bike and off and I think better not take the road to the Ferry, so I take t'other.

They was after me but they didn't catch me. Bet they took Ferry road."

"Go on," said Dorothea. "Go on."

She filled up his mug and Joe gulped again, goggling at his listeners over the rim.

"Well, I think no good my going off without seeing young Rob, so I wait a bit and make a round and come back and I don't see nobody till I come down by the Maltster's, and there were that young Rob on the staithe, and you wouldn't believe it but that young Rob run away. So I hop on and after him and catch him, and he say to leave him go, he ain't a Coot no more. . . . "

"That's another," said Bill gloomily.

" 'Coot or no Coot,' I say, 'you'll wish you was a dead one if you don't talk sense.' And I ask him if any boats been cast off. And he say no only them boats we cast off ourselves and I were mad as mad and just then there were that old farmer again behind me and two or three more up the road and young Rob he twist away and I jump on and ride for it and there was three or four tumbling over each other to stop me and one of 'em near had me off, but don't and I keep going to South Walsham. Nothing cast off there neither, but chap on the staithe say 'Ain't you one . . . ' and I don't wait. And then, coming into Acle there's my front tyre gone flat. Lucky that weren't in Ranworth. And I walk the last mile into Acle and I find our chap. . . . "

"The stomach-ache boy?" said Dorothea.

"That's him," said Joe. "He won't get no more stomach-aches out of being a Coot. He say right off he ain't a Coot no more."

"We got nobody left," said Bill. "The Coot Club's bust already. Only us three and Tom."

"And Dick and me," said Dorothea.

"No boats adrift at Acle," went on Joe, "nor anywheres else as he know. Well, I make him pinch what's wanted off of his brother's bike, and we mend that puncture in his yard while his Mum's up to the village, and she come back and see me and he were into the house in two shakes and I were off again. I could hear her going on for near a mile."

"And then?" said Dorothea.

"After them two goes at Ranworth I think better come back t'other way, and I cross Acle Bridge and round by Repps and through Potter hard as I could lick for fear they stop me, and back by Ludham. . . . Can I have another of them rolls?"

"That lot's all yours," said Dorothea, and poured him out yet another mug of cold tea.

"Well," said Tom, "that means that the only boats set adrift are the ones we know about. So we've wasted the whole day."

"It isn't really waste," said Dorothea. "It's exploring avenues. They always do it. You see Scotland Yard's in the middle and the avenues are all round. They explore them one after another. They go down one and there's nothing but . . . oh . . . a rabbit hutch. They go down the next one and there's only an empty orchard. And then they go down the last one and there's the villain and they catch him. What's that, Pete?"

Pete, who had been whispering to Bill, went pink.

"Go on, Pete," said Bill.

"Why not go down that one first? I say. We got no time for all the others."

"But we don't know which it is," said Dorothea. "And it wouldn't be detecting if we did. And anyway it isn't waste. We've learnt one thing for certain."

"What's that?"

"Why, we know for certain now that whoever cast all those boats off chose places where the Coots were. It couldn't happen that way by accident every time. Tomorrow we'll try to find the villain's bicycle. But I say, Dick, we ought to go home. And I've got to go to the *Death and Glory* to get *The Outlaw*. Joe's got the key."

"Gosh!" said Joe. "Didn't Pete bring that book for you this morning?"

"I put it out to bring," said Pete.

"Let's go there now," said Dick.

"We'll all go," said Tom.

"All right," said Joe, biting into a roll.

"Let him finish his grub," said Tom. He was looking at the map on which a pencilled line under the name of a place meant that it was an outpost of the Coot Club. "That means no one at Acle," he said. "No one at Potter, no one at Wroxham, no one at Ranworth. . . . There's only us at Horning left. . . ."

"There won't be us if we can't find who cast off them boats," said Bill.

Dorothea looked out of the door. It was beginning to grow dusk outside and the thickening mist made it seem later than it was.

"I say, we *must* go," said Dorothea. "Come on, William."

She went out of the door and waited a moment. William followed her. The others were crowded round Tom, who had taken down the map of the Northern Broads and was rubbing out the pencilled lines under the names of the places that had been outposts of the Coot Club and would be so no more.

"Come on, William," said Dorothea.

"We're just coming," called Tom. "I say, Dick, how soon will you and Dot be coming in the spring? We'll want everybody we can get if the birds are to have half a chance . . . ."

Dorothea and William started on their way.

CHAPTER XVIII

A SCRAP OF FLANNEL

DOROTHEA waited a moment at the drawbridge over the Coot Club dyke. There was nothing more that could be done that day and she wanted to get hold of *The Outlaw* and hurry home to be in time for Mrs. Barrable's supper, even if she herself did not feel hungry after all those sausage rolls. Bother those boys. "Coming," Tom had said, but they were still talking in Scotland Yard. She crossed over into the Farlands' garden, putting William on his leash for fear he might get interested in botany. She went through the garden, round the Farlands' boathouse and through the wooden gate into the Wilderness. Here she unleased the bloodhound, and the stout William paddled on ahead, sniffing, trotting, scratching among the osiers and then trotting on again. He had formed a high opinion of the Wilderness and the wet autumn mist gave a new flavour to its delightful smells.

Dorothea listened for the others, could not hear them, and went on picking her way through the damp grass along the narrow path beside the river while William, who scorned paths, was exploring through the willow bushes far ahead. It certainly was pretty misty. Her mind went back to that day of fog in the spring when the *Teasel* had lost her way on Breydon Water and William had been a pug-rocket. Everybody had given him good marks for that, but now, as a bloodhound, Dorothea had to admit to herself that the younger Coots were right in not taking William very seriously. William's interests came and went like patches of sunlight on a windy day with clouds. A bloodhound ought to think of one thing at a time. If only, for example, William were a little more like Dick . . . in one of his scientific moods, of course. Bother those boys! Dorothea wished she had borrowed the key from Joe. She would have had time to get the book and be back at Scotland Yard. . . .

She came to the place where the Wilderness dyke opened into the river. Here the path turned to the left along the dyke and Dorothea looked ahead of her through the mist for the first glimpse of the *Death and Glory*. There she was, just beyond the next lot of overhanging willows. Hullo! Dorothea quickened her pace. Tom and the others must have gone round by the road and been quicker than her. There was one of them already at the old boat, standing on the bank, leaning over and patting her enormous chimney pot.

"Hullo!" called Dorothea. "You've been jolly quick."

She got no answer out of the mist.

She called again.

Whoever it was at the green chimney pot turned suddenly and rushed off into the bushes. The next moment there was a startled squeal from William, a squeal of pain and fright and rage all mixed together, a shout, the crash of someone falling, another squeal from William and the noise of running feet.

"He's trodden on William!" cried Dorothea. "Hi! William! William!"

Steps sounded behind her.

"What's the matter?" called Tom.

"One of the others went round by the road," said Dorothea, "and I startled him and somehow he trod on William. . . ."

Tom looked over his shoulder.

"But we're all here," he said, and she saw Pete, Joe, Bill and Dick coming along behind him.

"What's up?" said Pete.

"There was someone at your boat," said Dorothea.

"Come on," cried Joe, and the crew of the *Death and Glory* rushed past Tom and charged along the dyke to get to their ship.

"Where is he?" said Bill.

"Can't see no one," said Joe.

"But there was a minute ago," said Dorothea. "Didn't you hear William squeal? He got trodden on. William! William!"

They had all reached the *Death and Glory*. Joe and his mates were already aboard looking here and there about their ship. Joe was in the cockpit. He had pulled the big key out of his pocket and was opening the cabin door.

"Door's all right," he said. "Nobody ain't been here."

"But I saw him," said Dorothea. "I saw him. I thought it was Tom. He was patting the chimney and I called out and then he ran away into the bushes and he must have fallen over William. And where is William? William! William! Come to heel!"

SOMEONE WAS PATTING THE CHIMNEY

Just then William, breathless and muddy, came out of the bushes, shaking his head as if he were worrying a rat. He came up to Dorothea and plumped, panting, on the ground.

"He's bitten him!" cried Dorothea. "Good dog. Good dog. I knew there was somebody here. And William's a bloodhound after all. Look what he's got."

William, after a little coaxing, gave it up, a torn and slobbery scrap of grey flannel.

"Somebody's trousies," said Pete. "It's like what Tom wear."

"Well, it wasn't me," said Tom. "I was behind her with you."

"Course it weren't you," said Pete. "I only say it's a bit of trousies like what you wear."

"And anyway," said Tom, "old William wouldn't bite me. He'd be much more likely to bite one of you."

"He wouldn't bite any of us, said Dorothea. "I don't believe he's ever bitten anybody before."

Dick, when his turn came, looked at the bit of flannel. "It may be another clue," he said.

"The villain himself!" said Dorothea.

"Which way did he go?" said Dick.

"He went off into the bushes," said Dorothea. "Just there. Then there was a crash and William yelled and he yelled too, not exactly yelling, just short, and then I heard him running."

"Come on," said Tom. "Let's go after him."

"With William," said Dorothea. "Good William. Worry him. Worry him. Come on. You've got to be a bloodhound again."

But William had had enough excitement and would take no interest in the search as the others worked their way through the bushes.

"Dick better go first," said Joe, remembering the detective work that Dick had done at Ranworth.

"Go on, Dick," said Tom.

It was easy tracking. Anybody could see the place where William's enemy had stumbled and crashed over the unsuspecting bloodhound. Anybody could see where he had charged on towards the road.

"He didn't make for the gate," said Tom.

"Why should he with that old lock on it?" said Joe. "Nobody do."

Dick stooping low moved slowly on.

"Oh, go on, Dick," said Tom. "We might catch him if we hurry."

"I didn't think of that," said Dick simply. "I was looking for more clues. He might have dropped something."

They found nothing. They came to the fence that divided the Wilderness from the road. No scraps of grey flannel had caught in splinters or nails. There was nothing to show exactly where their quarry had climbed over. They climbed over themselves and looked up and down the road. No one was in sight.

"Too late," said Dorothea.

"Dick's found something," said Pete.

Dick had stopped short close by the fence and was looking at the ground.

"What is it, Dick?" said Tom.

"Bicycle," said Dick. "He had a bicycle and stood it here, leaning against the fence. You can see where his handlebar rested and made a mark in the moss. And there's a bit of track. Look out. Don't tread on the marks. They're pretty dim." He went down on his knees. "If only it wasn't so dark. . . . I do believe it's the same bicycle. . . . Dunlop tyre."

Three torches leapt from the pockets of the Death and Glories and the tracks, such as they were, were lit by a blaze of light.

"Dunlop all right," said Bill.

"Look same as yours," said Joe.

"It may not be the same bicycle," said Tom.

"I'm sure it is," said Dorothea. "He went to Ranworth and now he's been here. Oh, if only we hadn't all come along the river. If some of us had come by the road we'd have found the bicycle and we could have looked to see if its pump had lost its tube."

"We might have caught him proper," said Pete.

"Wonder which way he went," said Joe.

But they could find no tracks on the hard road. They searched about but could find no other clues. Dorothea remembered Mrs. Barrable.

"Dick," she said, "we've simply got to go. But I must just get *The Outlaw*."

They climbed over the fence again and went back to the *Death and Glory*.

"But what were he doing?" said Joe. "That's what beat me. If it were the same chap. He come to Ranworth and push them boats off. We know that. But what were he after here? Pushing off

the *Death and Glory*? Dorothea and William stop
that for him. Good old Puggy!"

"I told you he'd be jolly useful," said Dorothea
over her shoulder. "The bloodhound leapt on his
quarry. With a fearful struggle the villain tore
himself free, little knowing that he had left in
the jaws of his pursuer the clue that at last would
bring him to the gallows."

"He ain't touched our mooring ropes," said Joe
as they came to the *Death and Glory*. "I know
that. I moor her myself and all's as I leave it."

Dick was looking again at the scrap of flannel.
"Grey flannel trousers," he said. "And rides a bicycle with Dunlop tyres. Probably lives in Horning
. . . this side of the river anyhow because of his
using the Ferry. And he's lost the indiarubber
tube from his pump. And one of his tyres has
got a puncture."

"That ain't much good," said Bill. "Lots of chaps
get punctures. My old back tyre's patches all over."

"And of course by now he may have got a
new tube for his pump," said Tom.

"We know a good lot about him anyhow," said
Dorothea, climbing into the cockpit on the way to
get her book.

"We'll have a look at every bike in the village
tomorrow," said Joe.

"Look here, Dot," said Dick. "What, exactly,
was he doing when you saw him?"

"Patting the chimney," said Dorothea. "At least,
that was what it looked like."

"You come and do it," said Dick, "and we'll
watch and see if we can guess what he did it
for."

Dorothea obediently hopped ashore again. This, after all was the way detecting should be done. "I was a long way off," she said, "so I couldn't really see. I thought . . . I say, Tom had better do it. . . . (She reached out towards the chimney). . . . I'm not tall enough. He was reaching out at first. . . . Yes. . . . Like that and . . . No . . . much nearer the top. Patting it. . . . And then his other hand was on the top too. . . . No. . . . Much higher. . . . "

"Oh, look here," said Tom. "My arms aren't a mile long."

"Just stay like that a minute," said Dorothea and ran back along the edge of the dyke to the place from which she had first seen the *Death and Glory* and her visitor.

"He was a lot bigger than Tom," she called, and came back. "And I think he must have had his knee on the roof of the cabin."

Dick was taking notes.

"I believe I know why he was patting the chimney," he said, doubtfully. "But it may have been something else."

"Go on," said Tom.

"He's someone who knows they light their stove in the evenings and he wanted to feel the chimney to see if they were at home."

"Why don't he look through the windows?" asked Bill.

"Somebody might be in the fo'c'sle," said Dick. "If the chimney was warm he'd know there was somebody about."

"If he want to see us why do he run off when Dot call out?" asked Bill.

"He were up to no good," said Pete.

"Like enough," said Joe. "If Dot ain't seen him we'd have come back to find the old ship floating down river like all them others."

"Perhaps it's a pity he didn't have time to send her adrift," said Tom. "If he had, then everybody would have known that it's somebody not us pushing boats off."

They considered this for a moment, and then Dorothea remembered Mrs. Barrable again.

"Come along, Dick," she said. "It's nearly dark already."

"I'll get your book," said Pete, and a moment later handed it out from the cockpit.

"It'll be quicker going by the road, won't it?" said Dorothea. "Come on, William. . . . No exploring. I'm going to put the leash on you."

"Let's just put the new clue with the others in Scotland Yard," said Dick.

"What if he comes again?" said Tom. "Hadn't I better stay?"

"Three of us," said Joe. "We'll settle him. All the better if he come again and we see his ugly face."

Tom, Dick, Dorothea and William went back to Dr. Dudgeon's where they hung a scrap of grey flannel beside the other clues, after which Dick and Dorothea took their bicycles and riding slowly, for the sake of the bloodhound, went home for the night.

*

In the *Death and Glory*, the three went early to bed.

"No good lighting the stove," said Joe. "No cooking after all that grub."

"Look here," Pete protested. "It's my turn to light that stove."

"All right," said Joe. "We know that. You can light it in the morning instead of the primus. And if you want to do some lighting you can light the lantern now."

Joe fed his white rat and dealt out a ration of chocolate, after which they lay on their bunks, eating the chocolate, watching the lantern and talking of the day's work.

"Better keep the lantern lit," said Pete at last, "case that chap come again."

"Good old pug," said Joe, turning over on his left side to get the light out of his eyes. "Wouldn't have thought a pug had had it in him."

"Tread on 'em," said Bill sleepily, "and all dogs is alike."

CHAPTER XIX

UNWANTED GIFT

I<small>T</small> was Pete's turn to light the fire and he had been looking forward to it. But lighting the fire in the evening is one thing and getting up to light it in the morning is another. Pete lay awake for some time thinking about it until both Joe and Bill, snuggling in their blankets, yelled at him to stir his stumps. Then, making up his mind to it, he threw off his blankets, rubbed his eyes, rolled out of his bunk and, kneeling on the cabin floor, opened the door of the stove. He thrust in a hand to claw out the ashes and bumped his knuckles.

"Who bung up that stove?" he asked indignantly.

First Joe and then Bill answered with a snore.

"It ain't April first," said Pete. "I near take the skin off my hand."

"I'll light the primus," said Joe, "if you don't get that fire lit. We want our brekfuss."

"Why do you bung up that stove then?" said Pete, and reached in again. "Whatever have you gone putting in it?"

He felt something rough under his fingers and something hard inside it. There was a muffled clink of metal on metal as he pulled out a small heavy bundle of sacking.

Joe opened an eye and watched him sleepily from his bunk.

"Lot of old iron," said Pete. "That's a game to play on a chap!"

"Did you put it in, Bill?" said Joe.

"Put what in?" said Bill, rolling over in his bunk on the other side of the cabin. "I say, look out for that soot."

Pete was opening the sacking on the floor by the stove.

"Gosh!" he said. "Shackles. Beauties!"

"Shackles!" exclaimed Joe and was out of his bunk in a moment, handling the shackles, new gunmetal shackles, shining like gold under a film of grease. "That's what that chap were doing. Putting 'em down our chimney."

Pete was counting them. "Couple o' dozen big 'uns," he said, "and eight little 'uns."

"Wrap 'em up," said Bill suddenly. "Wrap 'em up. We don't want to be doing with them shackles. What was that Tedder talking night before last? Saying we had shackles when we didn't have none. Shackles! Ain't you read that paper on the staithe? Wrap 'em up. We got to take them shackles along to Tedder's the first minute we done brekfuss. You get that fire alight, young Pete, and don't you touch nothing else till you get the soot off you."

The fire was lit. A kettle was put to boil and, meanwhile, there was hurried and worried washing in a bucket dipped from the dyke. They kept looking over their shoulders as they scrubbed themselves, as if an enemy might be lurking behind each osier bush.

"Somebody's patching everything on us," said Joe. "Casting off boats *and* stealing. Bill's right.

That chap put 'em down the chimney. We got no time to lose. Next thing that Tedder'll be coming and finding 'em. Go on, Pete. That kettle'll be near enough boiling."

Pete made cocoa from a tin of cocoa and milk powder so that there was nothing to do but pour boiling water on it and stir. They drank it without complaining that he had made it before the water really boiled, so that the powder of the cocoa tickled the roofs of their mouths. At least it wasn't too hot to drink. Their eyes were on the parcel of sacking on the cabin floor.

"Best put 'em out of sight," said Bill, and put the parcel away in the fo'c'sle.

"Overslept we have too," said Joe. "If that chap's put Tedder on, we'll have him here in two twos."

They ate a thick round of bread apiece and a stout slab of bacon, then another round of bread and marmalade. While they ate, their eyes kept glancing towards the fo'c'sle just because they knew the shackles were there. It was as if they had a keg of gunpowder aboard.

"Come on," said Joe, almost before they had done. "Take 'em to Tedder right away."

"Better take 'em to Tom Dudgeon's first," said Bill.

"Put 'em in Pete's fish-bag," said Joe.

They went along the river bank, through Mr. Farland's garden, over the drawbridge and so to Scotland Yard. The door of the shed was open. William was asleep on the threshold and Dorothea was busily writing at the table.

"Where's Tom?" asked Joe.

"They've gone on," said Dorothea. "They were

in a hurry to get to the bicycle shop. You're to
go after them. We want a list of all the bicycles
with Dunlop tyres. What's the matter? What's
happened?"

"Worst that could have," said Joe.

"I find it in our stove," said Pete.

"We know what that chap was doing with our
chimbley," said Bill. "Let her see 'em, Joe."

Joe emptied Pete's fish-bag on the floor of Scotland Yard and untied the twine that held the
parcel of sacking together. Dorothea looked at
the shining yellow shackles.

"What are they?" she asked.

"And you gone Able Seaman," said Joe. "Don't
you know? Them's shackles. New 'uns. Greased
from the store. Them's what was took from Sonning's at Potter, and Pete find 'em in our stove.
When he go lighting the fire."

"That chap were putting 'em down our chimbley
when you catch him," said Pete.

"Good, good!" said Dorothea.

"Why good?" said Joe.

"It all fits in," said Dorothea. "Don't you see? I
thought the villain was doing it on purpose . . . just
casting off boats where you were, trying to make
people think you'd done it. Now we know. It'll help
a lot. It shows it's all one person. Potter Heigham
made it look so funny. Because it's so far away.
But with things from Potter Heigham turning
up at Horning. . . . Somebody must have brought
them. . . . It's a Horning person. . . . We've only
got to find out who. And he's got a bicycle with
Dunlop tyres. And part of his pump is missing.
And a bit torn out of his trousers. And . . . "

The Death and Glories stared at her.

"What a good thing you found them," said Dorothea. "The villain meant to come with a search party and find them himself and then everybody would have thought you had hidden them."

"Come on," said Joe. "Let's get rid of 'em quick."

"I tell you so, first thing," said Bill.

"Let's count them," said Dorothea.

"Two dozen big 'uns," said Pete. "And eight little 'uns."

"Come along," said Joe, hurriedly wrapping them up again.

"What are you going to do with them?" said Dorothea. "They'll be safe here. Let's hang them with the rest of the clues." She pointed to the wall where drawings of tyre-treads, a scrap of grey flannel and a bit of indiarubber tubing hung, each on its nail.

"Tedder's after these shackles," said Joe. "We're taking 'em to him just as fast as we can."

"Perhaps it's safer," said Dorothea. "Tom and Dick'll be waiting near the bicycle shop."

They ran round the house and out of the Doctor's gate and hurried along the road to Mr. Tedder's.

Two big boys on bicycles were riding down the road.

"Here come George Owdon and his pal," said Pete.

The two big boys jumped off their bicycles and waited for the Death and Glories.

"Where are you going?" said George Owdon.

"Police," said Bill.

"Cast off any more boats?"

"We ain't cast off no boats," said Joe.

"What have you got in that bag?"

"Tell him," said Bill.

"Lot of shackles," said Joe. "Bet you it's them shackles what was took from Sonning's at Potter."

"You ought to know," said George.

"What do you mean . . . 'You ought to know'?" said Joe angrily.

"Well, don't you?" said George. "You've seen the notice. Taking them to Tedder? Yes. I suppose that's the best thing you could do."

The other big boy laughed.

"Yes," said George. "You take them to Mr. Tedder and perhaps he'll let you off easy."

"We haven't done nothing to be let off," said Pete.

"Well, if you count casting off other people's boats nothing, and stealing . . . nothing," said George.

"I find 'em in our stove," said Pete.

"Naturally you knew where to find them if you put them there," said George.

"Come on," said Joe. "Mr. Tedder's got more sense than some."

"Now then," said George. "No cheek."

They heard more laughter behind them as they hurried on their way.

"He's dead sure it's us, because of Tom Dudgeon casting off that *Margoletta*," said Bill.

"We never look at their tyres," said Pete a moment later.

"Look at 'em later," said Bill. "But it ain't them two. Tell you for why. George Owdon never cast off no boats. He shoot buttles and he take beardies' eggs but he's dead nuts against monkeying with boats. Look how he side with them Hullabaloos against Tom, and look how he work in with Tedder, watching to see no more get cast off by no one."

They saw Mr. Tedder's bicycle leaning against the railing of his little garden, and knew that he had not yet left his house.

"Dunlop," said Pete as they passed it and went in through the gate.

"There you are," said Joe. "And Mr. Tedder ain't cast no boats off neither."

Mr. Tedder, in his shirt-sleeves, opened the door to them.

"See here, Mr. Tedder," said Joe, and took the parcel of sacking out of the fish-bag.

"What's this?" said Mr. Tedder.

"Shackles," said Joe. "You was asking about shackles t'other night and we tell you we ain't got none. No more we hadn't. But Pete find this lot in our stove this morning. We very near catch the chap what put 'em down our chimbley. . . . "

"Come in," said Mr. Tedder and they followed him into his little parlour with the big picture over the mantelshelf showing Mr. Tedder and Mrs. Tedder on their wedding day, Mr. Tedder looking like choking in a high white collar and Mrs. Tedder holding a big bunch of flowers in such a way as to show the ring on her finger. Mr. Tedder went to a cupboard in the wall and brought out a writing pad, a pen and an inkpot. He sat down at the table on which he had put the parcel. The three small boys stood side by side on the hearthrug under the picture of the wedding pair.

Mr. Tedder opened the parcel and looked at the shackles.

"Where are the rest of 'em?" he asked.

"Them's all we found," said Joe.

Mr. Tedder looked at the clock, which had an inscription on it to say that it had been presented to him on the occasion of his marriage "by friends and admirers in the force".

"At ten fifteen, a.m.", he wrote, saying the words aloud as he put them down. . . . He looked up gravely at the small boys. "Now," he said. "You think again. . . . No good telling me a yarn like that. And don't you go thinking you can keep the rest of them shackles just because you give up a few you don't want."

"We don't want none of 'em," said Joe. "And we didn't take none."

"How'd they get into your boat? You tell me that," said Mr. Tedder.

"Down our chimbley," said Joe. "I just tell you we near caught a chap putting 'em down."

"We'd have found 'em last night," said Pete, "only we didn't light the fire. It was my turn this morning, and I find 'em soon's I ope the stove."

"Now look here," said Mr. Tedder. "You lie here at the staithe and boats get cast off. You go to Ranworth and boats get cast off there. Jim Woodall lose his new warp off of his wherry what you cast off and we find that in Jonnatt's shed close where you was lying."

"Oh, they found that," said Pete eagerly. "That were a brand new warp and Tom say Jim think it had gone in the river."

"Course they found it," said Mr. Tedder. "They found it where you put it."

"We never touch it," said Bill.

"And you go to Potter," went on Mr. Tedder, "and boats get cast off the night you're there, and Sonning's lose a gross and a half of new shackles, and then you come here and bring me some of the shackles. . . ." He stopped suddenly, picked up a shackle and looked at it. "First step," he said, "is identification. Ought to have thought of that. You can clear out now, all of you, and I'll see you again, soon's Mr. Sonning identify them shackles. Out you go. But don't go thinking we shan't get to the bottom of this. You think it over and tell me the truth next time. Sorry for your Dads, that's what I am. They're all honest chaps."

"We'd have done better to drop them shackles in the river," said Joe furiously as they went out.

Outside the gate Pete stopped, very red in the face. He went back to Mr. Tedder's door. Mr. Tedder was still there, thinking hard.

"Can you give me a bit of paper, Mr. Tedder?" he said. "I got a pencil."

"If you volunteer to make a written statement," said the policeman, "you'll have to sign before witnesses." He went into the parlour and came back with a sheet of paper from his writing pad.

Pete thanked him and joined the other two outside the gate.

"What's up, Pete?" said Bill.

Pete plumped down in the road beside the back wheel of Mr. Tedder's bicycle, and made as good a drawing as he could of the tread of his tyre.

The policeman came out just as he had finished.

"What's all this?" said Mr. Tedder. "What are you up to now? You leave that bike alone."

Pete, still red in the face, flourished his bit of paper. "Dunlop tyre," he said. "The chap what put them shackles down our chimbley have a bike and his tyres are Dunlop too."

Mr. Tedder had no idea what he was talking about.

"If you've been sticking a knife into my tyre," he said darkly.

The three hurried off to look for Tom and Dick. Mr. Tedder felt his tyre between his fingers and looked after them with a puzzled expression on his face.

CHAPTER XX

DUNLOP TYRES

Tom and Dick were in the doorway of Mr. Bixby's bicycle shop, where they were asking careful questions. Yes, they had been told, if they were wanting new tyres, there was nothing to beat Dunlops. Not that Palmers were not good too, if they had a fancy for something else. Old Mr. Bixby, who had been selling bicycles for nearly fifty years, looked hopefully at Tom.

"What about punctures?" said Tom.

"Any tyre'll puncture if you push a nail in it," said Mr. Bixby, "but there ain't the punctures nowadays there used to be. Roads better kept maybe. Fewer horses. And hedges not what they was. Thorns are as bad as nails, maybe worse, but you don't get the thorns lying about in the dust same as you used to get before the roads were all tarred."

Tom looked over his shoulder and saw the three younger Coots, who had come round the corner and were waiting close by. He took no notice of them and they knew they were not wanted, not while Tom was asking questions anyway. He was just working up to something.

"Do you get many punctures to mend?" he asked, and they saw Dick pull his spectacles off. This was the vital point.

"Not so many," said Mr. Bixby.

"Any lately?" asked Tom as if he had no special

reason for wanting to know.

"Why yes," said Mr. Bixby, jerking his hand towards a rusty old bicycle leaning up against his work bench. "I had that brought in day before yesterday."

"Dunlop tyre?" said Tom and he could not keep the eagerness out of his voice.

"Yes," said Mr. Bixby. "They mostly use 'em. Are you wanting a new bike?"

"Not just now," said Tom. "I shall some day. But mine's got a lot of wear in it yet."

"Wanting new tyres for it perhaps?" said Mr. Bixby.

"Not just now," said Tom.

"Oh," said Mr. Bixby. "You'll excuse me. I'm busy." And he went off to the back of his shop.

"It hasn't got a pump at all," said Dick, looking at the old bicycle by the bench. "I say. I wish we'd asked if anybody's been buying pump-tubes."

"We'll have to watch to see who comes to take it away," said Tom. "Look here, you Coots, we mustn't go about detecting all in a crowd.

"Something's happened," said Joe. "You know that chap what was at our chimbley last night?"

"Yes," said Tom.

"He put a parcel of shackles down," said Joe.

"I find 'em this morning in the stove," said Pete. "Near took the skin off of my knuckles."

"Where are they?" said Tom. "What have you done with them?"

"Took 'em to Mr. Tedder," said Joe.

"And that Tedder say we steal 'em," said Pete. "And George Owdon he think the same."

"Gosh," said Tom. "The Potter Heigham shackles."

"That's what we think," said Joe. "And Mr. Tedder's taking 'em over to Potter to make sure. Look. There he go."

Mr. Tedder now in full uniform came bicycling round the corner on his way to Potter Heigham. The parcel in its bit of sacking was fastened to his handlebars, and as he went by he gave them the sort of look that ought to be given to a gang of criminals by one whose business it is to put a stop to their crimes.

"Anyway," said Tom, pointing into the shop, "we've got to see who comes to fetch that bicycle. And if he's got a bit torn out of one leg of his trousers. . . . "

"We'd better not wait quite so near the shop," said Dick.

"And not all of us," said Tom. "The chap would see us and sheer off and get his bicycle another time."

They crossed the road and were debating who should stay on watch when someone whom they all knew came round the corner. He seemed in very good spirits. He always was. They saw him take off his black felt hat to the old lady from the sweet-shop. They saw him nod to the boy from the dairy who was collecting milk bottles. They expected a nod themselves and the usual cheerful inquiry as to how all the birds were getting on. But though they saw that he knew them, he neither nodded nor spoke to them, and instead looked suddenly grave.

"That's another what think we done it," said

Bill.

"But it's the old parson," said Tom. "He knows we wouldn't."

"He's going into the bicycle shop," said Dick.

Two minutes later they saw the old parson come out again. He was wheeling that rusty, ancient bicycle and saying good-bye and thank you to Mr. Bixby who had come with him to the door of the shop.

"Well, Reverend," said Mr. Bixby, "them tyres is a bit worn and you'll expect to get a few punctures in an old tyre. They don't last for ever. Now I got some nice new ones and they'll never be cheaper than what they are now. . . . "

"I'll have to give myself new ones for a Christmas present," said the old parson, mounted his bicycle and rode away.

"It weren't him pushing off boats at Ranworth in the middle of the night," said Bill.

"You don't catch old Reverend poking shackles down our chimbley," said Joe.

"Was his trousies tore?" asked Pete.

"It wouldn't be him even if they was," said Joe. "It just mean we got to look for some other bike."

"And I thought we'd really got it," said Tom.

Dick's mind was working already on another clue.

"It's a pity you took those shackles straight to Mr. Tedder," he said. "You ought to have taken them to Scotland Yard."

"We did take 'em there," said Joe. "But there weren't nobody on duty but Dot."

"And our bloodhound," said Pete.

"She did want to keep 'em," said Joe. "But we was dead certain sure they was some of them shackles from Potter, and we want to get rid of 'em quick."

"We couldn't really have kept them at Scotland Yard," said Tom.

"There might have been a clue with them," said Dick. "What were they like?"

"Just new shackles," said Joe. "Good 'uns. Grease still on 'em from the store."

"Grease?" said Dick. "There might have been fingerprints."

"Plenty of ours," said Bill. "We all had a look at 'em."

"Were they all alike?" asked Dick.

"Couple o' dozen big 'uns and six little 'uns," said Bill.

"Eight little 'uns," said Pete.

"But I say," said Tom. "There was a whole gross and a half of shackles stolen."

"That Tedder he ask where was the rest of 'em," said Joe. "He make out we was keeping 'em."

"Taking us for thieves," said Pete hotly. "And he got Dunlop tyres himself."

"Oh, shurrup Pete," said Bill. "We know it ain't old Tedder."

"Let's go and talk to Dot," said Dick. "Dot'll know why the thief didn't put them all down your chimney instead of only a few."

"Dot scare him off before he had time," said Joe.

"If we could find where he's hidden the rest of them, " said Dick.

They went slowly back to Scotland Yard. Seeing

the old parson ride happily away on the bicycle that, since it had Dunlop tyres and had lost a pump, they had been sure was the one for which they were looking, had damped the hopes of Tom and Dick. But they looked at such bicycles as they found on the way, and Dick noted in his pocket-book that the milkboy's bicycle had Dunlop tyres, and so had the bicycle of the district nurse. There were three bicycles against the wall of the inn. Two had Dunlop tyres and one Palmers. They waited to see their owners, but went on again when three young men in brown pullovers and baggy knickers came laughing out of the inn and rode away. "Foreigners," said Tom. "Just touring." There was a bicycle in the doorway of Jonnatt's, the boatbuilders. "Dunlop tyres," said Joe hopefully. But Tom read the owner's card on the toolbag, and they went on again. Mr. Jonnatt himself was hardly likely to have been riding over to Ranworth in the dark to cast off other people's boats. The clue of the bicycle marks at Ranworth seemed to have led to nothing at all. The shackles seemed more promising, but the shackles, tied to Mr. Tedder's handlebars, were already far away.

"There might easily have been fingerprints on them," said Dick again. "And really we ought to have photographed them before giving them up to the police."

"What if they ain't Potter shackles," said Peter.

"If they ain't Potter shackles," said Bill, "we could do with 'em ourselves. Any hope Mr. Tedder bring 'em back?"

"If they aren't claimed," said Tom, "you'll get them. You found them."

"They're bound to be the stolen shackles," said Dick. "That's why they were put down your chimney."

They were still talking about the shackles when they came to Dr. Dudgeon's and went round to find Dorothea and William looking after Scotland Yard.

"Hullo," said Dorothea, looking up from her writing. "You haven't done all the bicycles already?"

"Only a few," said Tom. "All Dunlops and not the one we want."

"Oh," said Dorothea. "And what did Mr. Tedder say when you showed him those things?"

"He say we steal 'em," said Pete. "He've taken 'em to be 'dentified at Potter. And I say, Dot, his bike got Dunlop tyres."

Dorothea considered for a moment. "I don't think it was him I saw at your chimney. Besides, William's quite friendly with him. And he never wears grey trousers."

"You didn't see any fingerprints on the shackles, Dot, did you?" asked Dick.

"I never looked."

"There's another thing," said Dick. "That paper said a gross and a half of shackles were stolen. Why did the villain put only a few down their chimney?"

Dorothea frowned, thinking hard.

"Likely he want the rest himself," said Bill.

"It's not that," said Dorothea. "Why didn't he keep them all? Perhaps he meant to put them all down the chimney, only he heard me and bolted. He may have dropped the others somewhere, only we didn't see them when we were hunting round after William got a bit of his trousers. We weren't looking for them really."

"It was pretty dark," said Tom.

"And misty," said Dorothea.

"Come on," said Joe. "Let's go and have another look."

All six detectives and their bloodhound went round to the Wilderness and made a thorough search. Even William did his best, hunting this way and that though, as Dorothea said, it was a pity there was no way of explaining to him what he had to look for.

They found nothing and gathered disheartened beside the *Death and Glory*.

"He must have managed to take them away," said Tom.

"If he brought them," said Dorothea.

"He must have all the others somewhere," said Tom.

Dick was looking closely at the chimney pot. "They dust things with some kind of powder," he said, "and then they photograph them. There ought to be fingerprints. . . . "

"Dick," said Dorothea. "He's coming again. I know he is. That's his plan." She turned to the younger Coots. "Don't you see? If he'd left the whole lot at once, people might think you'd found them. So he left just a few and you took them to Mr. Tedder. That's what he thought you'd do. And Mr. Tedder thinks you stole them but he isn't sure. Well, if the villain leaves another lot and you take that to Mr. Tedder too, it'll look more suspicious than ever. . . . As if you were just giving up a little at a time. He'll come again. He'll come again tonight. We must never leave the *Death and Glory* without a guard. Isn't that right, Dick?"

Everybody but Dick was ready to agree. Dick was thinking about something else.

"Feeling the chimney," he said. "Feeling to see if it was warm and if anybody was at home. He'll do just the same when he comes again. So the sooner he comes the better. . . . "

"We don't want no more of them shackles," said Bill.

"Go on, Dick," said Dorothea.

"Fingerprints," said Dick. "He'll come and feel the chimney."

"But it won't take no mark," said Bill.

"It would if it was wet paint," said Dick, pulling off his spectacles, polishing them hurriedly and putting them on again.

"Gee whillikins!" said Joe.

"Gosh!" said Tom.

"That's just what Scotland Yard would do," said Dorothea.

"I've got some paint," said Tom, "but not much."

"That won't take much if we lay that on thin," said Joe.

"And the villain comes lurking through the bushes," said Dorothea. "Watching for blood-hounds . . . he won't want to be grabbed again . . . and he'll come to the *Death and Glory* like he did before . . . and lean over . . . and feel the chimney . . . and there's nothing like wet paint, the way you leave a print on it if you touch it by mistake."

"Fine," said Tom.

"But he'll leave us with the rest of them shackles," said Bill.

"Who care?" said Joe. "If he get his fingers on our chimbley anybody'll see somebody bring 'em and not us."

"He won't come if he sees us anywhere about," said Dorothea.

"We'll all get right out of the way," said Tom.

"Let's get the paint on," said Pete. "I'll lay a coat on quick as nothing."

"Is it quick-drying paint?" asked Dick.

"Fairly quick," said Tom.

"We'd better put it on just before we go to the Admiral's," said Dick.

"I never told you," said Dorothea. "Mrs. Barrable wants us all to come to tea."

"We'd better watch he don't get a chance to bring them shackles before the paint's on," said Bill.

"He won't want to cart shackles about in daylight," said Joe. "A gross'll make a tidy parcel. There were a mist last night and he wait till near dark then."

"Grub at Scotland Yard," said Tom. "Then we'll have a proper go at bicycles. Then we'll put the paint on, and then we'll go to the Admiral's and lie low."

*

Bicycles in the afternoon were as disappointing as they had been in the morning. As Dorothea said, it was like the story of the man who hid a gold piece under a molehill and when he came to look for it found that the goblins had raised mole-hills all exactly alike all over the field. They were looking for one bicycle with Dunlop tyres and all the bicycles in the world seemed to have tyres of no other make.

Late in the afternoon they gave up, after making a long list of Dunlop-tyred bicycles, not one of the owners of which seemed likely to be the villain they were seeking. They did not mind much, for Dick's idea promised an even better result. Pete did the painting of the chimney, with the others posted as sentinels round the Wilder-ness, to make sure that nobody else had any idea of what was being done. Dick tried an experiment. The result was a splendid print of his hand, so that part of the chimney had to be painted again and Dick had to take his hand to Scotland Yard to get the paint taken off with turpentine borrowed from Mrs. Dudgeon. But there could be no doubt that the thing would work, and the whole Coot Club went off in high hopes to keep out of the way at Mrs. Barrable's.

*

Mrs. Barrable gave them a high tea so that the Death and Glories had no need to worry about supper. They told her some of what they were doing but not all, and she did not ask ques-tions.

"You see, Admiral," explained Dorothea, "you don't know who the villain is, and we don't know. And if you knew what we were doing you might be saying something to somebody and the villain might make a good guess without

you ever thinking you'd given him a hint. In the
books detectives never talk. At least, when they
do they're sorry afterwards and find themselves
in cellars with the water rising while the villain
plays the piano overhead to stop anybody from
hearing their cries for help."

"All right," said Mrs. Barrable. "Whatever you
are up to, I'd better not know. I'd never forgive
myself if a chance word of mine or William's. . . .
By the way, how much does William know?"

"He's bitten the villain once," said Dorothea.
"I think probably he'd know him again. . . . But
he won't talk. . . . I say, though, if ever you hear
him growling at anybody in particular please will
you let us know?"

*

It was quite dark when Tom and the Death and
Glories set out homewards. The Admiral had put
her foot down against letting Dick and Dorothea
go with them.

"Better go careful now," said Joe, when they
reached Dr. Dudgeon's house. "You going in,
Tom?"

"What do you think?" said Tom. "Not I. I'm
coming with you. Two of us go by the river and
two by the road. Give us a chance of catching him
if he's not been and gone. You chaps got torches?"

Tom and Bill went through the Farland garden.
Joe and Pete went by road.

"Hear anything?" Joe stopped with his hand on
the fence before climbing over into the Wilderness.

"Someone moving in there," whispered Pete.

" 'St!"

PAINTING THE CHIMNEY

They waited, listening.

"Come on," said Joe. "Don't make a row getting over."

Again they listened.

"Get him round the legs if he come this way," said Joe.

They crept through the bushes. A torch glimmered in the darkness.

"It's only the others," said Pete.

"Coots for ever," called Joe softly.

"And ever," came the answer.

The four of them met beside the *Death and Glory*.

"Now," said Tom and switched the light of his torch on the shining green chimney. Three other torches joined Tom's.

"Put 'em out. Put 'em out," said Joe. "Who's to see in all that glare. One light's enough."

Three torches went out. Tom climbed on the cabin roof and searched every inch of the chimney. The others watched the patch of light slipping this way and that over the green paint.

"Not a mark," said Tom. "He hasn't been."

The chimney was exactly as they had left it.

"May come yet," said Joe hopefully. "He's got all night to come in."

"Look here," said Tom. "If he does, one of you come and fetch me right away. I'll leave the string out of my window. You know what Dick said about looking at clues while they're fresh."

"We'll take turns keeping awake," said Joe.

"I'll keep awake," said Pete, yawning.

"No need," said Tom. "I was forgetting. He

won't come in the night. Not with you sleeping aboard. He wants to come when there's nobody here. Well, I'm off. See you in the morning."

They watched the glimmer of his torch through the bushes until it disappeared. Joe unlocked the cabin door. Bill lit the lantern. They made ready for the night.

"Tell you what," said Joe, when they were already in their bunks. "We'll out that lantern. If he do come we don't want to fright him off. And don't you go snoring, Pete, telling him the crew's aboard."

"I don't snore," said Pete. "I know who do."

Joe wriggled out of his blankets, blew out the lantern, and settled for the night once more.

CHAPTER XXI

MORNING VISITORS

In the cool September morning, when the sun brought no warmth through the willows, smoke was drifting from the *Death and Glory*. Joe, Bill and Pete, who had washed but not breakfasted, were standing on the cabin roof looking at the chimney. As a bit of new paintwork it was a great success. As a snare for other people's fingerprints it was a failure. There was not a mark on it.

Joe gently touched it with his thumb.

"Now you done it," said Bill.

"Very near dry," said Joe, looking closely at the faint print he had left on the shining surface.

"She were wrong, thinking he'd come again," said Pete.

" 'Sh!" said Joe.

Steps were coming through the bushes, and presently they saw Mr. Tedder.

"Morning," said Joe and Bill. Pete said nothing. He could not forget that Mr. Tedder had accused them of stealing and that, no matter what the others might say, Mr. Tedder's bicycle had Dunlop tyres.

"Morning," said Mr. Tedder. "I come here to look for you last night near lighting-up time. But you wasn't here. Wasted near an hour watching for you."

"That's why there's no marks," exclaimed Joe, glancing at the chimney.

"What's that?" asked Mr. Tedder.

"Don't tell him," squeaked Pete.

"Oh, nothing," said Joe.

"You say 'Don't tell him!'" said Mr. Tedder sternly. "I hear you. And you'd better tell and tell quick. I take them shackles to Potter yesterday, and Mr. Sonning identify 'em. Them shackles is part of the lot took from his shed."

"That's what we think, all of us," said Joe.

"Think!" said Mr. Tedder scornfully. "You know they was, and you come to me with a yarn about finding 'em in your stove. Who put 'em there if you didn't?"

"That's what we're trying to find out," said Bill.

Pete looked at Bill in horror. Was Bill going to give away secrets to the enemy, to one who might be the very villain they were trying to catch?

But Bill went on. "The one what put them shackles in our stove is likely the one that steal 'em and the one what cast all them boats off. And if everybody go patching it on us they'll never get him."

"Now look here, young Bill," said Mr. Tedder. "I give you every chance I can. I'm going to see Mr. Farland now, and I didn't ought to warn you first. I got to tell him what them shackles is, and I got to tell him who bring 'em to me. That'll be a lot easier for you if you own up now and hand over the rest of 'em. You got 'em put away somewheres."

"We ain't," said Joe.

Mr. Tedder thought for a moment. "I ain't got a search warrant," he said at last, "but I can easy get one."

"Search away," said Joe. "We don't mind. . . ."

"Well, if you're agreeable," said Mr. Tedder.

"Mind your head when you go in," said Bill. "Tom Dudgeon crack his every time."

Pete found himself holding Mr. Tedder's helmet. Mr. Tedder stooped down, and shielding the top of his head with a hand in case of accidents, crawled into the little cabin. The owners of the *Death and Glory* watched from the cockpit.

Bent double, the tall policeman looking along the bunks, lifted the straw mattresses, ran his eye along the shelves, and then, on all fours, crawled into the fo'c'sle and looked at the gear stored in the bows.

"What about them doors?" he said, looking at the cupboards.

"Ope 'em," said Joe, who was proud of the cupboards. "They ain't locked."

Mr. Tedder opened the cupboard doors.

"You got a lot of stores," he said.

"Plenty of everything," said Bill. "That's all soups below. Them's potted meat. That's salmon and shrimp. Them's jams. . . . " He had hurried in, and, as chief cook, was proudly showing off the larder.

Mr. Tedder began to back his way out, and Bill backed too, to let him come.

"Your Dads never give you the money to buy all that stuff," said Mr. Tedder, stretching to his full height again in the cockpit.

"We never ask 'em," said Joe.

"Where did you get the money?" said Mr. Tedder.

"Earn it," said Joe. "We tell you about that before and you wouldn't believe us. We earn it."

"Where?"

"Selling fish."

"When?" Mr. Tedder pulled out his note-book.

"That time we went to Potter," said Joe.

"Ar," said Mr. Tedder, sucked his pencil, and wrote.

"Them shackles is gone," he said presently. "Who buy 'em from you? We can have him up for receiving property knowing it to be stolen."

"Nobody buy 'em," said Joe.

"How do you know?" said Mr. Tedder. "Answer me that now. How do you know they ain't sold if you ain't got 'em?"

"Nobody buy 'em from us," said Joe. "And for why? 'Cos we ain't had 'em to sell."

Mr. Tedder sucked his pencil again. "Refused all information," he said solemnly, writing the words as he spoke them. "Well," he went on. "It'll be all the worse for you. I'm off now to see Dr. Dudgeon and Mr. Farland." He put his note-book in his pocket, looked from one to another of the three boys and then, in an almost friendly tone, said, "Now you think again. You just change your minds and own up."

"We ain't got nothing to own up to," said Joe.

"And you all sons of decent chaps," said Mr. Tedder mournfully. He went ashore, took his helmet from Pete and strode away through the bushes.

The three watched him go.

"Well, we got to get our brekfuss anyways," said Bill at last. "That kettle's boiling."

*

A shout of "Coots Ahoy!" brought the crew

of the *Death and Glory* tumbling up out of the cabin with their mouths full.

Dick and Dorothea were coming through the bushes from the road.

"Is it a good print?" asked Dick, when they were still a dozen yards away.

"Tom's just coming," said Dorothea. "We met Mr. Tedder going in to Dr. Dudgeon's. Tom's waiting to get the news. What did Mr. Tedder say when you showed him?"

"We ain't got nothing to show," said Bill.

"Tedder search our boat," said Joe. "He's dead sure we stole them shackles."

"Them shackles was from Potter all right," said Bill. "And Tedder think we got the rest of 'em."

"Well if he searched the boat he knows they're not here now," said Dorothea. "That's one good thing. And you showed him you had nothing to hide."

"He pretty near say we steal our stores," said Pete, bitterly.

Dick was on the cabin roof looking carefully over every inch of the green chimney.

"There ain't a mark on it," said Joe. "Only where I touch it with my thumb. Ain't likely to be a mark neither. That Tedder say he were hanging about here last night while we was at the Admiral's. That's why."

"Oh dear," said Dorothea. "And now he'll tell the whole place about the chimney and the villain will be careful to keep his paws off it."

"He won't do that," said Joe. "Pete squeak just in time. It were on the tip of my tongue to tell him how he muck things up."

"That's all right," said Dorothea with relief.

"There's enough paint for another coat," said Dick, looking in the tin.

"Good, oh, good," said Dorothea. "If Mr. Tedder frightened him off last night he'll be all the more certain to come this evening. Hullo, haven't you had your breakfast? The Admiral let us have ours early so that we could get here first thing. We're going to Ranworth. Dick wants some more photographs, and we've got our bicycles."

"I've got to take one photograph here," said Dick, "to show just what Dot saw the time William got the villain's trouser leg."

"What for?" said Bill.

"You'll see," said Dorothea. "It'll be very important evidence. Hullo. Here's Tom."

"No good," said Tom. "Dad's off seeing victims. He was talking to Mr. Tedder till the very last minute. I couldn't get him at all. We'll have to wait till he comes in for dinner. What about fingerprints?"

"There aren't any," said Dorothea. "But it's all right. It's not because the villain isn't coming. I'm sure he is. It's the only thing he can do. But he couldn't come last night because Mr. Tedder was hanging about here all the time. So he gave it up and slunk away. He'll probably come tonight."

"We'll put another coat of paint on this afternoon," said Dick. "Let's get that photograph. We'll want that anyhow."

"Wait just while we finish our brekfuss," said Pete.

"Pitch it in then," said Tom.

"We'll be finding the place to put the camera," said Dick.

The Death and Glories crammed down the rest of their breakfast, put off washing up till later, and hurried out to find that Dick had his camera standing on its tripod just where Dorothea had been when she first saw the villain, if it was the villain, patting the chimney.

One by one they squinted through the finder and saw the tiny picture of their ship snugly moored among the osier bushes.

"Now we want the villain," said Dick.

"What do you mean?" said Pete.

"Somebody's got to be in the picture doing just what Dot saw him do."

"I'm him," said Joe.

"No," said Dorothea. "Tom's bigger."

"Well, I'm not big enough," said Tom. "I tried the other night."

"That's just it," said Dorothea. "You reach out as far as ever you can and the photograph'll show you can't touch the chimney. And you're the biggest of us all. So the photograph'll be proof that it was someone else."

"Gee whizz!" said Joe.

"That's pretty good," said Bill.

"Tedder could reach all right," said Pete.

"Oh, shurrup, Pete," said Joe.

"Come on, Tom," said Dorothea. "You stand like that, and I'll go back to Dick and see if it looks right."

She ran back and stood beside the camera. "Leaning over a bit more," she said. "And his hand came much higher. Stay like that. . . . "

"Keep still," called Dick. "I'll have to give it nearly half a second because of all the trees. . . . Now. . . . "

There was a click, and then another.

"That's all," called Dick.

"Are you only going to take one?"

"I've only got two more to expose," said Dick, "and I want those to show the place where the villain pumped up his tyre at Ranworth. We're going on there now and then we'll be able to develop them right away."

"Let's all go," said Joe. "We can take Bill's bike, and take turns. One run. One ride proper, and t'other hang on."

But at that moment there were sounds of more visitors coming through the bushes from the road.

"Oughtn't to be allowed to padlock that gate," said a woman's voice.

"Only make people climb that fence for nothing," said another.

"Hullo, Mum!" shouted Pete.

"Hullo, Mum!" shouted Bill and Joe.

The three mothers were already close to the boat. All three were carrying baskets with loaves of bread and other food. All three looked rather grave, as they exchanged "Good mornings" with the detectives.

"Well," said Bill's mother, "I don't see you can be up to much harm in here."

"Nor I," said the mother of Joe.

"That Tedder's getting too big for his boots," said the mother of Pete.

"But there's things going on," said the mother of Bill.

Dorothea looked at the mothers and then at their three sons.

"We'd better be getting those Ranworth photographs done," she said. "You won't want us here while you're having a talk."

"Well, there is a bit to say," said the mother of Bill.

Dorothea caught Joe's eye, glanced at the chimney and back again, and saw that he understood. Not a word was to be said about that, even to mothers, because, if word got about the village, the villain was likely to hear it and be warned.

"Meet at Scotland Yard this afternoon," said Tom. "I'll have seen Dad by then."

"Where's the bloodhound?" asked Pete. "You can leave him here."

"We left him with the Admiral," said Dorothea, and went off with Tom and Dick.

*

"Scotland Yard?" said Joe's mother.

"Bloodhounds?" said Bill's mother.

"What's adoing?" said the mother of Pete.

And Pete, Joe and Bill, without giving away the secret of the chimney pot, found themselves telling their mothers how the Coot Club was doing the best it could and trying to find out who the villain was who had been casting off boats and stealing shackles and making people think that all his villainies were the work of virtuous Coots.

"But what's Scotland Yard doing in it?" asked Joe's mother.

"That's what that Dot call the shed against Tom Dudgeon's," said Joe.

"And that Dick he's got a lot of evidence, photographs and such," said Bill.

"But bloodhounds!" exclaimed Bill's mother.

"We ain't got but one," said Pete. "That's Mrs. Barrable's William."

"That yellow pug," said Bill's mother, laughing for the first time. "You won't make a bloodhound out of him."

"He get the villain by the leg," said Bill. "We got good evidence for that. If that chap he get weren't the villain he'd have been at Tedder's claiming for the bite."

"Wish he'd have got that Tedder," said Pete's mother. "He make as much to-do as if you was all murderers. He come round yesterday with a lot of fool talk about you stealing shackles from Potter, and there was your Dad sitting at his supper with a bit of good beef over his black eye, and he ask your Dad how he come by it. And your Dad up and tell him he come by it knocking spots off a fellow who say the same fool things as has just been said. He tell him his son don't steal shackles and he don't cast off boats and if Tedder want to say he do he'd better play fair and say it without his uniform on. And Tedder say he don't say nothing. He only make inquiries as directed. And your Dad say he's glad to hear it and Tedder's got his answer. Tedder go off then and say something about breach of the peace and your Dad was that mad I had to tell him spuds was getting cold to stop him going out of door after him."

"It ain't only Tedder," said Bill's mother. "The old Reverend came round and say he's sorry you're in trouble and what can he do about it . . . I tell him best he can do is close his ears to evil tongues."

"It's the whole village gone crazy," said the mother of Joe. "To hear 'em talk, you'd think you was the only boys in the place and just out of gaol at that. And what's all this Tedder say about you bringing him some of them shackles and keeping the rest. He want to know if you bring any home."

An angry chorus told just how the bloodhound had come to bite the villain, of the parcel found in the stove, of Tedder's visits and of his searching of their ship.

"Right down wicked, I call it," said Bill's mother. "He ought to be grateful, he ought, with you bringing of 'em back. Didn't, he'd be looking for 'em still. And there he go asking if we give you pocket money and how much. I tell him you have plenty which is what Mrs. Dudgeon tell me. And he say 'Ar' that silly, I could have slam the door on him."

A slow grin spread over Bill's face. He was thinking that detective work was not too easy even for real policemen.

She went on. "What are we going to do, I want to know? Your Dads say, best take you off the river, but Mrs. Dudgeon stick up for you and say why spoil your holiday if you ain't done nothing? And she say you'd be all right here. But with that Tedder and his shackles, I'm sure I don't know."

"We're going to find out who did it," said Joe. "Tom and that Dot and Dick they say we'll find out sooner'n Tedder, because he think it's us and we know it ain't."

"You be quick about it," said his mother. "Casting off boats and that is no good in a place like this, and Hannam's would have sacked your Dad if he weren't too good a boatbuilder to lose. There was some as said he must have knowed Jim Wooddall's rope was hid in Jonnatt's shed. And that Tedder's talking of the law, and if it come to summonses, whatever are we to do? . . . That's new paint you've put on your chimney?"

"It's dry now," said Pete.

"We did that apurpose," began Bill, but Joe slipped and caught him a buffet with his elbow just in time.

After that the mothers had to see inside the boat, and were a bit shocked to find the remains of breakfast until it was explained to them that there had been a lot of interruptions. Bill made them a cup of tea, and would not even let his own mother touch kettle or teapot. They sat in the cabin and were given gingerbread biscuits and were treated and behaved as honoured guests aboard ship. It was only as they were leaving that things turned dark again.

Bill's mother looked round as they were saying goodbye, to see that there was nobody else about. "Mrs. Dudgeon she say she don't think you done nothing. But what about her Tom? He cast off one boat this year, that we do know."

There was a chorus of protest from the Coots.

"All right then, all right," said Bill's mother. "If anybody ask we'll tell 'em you're finding out who done it. We'll tell 'em you'll be finding out before that Tedder and he'd better get you learn him his job."

"No, no, don't you say nothing," said Bill in horror. "Wait till we catch him first."

"You catch him then," said his mother. "For if it come to summonses there's nothing your Dads can do but take you off the river."

INSIDE THE CABIN

CHAPTER XXII

ANOTHER COAT OF PAINT

THE spirits of the Death and Glories had fallen low with the news that had been brought by their mothers. They fell lower when Tom came into Scotland Yard to say that Mr. Tedder had indeed been talking to Dr. Dudgeon about summonses.

"If we ain't quick it's going to be too late," said Joe.

"We aren't going to be too late," said Dorothea. "Just look at all the evidence we're getting."

"We ain't got them fingerprints," said Pete.

"If only that Tedder hadn't have hung around," said Joe.

"We'll get them tonight," said Dorothea.

"I've fixed it up for us all to have supper here," said Tom. "So as to give the villain a chance."

"What are we going to do now?" asked Pete. "Put another coat of paint on?"

"Not yet," said Tom. "You can find something or other to do. Dot's getting the evidence into shape. Dick and I are going to develop those photographs."

"If we're to be turned off the river," said Bill gloomily, "we'd best tidy up the ship."

"No harm in that anyways," said Joe.

So, while Dorothea wrote, Dick and Tom had a pleasant messy time in Mrs. Barrable's bathroom and the Death and Glories cleaned out their cabin, scrubbed their decks, overhauled their ropes, hoisted their sail to dry, made a neat stow of it, and washed down their topsides. The old ship was looking smarter than anyone would have thought possible and her crew were cheerful once again when Tom, Dick and Dorothea came along to say that the photographs had come out very well and that it was time to put a new coat of paint on the chimney ready for the villain's paws.

"Don't you get any paint on our clean cabin-top," said Joe.

"You leave me alone," said Pete.

Once again scouts were posted in the road, at the mouth of the dyke, among the osier bushes, at the gate of Mr. Farland's garden, to make sure that nobody, no matter who, should have any idea of what was being done, while Pete used the last of Tom's paint in putting a new thin coat all over the chimney.

"There weren't but just enough," he said when the painting was done and the sentinels were admiring his work. "We'll have to get another tin if we have to do it again tomorrow."

"We won't," said Dorothea. "He's in just as much of a hurry as we are. He's wondering why you haven't been summoned already, and he's thinking that if something doesn't happen soon he'll have to start all over again."

They stared at her.

"Do you know him?" said Joe wonderingly.

"I'm thinking his thoughts," said Dorothea.

"But it isn't a book, Dot," said Dick.

"It's the same thing," said Dorothea.

"Come along now," said Tom. "Let's get away.

And you mustn't be back here till after dark."

"They'd better go for a walk through the village," said Dorothea. "So that everybody'll know there's a chance of finding nobody at the ship." She had a last look at the *Death and Glory*. "What about the curtains?" she said. "Better have them closed, so that he can't look in through the windows and simply *has* to feel the chimney."

The orange curtains were pulled across the windows. Joe locked the cabin door and put the key in his pocket. Everything was ready. The detectives left the Wilderness and went back along the river bank to Scotland Yard.

They heard voices in the garden and found Mrs. Dudgeon sitting on the lawn by the river, and playing with "our baby" who was crawling on the grass.

"Well," said Mrs. Dudgeon, "and how are the Big Six getting on? An arrest to be expected shortly?"

"We think so," said Dorothea. "There's going to be a tremendous new clue tonight."

"You seem very sure about it."

"Dot is," said Tom.

Just then a pair-oared boat passed by going up the river, rowed by George Owdon and his friend.

"They've borrowed the Towzers' boat," said Tom.

"I wonder they aren't in bed," said Mrs. Dudgeon. "Mr. Tedder says they're out night after night watching for any more boats to be cast off. And those Towzer boys. I wonder if they've got any clues too."

"George Owdon think we done it," said Joe.

"So do a lot of people unfortunately," said Mrs. Dudgeon. "But I'm sure they're all wrong. If only they could find out who took those shackles."

"That's just what we're doing," said Tom, and stopped.

Dorothea looked at him and at Mrs. Dudgeon and then at the others. "We'd better tell her," she said. "Only it's terrifically important that she mustn't tell anybody else."

"Don't tell me if you don't want to," said Mrs. Dudgeon. "Tom, take care! Don't let him crawl so near the edge. We don't want him falling in before he's had time to grow webbed feet. How soon do you think he'll be big enough to let into your club?"

"There won't be any club," said Tom, "if things don't clear up. The Potter Heigham member's been made to resign, and the one at Acle, and the one at Wroxham. . . . Everybody's resigned except us."

"This is what we're doing," said Dorothea, and told about the painting of the chimney and of how last night it had not worked only because Mr. Tedder had been hanging about at dusk wanting to see the Death and Glories.

Mrs. Dudgeon listened to the end. "I don't want to throw cold water on it," she said at last. "But don't you think the thief will want those shackles for himself? Don't you think he just put that bundle down your chimney to throw suspicion on you so that he can safely keep the others or get rid of them somewhere else? I shouldn't be surprised if he has sold them in Yarmouth by now. I don't quite see why you should think he'll make you a present of another lot."

There was silence for a moment. Then Pete turned to Tom.

"An extra coat or two don't hurt," he said. "That paint ain't really wasted."

But Dorothea held her ground. "We don't think he stole them to sell them," she said. "We think it's all part of a deep plot. Why did he bicycle to Ranworth to put those boats adrift just the night they were there?"

"That may be a different person," said Mrs. Dudgeon.

Dorothea shook her head.

"There's no harm in laying your trap anyway," said Mrs. Dudgeon. "Real detectives lay dozens that don't come off and then the one that does makes all the others worth while. But don't put all your hopes on this one. There's another thing too. If he's the sort of person you think he is he must know what a lot of you there are. How are you going to let him know the coast is clear?"

"We've thought of that," said Tom. "I say, you don't want anything at the post office or Roy's? We're going to walk up there so that the whole village knows there's a good chance of nobody being in the Wilderness."

"Let me think," said Mrs. Dudgeon. "Why, yes. You can get me a two shilling book of stamps, and how would you like to have pears after supper? That'll give you two shops to go into."

"Well done, Mother," said Tom.

"Splendid," said Dorothea. "That's just the thing. So that if the villain sees us he'll never guess we're showing ourselves on purpose."

"You'll find my purse in my bag," said Mrs. Dudgeon. "On the dining-room table."

"We got money," said Bill.

Mrs. Dudgeon looked at him for a moment and then laughed.

"I'm glad to hear that," she said. "But I've got plenty too."

"How many pears?" said Tom.

"Better get a dozen," said his mother.

*

The mothers of the Death and Glories had been right about the feeling in the village. Tom, Dick and Dorothea could have gone to the shops and nobody would have noticed them. It was very different when they were with Joe, Bill and Pete. People hanging out washing in their gardens stopped to look at them. People sweeping their lawns leaned on their brushes and gravely watched them go by. Old ladies gossiping together pointed them out to each other and turned to have a better sight of them. Long before they came to the shops and the staithe the three small boys were red in the face and staring so defiantly at anybody who looked at them that it was not surprising that they heard one old lady say that they had the look of hardened criminals already. It was quite clear that news of the Potter Heigham shackles had got about and that the whole village had made up its mind that the Death and Glories were the thieves.

There was busy chatter going on in the Post Office when the six Coots filed in. Talk stopped dead. The old post-mistress gave Tom his book of

stamps without a word. Nobody spoke in the shop
till the Coots had gone out, when they heard the
chatter burst out again behind their backs.

"Drat 'em!" said Pete. "Drat 'em! Drat 'em!
They all think we done it."

"Well, you didn't," said Dorothea. "So they're
all wrong."

But that, though true, was small comfort.

It was the same thing at the greengrocer's. Old
Mrs. Halliday looked severely at the Death and
Glories, opened her mouth as if to say something,
but thought better of it and pretended that the
three small boys were not in the shop. She pursed
her lips, put the pears in a bag and handed them
to Tom as if he too was a criminal and she wished
to have as little to do with him as possible.

"Gosh!" said Tom when they got outside.

"I think it's perfectly horrid," said Dorothea.

"Let's get out of this," said Bill.

"Oh, but we mustn't," said Dorothea. "Not till
we've made sure everybody knows we're not at
the *Death and Glory*."

"But how will they know we aren't going
straight back there?"

"They won't. The villain will think he's got
a chance and he'll go and feel the chimney to
make sure. Won't he Dick?"

Dick was thinking of something else. He was
the only one of the six who was enjoying the walk,
because, as usual, his mind was far away. "I wish I
knew how they photograph fingerprints," he said.
"It's got something to do with powder ... very
fine powder. ... " And then, as he slowly realized
that Dorothea had asked him a question, he said,

"Sorry. I didn't hear what you were saying." For the first time on that walk, they all laughed.

They walked, from mere habit, out on the staithe and were stared at in a very unfriendly way by two of the boatmen outside Jonnatt's shed. They came on George Owdon and his friend tying up their rowing skiff.

"Tom and his young friends," they heard George Owdon say in a loud whisper.

"Had I better stay and watch the boat?" asked the friend.

"They won't dare to cast her off here now that we've seen them," said George, and they saw him put two extra half hitches on his painter when he had already made his boat fast.

"We'll be back before dark anyway," said the friend.

"Even them beasts!" said Pete, as the Coots, not letting it be seen that they had heard, strolled on their way.

They made a leisurely round of the busier parts of the village and then, sure that everybody would know that they had left the *Death and Glory*, went slowly back to the Doctor's house where they found high tea nearly ready for them.

"You know," said Mrs. Dudgeon as they came in. "I've been thinking over all you told me about these shackles and I was going to ask you to tell my husband too, but he's just telephoned to say he has to stay in Norwich for an operation and he won't be back till very late."

"We couldn't have told him," said Dorothea. "Not till we've got the proofs."

"It isn't only proofs that count," said Mrs.

Dudgeon. "I think perhaps if he had heard of
that plan of yours it might have helped to make
him a little doubtful about the evidence of Mr.
Tedder."

"Mother!" exclaimed Tom. "You don't mean
he's really thinking Tedder's right."

"Well, I did hear him say that Mr. Tedder was
putting up a pretty good case. . . . But, of course,"
she added hurriedly, "he hasn't heard your side."

"It's all right," said Dorothea. "I'm sure it'll
be all right after tonight."

"Well," said Mrs. Dudgeon, "I'm sure I hope
the villainous fly will walk into your spider's
parlour."

"He will," said Dorothea. "We've been all round
the village and if he's there he must know by now
that he's invited."

"It isn't so much what you say," said Mrs.
Dudgeon. "But I'd like my husband to hear the
way you say it. . . . And now let's forget all about
it. Even detectives forget their work sometimes.
It's only doctors who never can. Come along in
now and let's see who of the Big Six has got the
best appetite."

*

In about two minutes everybody was sitting
round the table in the doctor's dining-room,
stowing away bacon and eggs, tomatoes and
mushrooms. The talk had wandered far away
from Scotland Yard to the mountains of the
north, prospecting for gold and pigeons that carried daily messages home from a mining camp.
Dorothea was telling about their adventures in

the lakes and how they had thought they had
found gold but it had turned out to be copper.
Dick was explaining how they had made their
own charcoal. Tom kept asking questions about
the boats on the lake. Joe and Bill and Pete were
asking about the birds. Dorothea told them about
the hawk that had tried to get one of the pigeons.
"Marsh harrier likely," said Joe. Dick said, "No.
It was a kestrel," and told them there were lots
of water-hens up there, but no great flocks of
coots, and no spoonbills, but plenty of herons and
kingfishers, and no harriers but buzzards flying
round the crags. "Crags?" said Joe, and Dorothea
explained. "What about beardies?" asked Pete,
and on hearing that there were no bearded tits
in the Lake Country said he reckoned they were
better off here.

They drank their tea, made a huge apple tart
look sorry for itself, and finished up with the pears.
Time flew on. "Our baby" was taken upstairs to
bed, and Mrs. Dudgeon suggested that they should
play darts, at which game Joe was much the best
and Dick the worst, though he was quicker than
the others in calculating what numbers to aim at.
Then, in the dusk, they went out into the garden,
half hoping to hear a noise in the Wilderness, and
yet knowing that it would have to be a loud noise
if they were to hear it, and that the villain, if he
were there, would be doing his best to make no
noise at all.

"Let's scout along and see," said Pete.

"And scare him off," said Joe scornfully.

"We mustn't go anywhere near till we have
to," said Dorothea and they went into Scotland

Yard and lit a lantern and sat there, and wished Joe had his white rat with him.

"Have you got your mouth organ?" asked Dorothea.

"I got that," said Joe, pulling it out of his pocket.

"Why not play it?" said Dorothea. "That'll encourage him if he's passing in the road. He'll know you're here and he'll guess the others may be. But he won't be sure, and he'll creep through the bushes. . . . " As she spoke, without knowing it, her hand reached out to feel an imaginary chimney.

"Here she go," said Joe, and staring straight in front of him with glassy eyes, moved the mouth organ to and fro, holding it to his lips with both hands. "Daisy, Daisy, Give me your answer do" came from the instrument and set Mrs. Dudgeon smiling in the house and hoping at the same time that it would not wake "our baby" so that she would have to go out to Scotland Yard and stop it. But "our baby" took it for a lullaby and slept on, and in Scotland Yard Joe played his mouth organ till he had no more breath and no more tunes and the dusk outside had turned to dark.

Mrs. Dudgeon came out at last and hurried Dick and Dorothea off home. "Mrs. Barrable will be wondering what we've done with you," she said. "And William can't be very good company."

"But ain't you and Dick coming to see?" said Joe. "Let's slip along now."

For a moment, Dorothea was tempted. Then, sadly but firmly, she made up her mind. "The longer you give him, the more chance," she said.

"You wouldn't be able to do anything about

it till the morning anyway," said Mrs. Dudgeon.
"And I expect you'll be down here pretty early."

Dick and Dorothea went home. Tom and the
Death and Glories stayed on at Scotland Yard.
From time to time someone looked out to see
that the dark was growing darker. Joe and Tom
were putting an eye-splice in one end of a length
of rope and a sailmaker's whipping on the other,
to make a new mainsheet for the *Titmouse*. Pete
and Bill were looking at the pile of separate bits of
paper on which Dorothea had made careful notes
of each bit of evidence they had collected.

"Wonderful how she do it," said Bill.

"Out of school too," said Pete. "Even Tom
couldn't do it."

"Bet he could," said Bill. "Tom, could you have
write all that if that Dot not been here to do it?"

"Not me," said Tom cheerfully. "I say, Joe,
get the twist out of your end."

"That eye-splice is all right," said Joe, looking
over Tom's work.

"Those last tucks ought to be tighter," said Tom.

Steps sounded on the path outside.

"Tom!"

"Coming!" called Tom.

"Bed-time," said Mrs. Dudgeon coming to the
door of Scotland Yard.

"I'll just run down to the *Death and Glory*,"
said Tom.

"In the morning," said his mother. "I want
you in bed before your father comes home."

"But what if Dick's dodge has worked?" said
Tom.

"I don't expect it has," said Mrs. Dudgeon . . .

"But ... Well, if it has they can come back and let you know. I'd like to know too. Now, off you go, you three."

Tom blew out the lantern. In the dark outside, Pete tried his torch.

"If there's anything happen we can come back and tell Tom?" said Bill.

"Didn't you hear her?" said Joe.

"Yes. You can come back. But don't make too much noise if you do. Good night. Good night."

Tom and his mother went round the house and in, while the crew of the *Death and Glory*, using one torch to save the others, went to the drawbridge, crossed quietly into Mr. Farland's garden, and made their way round his boathouse and so along the river bank. Cautiously, silently they crept towards their ship.

*

Three minutes later, they scrambled over the fence into the road and with all three torches blazing raced back to Dr. Dudgeon's as hard as they could go.

CHAPTER XXIII

THE VILLAIN LEAVES HIS MARK

THEY charged into Dr. Dudgeon's gate and round the house. There was a light in the window of Tom's room. Tom was not yet in bed.

"Tom!" called Joe.

"Coots for ever!" shouted Bill.

Pete said nothing but pulled as hard as he could at the string that was hanging from the window.

Tom put his head out.

"Stop pulling," he whispered. "You're lugging my bed across the room. And don't make such a row."

"Tom," whispered Joe, in the sort of whisper that is meant to carry from the ground to an upper window. "He's been at our chimbley."

"All five fingers," whispered Bill.

"We ain't looked in the stove yet," said Pete.

"I'll be down in a minute."

"Coming down the rope?" said Joe hoarsely.

"No," said Tom.

Two minutes later he joined them in the garden, and they set off at a run back to the Wilderness.

"Dad's not in yet," said Tom, "and Mother says I must come straight back. What sort of print is it?"

"Good 'un," said Joe.

"Might have done it apurpose," said Bill.

It was a curious thing but, as they hurried

through the osier bushes in the dark, Pete found himself wondering if the print were there at all. He had the oddest feeling that when they came to look at the chimney again they would find nothing but smooth green paint. What would Tom say then, dragged out in the night all for nothing?

Tom was first at the chimney, and, in the light of his torch, Pete saw the print again. It was there all right, and what a print! Thumb and all four fingers plain to see, and below them a long smear made by someone pulling his hand suddenly away.

"Gosh!" said Tom. "It's a beauty."

"Look out, don't go clumping," said Joe as they climbed on the cabin roof. "You'll have us all through."

"Look out for the paint," said Bill, as Pete worked his hand in under the mushroom top to feel if the chimney was full to the brim with shackles.

Joe had jumped down into the cockpit and was unlocking the cabin door.

"Half a jiff while I get that lantern lit," he said.

The others with lit torches crowded in after him. Joe wrestling with the lantern blocked their way. One match flared and went out and then another. Then the wick of the lantern burned up and Joe hung it from its hook.

"Let Tom ope that stove," he said. "So it won't be us find 'em."

There was a tight jam in the cabin in front of the stove. Tom crouched before it, lifted the latch of the door and swung it open.

The stove was empty, except for the ashes of their last fire.

"Stuck in the chimbley," suggested Pete.

Tom thrust his hand up inside the stove and brought it out black with soot.

"Somebody shine a torch down the chimney," said Tom. "No good shining it up with that cap on the top." Bill scrambled for the door and Tom called after him, "Don't touch the chimney. We'll want to let the paint dry with that print."

"I ain't a roaring donkey," said Bill.

They heard his footsteps overhead. There was a pause and then a glimmering of light came down the chimney lighting up the dead ashes in the stove.

"There's nothing there," said Tom.

"That's a rum 'un," said Joe.

"We come too soon," said Pete. "Reckon that old villain hear us and run for it."

"Let's have a look round on deck. . . . All right, Bill. Nothing here," Tom shouted up the chimney.

But there were no shackles to be seen on deck and few places where shackles could be hidden. There was a bollard on the foredeck, a coil of rope and a small hatch. The sail, neatly stowed along its spar, lay on the roof of the cabin, and the pair of oars that in the *Death and Glory* served as engines. Otherwise the cabin-top was clear but for the mast tabernacle and the green-painted chimney pot. They turned their torches again on that print of the enemy's hand.

"That Dick and Dot ought to see it," said Joe.

"Too late to yank them out now," said Tom. "They'll be in bed. What are you doing, Bill?"

FIVE FINGER PRINT

Bill had left the others on the cabin-top and the light of his torch was playing round the cockpit.

"Look ahere. Look ahere!" he suddenly shouted.

"What is it?"

"Them shackles," shouted Bill.

The others scrambled aft. Right in the stern, under the little bit of an after deck, in the place where usually was nothing but a bucket and a warp, the light of Bill's torch was playing on a pile of new shackles strung together on a bit of tarred marline.

"Gee whizz," said Joe. "We got him. Yank 'em out and let's see."

"Don't touch them," said Tom, just as Bill was reaching in to bring them out. "Scotland Yard'll want a photograph. Don't touch them till we can get Dick."

"Couple o' score of 'em," said Joe.

"Can't we pull 'em out and count 'em?" said Pete.

"Better not," said Tom. "Let's have a look for any more."

They shone their torches this way and that under the seats, but found nothing else that did not belong to the boat.

"What are we going to do with 'em?" said Joe. "Take 'em to Tedder and be told we stole 'em?"

"I'm not going to Tedder with 'em," said Pete.

"Look here," said Tom. "I think I'd better ask Dad. But don't touch them till Dick and Dot have seen them. It was Dick's idea trying to get the fingerprints. Leave them where they are till the morning."

"What if that Tedder come and find 'em here?" said Pete.

Tom thought for a moment. "I'll bolt up to Mrs. Barrable's before breakfast and get Dick and Dot here first thing. Dick'll get them photographed and then if Dad says we've got to take them to Tedder we'll have to. I'll come too. We'll all go. And if Mr. Tedder comes first . . ."

"He may come in the night," said Pete.

"And if that old villain tell him where to look . . . ," said Bill.

"You'll have to get word to me quick," said Tom. "And I'll tell Dad what's happened. But we won't touch them now. Not till Dick and Dot have had a sleuth at them. And I've got to bolt. I promised I'd come straight back."

"What if that chap come again?" said Pete.

"Get a sight of him if you can. But he won't. At least I shouldn't think so. He's probably too busy getting the paint off."

"That'll be another clue," said Joe. "He'll be properly stinking of turps."

"We can't go round sniffing for him," said Bill.

"We can't do anything till morning," said Tom. "Good night."

*

The crew of the *Death and Glory* watched Tom's torch flickering through the osiers until it disappeared for the last time. They had a last look at the print of the villain's hand on their chimney. They had two or three last looks at that little heap of shackles that had been pushed in under the after deck.

"Wish it was morning," said Pete.

"You turn in and go to sleep," said Bill. "What'd your Mum say?"

But when they were in their bunks and rolled up in their blankets, Joe was the only one who fell asleep at once.

"Think of that chap come pawing our chimbley," said Pete. "How'd that Dot know he'd be coming? That's what beat me."

"It's having 'em aboard I don't like," said Bill. "Wish Tom had took 'em. And that's not the lot neither. He've the most of 'em to bring."

The thought that a stranger had been at their boat, had been aboard, and might come again, and had left aboard something that was certainly not meant as a sign of good will, somehow made their boat feel less like home. She was the same old *Death and Glory* but that night, for Bill and Pete, she felt quite different. For a long time they did not get properly to sleep, but dozed and woke to listen for strange hands feeling round her.

*

In the morning Bill was the first to wake. He screwed himself round to look up at the old clock thinking he would have time to turn over and go to sleep again. Then he remembered. He tugged the blankets off the others and hurried out.

Yes. There was the pile of shackles well in under the after deck. He climbed on the roof to look at the hand-print on the chimney. "Give himself away that time," he said gleefully as Joe, rubbing his eyes, came out and joined him.

Pete came out too, blinking in the morning sunshine. He looked first at the print on the chimney which, in daylight, did not seem so clear as it had last night in the white gleam of the torches. Still, it was there all right, and proof that somebody had indeed laid his paw on the chimney. Pete turned and crouched in the cockpit to look in under the after deck.

"Let's get on with it," said Joe. "Tom'll be up at the Admiral's by now and they'll be along all three before we had our grub."

"Hope they come before that Tedder poke his nose in," said Bill. "If he come and find them shackles now . . . "

"Your turn," said Joe. "Primus to save time. Boiled eggs. Two apiece and put 'em in the kettle when that start boiling. We got no time to lose."

Less soap than usual was used in the morning wash and it was a quick breakfast. Everybody was in a desperate hurry to get done and be ready for the rest of the detectives. And everybody was in a desperate stew lest Mr. Tedder should come first.

Tom, Dick and Dot arrived together, on the run. Dick and Dot went straight for the chimney. Tom had urgent news for the others.

"I say," he said. "I told Dad about the shackles and about your not wanting to take them to Tedder after what happened last time. He says he'll take them for you. He's coming along here just before he goes off on his rounds. You don't mind do you? Dorothea says it's all right."

"Good," said Joe. "That Tedder'll think twice before he say the Doctor steal 'em."

Dorothea, looking at the chimney and its print,

felt much as she felt when reading over a good bit in one of her own stories. She had been sure the villain would come, and now it was almost as if he were obeying her orders. "I knew he'd do it," she said. "And hasn't Dick's idea worked beautifully . . . the wet paint, I mean."

"Going to photograph it, Dick?" asked Tom.

"Of course he must," said Dorothea. "But where are the shackles? You haven't moved them, have you?"

"Ain't touched 'em," said Joe.

"That's how I find 'em," said Bill, and all six detectives peered in under the after deck.

"I'll get a photograph of the chimney all right," said Dick. "But I don't know about the shackles. Nothing'll show much. It's too dark in there, and . . . "

"But it's like the corpse," said Dorothea. "Scotland Yard always wants a picture of that to show just where it was found."

"I'll have a shot," said Dick.

He fixed the camera on a box on the cockpit floor to get it at the right level, and moved the focusing lever to the spot marked "3 to 10 feet".

"I'll give it half a minute," he said, "just to give the shackles a chance of showing. And then I'll take a photograph from the top of the cabin to show the whole cockpit."

"And we can mark it with a cross to show the place where the shackles were found," said Dorothea.

Dick took his three photographs, while the others waited, reminding him in chorus to wind on the film after making each exposure. With pictures as serious as these it would be dreadful if one came out on top of another.

"Done?" said Joe. "Shall I get 'em out?"

"Go ahead," said Tom.

Joe reached in and pulled a heavy bundle of shackles out into the light.

"Green paint," cried Dorothea.

"Look at that now," said Bill.

There was no doubt about it. Some of the new gunmetal shackles were smeared with the same green paint that Pete had put on the chimney.

Dick had a close look at the shackles, pulled off his spectacles, polished them with his handkerchief and put them on again.

"What is it, Dick?" asked Dorothea, who knew the signs.

"Clue," said Dick. "Let me just try."

He went ashore and stood on the bank opposite the *Death and Glory*'s chimney and leant out as if to touch it. Then he began searching the ground at his feet.

"Here's where he put them down," he said. "You can see there's been something heavy in the grass. He must have put them down while he was feeling the chimney. He wouldn't want them to clink or anything in case there was somebody at home. Then he got his hand all over paint. Then he must have picked up the shackles and got some paint on them. He wouldn't know if it was pretty dark. The next thing he did was to get into your cockpit and push the shackles into that hole."

"Under our after deck," said Joe, who liked things aboard his ship to be given their proper names.

"Let's see if he left any paintmarks on the way," said Dick.

"Here you are," shouted Pete. "On the edge of the coaming. But maybe I do it when I done painting the chimbley."

"More likely the villain," said Dorothea. "Go on, Dick." She knew his mind was running ahead like a hound with its nose on a fresh scent.

"He went ashore again," said Dick. "He'd have to get out of the Wilderness. He wouldn't go our way through the garden. He'd go the way he went that time Dot and William saw him. We ought to track him."

"Come on, quick," said Dorothea.

"You go first, Dick," said Joe. "Let's see how you do it."

"Spread out a bit," said Dick, "so as not to miss anything."

Crouching low and peering at the ground, the six detectives worked their way through the osier bushes to the fence that shut off the Wilderness from the road.

"A whole lot of people have been along here," said Dick.

"Course there has," said Pete. "There was our Mums yesterday, and that Tedder and all of us. . . ."

"But Tom didn't bring his paint this way," said Dick in triumph. There, on the top bar of the fence, was another smear of green. "Here's where the villain got across," said Dick.

"And then what?" said Dorothea.

"Don't get over just here," said Dick. He went a few yards along the fence and climbed over, jumping clear so as to land a foot or two beyond it. Then he worked carefully back looking at every inch of the ground under the fence.

"Here it is," he said suddenly. "More bicycle tracks."

The others crowded to see.

"Dunlops!" said Pete. "Same as that Tedder's."

"We can't know for certain they're his," said Dick. "But he had a bicycle the night William got him, and he had a bicycle at Ranworth." He thought for a moment, pulled off his spectacles, looked at them with eyes that hardly saw them and smiled with the happiness of the successful scientist. "Yes," he said. "He got on his bicycle and rode away. And we know another thing about his bicycle now."

"What?" asked everybody at once.

"It's got some green paint on the grip of the right handlebar."

"How d'you know?"

"He'd got a lot of paint on his hand. . . . That's a big smear on the fence and it wouldn't all come off the first time he touched anything. Of course we don't know how he took hold of his bicycle when it was leaning up against the fence. There may be other smears on it too. But there's sure to be some on his right handlebar."

"Why the right one?" said Dorothea.

"I know that," said Pete. "That were his right hand on our chimbley. Thumb and fingers go so. . . . " He put his own right hand on one of the posts of the fence.

"We got him now," said Joe.

A motor car hooted somewhere up the road.

"That's Dad coming out of our gate," said Tom.

The Doctor's car passed them, went on to the Ferry Inn to find room to turn round, came back and pulled up beside the detectives.

"We've caught him," cried Dorothea as the Doctor got out. "We've got his fingerprints, and there's the green mark where he put his hand on the fence."

"Look here," said Dr. Dudgeon, "I'm in an awful hurry. I ought to be on my rounds and instead I'm leaving my patients to die in dozens. So don't waste time. I'll take those shackles to Tedder for you. It doesn't matter how you come to have them, but you are putting yourselves in the wrong by not letting him have them at once. And I want to have a look at those fingerprints. Come along quick and tell me all about it."

"Look at the paint on the fence first," said Dorothea.

The Doctor looked at the smear of paint.

"How do you say it got there?" he asked. "You begin at Ranworth and tell me the whole story. Never mind the things that happened before that."

They told him everything they could remember, of bicycle tracks, of the figure Dorothea had seen, of William's trophy of grey flannel, of the painting of the chimney. Dr. Dudgeon listened carefully. Presently he stepped over the fence. The others scrambled over and took him through the bushes to the *Death and Glory*.

He had a good look at the chimney.

"Who's got the biggest hands?" he said.

"Mine," said Joe.

"What about Tom's?" said Pete. "And Tom's ain't big enough."

"Let's have a look at them," said Dr. Dudgeon. "And yours, Tom."

Tom and the Death and Glories showed their hands.

"Green paint on yours, Pete."

"I paint that old chimbley," said Pete. "That stuff don't come off so easy."

"Um," said Dr. Dudgeon. "That's a fair sized hand. Bigger than any of yours."

"That settles it, doesn't it?" said Dorothea hopefully.

"I'm not sure that it does," said Dr. Dudgeon.

"Green paint on the shackles," said Dick.

Dr. Dudgeon looked gravely at the shackles. "Look here, I may as well tell you. Tedder wants to take out a summons right away."

"We're sunk," said Joe bitterly.

Dr. Dudgeon looked at him but for a moment said nothing.

"I don't know what to think," he said at last. "It isn't only shackles."

"But they didn't do any of the things," said Dorothea.

Dr. Dudgeon smiled at her. "I've told Tedder he hasn't got enough evidence."

"And we've got lots and lots," said Dorothea.

"Tedder says nobody but you could have got those shackles. He told me yesterday he was sure that you had a lot more, and he thinks that if he had a summons for you the truth would come out. And when I take him this new lot. . . . And I've got to take them to him. Now look here.

You think you've got a lot of evidence. Well, what about consulting a lawyer? Put the whole thing in front of him and see what he says?"

Dorothea's eyes sparkled. "We'd simply love to," she said. "Of course that's what we ought to do."

"But what lawyer?" said Tom.

"I'll ring up Uncle Frank and ask if he'll see you."

"But he's on the other side," said Tom. "Haven't you seen the notice?"

"That's just why I'd like him to see you. Well? Have you any objection to telling him everything you've told me?"

The detectives looked at each other and then, somehow, all five boys were looking at Dot.

"We'd love to show him everything," she said.

"Right," said Dr. Dudgeon. "I'll telephone to Mr. Farland. You come home for lunch, Tom, and I'll tell you then if you can see him or not. Of course, as Sonning's lawyer, he may say he'd rather have nothing to do with you."

"You tell him he's got to, Dad," said Tom. "But, I say, what are we to do if Tedder comes charging along as soon as you've given him the shackles?"

"I'll tell him to leave you alone for this morning," said Dr. Dudgeon, picking up the bundle of shackles and turning to go. "He hasn't got his summonses yet."

"You won't let him have them, will you, Dad?" said Tom.

"Not till I've heard what your lawyer has to say." He was gone.

There was a long silence, as they stood by the *Death and Glory* looking at the chimney with the five fingerprints that seemed not to have settled things after all.

"Tom," said Joe at last. "Your Dad don't think we done it, do he?"

"He can't think that," said Dorothea.

Tom looked very unhappy.

"It's those boats," he said. "And partly it's that beastly old *Margoletta* I had to cast off last spring."

"But he said himself that if boats were cast off at Ranworth he'd think it was someone else," said Dorothea.

"It's with so many things all together," said Tom.

"I wish he hadn't been in such a hurry," said Dorothea. "There was lots more evidence we could have told him if he'd only waited."

"How could he wait?" said Tom, defending his father. "How could he wait with victims dying in all directions?"

"We'll have to show Mr. Farland every single thing," said Dorothea.

"I'd better go home and develop those photographs," said Dick.

CHAPTER XXIV

THINGS LOOK BLACK

Dɪᴄᴋ and Dorothea were at Mrs. Barrable's. Joe,
Bill and Pete were eating corned beef in the *Death
and Glory*. They were to meet Tom at Scotland
Yard after he had seen his father and learnt
whether Mr. Farland would see them or not. Tom
Dudgeon was waiting about for his father to come
home.

Usually the ringing of the bell for meals found
Tom in the middle of something really important,
and he knew from long practice just what it felt
like to slip late into the dining-room, hoping that
people would be talking hard and not noticing
that his chair was empty and, perhaps, that a
little more time spent on the washing of his
hands would not have been wasted. Today Tom
was waiting in the garden, hands washed, ready
to go in, and when he found that a patient had
waylaid his father at the gate and been allowed
to come in and have a cut dressed, he felt it would
have been a good thing if that particular victim
had bled to death instead. He heard the hoot of
the car, followed by the ring of the dinner-bell. He
dashed hopefully into the house and there was the
wretched patient going with the Doctor into the
consulting room.

"Oh, bother!" said Tom.

"What's the matter?" asked his mother, who

was coming downstairs with "our baby".

Tom pointed over his shoulder. "Dad's got a victim in the consulting room."

"Tom, I've told you a hundred times not to call them victims."

"Sorry," said Tom. "But this one may keep him ages."

"No he won't," said his mother. "I've seen him. It's only a bad cut. Not even stitches, I should think. Just disinfectant and a dressing. And that sort of thing can't wait."

"Well I wish the victim . . . sorry . . . I wish he'd chosen another day. Dad's simply bursting with important news. How's our baby?" and Tom set his small brother gurgling by tickling him under the chin.

"We'd better begin lunch," said his mother and began to mix a salad.

Presently they heard the front door close behind the patient, the sound of running water in a basin and Dr. Dudgeon's cheerful whistling.

A minute later, Dr. Dudgeon came in. Tom looked up eagerly. His father helped himself to cold meat and boiled potatoes at the sideboard, and sat down. Mrs. Dudgeon had already put a helping of undressed salad by his place. Dr. Dudgeon took a large wooden spoon and put a pat of mustard in it. Then he pulled the cruet towards him and carefully added olive oil and a little vinegar. He always liked to mix his own salad dressing. Tom watched and waited. Dr. Dudgeon took up a fork and began stirring the mixture in the spoon. Tom waited and watched. It was as if nothing in the world mattered except salad dressing, or as if, thinking of something else, Dr. Dudgeon was going to stir the oil and vinegar for ever. He stopped at last, but only to add a little pepper and stir again.

"Get on with your meat, Tom," said Mrs. Dudgeon.

Dr. Dudgeon looked up and saw Tom's anxious face.

"I've talked to your Uncle Frank," he said. "He won't be in till late tonight. But he'll see you first thing tomorrow morning before he goes to his office.

"Oh good," said Tom. "We were awfully afraid he wouldn't. Did you tell him about the finger-prints?"

"I did."

"And what did he say?"

"He said it was a very ingenious idea."

"So he knows now they didn't take those shackles?" said Tom.

"He said he wouldn't make up his mind about that till he'd heard what you've got to say," said his father. "And I wish I could make up my own mind about it too," he added.

"But you saw it yourself," said Tom.

"So I told him, but he said that a mark on a chimney last night doesn't clear them of things they are said to have done on half a dozen different days."

Tom's face fell.

"You don't really think those boys did it," said Mrs. Dudgeon.

"On the face of things, it looks as if they did," said Dr. Dudgeon. "It's only that they seem such decent boys, and have got you on their side, and Tom."

"And Mrs. Barrable, and Dick and Dorothea," said Mrs. Dudgeon.

"I know," said Dr. Dudgeon. "But there you are. Frank tells me that he's more than half convinced that Tedder is right. There have been no cases of boats being cast off here until this last fortnight, except that unlucky business Tom was mixed up with in the spring. And now there have been half a dozen. Each time it has happened in a place where those boys were close by and in a better position to do it than anybody else. Most of the cases were here. That case at Potter Heigham is the first they've had there since anybody can remember. It's a biggish coincidence to get over, that the night those boats were cast off happens to be the one night these boys had taken their boat to Potter Heigham. The same thing with Ranworth. I admit I was puzzled about boats going adrift there after all the other things had happened, and you would have thought they'd have been very careful to do nothing of the sort. But the shackle business is even more unfortunate. The shackles were stolen at Potter Heigham the night they were there, and you must see it looks a little odd that they should find first one lot of them and then another."

"But Dad, Dot's idea explains it all, and you've forgotten about the chap she saw touching their chimney."

"You'll tell your Uncle Frank about that. I'm only pointing out how things look to an outsider."

"But don't be an outsider, Dad," said Tom. "You ought to be on our side."

"If you'd heard me talking to your Uncle Frank you'd have thought I was," said Dr. Dudgeon. "I told him it seemed to me that you and your Scotland Yard had got together a lot of evidence pointing the other way."

"What did he say?"

"Do you really want to know?"

"Of course I do."

"Well, he said 'Clever lads! But that doesn't mean they're very good ones'."

"I'm glad you're a doctor not a lawyer," said Mrs. Dudgeon.

"It's lawyers they'll have to deal with," said Dr. Dudgeon seriously.

"He doesn't really think they did all the painting of the chimney and that just for show," said Tom. "Why, it wasn't even their idea. It was Dick's. Besides you've only got to look at the print to see their hands aren't big enough to make it, and you could compare the lines or whatever it is detectives do."

"He only means they could have done it," said Dr. Dudgeon. "They could have got a friend to make that mark."

"I'll have a talk with him myself," said Mrs. Dudgeon. "It's idiotic. Those boys would never think of such a thing."

Dr. Dudgeon went calmly on with his cold meat and salad.

"Don't be too hard on Frank," he said presently. "To hear our good policeman talk you'd think poor Frank was in league with the boys himself."

Tom, who had been with difficulty trying to eat his dinner looked up.

"Yes," said his father. "Our Mr. Tedder has been rather pleased with himself as a detective, and with all the help he's had from the people who've been out at all hours of the night watching the river and hoping to catch someone casting off a boat, he thinks he's got the mystery solved."

"But he's all wrong," said Tom.

"He thought that first lot of shackles settled it," said his father. "And he's pretty well fed up with your Uncle Frank for telling him that he'd rather not prosecute at all than not be absolutely sure of his ground. It seems Uncle Frank told Tedder that he and his watchers have made rather a mess of things, and that they'd have done much better to lie low and catch those lads actually pushing a boat off. Instead, everybody from Wroxham to Yarmouth knows they've been keeping an eye on the staithe and patrolling the river, so naturally the casting off of boats has come to an end. Frank saw him this morning. That was before they knew about that second lot of shackles, and you should have heard our Mr. Tedder on the subject when I handed them over. You know how he talks. 'Proof! Why them shackles is proof enough to a blind cow, and them boys is too artful to push a boat off where we could catch 'em at it. And I talk straight to Mr. Farland and tell him so, and he say he'd be better satisfied if we catch 'em in the act. What's he want more'n them shackles? And what am I to say to the chaps who been watching at nights? Am I to tell 'em Mr. Farland'd be better pleased if more boats been cast off?' Mr. Tedder was feeling very ill-used, I can tell you, and was holding an indignation meeting all by himself."

"But when you gave him the new lot of shackles and told him about the mark on the chimney and the green paint?"

"He said he'd known all along they had the rest of the shackles put by."

"But what's going to happen, Dad?"

"Nothing, till you've shown Uncle Frank all your evidence. But if when he's looked at it he isn't convinced, he thinks he ought to let Tedder have his way. He's going to hear both sides tomorrow. I gather Tedder is putting his case together and your young friends had better do the same with theirs. But I'm very much afraid the strongest point they've got is that no one has actually seen them pushing a boat off."

"Oh Gosh!" exclaimed Tom. "We ought to have started our own watchers right at the beginning, the day that first boat was cast off, and then we might have caught whoever it was pushing off one of the others."

"You seem very sure your Coots had nothing to do with it. Are you sure of all three of them? You see any of them could have done it without telling the others."

"They wouldn't," said Tom. "Not one of them. Boats matter more than anything else to them. More than birds. Not one of them would do it."

"More than birds?" said his father, knowing very well that Tom was thinking of how he himself had cast a boat off to save a family of coots and their nest.

"They had nothing to do with that time," said

Tom. "They didn't know what I was going to do
. . . and . . . just look how they salved her in the
end even though those beastly Hullabaloos were
still in her."

"I know," said his father. "Well, put your evidence together as well as you can. I wish you luck.
You and your young Portia. Everything's going to
depend on tomorrow morning, and I can tell you
I don't look forward to being on the Bench when
your young friends are brought up and charged
with theft."

"But they haven't done a single thing," said
Tom.

"Well, you convince Uncle Frank," said his
father.

CHAPTER XXV

THE LAST CHANCE

Five detectives and a bloodhound were waiting in Scotland Yard. Three damp photographs were drying on the window. The one of the whole cock-pit had come out very well, and so had the one of the chimney. You could see the mark left by the hand of the villain, small though it was in the picture. The photograph of the shackles in the darkness under the after deck was a failure as Dick had thought it would be, but they had decided that it did not matter so much. Dick had bought a bottle of red ink on the way back after lunch, meaning to mark with a cross the place where the shackles were found as soon as the photographs had dried. Dorothea was already using the red ink to mark in the photographs of Ranworth the place where Dick had found the tracks of the bicycle. William was asleep. The others were watching the door and wondering why Tom was so long over his lunch.

"Is he going to be all day?" said Joe.

"Bet something's gone wrong," said Bill.

"Eating and eating," said Pete.

And then they heard running footsteps and the next moment Tom came in.

"We've made the most awful mistake," he said.

"What's happened?" said Dorothea. "Won't Mr. Farland see us?"

"Go on Tom, said Joe.

"No, it's not that," said Tom. "We started detecting too late. We ought to have begun right at the beginning. We ought to have done what Tedder and the others did and started watching after the very first boat was cast off and then we'd have had a chance of catching the villain in the act."

"How was we to know there was going to be any more cast off?" said Bill.

"I know. I know," said Tom. "But Uncle Frank told Tedder that if only he'd caught you casting a boat off, he'd feel happier."

"Why?" said Pete. "He don't WANT boats going adrift."

"No. But he meant he'd feel there was more proof if only you'd been caught in the act. So of course if only we'd caught the villain in the act everything would have been all right. And we've had chance after chance if only we'd thought of it."

"Well, it's not too late," said Joe.

"Yes it is. We've got to take all our evidence to Uncle Frank tomorrow morning. Before he goes into Norwich. And Tedder's going to take his. And if ours isn't good enough it's all up. Dad says Tedder's furious because of Uncle Frank not thinking he's got enough already. And now he thinks that last lot of shackles settles it."

"But it proves it wasn't us," said Dorothea.

"Tedder thinks it proves just the opposite."

"What's the good of anything," said Pete, "if that Tedder don't believe a word we say?"

"If only we'd begun detecting at the beginning," said Tom.

"What else did Dr. Dudgeon say?" asked Dorothea. "Try to remember every single thing."

In no sort of order, just as it came into his head, Tom told everything he could remember. He told how Mr. Tedder thought he had proof enough to take out summonses. He told how his own father was not sure one way or the other. He told how once more Mr. Farland had made the policeman furious by saying that all the hard work he had done as a detective was not really enough to prove his case. "But all the same Uncle Frank thinks it was the Death and Glories at the bottom of everything. And if we can't persuade Uncle Frank tomorrow that it wasn't, Dad thinks he's got to let Tedder have his summonses. Dad's pretty upset about it too. He called you Portia by mistake, instead of Dorothea."

Dorothea blushed. She understood, but she did not explain.

"We've got a lot of evidence that it wasn't the Death and Glories," said Dick.

"But it doesn't show who it was," said Tom. "And tomorrow's the last chance. . . . What's the matter, Dot?"

Joe, Bill, Pete, Dick, and even the bloodhound, William, all turned to look at Dorothea, who was sitting at the table, pulling at one of her own pigtails and scowling most horribly.

"I'm being the villain," said Dorothea.

"How?"

"I'm just being him and thinking what he thinks."

"Bet he ain't got no plait to pull," said Joe, but was instantly ashamed of himself when he saw the serious way Dick was looking at his sister.

"Whoever he is," said Dorothea, "he knows everything we do. He knew when you went to Potter Heigham. He knew when you went to Ranworth. He knew when you hid the *Death and Glory* in the Wilderness."

"That's right," said Joe. "Look how quick he were coming with them shackles. And there was that Tedder on to us first thing."

"Let her go," said Dick. "That's the way detectives find things out."

"He probably knows everything Tom's just told us. . . . No, I don't mean he's listening. . . . " Pete, looking hurriedly round, had stolen to the door. "Of course he might be. . . . "

"Nobody here," said Pete.

"The villain's in just as much of a stew as we are," said Dorothea. "His deep laid plans have come to nothing. He's got to do something at once. Time is going on. Tomorrow the innocent people he had hoped to send in chains to the gallows are going to see a solicitor and lay the proofs of their innocence before him. . . . "

"Do he know what proof we got?" asked Pete.

"If he doesn't he's probably thinking we've got more than we have. You see, he knows he's guilty even if no one else does. So he knows what lots of proofs there must be to find if only we knew where to look for it," said Dorothea. "He's probably heard Mr. Tedder raging about what Mr. Farland said to him. He's wishing there were other boats near the *Death and Glory* so that he could push them off and get the Death and Glories blamed for it. You've been back from Ranworth three whole days and nothing's happened. Nothing new. And Mr. Farland saying you ought to have been caught in the act. 'Ah', says the villain to himself, 'another lot of boats adrift and nothing would save them.' He strides up and down, planning furiously, and his friends shrink from him in fear."

"You don't know who he is, do you?" said Pete hopefully.

"We've got a lot of clues," said Dick.

"Bad luck everybody using them Dunlop tyres," said Joe.

"We know a lot about him beside the tyres," said Dorothea. "We know he's somebody who's got some reason for wanting people to think it's Tom or the Death and Glories. We're pretty sure he's somebody who lives near here, because if he didn't he couldn't get to know so soon what you and Tom are doing. Then, the thing to ask is, what is going to happen if we can't prove it isn't any of you?"

"We'll be taken off the river," said Bill.

"Bust up of the Coot Club," said Tom.

"Well," said Dorothea, "who is there who lives near here and has a bicycle with Dunlop tyres and would be glad if the Coot Club got busted?"

"There's only George Owdon," said Bill. "He'd be glad enough if there wasn't no bird watchers on the river."

"It can't be him," said Tom. "He was one of the people keeping watch on the staithe that night when you were all at Potter Heigham."

"Tom," said Joe suddenly. "When you go to Potter that time, to put the Coots on the look out, what did you say to young Bob Curten?"

"I told him everybody was wrong in thinking you'd cast off those boats, and I asked if any other boats had been cast off, and I told him to let us know quick if any more boats got cast off. But it was no good because he said he isn't to have anything more to do with the Coot Club."

"You didn't say anything about that George Owdon?"

"Of course I didn't," said Tom. "Why should I?"

"I'm off," said Joe. "Look here, Pete, if I don't get back, mind you give old Ratty his supper."

"What are you going to do?" asked Tom.

"I got an idea," said Joe. "Bill, I'm taking your bike."

"Where are you going?"

"Potter Heigham."

"They'll grab you sure," said Pete. "That Tedder say the chaps at Sonning's was fair mad about them boats, let alone them shackles. They'll half kill you and ask questions after."

"They'll have to catch me first," said Joe. "I got to go. I got to go now. Tomorrow'll be too late."

Dorothea's eyes sparkled. "If we could prove George Owdon was there," she said.

"But everybody knows he wasn't," said Tom.

"All the better if we could prove he was, and he may have been there even if we can't prove it. But don't get caught, Joe. . . . "

Joe had already gone.

Dorothea was scowling again.

"What's he thinking now?" said Tom.

"Shackles," said Dorothea. "You see he's still got some. That notice said a gross and a half. How many's that?"

"144 and 72," said Dick. "That's 216."

"He must have about a hundred and fifty left," said Dorothea, "and he's wondering what to do with them."

"I'm going to the ship," said Pete. "We don't want any more of them shackles aboard."

"Come on," said Bill. "We'd better keep watch."

"But we're just getting at something," said Dorothea. "And anyway he won't do anything in daylight."

"Pete's right," said Tom. "Nobody could see what he was doing once he's got into the Wilderness. And if he's desperate. . . . Look here. Let's shift her to the river. Nobody would dare to touch her if she's in full view from everywhere. And there's no point in keeping her hid when Tedder and everybody knows where she is."

"But you'll come back here," said Dorothea.

"It won't take a minute to shift her," said Tom. "And you can go on being the villain. It would be too awful if there's another lot of shackles."

"I'm coming too," said Dick.

"All right," said Dorothea. "I'll be looking through the evidence."

Pete ran on ahead and looked all over the *Death and Glory*, but found no shackles. Then, when the others came, they put the anchors aboard, and brought her down the dyke, clear of the osiers, and moored her again just above the place where the dyke joined the river. There she could be seen by anybody on the water or on the banks and no one was likely to risk playing tricks with her, at any rate before dark.

"You'll have to keep a watch on deck all night," said Tom, as, with easier minds, they went back to Scotland Yard.

They came back to find Dorothea full of a new idea.

"I don't believe he'll bother about the shackles," she said. "You see there was the bloodhound the first time and getting his hands all over green paint the second. He may think another try would come off worse. And anyway he's got what he wanted, because everybody thinks you stole them. He's trying to think of something else. He's bothered because of what Mr. Farland said to Mr. Tedder. He's in an awful hurry because of tomorrow. He's trying to think of something that could happen tonight."

"Well there ain't no boats near us," said Pete.

"I wish there was one," said Dorothea. "He'd be absolutely certain to push her off tonight. . . . If only there was. . . . The detectives would lurk in the bushes listening and watching. And then, just as the villain creeps up in the dark to push her off, they would leap out and shine their torches on the villain's guilty face."

Dick jumped. "I say," he said. "We could do something even better. I've still got a lot of that flashlight powder."

"Torches are better," said Tom.

"Not to take a photograph," said Dick. He pulled his spectacles off at the thought. "We could wait in hiding with the camera all ready and then, just as the villain was pushing off the boat, we could fire off the flash and get a photograph of him in the very act."

Dorothea clapped her hands. "Simply lovely," she said.

"Gosh!" said Tom. "That would settle it."

"But how'd we know which boat he's going to set adrift?" said Bill.

"And there ain't no boats anywhere's near," said Pete.

"What about Mr. Farland's *Flash*?" said Dorothea. "If we could only borrow her and moor her somewhere."

"Uncle Frank would never lend her," said Tom. "He's laid her up for the winter already, because of Port and Starboard being in Paris. And besides, he thinks the Coots are guilty, so he wouldn't lend her anyhow. He'd think it was some new trick."

"It's an awful pity," said Dick. "We'd have to have a boat in a good place to be cast off from, for one thing. And fairly near the *Death and Glory* for another. And we'd have to get everything ready before dark . . . focusing the camera and all that. But if only it worked and we got a photograph of the villain in the very act, it would be as good as all the clues put together."

"It's no good talking about it," said Tom. "It would be a fine idea if there was a likely boat, but there isn't. You came to the Wilderness so as to be away from places where there are boats to be cast off. And if there's no boat the villain can't cast one off. He'll be doing something else."

"We've got so little time," said Dorothea.

"Nine o'clock tomorrow morning," said Tom. "Nothing much can happen between now and then. We ought to get ready every bit of evidence we've got."

"I've been going through it," said Dorothea. "Let's start at the beginning, and do it in a new way. I'll write down our evidence opposite each case." She wrote down "Cruiser at the staithe" and said, "Evidence?"

"We only know there was someone there that night beside the Dead and Glories and me."

"Evidence?" said Dorothea again.

"Someone was there, to throw that brick back through the window of the sail loft."

"That's something," said Dorothea. "And the next case. . . . "

"That was the boat we rescued with her mast stuck in the trees."

"Evidence?"

"We were with the eelman up river when she was cast off. We were on our way back when we found her. Only George Owdon saw us tying her up and thought we were casting her off. . . . "

"George Owdon," said Dorothea. "It isn't exactly evidence, but I'll put it down. . . . 'G.O. was on the staithe'."

"He just come biking on his way to Norwich with that pal of his," said Pete.

"Never mind," said Dorothea. "What about that first case? Wasn't he there in the morning when people thought you had cast off the cruiser?"

"He think we cast her off," said Pete. "He say so loud enough. At least he think it were Tom."

"G.O. in the morning thought it was Tom," wrote Dorothea. "Next case."

"Potter Heigham," said Tom.

"Potter Heigham," wrote Dorothea. "Evidence?"

"Them shackles," said Bill.

"The shackles are evidence in the wrong way," said Tom. "Everybody says the Death and Glories couldn't have got the shackles if they didn't steal them."

"That's what the villain wants them to say," said Dorothea. "We know the villain put the shackles in the *Death and Glory* so that they would get the blame."

"Down the chimbley," said Pete, looking at his fist. "I very near skin my knuckles."

"And there's more than that," said Dorothea thoughtfully. "I saw someone at your chimney. . . . And then there's the bit of flannel torn by our bloodhound from the villain's trousers. If we only knew. I wish Joe would hurry up and get back."

Pete gently tickled the roll of fat round William's neck.

"That's all the evidence we got with the first lot of shackles," said Tom. "But we've got Dick's paint trap with the second lot. There's the print on the chimney . . . and then the green paint on the shackles."

Dorothea wrote busily.

"Will it be an awful job to take the chimney off the boat?" asked Dick.

"Easy," said Bill. "It just fits over and there's two chocks to hold it. I can have them screws out in two ticks."

"We'll have to take it with us," said Dick.

"Chimney pot," wrote Dorothea. "Evidence to be produced in court." She said the words aloud.

"Court!" exclaimed Bill. "If they takes us to court we're sunk. It don't matter what happen. If they take us to court there'll be no more Coots."

Dorothea scribbled "If necessary" after "to be produced in court," and said, "We'll have to show it to the lawyer anyhow."

"Shall we go and get it off now?" said Dick.

"We'll be lighting the fire tonight," said Bill. "I can have them screws out quick in the morning."

"When Mr. Farland sees those fingers on the chimney," said Dorothea, "he can't help knowing that there was someone there."

"That's about all we've got about Potter," said Tom. "Unless Joe gets something out of Bob Curten. . . . But I don't see what he could get. Bob was as certain as the rest of them that the Death and Glories cast those boats off."

"What came next?" said Dorothea. "Ranworth. . . . "

"*Sir Garnet*," said Pete. "That night after you come and we was all in the old ship and old Simon tell us to keep an eye on the wherry, and we did and saw her warps was made fast proper, and yet off she go in the night and Jim Wooddall's new warp turn up in Jonnatt's boatshed."

"*Sir Garnet*," wrote Dorothea. "Evidence?" She waited.

"We ain't got none," said Bill. "Everybody go for us and we was lucky getting away. If that George hadn't have spoke up for us. . . . "

"George Owdon again," said Dorothea eagerly. "Go on. What did he say?"

"He tell 'em he didn't see what harm we could do in Ranworth, and we just push off while they were arguing."

"Dot," said Tom. "That ought to go with the

Ranworth evidence. Don't you see? George Owdon knew they'd gone to Ranworth."

"What's the good o' that?" said Bill. "Everybody on the staithe know where we was going. George only say to let us go. By the time they done shouting I wonder chaps didn't know in Ranworth we was coming before ever we get started."

"All the same," said Dorothea. "That's George Owdon again. He comes in a bit every time except when you were at Potter Heigham."

"No good," said Bill. "What about that Tedder? Tedder come in the first time and every time after. He keep track of us and come knocking on our cabin-top before we'd hardly got into the old Wilderness. But he ain't evidence, no more'n George Owdon."

"What else at Ranworth?" said Dorothea.

"Tyre prints," said Dick, "and bicycle pump."

"We know somebody come over the Ferry that night," said Bill.

"We've got a list of the people who use Dunlop tyres," said Tom digging it out from among the papers on the table. "Beginning with me and Bill, and Mr. Tedder, and the old parson. It's about a mile long. We'd have done better to make a list of the people who don't use Dunlop tyres. It would have been a lot shorter."

Dorothea was looking through the list. Her finger stopped at a name. "George Owdon's got Dunlops," she said.

"Everybody has," said Tom.

"Don't see how that matter," said Pete.

"Well, if he had Palmers," said Dorothea, "we'd know it wasn't him at Ranworth."

"Why," exclaimed Pete. "You ain't really thinking it's him."

"In detective stories," said Dorothea, "they don't rule out anybody. It's usually the most unlikely person."

"Gosh," said Pete. "I bet it *was* Mr. Tedder. Look at the way he try to patch it on us. Policeman too. Nobody'd think it were him. And he use Dunlops. I saw 'em."

"I'd better make a fair copy," said Dorothea. "So as to be sure of not forgetting anything when we're putting our case before the lawyer."

"Mark at the side where we have a clue to show him," said Dick. "We'll take them all with us."

She set to work, with the others looking over her shoulder and making suggestions from time to time. She had not nearly finished when Joe, hot and dusty from his ride, came into Scotland Yard in triumph.

"How long have I been?" he asked. "George Owdon could do it quicker."

"What did you find out?" asked Dorothea, jumping up from the table.

"Real evidence," said Joe.

"What happened?" said Tom.

"They didn't catch you?" said Pete.

"Nobody see me till I were off again," said Joe happily. "They shout after me then but they was too late."

"Did you find Bob?"

"I find him, and his Dad had tell him never to speak to none of us, but I soon settle that. I say to him, 'Young Bob,' I say. 'Have you seen that

George Owdon about?' And what do you think he
say? He say, 'No, I ain't seen him this ways not
since that night you was here casting them boats
off.' So I clout his head and tell him we don't cast
off no boats. And he say Tom Dudgeon tell him
that but everybody think we do. And I tell him
he got to be here tomorrow morning to go with
us to Mr. Farland, but he say he can't do that.
So I make him write it down and here it is." He
held out a scrap of paper. Dorothea took it.

"Read it out loud," said Dick.

Dorothea read, "I swear I see George Owdon by
Potter Bridge the night before you come through.
Bob Curten."

"That's right," said Pete. "He see us come
through the bridge next morning. He were shouting and signalling, but we was in tow."

"George Owdon comes in every time," said
Dorothea.

"He'll be putting the rest of them shackles
aboard," said Joe.

"We've shifted her out of the dyke," said Tom.

Joe turned and made for the door. "I'll just see
she's all right," he said. If anybody else had been
mooring the *Death and Glory*, Joe wanted to have
a look at her anchors for himself.

"But we ought to go through the evidence with
you," said Dorothea, too late for him to hear her.

"Let's all go," said Pete.

Dorothea took her rough copy with her, and
they went along the river bank to find Joe, who
had had a look at the anchors, feeling the *Death
and Glory*'s mooring ropes to make sure they were
not stretched too taut.

"IT'S THE *CACHALOT*"

Sitting in the cockpit and on the cabin roof they went through the evidence with Joe. He had nothing to add, though, after his ride to Potter Heigham, he tried hard to think that they had proved George Owdon was the villain. The others saw only too clearly that they had only proved that somebody else could have done the things the Death and Glories were accused of doing. They had no real proof that any particular person had done them. And, worst of all, they had not proved that they had not done them themselves.

"It's a lovely lot of evidence anyhow," said Dorothea, sitting on the cabin roof beside Joe. "But it's not enough." She frowned. "And somewhere in the village the villain is thinking of the evidence he's piled up against us, and trying to plan something else to make sure before tomorrow. If only we could borrow a boat."

"The fingerprints are good," said Dick. "And the tyre prints. And the bit of bicycle pump. But a photograph of the villain would be better than anything."

"We simply must get something more," said Dorothea.

"Do you think he'll come and put those shackles aboard after dark?" said Dick. "I could wait with the camera in that bush, and somebody else would have to fire off the flashlight just about there. . . . " He pointed. "You see we'd have to be careful that the flash isn't in front of the lens. You get nothing but fog if it is. That's what was wrong when I tried it with the Admiral."

"No hope," said Tom. "Not unless the Death and Glories were sleeping somewhere else. The villain would never risk being caught like that, with the shackles."

"I do wish there was a boat we could borrow," said Dorothea again.

"Most everybody's taking their boats off the water by now," said Joe. "Come October and there won't be a boat about except fishermen and us . . . and there won't be us if Sonning's take us into court."

Just then there was a faint drumming somewhere down the river. Presently a smallish white motor cruiser came chugging upstream round the bend by the Ferry. Pete, in the cockpit of the *Death and Glory*, looked at her through his big telescope.

"It's the old *Cachalot*," he said.

CHAPTER XXVI

A KID FOR THE TIGER

THE fisherman at the wheel of his little cruiser saw the *Death and Glory* and recognised her crew. He swung the *Cachalot* towards the bank.

"Hullo you chaps!"

"Hullo . . . Hullo!"

"That's the one what bought our fish," said Pete to Dorothea.

"Got any use for some maggots?"

"RathER," said Pete.

"You can have what I've got left," said the fisherman. "I'll be bringing a fresh lot tomorrow."

"Maggots beat worrams hollow," Pete explained to Dorothea.

"Bring her in here," called Joe as he and Bill jumped ashore.

The *Cachalot* slid up beside the bank and Joe and Bill took her rond anchors and made her fast.

"You fishermen too?" asked her owner, looking at Dorothea, Dick and Tom.

"Just friends," said Dorothea.

"I don't know how the cellar is," said the fisherman. "But I'll have a look." He disappeared into his cabin and came out again with half a dozen oranges. "Catch!" Oranges flew through the air. Tom, Joe, Bill, Pete, and Dorothea caught theirs. Dick was not expecting his, but saved it from going in the river.

"Best I can do today," said the fisherman.

"Of course, if I'd known I was meeting you. . . . Never mind, I'll be stocking up tomorrow when I come back." He looked about him. "Nice mooring you've got here. How far are we from where the Wroxham bus stops?"

"Not above ten minutes," said Pete. "And not hurrying neither."

"Would you keep an eye on her if I left her here?" asked the fisherman. "I've got to get back to Norwich for the night and they tell me there's a gang of young toughs about here casting off boats. I don't much like the idea of leaving her at the staithe."

The Death and Glories looked grimly at each other.

"We never cast no boats off," said Bill.

"Never thought you did," said the fisherman.

"Everybody think we do," said Joe.

"What!" exclaimed the fisherman. "Are you the toughs they were telling me about? Well, I'd trust you not to cast off the old *Cachalot*. Set a thief to catch a thief, eh? And poachers make the best gamekeepers. . . . "

"It's not us at all," said Tom. "Only once I did cast off a boat because some people had moored her over a nest we were watching and so now because boats are getting sent adrift everybody thinks it's us. . . . The Coot Club. . . . " he explained.

"And you know that money you give us for that great old pike," said Joe. "They're saying we stole shackles at Potter that day we was there, and sold 'em and that's the money."

"What's all this?" said the fisherman.

Bit by bit, they told him the whole story. He laughed when he heard about Scotland Yard but, seeing Dorothea's face, he was serious again in a moment.

"It would do most beautifully if he didn't mind," said Dorothea privately to Dick, with her eyes on the fisherman's cruiser.

They told him about the flying brick that had shown there was someone else about when the first boat had been sent adrift. Pete showed the gap where the tooth had been. They told him of the bicycling visitor to Ranworth, of the shackles in the stove, of the fingerprints on the chimney (which he examined with interest), of the second lot of shackles, of their certainty that someone was doing things on purpose to get the Coot Club blamed for them. They told him that they had only till tomorrow morning to clear themselves, when they had to see a lawyer who believed them guilty and lay their evidence before him. They told him finally of Dorothea's plan.

"We could lay a mudweight out in the river," said Joe, "so she wouldn't go far even if he do push her off."

"You mean you would be lying hid watching the *Cachalot* being the bleating kid and so you would see who the ravening tiger was if you could catch him in the act of sending her adrift?"

"That's just it," said Dorothea. "It's just the one thing that's missing. You see we've got all that evidence we told you about but it isn't enough. If only we could catch him at it people would simply have to believe."

"And we've only got until tomorrow," said Tom.

"And if we can't prove it isn't them they're going to get prosecuted for what they didn't do, and the Coot Club'll be smashed up. And it's all just about as unfair as it possibly could be."

The fisherman was silent for a moment, looking at his ship.

"She can't take much harm," he said. "What do you want me to do? Leave her here?"

"No, no," said Dorothea. "They'd know we'd be on the look out and the *Death and Glory*'s too near. She ought to be in a more tempting place . . . near but not as near as all that."

"Put her where you like," said the fisherman.

For some minutes everybody was talking at once, suggesting possible places. The staithe was rejected at once, because it would be difficult for the detectives to be there without being seen by the villain. Dr. Dudgeon's mooring alongside his front lawn was rejected because the villain might think the risk of being seen was too great. Finally Joe had his way.

"That's a good place just beyond that ditch what run to the road below the Ferry. Good bushes there for a hide, and soft banks case she do break away. But she won't take no harm anyways, not if we have a mudweight down."

"What if your villain never knows she's there?" asked the fisherman. "No good putting a bait out for pike if you put it in the weeds where the pike can't see it."

"Couldn't you say a word to Mr. Tedder . . . he's the policeman . . . and tell him where you've left her?" said Tom. "And if you went into the Swan and just happened to mention it."

The fisherman laughed again. "I'll be doing that anyway," he said. "They may have a message for me from Norwich. . . . Hullo, what are you doing?" he said to Pete, who was collecting the orange skins.

"We always bury peel," said Pete.

"Rule of the Coot Club," said Tom.

"Well," said the fisherman, "it's a pretty good rule, and it'll take a lot to make me believe that you chaps cast off other people's boats."

"I tell you we doesn't," said Joe.

"So you did," said the fisherman. "All aboard, and pilot me down to your mooring. The old *Cachalot*'s done a bit of fishing, but she's never been a bait before."

There was a general move towards the *Cachalot*. It was stopped by Dick. He was polishing his spectacles, always a sign of thought, and he said, "We'd better not, don't you think? If someone saw us all sailing with you the villain might get to know. . . . "

"Pike begin looking for a hook, eh?" said the fisherman.

"We'll meet you down there," said Tom. "Just give us time to get round by the road."

*

Below the Ferry and about thirty yards beyond the narrow, deep ditch that keeps cattle from straying off the meadows, the six detectives and William (who was a little out of breath and lay panting, showing his pink tongue) waited for the *Cachalot*. They had chosen the bushes where the watchers were to lie, and picked a good mooring place for the little cruiser a few yards further downstream.

"Here she come," said Pete.

"I half thought he'd change his mind," said Tom.

"He's all right, that chap," said Joe.

The *Cachalot* passed them, swung round and came in towards the bank.

"Don't stop your engines," called Joe. "We'll want to lay that weight out first."

"Hop aboard," said the fisherman, "and put it where you want it. Give your orders. . . . "

"Starboard your hellum and slow ahead," sang out Joe, high on the *Cachalot*'s foredeck, with the mudweight at the end of its rope all ready to lower.

There was a splash as the weight went down.

"Port your hellum and get her nose to the bank," called Joe. The fisherman obeyed, but the weight began to pull before she touched and Joe had to make a flying leap with the forward anchor. After that everything was easy with so many helpers, and presently the *Cachalot* was moored fore and aft with her two rond anchors well dug in. No one looking at her from the shore could have guessed that on the further side of her a rope ran down to a weight on the bottom, so that if she were set adrift she would lie just where she was, only a few yards further from the shore.

"She'll be right enough there," said Joe, "even if they do push her off. We'll see to that."

"I don't think she'll come to any harm," said Tom.

The fisherman dived into his cabin and came out with a small suitcase. "And what do you want me to do now?" he asked, smiling. "The bleating of the kid excites the tiger. I suppose you want me to bleat all I can to let the tigers of the neighbourhood know the kid is waiting for them."

"That's just it," said Dorothea.

"We ought to make sure the whole place knows where she is," said Tom.

"I've got to get that bus," said the fisherman. "I don't see how I can come back here to report the effect of the bleating. One of you had better come with me to make sure it's up to standard."

"I'll go," said Pete.

"That's it," said Joe. "Pete go to carry his bag."

*

The fisherman wanted to carry his own suitcase, but Pete thought better not. It weighed very little anyway, and Pete got it up on his shoulder where it was not so awkward as when banging round his knees.

"Hadn't I better tell them all about that money?" said the fisherman.

Pete thought it might help, but then remembered something else.

"Better they don't know you knows us," he said. "We don't want 'em keeping off the *Cachalot*."

The fisherman stopped and wrote his address on a card. "Right," he said. "But you take this and tell them to talk to me if there's any more trouble about the money."

"There won't be none," said Pete grinning. "Not if that kid bleat proper and Scotland Yard catch the tiger in the act."

"I rather wish I could stay aboard tonight

and help to catch him," said the fisherman.

"He'd know you was aboard and keep off," said Pete. "He'd never have sent *Sir Garnet* adrift if Jim Wooddall and old Simon hadn't have gone home for the night."

Pete was feeling more cheerful than he had felt for days. Here at least was someone who was wholly on the side of the Coots, and didn't think that if it wasn't Tom it must be the Death and Glories and that if it wasn't the Death and Glories it must be Tom.

As they walked along together he showed the fisherman Mr. Farland's house and where Tom Dudgeon lived, and when they came to Mr. Tedder's, he stopped and pointed silently to the sign over the door. "POLICE".

"Right," said the fisherman.

"I better wait out here," said Pete.

Mr. Tedder was taking his tea and came to the door when the fisherman knocked. Pete could not hear what was said, but he saw the fisherman point towards him, and then he saw that Mr. Tedder was talking very earnestly. Presently the fisherman came back, looking grave. He did not smile till they were out of sight from Mr. Tedder's door.

Then he chuckled. "Well, well," he said. "I seem to be taking a frightful risk. But your policeman tells me I *may* be all right, because some of the boat-owners along the river are keeping a look out at nights. . . . "

"That's George Owdon," said Pete.

"And he'll pass the word to them, but he'd rather I'd brought my boat up to the staithe where he could have kept an eye on her himself."

"Fat lot of good that do *Sir Garnet*," said Pete.

"I told him it was too late now, but that I was much obliged to him. Good bleating, eh? And now for the lads of the village. You slip round the corner and wait for me where the bus stops. At the cross roads, you said?"

The fisherman went into the inn. Pete took the suitcase to the cross roads and sat down on it. He waited five minutes. He waited ten. He began to think the fisherman had forgotten him and his suitcase and the bus. But then old Miss Evans came along with another old lady who had been over for the afternoon from Wroxham.

"We're in plenty of time," said the second old lady, and Pete remembered that the fisherman would have asked what time the bus went as soon as he had gone into the inn.

Then he saw that Miss Evans was talking about him. Her friend was a little deaf and he could not help hearing what Miss Evans said.

"You wouldn't believe it, my dear. There was a time when I would have said there was no honester village in Norfolk. And now these boys. . . . They tell me it's a regular gang. They stop at nothing, so they say. And there are those among them who ought to know better. Our own doctor's son . . . Boys were better brought up in our young days. . . . "

Pete grew hot about the ears, but then he saw the fisherman coming, and he hopped up and went to meet him.

"I've heard enough about you lads to put you all in gaol for twenty years," the fisherman laughed. "They told me I'd be lucky if I found the *Cachalot* again this side of Yarmouth. They told me you were actually caught casting off a yacht from the staithe in broad daylight."

"We wasn't," said Pete.

"One of the maids said she thought there was a doubt about that because she'd seen you pulling the boat away from some trees higher up the river. . . . "

"Which of 'em?" said Pete eagerly. "That's evidence, that is."

"Red haired one," said the fisherman, "but they all said that was her kind heart and she had to admit she wasn't really sure. Anyhow, by the time I left I might have been the bleating kid myself, they were all so sorry for me, and even the red haired maid said she thought it was a pity about my boat. Somebody ought to have warned me. Well, here's my bus. Good luck to you. Catch your tiger and don't let him maul the kid more than you can help. See you in the morning."

He took his suitcase and was gone.

Pete, grinning to himself, went back through the village. Bill was on the look out for him in the road by Dr. Dudgeon's and they went in to find the others at Scotland Yard.

"Did he manage it all right?" said Dorothea.

"He tell Mr. Tedder, and he stir 'em up proper at the Swan. Only hope he ain't stir 'em up too much. Won't do if we have half the village watching on the bank."

"Now look here," said Tom. "This is the plan. . . . "

CHAPTER XXVII

SETTING THE TRAP

THE plan was simple enough. One of the detectives was to lie hid with Dick's camera in a bush close by the *Cachalot*. A little further from the *Cachalot*, so that the flash should not shine into the lens of the camera, a second detective was to lie in the long grass with the flashlight apparatus. When the villain had come and was in the act of casting off the boat, the second detective was to let off the flash and run for his life. The villain would naturally dash in pursuit of him, so that the first detective, sitting tight in the bush, could wait till the coast was clear and then get safely away with the camera.

"Two hour watches," said Tom. "Dick and I take the first watch, it's his camera, and I can run faster than any of you. And Dot says he's likeliest of all to come just after dark."

"Who come next?" said Pete.

"Dot and Joe. Joe to let fly with the flash and bolt and Dot to look after the camera."

"You and me after them," said Bill. "You'll have the camera."

"You've only got to open the shutter as soon as you hear the villain," said Dick, "and close it again after the flash.... And I'll fix the flash all ready so whoever's got it has only to pull the trigger."

"You'll take awful care of the camera, won't you?" said Dorothea.

"The camera'll be all right," said Dick, "if whoever has it keeps quiet."

"You'd better nip home now and get it," said Tom.

"I'd better come too," said Dorothea, "to explain to the Admiral that we'll have to be late. And we've got to take William home. He'd only bark if we had him in the ambush."

"What about the shield for the flashlight?" said Dick.

"We'll have that ready by the time you're back," said Tom.

"Shield?" said Pete.

Dick explained. "We'll have to let off an awful lot of powder for the flash. The shield's so that it doesn't burn anybody's hair off. It'll be a pretty big explosion. The label says it's dangerous to use more than a small lot, and we'll have to use ever so much more because of it being in the open air, and because of not being able to have it near the object. It's going to be like this. . . . " He pushed a drawing into Pete's hands.

"Come on," said Dot.

"Tell her, Mother wants you to have grub here," said Tom.

Dick and Dorothea were gone.

Tom, helped by Joe, set to work with a pair of garden shears on a big square biscuit tin. "It's all right," he said. "They probably won't be doing any more pruning this year." He cut one side of the tin out altogether, and then cut along the bottom of two of the remaining sides so that they could be bent back. Then, with a chisel, he punched out a square hole in the bottom of the tin, for the handle of the flashlight apparatus. All this took a long time and blistered even Tom's rope-hardened fingers. Meanwhile Pete and Bill took turns to hide by Dr. Dudgeon's gate and keep a look out on the road.

Pete was the one who saw Mr. Tedder bicycling down the road towards the Ferry.

"Tedder's gone down to have a look," he reported joyfully.

"Good," said Tom.

Pete stayed to watch the work and Bill took his place among the bushes. He presently reported seeing George Owdon and his friend bicycling the other way. "Reckon they been down to have a look too. And there's a pack of others gone down. I see three chaps from Jonnatt's. And Jack what work at the butcher's. And that milk-boy. Fine idea stirring 'em up at the inn. He make that kid bleat all right. But if all them chaps don't clear out before dark we can't set our trap."

"Hope it's all right," said Joe, looking at what was left of the biscuit tin.

"It'd be a job to alter it," said Tom. "But it's just like what Dick drew."

Dick and Dorothea came back with the camera and the flashlight apparatus, hidden in a basket under some roses from the Admiral's garden, just in case anybody should guess what they were planning. They came with long faces. The Admiral had put her foot down. Dorothea was not to be allowed out after dark.

"She said ambushes are all right for boys and

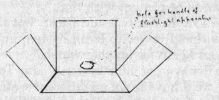

HOW THEY CUT UP THE BISCUIT TIN

hole for handle of flashlight apparatus

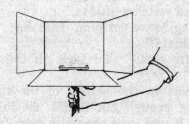

THE APPARATUS IN ITS SHIELD

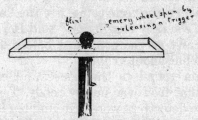

flint

emery wheel spun by releasing a trigger

THE FLASH-POWDER GOES IN THE
TRAY AND IS FIRED BY A SPARK
BETWEEN THE WHEEL AND FLINT

THE FLASHIGHT AND ITS SHIELD

if there was a row I'd only be in the way. I told
her it was my idea in the beginning, but she said
I'd have to be content with that."

"She's right, really," said Dick, "but the worst
of it is that I've got to be in by ten, and I can't
come out again for another watch."

"We'll have got him by ten," said Tom. "But
if not, we'll have to fix up different watches. Bill
and Pete take second watch and if they haven't
got him, I'll come out again down the rope and
take third watch with Joe."

"So long as we get him," said Joe. "How's this
for the shield?"

"Exactly right," said Dick. "If that hole's big
enough."

The hole in the bottom of the tin was not
quite big enough but it did not take long to
make it bigger, and presently each in turn was
trying his hand at holding the apparatus at arm's
length, in its shield, and pulling the trigger that
would, when the time came, fire the flash.

"Time's simply buzzing on," said Dorothea.

"We can't go there till just before dark," said
Tom. "What about grub?"

He ran round to the house and came back
to say that food was nearly ready. Ten minutes
later the detectives were drinking tea and eating
poached eggs. It was a hurried, silent meal. Dr.
Dudgeon was out. Mrs. Dudgeon said, "You must
be up to something." Nobody answered, and she
laughed. A little later she asked if they had all
their evidence ready for Mr. Farland to see.

"All but one bit," said Dorothea.

Pete looked at her with horror over his mug.

They went back to Scotland Yard. It was already getting dusk.

"We must get there while it's still light enough to see," said Dick.

"Somebody'll have to scout along to make sure it's all clear," said Tom.

"Let me," said Dorothea. "It won't matter if anybody does see me."

They waited while Dorothea sauntered away to the Ferry, as if going for an evening stroll. As soon as she came back to say that there was no one near the *Cachalot*, five detectives started on their way. They went through the Farland garden and by the river as far as the *Death and Glory*, where they left Dorothea on guard. Separately, one by one, they left the Wilderness and, taking care not to be seen, Indianed past the Ferry and the Ferry Inn to the place where the *Cachalot*, innocent bait for the villain, lay moored beside the bank.

Dusk fell. The Death and Glories crouched in the grass on the meadow side of the bank, watching. Lights were already showing in the windows of the inn. Someone was playing a gramophone. Everything was ready. Dick had broken away a few twigs so that his camera, focused on the *Cachalot*, had a clear view from its place in the bush. He had fixed it on its tripod, with the legs at half length.

"Sure you're all right?" said Tom.

"I'm all right," said Dick from inside the bush. "But you ought to be lying low and the others ought not to be here. The villain'll never come if they are hanging about."

"You clear out now," Tom whispered to the Death and Glories. He lowered himself carefully to the ground so as not to spill the flashlight powder. "Lucky it's a dry night. Look here, though. I've brought an oily to lie on. I'll leave it for you, Bill, if the villain doesn't come in my watch."

"Tell Dot she ought to go home," said Dick.

"Coots for ever," whispered Pete and the Death and Glories slipped quietly away, crossed the ditch, made their way round the inn, climbed over the fence into the Wilderness and came to the *Death and Glory* to find Dorothea sitting in the cabin nervously sorting papers by the light of the hurricane lantern.

"Is Dick well hidden?" she asked.

"You could walk right up to his bush and not know he were in it," said Joe. "It's Tom that's a bit showy till it come dark."

"I shouldn't think the villain would be armed," said Dorothea. "He won't be expecting anything. He'll just creep along and pick up the anchors and push her off and then there'll be one awful whoosh and when he's done blinking the photograph'll be taken. If only he doesn't get hold of Dick and the camera. I say, you do think Dick'll be all right? It's his spectacles. He won't be any good if there's a fight."

"There won't be no fight," said Joe. "Not for Dick. He've to sit tight and make sure of the photo. And Tom got to run, not fight. He got to draw the villain after him so Dick get home with the camera."

"Of course Tom's been an outlaw before," said Dorothea. "But what if he gets caught. The river's so handy. A splash. . . . A groan. . . . Just a few bubbles in the dark. . . . "

"There'd be more'n a few bubbles if anybody push Tom Dudgeon in the river. Take a tidy villain to push him in," said Pete. "And if it's that Tedder. . . . "

"Course it ain't old Tedder," said Bill.

"Well, if it is," said Pete. "He've no more chance of getting Tom in the river than he have of growing wings and flying. Tom'll keep out of his reach all right."

"Dark, too," said Joe. "Tom could run that bank blindfold. He'll have the villain in the river more likely."

"They'll be all right," said Bill, "once it come dark."

"Course they'll be all right," said Joe. "It's pretty near dark now."

Dorothea took one glance out of the cabin door, and gathered up her papers. "I've got our case nearly ready," she said. "I'll get it done tonight. The Admiral'll let me sit up till Dick comes home." She went out into the cockpit. "It really is pretty dark," she said. "It may be happening now, this minute. It's awful having to go."

"Dick say to remind you," said Joe. "Me and Bill'll run you to the road. Pete can stand guard here. You hang on Pete, till we come back."

"What am I to do?"

"Watch down river for that flash," said Joe.

*

Pete sat on the roof of the cabin. He was glad they had taken the boat out of the dyke and moored her to the river bank. Black dark in there under the willows, but out here, though it was dark enough, there wasn't any need to put out a hand to make sure something wasn't going to touch your face. The glow from the lantern in the cabin shone through a window by his knees, and dimly lit some rippled water and the faint ghost of the further bank. Upstream there were lights in some of the houses, and a party of late visitors had tied up to the opposite bank. He could see the awning over their boat, lit from inside and glowing like a giant paper lantern. He looked downstream towards the Ferry. Lights showed in the inn and there was a glow in the sky over distant Yarmouth.

Presently he heard voices on the bank and, after one anxious moment, knew them for the voices of Joe and Bill returning.

"No flash yet?" said Joe.

"No," said Pete.

"That Dot say she think the villain'll come smelling round here to make sure we ain't got no alibis before he go for to cast off the *Cachalot*."

"What she mean, alibis?" said Pete.

"She say he want to be sure we're here, because he wouldn't want to go casting off the *Cachalot* and have it turn out we was all with Tom at the doctor's, so it couldn't be us what done it."

"She have a head on her, that Dot," said Bill. "When it's our watch she say Joe have to keep the fire up and the lantern lit and the curtains close and the door shut and talk away and talk away like as if we was all three here."

"You come on below," said Joe. "You and Bill better get a bit of sleep. Else you'll be sleeping when the villain come. Nice fools we'd look if you wake up in that bush and find the *Cachalot* adrift and that old villain gone and you not knowing who done it after all."

"I'm not sleepy," said Pete.

"What about you, Joe?" said Bill. "If he don't cast her off quick, I bet he won't touch her till pretty late. Come midnight, he'll think the coast's clear. It'll be our watch then."

"It's your watch next," said Joe.

They went into the cabin and lay on their bunks. But it was hard to sleep with the trap set, the kid waiting for the tiger, and Dick and Tom lurking in the dark.

"Lucky it's a dry night," said Joe.

"Why?" said Pete.

"Dick say flash powder won't fire if that get damp."

For some minutes there was silence then Bill chuckled.

"Eh?" said Joe.

"I'll shift that plank over the ditch," said Bill. "That'll give that old villain something to think about in black dark bursting after me."

"If Joe's to keep on talking with us gone," said Pete. "Ain't he to get any sleep at all?"

"I don't want no sleep," said Joe. "When we was eeling that night, it weren't me started snoring."

"What about something to chew?" said Bill.

That was better. Not one of them could get to sleep, no matter how they tried. So Bill got some chocolate out of the cupboard in the fo'c'sle and divided it into three equal bits. They lay there, munching chocolate and talking. They talked of what they would do during winter week-ends free from school. They talked of fishing and of trying to catch big pike for themselves. They talked of building a locker for food on the after end of the cabin roof. They got up and looked at Dick's picture of the *Death and Glory* sailing. They talked of what the Coot Club would be doing in the spring. "Maybe there won't be no Coot Club," said Bill. They talked of Dick and his plan to photograph the birds. "Starting with a nightbird," chuckled Joe. "Gosh, if only he get him," said Pete. And every now and then talk stopped, tongues held bits of chocolate still, and they listened. And slowly, slowly the hour hand on the old alarm clock (that would no longer ring) crept round. . . . Nine, ten minutes past, half past, a quarter to, ten to, and minute by minute on to ten.

"Come on, Pete," said Bill.

"Off you go," said Joe.

They opened the door, crept out into the cockpit and listened. Nothing was moving anywhere near them.

"Slip away quiet," whispered Joe. "And look out you don't spoil everything when you get down there. Fine if the villain come along just when you're changing places. Pete, don't you go flashing your torch more'n you can help."

*

Pete and Bill crept off through the osiers. Behind them, they saw the light in the cockpit go out as Joe, left alone in the *Death and Glory*, closed the cabin door behind him. There was left only the orange glow of the curtained windows.

"Steady on, Bill," said Pete. "I can't see a thing."

"Don't light your torch," said Bill. "Hold your hands well out forrard, and keep swimming with 'em, so's you'll touch things before bumping 'em."

They climbed over the fence into the road and found things easier with every step. Dark it was but after a few minutes the darkness seemed less solid. They could see the shape of houses and trees against the starry patches of the sky.

"Come on," said Bill. "They'll be thinking we ain't coming."

"Don't go so we can't hear things," whispered Pete.

They came to the Ferry Inn, with its lighted windows, and slunk suddenly off the road, out of the way of a couple of men strolling home.

"Closing time," whispered Bill.

They hurried on again.

"We'll follow the bank," whispered Bill. Beyond the garden of the inn they crept along the narrow footpath at the side of the river, startled now and then by the splash of water rats as startled as themselves. They came to the ditch, found the plank and went carefully across it.

"Half a minute," said Bill. "I'm going back. You lift this end and I'll lift t'other. So's I can shift it easy if I got to run for it."

They shifted the plank and went on.

"Pretty near now," said Bill. "That your teeth chattering? Pity we ain't outed a few more of 'em."

"They ain't chattering," said Pete.

"Better give 'em the password," said Bill. He

stopped and said very quietly, "Coots for ever!"

"And ever." Tom's voice came from close to Bill's feet, and at the same moment, Pete saw the dim white bulk of the *Cachalot* moored against the bank.

"No tiger yet," said Tom. "Here you are. Get down in my form. Here's the thing. It's wound up already. Got it? I'll put your finger on the trigger. Pull that and off it goes."

"I got it," said Bill.

Pete was feeling his way into the bush and Dick, who had been a couple of hours in the dark and could see much better, was pulling him into place.

"Whatever you do don't upset the camera," he whispered. "Here's the release." He pushed the end of it into Pete's hand. "Press the button to open it. Press it as soon as you hear anybody. And press it again when the flash dies down."

"We mustn't wait about," said Tom. "Or we might put him off."

"Look out for the plank over the ditch," whispered Bill. "Me and Pete leave that loose so's I can drop one end if that old villain come chasing after me."

Tom chuckled.

"Pete knows he's to stay where he is whatever happens, doesn't he?" said Dick.

"He know," said Bill. "He's to lie low till all's clear and then bring the camera along."

"Come on," said Tom. "Give the tiger a chance . . . if he's coming. And I've got to show up at home. Ow! I can hardly move. I've got cramp in both legs and five fingers."

"Dot's dead certain he'll come some time," said Dick. "But I say, Pete, you will be careful with that camera? I wish the Admiral would let me stay. . . . "

"He'll be all right," said Tom. "Come on Dick. Joe and I'll be back at twelve."

"Joe think that tiger won't be showing up till after then," Pete's voice came out of his bush.

"He won't show up at all if you chaps don't clear out," said Bill. "Pete and me's all set. Good night."

"Back at twelve," said Tom.

"Look out you don't meet that old tiger and scare him," said Bill.

There was silence.

Tired and cramped, Dick and Tom were creeping away to the road and their beds. Two fresh detectives were watching in their lairs.

CHAPTER XXVIII

BLINDING FLASH

Tom and Dick had gone home to their beds. Bill and Pete were waiting in the dark.

Pete, squatting on the ground under the bush, shifted his weight from one foot to the other. In there it was very dark indeed but, looking out through the peep-hole that had been made for the camera, he could dimly see the *Cachalot* where she lay moored beside the bank. He could not really see her, but he could just see that she was there. He fingered the press-button that was to open the shutter when the moment came. He let go of it for fear he should press too soon.

Bill was lying in the grass on the side of the dyke a little way behind him. He lay so still that for a moment it came into Pete's head that he was alone and that Bill, too, had gone after the others.

"Bill," he whispered.

"What's up?" hissed Bill.

"Nothing."

"You all right?"

"Yes," said Pete.

"You know what you got to do. Press that thing the first moment you hear anything. Don't you go waiting for me to tell you. I'll be letting flash like Dick say . . . if powder keep dry. If it don't light, we're sunk. You just got to keep that camera open till that flash die down. That's what he say. . . . "

"And then what?" said Pete, though he knew
already.

"You sit tight. Nobody won't see you under that
bush in black dark. That'll be me he come after.
I'm to go bolting, making all the noise I can. And if
that old villain come after, well . . . " Bill chuckled
quietly. "We shift that plank. . . . Anyways that
don't matter what happen so long's he don't get
Dick's camera. You sit tight till all's clear and
then nip out and bring it along and we take it to
Dick. But whatever you do don't be copped with
it . . . Sh!. . . ."

Pete held his breath and listened. It was nothing. Only that old horse in the meadow ablowing
through his nose. A twig tickled the back of Pete's
neck. He put up a hand and snapped it off. He
heard Bill start.

"It's only me," said Pete.

"Don't make such a blame row," said Bill.

Pete felt again for the thin, springy tube from
the camera and for the press-button on the end
of it. He found it and let it go again. Silly to go
breathing so fast. Nothing to worry about, not
really. He made himself breathe slow and regular, with the result that he nearly fell asleep. An
old bream turned with a quiet splash somewhere
out on the river and Pete listened for it to splash
again. He heard a rabbit stamping the ground and
all but pressed the button, but guessed what it was
in time. He heard, far away in the meadows below
the level of the river, the lumbering tread of the
old horse. He heard a car on the road Ludham
way. That light in the sky must be over Yarmouth.
Something small ran close by him. One of them

old rats. Nothing was going to happen. It was all
for nothing, and Pete wished he was rolled round
in his rug in his bunk in the *Death and Glory*.
That Dot was too clever with her plans. Why,
they might lie a month of nights and nobody'd
come meddling with the old *Cachalot*. Why should
they? And even if that Dot were right, whoever it
were casting boats off would have his eyes open
and likely had seen the detectives making ready.
Sleeping in his bed he'd be, not getting cramp like
us. Pete wondered if Bill was thinking the same.
What would the others say if, after all, they were
to go home?

"Bill," he whispered.

There was no answer whatever. Just for a
moment he thought that Bill had gone. And then
he heard voices.

The voices were coming from the direction of
the road. Coming nearer. Whoever it was must
have come into the meadow from the road and be
walking along the near side of that ditch. There
was a scrambling noise. They were coming up the
bank from the low meadow. Steps came nearer
along the bank. Tom and Dick back again, or
could it be Tom and Joe? Had time gone on that
fast? And then Pete froze. He could not hear what
was being said, but he somehow knew that these
people who were coming were not the Coots. And
not one villain; but two at least. They were talking
low and coming quick. Were they going to walk
right over Bill?

Looking over his shoulder through the leaves,
he saw the faint glimmer of a torch flashed at
the ground. There it was again. Whoever these

newcomers might be, they would see Bill, lying
there in the grass, even if they did not stumble
over him.

Nearer the steps came and nearer. Pete
watched for that faint glimmer of the torch.
He heard no more talking. Suddenly the torch
showed only a few yards away. The newcomers
were close to him, almost on the top of Bill.

Funny the way they were using that torch.
He never saw more than a glimmer of it, as if
they were shading it so that it should not be seen
by anybody but themselves. Dot must have been
right. It could be nobody but the villains. They
had fallen into the trap and were on their way
to cast loose the *Cachalot* just as she had said
they would. But if they were going to tread on
Bill now the game would be up and the trap laid
for nothing.

"Close here," said a voice startling Pete so
much that he very nearly gave himself away.
They had passed Bill. They were between Pete
and the river, going close by his bush. What if
Bill had heard them coming and had wriggled
down into the meadow so as not to be caught by
them? He would never be able to get back to fire
that flash. Pete felt the press-button in his hand.
Press it or not? No good if there was to be no
flash. . . . Yet. . . . What had Bill said? Press it if
he heard anybody there. He pressed. There was
a faint click as the shutter of the camera opened.
It sounded to Pete, crouching under his bush in
the dark, as if everybody in the world must have
heard it. But nothing happened.

Then he saw a glimmer from the torch again,

this time on the smooth white-painted sides of the *Cachalot*. It went out. There was nothing but black darkness. People were fumbling along the bank.

"It's them. It's them," Pete whispered to himself, and kept his finger pressed hard on the button. Why didn't Bill fire that flash and be done with it? If only Bill would give a sign, a whisper . . . anything, just to let him know that he was not alone, within a yard or two of the villains and able to do nothing . . . nothing. As near as all that and he did not know who they were.

He heard the faint clink of a rond anchor on the *Cachalot*'s deck. Gosh! In another minute they'd have her adrift and be gone and everything would be too late, and there'd be another boat cast off and everybody believing the Coots had done it.

There was another faint clink.

That would be the other anchor.

And then, suddenly, there was a click in the grass close behind him and a tremendous hissing flare of white light. A tuft of grass glittered silver. Trees across the river showed in the darkness. The *Cachalot* gleamed for a moment. Pete blinked in spite of himself. He had seen a white face that might be anybody's . . . figures leaning out from the bank . . . pushing. . . . And then the white light had died away and he was staring into darkness blacker than before.

A voice shouted. "After him! Quick! Don't let him get away! . . ."

The torch flashed close by him. Somebody, stumbling in the dark, brushed against the

branches behind which Pete was lurking. Somebody else rushed past.

Behind him there was a noise of running, wild,
helterskelter running. Bill must be bolting for his
life.

"We saw you," somebody shouted.

Suddenly, close one after the other, there were
two heavy splashes, followed by curses and more
splashing.

"They're in the ditch," said Pete to himself.
"That give Bill a chance." He remembered that he
was still squeezing the press-button of the camera.
He released it. What had Dick said? Press again
after the flash die down? He pressed again and
heard the shutter click.

He listened. The noise of the chase was already
far away.

"Bill'll give 'em a run," said Pete to himself.
"See in the dark like a cat Bill can. Better'n Joe.
And they can't likely. There's a lot of good mud
in that ditch." He chuckled and found his teeth
chattering at the same time.

He began to think of what he ought to do. Sit
tight till all's clear, they had said. Well, he had
done that. First of all there was the camera. He
felt for it carefully. Yes, it was all right. Still standing on its tripod. Might easily have got smashed
up when that one come blundering by. He felt its
legs. He did not know how to make them shut up.
He would have to carry the camera just as it was.
No matter for that. In the cabin of the *Death and
Glory*, with a decent light, perhaps Joe would get
the legs off it. Or they could take it to Dick. Pete
waited a little longer. All was quiet. He crawled

out from under his bush and stood up, getting used to the darkness which had seemed very black after that white flash. Holding the camera in one hand, he felt for his torch with the other, but decided it was not safe to use it for fear of bringing the villains rushing back. He peered out from the bank. Yes, there she was, anchored in the river. They had cast her off, but the mudweight had held her. The *Cachalot* was all right.

Bother that camera. Worse than a fishing rod it was. Two of the legs closed together and caught his finger. He felt for the third leg, closed it against the other two and held all three together. Then, with his right hand pawing into the dark so as not to run into anything and hurt the camera, he set out for the *Death and Glory*, stopping every few steps to listen. Them villains might be coming back if Bill had given them the slip.

He met no one on the bank, but did not try to cross the ditch. Instead, he slipped along at the side of it till he came to the meadow gate and then hurried along the road at a good pace, glad to have firm ground under his feet. He passed the Ferry Inn, where there was still a light in an upper window, came to the fence along the edge of the Wilderness, climbed over it, and began feeling his way through the osier bushes along the side of the dyke. He stopped suddenly. Someone was talking in the darkness ahead. Lucky he hadn't dared to use his torch. Lucky he hadn't yelled out "Ahoy, *Death and Glory*!" He very nearly had, just to hear his own voice and not feel so horribly alone.

Someone was talking angrily.

THE MOMENT

"He's there all right," said a voice. And then came a noise of loud banging on a door.

Pete crept on. Were they trying to break into the old boat?

The flashing of torches showed him where the *Death and Glory* lay, moored at the mouth of the dyke. But what were those figures in the cockpit?

"You may as well come out now as later," said a voice.

Pete stopped dead. Was Bill back in the *Death and Glory*, or was Joe there alone? For a moment he thought of charging to the rescue. Then he remembered the camera. It was Dick's camera. More than that, it was at the moment the most important thing in the world. "Bring it along and we'll take it to Dick," Bill had said. "But whatever you do don't get copped with it."

There was only one thing to do and that was to get the camera with its precious photograph safely into Dick's hands.

He turned and on tiptoe went back to the road, climbed over the fence and made for Mrs. Barrable's. How late was it? He did not know. There were still lights behind the blinds in some of the houses, but not in all, and when he came to Mrs. Barrable's he found every window dark. They had gone to bed long ago. Wake them? He felt at his feet for a handful of gravel. If only he knew which was Dick's window. Should he bang at the front door and hope Dick would be the first to hear him? That Dick ought to have string hanging down from his window like Tom. Then he thought of taking the camera to Tom. But what if he should meet the villains on the way there and be caught with the camera in his hands? He had a better idea. He would run home, leave the camera at home where no villains would think of looking for it and he could then go back to the *Death and Glory*, tell the others it was safe and get up early and take it to Dick first thing in the morning.

He hurried along, turned the corner and came to his own house. Here he had hoped all would be in darkness, but he found a light still burning in an upstairs window. Well, they didn't lock the door at night, that was one thing. He slipped round into the back yard, opened the scullery door, and, putting the camera on the floor for safety's sake, felt his way across the room. He found the switch and turned on the electric light.

"Who's there?"

"It's only me, Mum."

"PETE! What in the name of goodness are you doing?" His mother was already coming downstairs. "Why aren't you asleep hours ago? Something wrong with your boat? Joe and Bill both promise me you go to bed regular."

"It's all right," Pete explained. "I've just got to leave something for Dick. I'll fetch it in the morning."

"You won't," said his mother. "Do you think I'm going to let you go off again, wandering round the village in the middle of the night? You'll go to your bed here this minute and don't let me hear a peep out of you till I wake you."

"But, Mum, I've got to go back. Chaps trying to break into our boat. . . . "

"You won't stop them," said his mother. "Do

you know what time it is? Now then, into bed
with you."

"But. . . ."

"If you're not into bed in two minutes you'll do
no more boating this year. I'll begin to think Mr.
Tedder's right."

Pete found himself upstairs and beside his bed
without knowing how he got there. He wriggled
away. "There's that camera," he said.

"What camera?" said his mother.

"I left it on the floor," said Pete.

For one wild moment he thought of slipping
out again and bolting for it. But his mother came
down with him into the scullery and herself picked
up the camera.

"Where did you get this?" she asked.

"It's not mine. It's that Dick's," he said, "and
Dick's got to have it first thing."

"I'll take care of it," said his mother. "You
can take it to him in the morning. Into bed with
you now. Upstairs. Be quick. I'll stay with you till
you're under the blankets."

And Pete, ex-pirate, salvage man, member of
the Bird Protection Society, member of the Coot
Club, detective and part-owner of the *Death and
Glory*, found himself being tucked up and even
kissed.

"Not another peep out of you," said his mother,
as she closed the door on him.

For a minute or two he lay, wondering what
best to do. And the next thing he knew was the
morning sun shining through the window.

CHAPTER XXIX

SIEGE OF THE *DEATH AND GLORY*

Joe had his orders. He was to keep the lantern lit in the *Death and Glory* and the door closed, so that anybody who came to spy would think that the crew were at home. He stoked up the fire, played a tune or two on his mouth organ and then got old Ratty out for company.

Old Ratty sat on the table and Joe gave him a nut and began eating nuts himself. But Ratty did not eat fast enough for Joe, and presently Joe put the bag away because he was eating a great deal more than his share. Then he and Ratty played an old game of theirs, Joe putting the rat into his sleeve, and the rat working its way up the sleeve and coming out somewhere else. Joe looked up at the old alarm clock. It must be nearly an hour since Bill and Pete had gone off to take their places watching for the tiger.

Suddenly Joe stiffened. What was that, moving on the rond outside? The curtains made it impossible for anybody to see in, though they let plenty of light through. Anybody outside could see that the lantern was burning. Joe waited. There was just the slightest movement of the boat. Someone was touching her, trying to look through the windows, or feeling the chimney.

"Bed-time, Bill," said Joe loudly. "Young Pete ought to be asleep."

He listened, but could hear nothing.

"Hurry up," he said. "It don't take half an hour to get a pair of boots off."

Again he listened. He waited a long time. Then he put old Ratty back in his box, watched the long tail curl out of sight into the cotton wool, and put the box on the shelf over his bunk. Nothing seemed to be stirring outside. Gone, whoever it was. Mighty quiet too. Almost it looked as if that Dot had been right and the villain had come, as she had said he would, to make sure first that the Death and Glories were at home, before going on to cast off the *Cachalot*. Cautiously, Joe opened the cabin door, waited a moment and crawled out into the cockpit.

If that had been the villain, he must be getting near the *Cachalot* by now. And Bill and Pete were there waiting for him, ready to spring the trap. Would it work, or would it not? Bill would do his part all right. But Pete? Joe for half a minute thought of trying to join them. But what would be the good of that? Upset the whole plan for nothing.

It was a dark night, and down river there was nothing to be seen but a soft curtain of blackness, with just that dim glow over far away Yarmouth. Joe tried to make up his mind just where in that darkness the *Cachalot* must be, with the detectives lurking beside her, one ready with the camera, the other with the flashlight outfit in its biscuit-box shield. What if the powder didn't catch? And that Pete! Never taken a photo in all his life. Much better, thought Joe, if we'd all laid for them and dashed out and caught them in the act.

And then, suddenly, a white flare lit up the darkness beyond the Ferry. Trees and the inn showed suddenly black against a silver glow. Then all was dark again.

"They've done it," said Joe to himself. "They've done it. Gee whizz! And now what! Was that a shout?"

He jumped ashore and started off along the dyke towards the road. He stopped, listened, and turned back. His orders were clear enough. To stand by the boat. He stood on the bank, with a hand on the gunwale of the *Death and Glory*.

What was happening? Had Bill got away? What if the villain had caught Pete, camera and all? Again he thought of bolting to their help.

Then he heard running footsteps on the road from the Ferry.

He got aboard. Nearer and nearer the footsteps were coming. They hesitated. They came on again. They stopped. He could hear other footsteps, racing down the road. Then in the Wilderness, close to the *Death and Glory*, someone was crashing through the willow bushes. The next moment, there was Bill clambering aboard, panting fit to burst.

"Two of 'em," panted Bill. "Near trod on me, they did. Quick. Quick. Into the cabin. They'll be here in two ticks. Close behind. . . . "

"Pete," said Joe. "What about Pete?"

"Lying low till they gone," said Bill. "He's all right. There was only the two of 'em and they both come after me. Heard 'em splash one after t'other. I drop that plank in the ditch for 'em. Go on. Get the door shut. . . . Get the key inside. . . . "

Bill lay puffing on his bunk. Joe fumbled desperately with the key. Already he could hear people stumbling through the bushes. He caught a glimpse of a torch. And that old key, which always fell out when he didn't want it to, was sticking in the lock on purpose. It came loose at last, Joe put it into the lock from inside, closed the door, locked it, plumped down on his bunk and waited.

"They're close here," he said. "Who are they? Did you see 'em?"

"That thing fair blind me," said Bill. "But there was two of 'em. And they cast her off. I see that."

"But who are they?"

"I don't know."

Somebody's fist banged on the roof of the cabin above their heads.

"Come out of that," said a voice.

"That sound like George Owdon," said Joe.

"You talk," whispered Bill. "Gimme time to get breath."

"Who's there?" asked Joe as sleepily as he could.

"River watchers."

"All well here," said Joe.

"We'll give you all well." The boat lurched as the visitors stepped aboard. Hands pawed over the door. "They've got the door locked," said a voice. "Run him to earth all right. Shine your torch here. You can see the key's in the lock." There was a sudden angry rattle at the door.

"You clear off and leave us alone," said Joe. "We want to get to sleep."

There was a long silence. Then the noise of muttering in the cockpit. Then someone spoke aloud.

"He's there all right."

"I bet that's George Owdon," whispered Joe.

"They'll have the door in in a minute," whispered Bill, as someone outside started hammering on the door and then kicking at it.

"You may as well come out now as later," said a voice and there was such a banging on the door that Joe, for a moment looked anxiously at the hinges.

"Stop that," he shouted angrily.

There was whispering in the cockpit, and then a curse as someone tripped over the bucket which Joe had left there after the last washing up. Some sort of argument went on in low voices. Bill thought he heard the word "camera". There was more muttering and they heard someone say, "I tell you we've got to make sure."

"Shall I let 'em in now?" whispered Joe.

"No," said Bill.

"We don't want 'em to go without our seeing 'em," urged Joe. "Case that photo don't come off. Pete ain't no expert like that Dick."

"Keep 'em busy," whispered Bill. "Give Pete time to get clear. We don't want 'em to go and catch him with the camera. More row they kick up the better. Warn Pete not to come here."

"Who are you?" shouted Joe.

"You'll see soon enough. Are you going to open this door?"

"What for?" said Joe. "We ain't invited anybody."

"We'll break it in then."

"You'll have a job," said Joe.

The answer was a still more violent rattling

of the door. Then there was another whispered debate in the cockpit, ending as before with the words, "I tell you it isn't safe not to make sure."

The next thing heard in the cabin was the splash of the bucket over the side. Then steps on the cabin roof. . . . Then . . . as Bill said afterwards, it was like the end of the world. There was a loud hiss of water on hot coals. . . . The door of the stove flew wide open. . . . The cabin was full of smoke and scalding steam. . . . Bits of coal flew in all directions and lay hissing where they fell. Water poured from the stove.

"You all right?" Joe gasped.

"Beasts!" shouted Bill. "Beasts!"

Again the bucket splashed over the side, steps sounded on the roof, and another deluge of water poured down the chimney and out over the cabin floor bringing cinders with it.

Bill choked.

Joe, coughing and spluttering, reached for the door.

"We'll open."

He unlocked the door. It was pulled wide. A hand reached over his head, grabbed him by the collar and hauled him out of the cockpit.

Bill, struggling to escape from all that smoke and steam, was in the doorway. He too was hauled out.

"Any more?" said George Owdon. "Three of you, aren't there? Where's the third?"

"You can see he ain't here," said Bill.

"You ain't got no right to make a mess of our boat even if you are river watchers," said Joe.

"We know now who was casting boats off," said Bill.

"Shut up."

"Been swimming?" he asked.

A large hand swung round and caught him on the side of the head.

"Who are you hitting?"

"You . . . and you'll get some more if you start any cheek. Come on, George. Better make sure."

"Wait till the smoke's cleared . . . You'd have done better to open the door when we asked you."

The smoke and steam were drifting out of the cabin and the lamp, burning clearer now, showed the dreadful mess that had been made.

"You might have set the ship afire," said Bill.

"Ship!" jeered George Owdon. "A lot you cared what happened to the 'ships' you cast adrift."

"We didn't," began Joe, but Bill gave him a nudge and he said no more.

"I'm going in now," said George Owdon. He stooped and went in, hitting his head on a beam as he did so. "Harder'n ever Tom hit his," said Joe with some pleasure telling about it afterwards.

"What's he doing?" asked Bill.

"Shut up," said the other big boy, George Owdon's friend, who was standing guard over them in the cockpit.

In the cabin, George Owdon was looking this way and that. He pushed his way forward, opened the cupboards, pulled everything out on the floor, tore the blankets off Pete's bunk, came back, hitting his head again, and hunted along the cabin shelves, sweeping things off them as he hunted.

"Hullo!"

Joe and Bill, watching the sack of their cabin, heard George Owdon exclaim.

"Got it!"

He had found the square wooden box on the shelf over Joe's bunk.

"Don't you touch that," shouted Joe. But George Owdon was already feeling in it and pulling out the cotton wool. The next moment there was a yell, and he had flung the box into the forepart of the boat and was sucking a bleeding finger.

Joe broke free from his captor and plunged into the cabin, pushed past George Owdon and picked up the box. It was empty, but he saw something white close under the deck in the very bows of the boat.

"I'll kill that rat for you," shouted George Owdon.

"You won't," said Joe. "All right, old Ratty. It's all right."

"Leave him alone," said the big boy in the cockpit, who still had Bill by the collar. "You're sure it's not there?"

"I thought it was in that box," said George Owdon, looking at his bitten finger by the light of the hanging lantern.

"Come on then," said the other boy.

"You wait till morning," said Joe angrily. "We'll tell Mr. Tedder what you done to our boat."

"I'll tell him I caught you casting loose that cruiser," said Bill.

George Owdon laughed. "Who'll believe you?" he asked. "We've got something to tell Mr. Tedder too. We saw you unmoor that boat and put her adrift. You saw him, didn't you, Ralph?"

"Swear to him any day," said the other boy.

"Now what about Mr. Tedder?" said George. "This'll settle it. We were watching for you and we saw you take those anchors up and push her off. That was all he said he was waiting for, for someone to catch you in the act."

"Liars!" gasped Bill.

"We'll tell him first," said Joe.

"Come on, George," said the second boy. "We'll go and tell him now."

The two of them went ashore and disappeared in the dark.

"Are rat-bites poisonous?" Bill heard George say.

"Hope that one is," shouted Bill.

There was the sound of a scuffle. "Let go." Bill heard George's voice.

"Never mind him," he heard the other boy say. "Now you listen to me. What's the name of that kid? We've both got to say we saw the same one."

They were gone.

Bill joined Joe in the wrecked cabin. Joe was talking to the white rat, persuading it to come back.

"I say, Joe."

"Yes.... Come on, Ratty, old chap. There ain't nobody to hurt you."

"I say, Joe. What if that Tedder believe him?"

"Well, you saw him pushing the boat off."

"Not to swear," said Bill. "There was that light right afront of my eyes, and I didn't see nothing not hardly. I didn't know who they was till they come drive us out of our cabin."

"What about Pete?" said Joe.

"I were frightened all the time he'd come walking in on us," said Bill. "If they catch him with that camera, we're sunk. And if he bungled that photo we're sunk too. Pete may have seen 'em, but that's not much good if he did. Our word against theirs, and everybody in the place believing it's us anyhow."

"If Pete come along, he sheer off when he hear 'em," said Joe. . . . "Good old Ratty. . . ." He had got the white rat on his knee by now and was stroking it and tickling it behind its ears. "Pete's got sense. He'll likely be watching for 'em to go. He'll be along, soon as he think the coast's clear. Pete's lucky. His is the only dry bunk in the ship. That water splash over everything. Take us a week of Sundays to put all straight. What was that George looking for, throwing things about?"

"That flashlight make 'em think," said Bill. "He were looking to see if we got a camera. That's why they don't say they seen us till they make sure we ain't got a photograph."

"And if they'd found it?"

"They'd have put it in the river, or spoil the picture somehow."

"Do you think Pete take that photo?" asked Joe. "Didn't, we're no better off than we was."

"I don't know," said Bill wearily. "That light startle me when I pull that trigger, and if it startle Pete too he'd be too late maybe."

For some time they were busy, putting things back into their places by the light of the lantern, mopping up the mess on the floor, clearing the bunks.

"It's the end of the old Coot Club," said Bill in deep gloom. "We was being a bit too clever. You see, if they asks me I can't say I weren't there. And it's them being river watchers and helping Tedder and all that."

"All right if Pete get that photo," said Joe. "Wish he'd show up. Shall I give him a shout?"

"Better not," said Bill, but he went out into the cockpit, turned his torch on and waved it to and fro for a signal, in case Pete might be lurking somewhere near.

"I'm lighting up that fire again," said Joe. "He'll be clem cold hanging about. Dry things up a bit too."

They got the fire burning again, boiled a kettle of water and made cocoa.

"No good going looking for him," said Bill. "Pete know enough not to get caught. Pull the curtains. Leave the door open. So he'll see all's clear. Gone to Tom's likely. Maybe Tom'll be coming with him. Well, there's cocoa for all."

They sat by the fire in the cabin, sipped their hot cocoa, told each other all the many things they might have done to George Owdon and his friend if only they had thought of them in time, and in the end dropped asleep where they sat.

CHAPTER XXX

"ALL THE EVIDENCE WE GOT"

"Wake up, Bill. Where's that Pete?"

Joe was shaking Bill by the arm. Sunlight was slanting through the orange curtains.

"Wake up. That Pete ain't come back."

"Leave go my arm." Bill woke slowly. He sat up and stretched out an arm, stiff and cramped after the night. He blinked at Joe and stared sleepily at his own feet, wondering to find them in sea-boots. Suddenly he remembered the battle with the besiegers, the tremendous flash in the darkness, the splashes of the pursuers in the ditch behind him, and Pete, left with the camera in his hiding place on the bank of the river.

"Ain't he come in?"

"Ain't you heard me tell you?"

"Gone to Tom's. Tom'll have give him a doss down."

"Come on then."

Rubbing their eyes, they hurried along the bank, through Mr. Farland's garden, over the little drawbridge and so to Dr. Dudgeon's. They could hear the clatter of crockery and pans and someone singing in the kitchen.

"Tom! Coots!"

There was no answer as they stood by Scotland Yard looking up at Tom's window.

Bill gave a hard tug at the string. A moment later, Tom, still in pyjamas, looked out.

"You nearly had my hand off that time," he said sleepily, and then, waking up . . . "Look here . . . Why didn't you fetch me when it was my watch? Why? What? What's happened?"

"They come all right," said Bill. "But everything go wrong."

"Didn't the trap work?"

"I couldn't see a thing after I let go that flash," said Bill. "But they was there all right. And I bolt, like you said, and they go in the ditch clopwollop, and the next thing were that George Owdon and that other banging at the *Death and Glory.*"

"Three cheers," said Tom. "We've got them."

"We ain't," said Joe. "They say they see Bill pushing off the *Cachalot.* But where's that Pete?"

"Did Pete get the photograph?" asked Tom.

"Ain't Pete with you?" said Joe.

"Of course he isn't."

"Pete lie low, like you say," said Bill, "and we ain't seen him since."

"Perhaps he went to Dick's."

"He'd never go to Mrs. Barrable's, not in the middle of the night," said Bill. "Dick ain't got a string from his window."

"Why didn't you come here last night?" said Tom.

"We fall asleep. That's why," said Bill.

Joe was already running for the road. "Come on, Bill," he shouted over his shoulder. "We tell young Pete to lie low and he never dare shift. He's by the *Cachalot* yet. Been there all night."

Bill pelted after him.

Side by side they ran down the road to the

Ferry, round the inn, through the gate and across the meadow to the bank of the river.

There was the *Cachalot*, anchored just out of reach from the bank. Pete or no Pete, Joe was delighted that his idea had worked out so well.

"She lie beautiful," he said. "Lucky we put that weight down to hold her. Might have been anywheres by now."

"Pete," shouted Bill.

There was no answer.

They came on the apparatus Bill had used to fire off the flashlight powder. It was lying beside the path, with the biscuit-box shield, just where Bill had dropped it before racing off with the villains close behind him. Joe picked it up. It was wet with dew, but Dick would surely want it again. Bill rescued Tom's oilskin.

They pulled aside the branches of the willow bush, where the photographer had lurked in hiding. There was no sign of Pete or of the camera.

"And he ain't come to the *Death and Glory*," said Bill. "Nor yet to Tom's. Joe! You don't think they get him? May have been more of 'em than them two. I never think of that."

"Silly young turmot," said Joe. "What if he tumble in the river getting away?" He did not believe it when he said it, but saying it somehow made it seem possible, and both of them looked anxiously along the bank.

"He've been out all night," said Bill. "Joe. We got to tell his Mum."

"If them chaps fright him," said Joe, "he'd likely run t'other way."

They looked down the river and this way and that over the low-lying meadows. There was never a sign of a wandering photographer.

"He'll be all right," said Joe doubtfully.

"We got to tell his Mum," said Bill.

"Well, he ain't here," said Joe.

They had a last look round and hurried back to the village. If Pete's Mum had to be told, the sooner it was done the better.

"Wish that Dot never think of that trap," said Bill. "That turn out wrong all ways."

"What about telling Tedder?" said Joe, as they passed the policeman's house at a good jog trot.

"No use us telling him," said Bill. "Pete's Mum'll do that. You don't really think he tumble in? . . . Pete's not one for that. . . . It were a black dark night. . . . I couldn't see nothing hardly, after that flash. . . ."

"Think they'll drag the river?" said Joe.

Bill did not answer and they ran grimly on, round the corner by the inn, and so to the row of cottages, one of which was Pete's home.

Pete's mother was on her knees scrubbing her doorstep. She looked up at them. "Well," she began, as if she had a good deal to say.

"We lost Pete," said Joe.

"Down river below the Ferry," said Bill.

"Lost him?" she said. "You just miss him. But didn't you two promise me that if he come in that old boat you'd see he go regular to bed?"

"Just miss him?" said Joe eagerly. "Has he been here?"

"He go out just before you two come. Rapscurry-hurrying he were too. But what I want to know is

what you was doing with him running loose at all
hours of the night?"

Pete was all right. There were other things
to think of now.

"Have he got a camera with him?" asked Bill.

"He didn't hardly finish his breakfast before
he got off with it."

"He've gone to Dick's," said Joe. "Come on."

"There's going to be no more of that. . . . " said
Pete's mother, but they never heard what there
was to be no more of, for they were off again on
their way to Mrs. Barrable's.

*

They never got there. Turning the corner of
the road they met Dorothea hurrying down to
Scotland Yard. She was almost running, carrying
a small suitcase.

"Oh good," she cried. "Come on, quick. Tell
me what happened. Pete said there were people
at the *Death and Glory* last night, and he went
home with the camera, and his mother put him
into bed. But what happened?"

"Did he get a photo?" asked Bill.

"He doesn't know if he did or not," said Dorothea. "And Dick and he have rushed back to
develop the film. They're coming after us. We
can't wait for them. We're going to be late if
we don't hurry. We've got to get all the evidence
together and take it to Mr. Farland. And if we're
late he'll be gone to Norwich. But do tell me what
happened."

"Didn't Pete say?"

"About people coming to cast off the *Cachalot*?

Yes. Yes. But he didn't know who they were. Did you see them?"

"That flash put me blind," said Bill. "But they was there. Two of 'em. I race back to the old ship. And they was after me. George Owdon and that other."

"Hurrah!" cried Dorothea. "I knew it was George Owdon. So it's all right after all."

"Just what it ain't," said Joe. "That George he's going to say he see Bill pushing her off."

"But didn't you see him?"

"Must have been him," said Bill, keeping up with Dorothea. "But with that flash I didn't see nothing. I up and run in the dark, and they after me. Into that old ditch they go good and proper. But I didn't see nobody, not till they smoke us out and there they was in our cockpit."

"What about Tom?"

"Bill's watch and Pete's," said Joe. "Wish we'd all have stayed."

"We're sunk," said Bill, "if Pete ain't got that photo."

"We aren't," said Dorothea. "We can't be. Not with all our evidence."

They were hurrying now along the main street of the village. Shops were opening. People taking down shutters turned to stare at them in an unfriendly way. Outside Mr. Tedder's two bicycles were propped against the fence.

"That George Owdon's in there now," said Bill.

Dorothea stopped, turned and darted to the bicycles. She looked first at one and then at the other.

"Look! Look!" she cried. "Dick was right." She

pointed at a small smear of green paint on the grip of the right handlebar of one of the bicycles. "We can prove everything. It's going to be all right. Come on."

They hurried on to Dr. Dudgeon's. Tom was on the look out for them.

"Pete's all right," Bill called out as soon as he saw Tom.

"Where's Dick?" said Tom.

"Developing with Pete," said Dorothea. "They're coming after us. And there's green paint on George Owdon's handlebars."

"It's close on nine already," said Tom. "We can't wait for them. Uncle Frank'll be gone if we don't look out. Look here. What did happen last night?"

Bill and Joe tried to tell all they knew. Dorothea began gathering the clues and packing them into her suitcase. There was the scrap of grey flannel with its label, Dick's drawing of the tyre-treads, the affidavit of Bob Curten, a sheaf of notes and the summary of all the evidence that she had finished before going to bed the night before.

She interrupted the others. "There's just one thing," she said. "I asked the Admiral about lawyer's fees."

"We got pots of money," said Joe.

"We can pay," said Bill.

"I don't see that," said Dorothea. "We're all in it."

It was arranged that the six detectives should contribute equal shares.

"We'll put in for Pete," said Bill.

"And I've got Dick's as well as mine," said Dorothea, digging in her purse. "I don't suppose

Mr. Farland'll mind a postal order. There isn't time to go and change it now."

"What about the map?" said Tom.

"Better bring it," said Dorothea. "Push the pins well in so that they don't fall out."

The map, with the black flags showing where boats had been cast off, was taken down and carefully rolled up.

"We haven't put a flag in for the *Cachalot*," said Dorothea.

"If Pete ain't took that photo right, the *Cachalot*'s going to be worst of all," said Bill.

The map was unrolled. Another flag was put in its place and the map was rolled up again.

"All the evidence we got," said Bill. "It ain't much, not if them two say they saw me cast her off."

"And there's the chimney," said Dorothea. "Have you taken it off the cabin roof?"

Bill and Joe answered never a word but raced for the *Death and Glory*.

Tom with the rolled up map and Dorothea with her suitcase came hurrying after them, to find them both on the roof of the cabin, Bill biting into a huge slice of bread and Joe working away with a screwdriver in one hand and a hunk of bread in the other.

"Haven't you had breakfast?" said Dorothea.

"That ain't no matter," said Joe. "Tip her gently, Bill."

The chimney left its seating without accident, and a moment later they were on their way.

They came into Mr. Farland's garden.

"We'd better just have a look in the road to see if they're in sight," said Dorothea.

They went to the gate and looked down the road.

"Must have got a photo," said Joe hopefully. "Not, they'd be here by now."

"No good waiting," said Tom.

Followed by the rest of the detectives, he walked up to the front door of Mr. Farland's house and rang the bell.

CHAPTER XXXI

IN THE DARK ROOM

For the first few moments Pete could not see a thing. Black darkness everywhere, except the dim red glimmer of the lamp which seemed to throw no light at all. Then, dimly, he saw Dick's face in the red glimmer, and caught a red reflection off Dick's spectacles. Then he saw hands, glowing red, working at the camera. He saw the spool of film lifted out.

"We needn't bother with much of it," said Dick. "The photograph'll be at the inside end. We can throw the rest away."

"Won't you be able to use it?" said Pete.

"No," said Dick. "And it doesn't matter a bit if only you didn't move the camera and had the shutter open."

"I ope the shutter all right," said Pete.

"Hold this end," said Dick, unrolling the film.

"But there's nothing on it anywheres," said Pete.

"Undeveloped," said Dick.

A pair of scissors shone in the red light and a length of film curled up to Pete's fingers.

"Just drop it on the floor. . . . Now. . . . You pour the developer into the dish. . . . Yes. . . . That's enough. And put the stopper back in the bottle. Better put it at the back of the table so that we shan't knock it over. . . . Now, let's see. . . . "

Holding each end of a short strip of film, milky

white, but tinted rose by the lamp, he plunged it
into the dish of developer and began moving it to
and fro.

"Don't it stink?" said Pete.

"The hypo's almost worse," said Dick. "I say.
We'll have to wash it and I never filled the bowl.
Never mind. We can do it under the tap. And the
hypo isn't ready. That's the worst of being in a
hurry. Look here. Look! You did have the shutter
open. That end of the film's getting darker with
a pale edge and all the rest's still milky. We've
got something anyhow. . . . Feel on your left for
that packet. Shake some hypo crystals into the
glass dish. Add water, not too much, and joggle
to dissolve them. . . . "

The faint red light from the lamp seemed to be
getting stronger every minute. Pete's eyes were
getting accustomed to it. He had no difficulty with
the hypo crystals, and very little with adding the
water, though he could not be sure he had put in
enough without dipping the tip of a finger to feel.

"You got the boat all right," said Dick. "I do
believe you did." His voice trembled. "Look out
for that hypo. Don't bring it too near. One drop
in the developer would spoil it. . . . Put it down
on the table. . . . But see that. . . . That big lump
of black's the boat. It can't be anything else."

"But the *Cachalot*'s white," said Pete.

"Not in the negative," said Dick. "Everything
comes the other way round. And then it comes
right again when you print it. Look. That'll be
trees on the other side of the river and all that
white's probably the black water. . . . "

Pete peered into the dish at the film, but Dick

DEVELOPING

did not dare to hold it still for more than a second at a time.

"It don't show them villains," said Pete.

"You can't tell yet," said Dick. "There's something. . . . "

"But it's all going dark," said Pete. "It's going dark all over."

"Nearly done."

For a few moments longer, Dick worked the film to and fro in the developer. Then he picked it out, let it drip, and then, just for a half second, held it so that the faint red light from the lamp shone through it.

"It shows them," he cried. "We've got them!"

"Where? Where?" said Pete.

"Turn on the tap," said Dick. "We've got to wash it and then we'll put it in the fixing. After that it'll be safe to have a proper look."

For a minute or two the water from the tap sluiced this way and that over the film. Then Dick lowered it into the dish with the hypo solution and worked it to and fro as he had done when it was in the developer.

"What's the time?" he said. "Where's the Admiral's watch?"

"I've got it," said Pete, and held Mrs. Barrable's watch in the red glow of the lamp.

"Five past nine," said Dick. "They'll be at Mr. Farland's already. And we've got to get it dry and take a print of it."

"What's that milky stuff?" asked Pete. "Melting away like a bit of snow. You haven't let spoil it?"

"Fixing," said Dick. "When that's all gone, it's

done." He lifted the film and held it to the light.
"Nearly done now. You can open the door. . . . "

Pete fumbled for the door handle and found
it. "Sure?" he asked. It would be too awful if they
spoiled the picture at the last minute.

"All right," said Dick.

Pete opened the door and blinked. The white
light of day pouring in seemed to douse the red
lantern almost to darkness. Dick came to the door
and held up the film so that they could both look
through it.

Pete stared. It was the first negative he had
ever seen. He could make nothing of it. There was
that lump of black and a big funny-shaped bit of
white that you could see right through, and, yes,
those must be trees all right, all those little dark-
ish spots. Leaves they must be. And branches. . . .

But Dick, usually so quiet, shouted. "Two of
them," he cried. "Two of them. You've got them
just as they were pushing her away from the
bank." He shot back into the dark room and
began sluicing the negative under the tap.

"Who are they?" asked Pete.

"Can't tell till we print," said the photographer.
"We've got to get the hypo washed off, and then
dry it. . . . I say. Could you bolt down and ask
the Admiral for some methylated spirit? She's got
some for her primus. It's the quickest of all ways
of drying."

Pete bolted, found Mrs. Barrable, and told her
what Dick wanted.

"Well," said Mrs. Barrable. "And was it a success?"

"Dick say we got two of 'em pushing her off."

"Not really? Sure it's not Joe and Bill?"

"Joe weren't there," said Pete seriously. "And Bill, he were working the light."

"Who are they?"

"I couldn't see nothing, not properly," said Pete. "But Dick say we got 'em all right."

"Well, I *am* glad," said Mrs. Barrable. But she had heard the hurry in Pete's voice when he had asked for the methylated, and she had been getting it even while she was asking her questions. Pete took the bottle, thanked her, and raced upstairs again. He found Dick holding the negative by one corner, and collecting the wet from its edges on a bit of blotting paper. He had already used the scissors to cut away the rest of the film.

"There's a clean dish at the back of the table," said Dick. "Pour some into that."

A few minutes later, in a smell of methylated that reminded Pete of Bill's Christmas pudding, Dick was holding up the negative and blowing at it to speed its drying.

"Lemme look," said Pete, and then, as Dick held the film so that he could look through it, gasped with surprise. "Gee whizz!" he said. "Niggers!"

"Not when they're printed," Dick laughed.

"Look like niggers to me," said Pete.

"You wait. . . . I say, what's the time now?"

"Quarter past nine," said Pete, looking at Mrs. Barrable's watch.

"Oh gosh," said Dick. "And we can't print it till it's dry or it'll stick to the paper." He went on blowing at the film, and waving it in the air.

"It's beginning to dry all right," he said a moment later.

"We're going to be late," said Pete.

"Tell you what," said Dick. "We can let it print while we're taking it along."

"How?" said Pete.

"We'll have it in the frame and hold it to the sun while we run. A few minutes'll be enough to let us see who they are."

"Dick." Mrs. Barrable called up from downstairs. "Aren't you going to Mr. Farland's? It's long after nine."

"I know," said Dick desperately. "But we've got the evidence at last. At least we will have in a minute."

Minute after minute went by, and looking sideways at the surface of the film he could see a damp spot that shrank with dreadful slowness, though Dick did all he could to hurry it, even holding it as near as he dared to the warmth of the lantern.

It was ready at last. He took a printing frame, opened a black envelope, took out a piece of printing-paper and laid it against the negative, pressed negative and paper against the glass, closed the frame, looked to see that the negative was squarely on the paper and said, "Come on, Pete."

"Let's have a look," said Pete.

"It's a pretty dense negative," said Dick. "Sometimes you can see a lot when they're printing. This one you can't. We've got to wait till the sun's got at it. When the edges of the paper turn black."

"All right if we ain't too late," said Pete.

A minute later they were out of the house and running together down the street on their way to join the rest of the detectives who were showing their evidence to the lawyer. Dick, as he ran, held the printing frame in the full light of the sun.

SHACKLES

CHAPTER XXXII

THE LEGAL MIND

"WHAT'S that?" asked Mr. Farland as soon as Bill and Joe came into the room carrying the big green chimney pot between them.

"Evidence," said Tom, unrolling the map and putting it at the end of Mr. Farland's long table.

"We've got lots more," said Dorothea, patting her suitcase.

Bill and Joe, carefully dusting the chimney pot with their hands, stood it upright on the carpet.

Tom looked anxiously out of the window, not that he could see the road or even the gate through which Dick and Pete would come, for the window looked the other way, over the river, but just for peace of mind. From what Joe and Bill had said it was clear enough to him that Dorothea had been right and that they knew now who the villains were. But it was also clear that the trap they had laid was going to work the wrong way, and that if George Owdon and his friend stuck to it that they had seen Bill cast off the *Cachalot* the Coot Club was going to be not better off but worse.

It was going to be Bill's word against George's, and with all that had gone before he did not think Bill's word had much chance of being believed. Tom knew very well that Mr. Farland himself had thought from the first that the Coots had been at the bottom of all the mischief that had been going on. And unluckily it had been Pete's turn with the camera. If it had been Dick's there might have been some chance. But Pete had never taken a photograph in his life.

"Won't you sit down?" said Mr. Farland to Dorothea.

"I think I'd rather stand," said Dorothea. She took something from her pocket and laid it on the table in front of Mr. Farland. It was a small screwed up bit of paper, one of Mr. Dudgeon's prescription forms.

Mr. Farland took it. "More evidence?" he said, unscrewing the paper. "What on earth's this? They haven't been accused of taking money."

Out of the paper came a postal order for two shillings, a two-shilling piece, a shilling, three sixpences, and couple of coppers.

"I think it's the proper fee," said Dorothea.

Mr. Farland had not for nothing been a lawyer all his life. He bowed gravely to Dorothea, but no one could have told what was in his mind as he smoothed out the bit of paper and laid it flat on his table, smoothed out the postal order and laid it on the bit of paper, and piled on it the two pennies, the two-shilling piece, the shilling and the three sixpences, exactly on the top of each other.

"I am sure that you quite understand the position," he said at last. "Sonning's, the boatbuilders at Potter Heigham, employ my firm as solicitors. They have been put to considerable trouble by having a number of their boats cast off from their moorings and sent drifting down the river. They have missed a quantity of boat's gear (shackles,

to be exact) from one of their sheds. They have
appealed to the police and to others to find out who
is responsible for all this. On two occasions a small
number of the missing shackles have been handed
to the police here by one of you two lads. . . . " He
looked straight at Bill and Joe. Until that moment
he had seemed to be looking at a picture on the
wall behind their heads. "On the second occasion
the shackles were given to a magistrate, Dr.
Dudgeon, who, on your behalf, took them to the
police. Now, we have been having the same sort of
trouble here. No stealing, certainly. But I am told
that every boat that has been sent adrift was lying
somewhere near that boat of yours. And that your
boat was at Ranworth when boats were sent adrift
there. And that your boat was at Potter Heigham
when the same thing happened there and all those
shackles were stolen. Stolen is an ugly word, but
stolen they were."

He paused. It certainly sounded terribly as
if Mr. Farland had already made up his mind.

Bill was just going to say something, when
Mr. Farland spoke again.

"Now then," he said. "I've told you how we
stand. I'm ready to listen to what you have to
say, but if you have come to me to ask me to get
you out of your difficulties, I don't see that I can
do anything."

"But it isn't like that at all," said Dorothea.
"They simply didn't do any of those things."

"Miss Callum," began Mr. Farland.

"Oh, look here, Uncle Frank," said Tom.

"Miss Callum," said Mr. Farland again, and
went on, "if these boys had no hand in all this,

somebody else had. Now, have you any idea who?"

Dorothea hesitated.

"We think we know," she said.

"Think isn't enough," said Mr. Farland.

"We're sure we know," said Dorothea.

"Take that first occasion," said Mr. Farland. "When a motor cruiser was cast off from the staithe. Theirs was the only other boat moored at the staithe that night."

"There was someone else there," said Tom.

"That was the night we outed Pete's tooth for him," said Joe, "and there was somebody there in the dark and he bung the brick back through the window."

"Did any of you see this other person?"

"No," said Tom. "We couldn't. It was already dark."

"You can't, on the strength of somebody whom you didn't see having been there some time before the cruiser was sent adrift, get away from the fact that all that night their boat lay there, and was still there in the morning, when the other boat was drifting down the river."

"But don't you see?" said Dorothea. "It was done by an enemy."

"Why then did the enemy cast off the other boat instead of theirs? He must have known the difference."

"He did it because he hated the Coot Club," said Dorothea, "and he wanted Tom and the others to get blamed for it."

"It's that George Owdon," said Bill. "We always think it were and now we know for dead certain sure."

"But look here," said Mr. Farland. "George Owdon was watching the staithe here, when you lads were casting off the boats at Potter."

"We ain't cast off no boats," said Joe doggedly.

"We've got evidence," said Dorothea. She put her case on the floor, opened it, rummaged in it for a moment, and laid young Bob's affidavit on the table.

Mr. Farland read it."I swear I see George Owdon by Potter Bridge the night before you come through. Bob Curten."

"Was he in two places at once?"

"Bike," said Joe.

"And what about Ranworth?"

"Bike again."

Dorothea took Dick's drawing of the bicycle tracks out of her case. "We found bicycle tracks on the soft ground by the staithe at Ranworth," she said. "This is the place." She put the drawing and a photograph on the table. "It's a Dunlop tyre. And we know someone crossed the Ferry that night. And we know George Owdon's got Dunlop tyres. . . . "

Mr. Farland looked at drawing and photograph. "Almost all bicycles have Dunlop tyres," he said. "What make of tyre does Tom use? . . . But never mind that. They tell me you lads were actually seen casting off a yacht from the staithe."

"We salvage her," said Joe. "We was tying her up when we was seen . . . not casting her off. It's only that George Owdon say we was."

"There's another thing," said Mr. Farland, looking at some notes on the table before him. "George Owdon and his friend have been giving up a lot of

their nights to watching just to prevent this sort
of thing happening. I have to ask myself, 'Isn't it
likely that you have a grudge against him on that
account?'"

"Not half the grudge he got against the Coot
Club," said Bill.

"That birds'-nesting affair?" said Mr. Farland
thoughtfully.

"When he try to get them bitterns," said Joe,
"and we fetch keeper just in time."

Mr. Farland stroked his chin. "Yes," he said.
"You don't like George Owdon and George Owdon
doesn't like you. But that doesn't prove anything
much. Now, what about those shackles?"

"We never steal 'em," said Joe. "Pete find that
first lot in our stove and Bill find that second lot
in our cockpit, and the one what put that second
lot in our boat is the one what print his hand on
our chimbley like Dick say he would."

"What's that?"

Dorothea explained. "You see, that first time
we knew someone had been there. I saw someone
feeling the chimney, and then he heard me and
ran away in the fog and fell over our bloodhound.
And William got a bit of his trousers." She laid
the scrap of flannel on Mr. Farland's table. "And
the next morning they found some shackles in the
stove and took them to Mr. Tedder. And then Dick
thought that if we kept the chimney covered with
wet paint we'd get a fingerprint if whoever it was
did it again. And we did get a fingerprint. There
it is. And there was some of the green paint on
the second lot of shackles."

"Not quite good enough," said Mr. Farland. "If

Bill or Joe or Pete had been messing about with green paint they'd be likely to get some on the shackles themselves."

"Ask George Owdon to fit his hand to that print," said Joe. "It's a sight too big for us."

"And we've got a photograph showing that even Tom couldn't reach from the bank," said Dorothea, dipping in her suitcase.

"It's no good, Uncle Frank," burst out Tom. "If you don't want to believe them. If only Port and Starboard were here, they'd tell you."

"There's green paint on George Owdon's bicycle," said Dorothea.

A bell jangled somewhere in the house. A moment later the door opened, and Mrs. McGinty, Mr. Farland's housekeeper, came in and said, "Mr. Tedder to see you, Sir. Urgent."

Mr. Tedder came in, but he did not come alone. With him came George Owdon and his friend.

"We ought to have gone to him right away," said Bill. "Didn't I tell you?"

"Shut up, Bill," whispered Tom.

George Owdon and his friend had just for one second looked taken aback when they saw Tom and Dorothea and Bill and Joe standing in the room. But only for a second. Then they stood quite at their ease, listening to Mr. Tedder.

Mr. Tedder had the air of the detective who has run his criminal to earth. "Open and shut," he said. "We know who done it now. Got all the proof we was needing. From information received Mr. Owdon and" (he looked in his note-book) "Mr. Strakey kep watch on the cruiser *Cachalot* last night where she were moored below the Ferry. At ten forty-three p.m. they hear footsteps approaching. At ten forty-seven. . . . "

The door opened again and Pete and Dick, very much out of breath, slipped into the room.

"I'm very sorry we're late," said Dick, and dodged past the others to the window, where he stood in the sunlight with both hands behind his back.

Pete looked from face to face, and stood by Bill and Joe. They looked at him, but could make nothing of the violent nodding of his head.

"At ten forty-seven," went on Mr. Tedder, "the witnesses, Mr. Owdon and Mr. Strakey, hear anchors bein' put on deck. At ten forty-eight they jump up out of their place of concealment and catch the guilty party apushing of the *Cachalot* off of the bank. He dodge 'em and they give chase and run him till he lock himself into his own boat. Not being official they couldn't take his name and address, but they catch him proper, and report to me, and sorry I am, young Bill, for your Dad's as decent a man as there is about this place."

Mr. Farland looked at Bill.

Bill spluttered. "But it was t'other way about. It was Pete and me catch them two pushing of her off."

"He said he was going to say that," said George Owdon.

"One minute," said Mr. Farland. "You see that chimney pot, Owdon. Would you mind just fitting your hand to that mark?"

"Certainly," said George Owdon. "It'll be a perfect fit, too, for I made it myself."

"How was that?" asked Mr. Farland.

"Ralph and I knew pretty well all along that it was these boys who had been playing the mischief with the boats, and one evening when there was a bit of a fog, we expected they'd be up to something, so I went to their boat and felt the chimney to see if they were at home, or if we had to go to see what they were doing elsewhere."

"And you found them not at home?" said Mr. Farland.

Dorothea almost groaned. Here was one of their best bits of evidence and it did not seem to be evidence at all. She looked at Dick, but Dick had his back to her. He was looking at something in his hands.

Mr. Farland turned to Bill. "About this affair last night. Did I hear you say you saw these boys pushing off the *Cachalot?*"

Bill waited a moment. "Not what you call see 'em," he said, "not till they chase me to the *Death and Glory* and we had to ope our door along with their emping buckets down our chimbley.

"So you admit that you were near the *Cachalot* at the time they say. Why did you run away if you were doing no harm?"

"Didn't want 'em to catch Pete," said Bill.

George Owdon looked at his friend. Mr. Farland looked at George.

"How was it you didn't see Pete if he was pushing off the *Cachalot* with Bill?"

"He wasn't," said George.

Mr. Farland turned to Pete. "Were you there?" he asked.

"Yes," said Pete.

"What did you do when Bill ran away?"

"Sit tight," said Pete. "That's what they tell me to do."

"Did you see those two pushing off the *Cachalot*?"

"Not to know 'em," said Pete. "But someone push her off. We do know that. We . . . . "

Mr. Farland turned again to George. "Dark night wasn't it?" he said. "You had torches, I suppose."

It was George's friend, Ralph, who answered. "With that great flare they made we couldn't help seeing him."

George, for the first time, stopped smiling and gave his friend an angry look.

"Flare?" said Mr. Farland. "They lit a flare just when they were pushing the boat off?"

"Not exactly," said George. "If Pete was there too, that perhaps explains it. We didn't understand it at the time. There was a white flare, and we saw Bill pushing the boat off. He must have see us at the same moment, for he bolted and we ran him to earth in their old boat."

"What was the flare like?" asked Mr. Farland.

"Like a photographic flashlight," said George.

"Did you light a flare?" Mr. Farland asked Pete.

"I did," said Bill.

"But how could you light a flare when you were pushing off the *Cachalot*?" asked Mr. Farland.

"I tell you I weren't pushing of her off."

"We saw you," said George Owdon.

"Why did you light the flare?" asked Mr. Farland in the same quiet, even tone that he had used all the time.

"We was taking a photograph," said Bill. "To catch whoever it were pushing the *Cachalot* adrift."

"They hadn't got a camera," said George.

Mr. Farland swung round.

"How do you know?"

Neither George nor his friend answered that question. There was a stir by the window. Dick was fumbling with something in his hands. "It's done," he said. "It'll go black if you keep it in the light. But I can print another." He dropped his printing frame on the floor, pushed his way to the table and laid a photograph in front of Mr. Farland. Then he tore his spectacles off and began wiping them, and then, with his spectacles in one hand, groped blindly over the carpet for the dropped frame.

"Come on," said George's friend.

"Not just yet," said Mr. Farland, without lifting his eyes from the photograph. "Just shut the door, will you, Tedder? This is very interesting."

Tom, Bill, Joe, Pete, and Dorothea strained their eyes to see what there was on that small piece of shiny paper lying on Mr. Farland's blotting pad. George and his friend were also doing their best to see from where they stood.

"A very remarkable likeness," said Mr. Farland. "What do you think, constable?"

Mr. Tedder looked at the photograph.

"Well, I'll be danged!" he said.

Mr. Farland thought for some minutes.

"The value of evidence," he said, "fluctuates with its context." The six detectives heard the words but had not the smallest idea what he meant. He went on. "This photograph will in any court of law" (here he looked gravely at George and his friend) "serve as proof that the boat that was cast off last night was cast off by George Owdon and . . . "

"Strakey," said Mr. Tedder.

"Strakey," said Mr. Farland. "But that is not all. It gives an entirely new value to a great deal of other evidence that, without it, I should have been justified in dismissing as unconvincing. Owdon, am I right in thinking that you ride a bicycle?"

George nodded.

"And it has Dunlop tyres." He laid Dick's drawing on the table in front of him. "This," he said, "concerns the Ranworth affair. It also has reference to the theft at Potter Heigham. One of our witnesses is prepared to swear that George Owdon was at Potter Heigham on the night that the theft was committed. Again the fact that Owdon and, er, Strakey did in fact cast off the boat last night and informed the constable that they had seen the boat cast off by someone else, who in fact was in the public interest recording by means of photography the truth of that case, suggests with other evidence that might otherwise be unmeaning that Owdon and Strakey were deliberately trying to manufacture evidence to bring innocent persons into disrepute and even into danger of punishment by law. Have you anything to say, Owdon?"

"It was his idea," said George Owdon.

"I knew nothing about it except what you told me," said Ralph Strakey.

Mr. Farland looked from one to the other of them and back again.

"Apart from the first lot of shackles," said Mr. Farland, "which you dropped down the chimney of these boys' boat on the day when you suffered, I think, some damage to your trousers . . ." (George stared at the scrap of grey flannel at which Mr. Farland's finger was pointing). "Apart, I say, from the first lot of shackles, and the second lot on which you left some green paint that had covered your hand when you felt their chimney to make sure that your victims were away, there are more than a gross that have not yet been recovered. Where are they?"

"Box in the tool-shed," said George. "Look here. I'm not going to stand any more of this. I'm going."

"I shall not keep you," said Mr. Farland. "But, before you go, let me tell you that I shall be calling on your uncle when I return from my office tonight. Between now and then I shall expect you to write an exact confession of all that you have done in this damnable, yes, damnable, plot to bring discredit on the innocent. As solicitor to the firm you robbed I shall have to decide whether or not I advise them to prosecute. My decision will depend on the completeness of the document that you will have ready for me before I see your uncle. It had better be signed by your accomplice as well as by yourself. You can go."

George Owdon and Ralph Strakey left the room without a word. As Joe said afterwards, "If they'd have had tails they'd have tripped on 'em."

Dorothea gasped. It was as if she had not breathed for the last five minutes. Tom had turned very red. Dick was again blindly rubbing at his spectacles. Bill and Joe were staring at Mr. Farland as if they saw him for the first time. Pete found he had tears in his eyes. He blinked angrily. "Might have been us," he said. "Only we didn't do it."

Police Constable Tedder cleared his throat.

"I'm sorry I ever thought it," he said. "Ought to have knowed different I ought. If anybody say a word against you young chaps again I'll know what to say to 'em. My garden's open to you day or night, for worrams, so you leave they chrysanthemums alone."

Mr. Farland was smiling now. He said, "They'll forgive you, Tedder. It was a wicked plot and a clever plot, and many people have been taken in by it beside you. It wouldn't be a bad thing if the truth got about, though as a solicitor I suppose I ought not to say so."

"I'll tell 'em at the Post Office," said Mr. Tedder. "I'll tell 'em at the store. I'll be up the village, come opening time. Chaps'll be rare pleased to hear that bit of news."

"And I'm late for my office," said Mr. Farland. "Well, I know some others who'll be pleased. I'll be writing to my daughters tonight. And, if I may, I should like to congratulate the detectives. . . . " He looked to see that Mr. Tedder had already gone. "I'm ashamed to think that if you had left it to the law things might have gone badly with you."

The door opened, and Mrs. McGinty came

in and said, "There's a gentleman to see you, Sir, urgent. . . . " but she had not got more than three words out of her mouth before the owner of the *Cachalot* was in the room beside her.

"They tell me these boys are accused of casting off my boat," he said. "I've come to say I lent her to them and they're free to cast her off if they want and not get into trouble about it."

"They're not in trouble," said Mr. Farland.

"It's all right," said Dorothea. "Everything worked beautifully. They fell into the trap, but if the photograph hadn't come out we might have been done at the last minute. Scotland Yard's won in the end. I knew it would."

Mr. Farland picked up the photograph and passed it to his latest visitor. Then he saw the little pile of money on the table.

"Six and eightpence," he said, "is a solicitor's fee. You are quite right." He bowed to Dorothea. "But, in this case, as I told you, I could hardly be solicitor for the accused. I seem, indeed, to have been acting as judge. And the one thing you mustn't do in a court of law is to try to bribe the judge. You had better put this money away before I see it. . . . "

"Your boat's all right," said Joe to the owner of the *Cachalot*. "They push her off but they never see she were anchored. She lie there beautiful, just off the bank. We'll put you aboard if you'll come along to the *Death and Glory*."

"I shall be getting the sack from my partners if I don't leave you," said Mr. Farland.

"Thanks a million times," said Dorothea.

There was a chorus of thanks from the others.

Dorothea collected the clues and put them back in her suitcase.

"What are you going to do with them?" asked Mr. Farland.

"Taking them back to Scotland Yard."

"I may have to ask you for them again," said Mr. Farland. "But I think not. I fancy they won't be needed."

"Wake up, Bill," said Joe. "You take t'other end of our chimbley."

"Gosh, young Pete," said Bill. "You give us a fright."

They all went out together into sunshine that seemed extraordinarily friendly. A light breeze was stirring the river and they could see the water sparkling through the trees.

"Come on," said Tom. "Let's all go sailing."

THE END

WHAT HAPPENED TO
THE FISH

WHAT HAPPENED TO THE FISH

Months later, when the worst of the winter was over, the Death and Glories, once more at peace with all the world, were lying at Horning staithe. It was a Saturday morning. They had come aboard after school the night before. Smoke was drifting from their chimney in the crisp air of late February, when Pete, on the look out, saw the *Cachalot* coming up the river, and called the others to come out.

"That fare to be a coffin he got on deck," said Pete.

"Never," said Bill.

It certainly looked like it, a long, narrow packing-case, roped down between the rails along the *Cachalot*'s cabin-top.

The *Cachalot* came close alongside.

"Ahoy, you," called her owner. "Busy?"

"Not all that," said Joe.

"Hop aboard. I'll bring you back in the afternoon. I'm just taking your fish to the Roaring Donkey, and you chaps ought to be there."

"Tell you that were a coffin," said Pete.

In two minutes they were aboard and the *Cachalot* had swung round and was on her way.

"Lay at Thurne Mouth last night," said the fisherman of the *Cachalot*, "but I didn't want to hand over without you."

"What about Tom?" said Joe.

"Take him, too, if you like," said the fisherman, "and that girl and the other boy, the one with the glasses."

"They ain't here," said Bill. "Won't be till Easter. But we can get Tom."

They were unlucky. The *Cachalot* stopped by Dr. Dudgeon's lawn only for them to learn that Tom was out. "Never mind," said the fisherman. "He can bicycle over any time. The fish'll still be there. . . . By the way," he asked, as they started off again, "what happened to the tiger who was taken in by the bleating of the kid?"

The Death and Glories looked gravely at each other.

"Them two," said Joe, "George Owdon and that other. They go away next morning and we never seen 'em since."

There is no need to describe their run down the Bure and up the Thurne. On that cold February morning, they took turns in steering the *Cachalot* and in going into her cabin to sit by the stove and get the tingle out of their ears and noses.

They passed under the bridges at Potter Heigham, getting friendly waves from a couple of Sonning's workmen as they passed. Bob Curten, once again a full member of the Coot Club, waved from the road bridge and they waved back. They tied up at the mouth of the dyke leading to the Roaring Donkey.

The long packing case was taken off the top of the cabin and the great fish, once again, was carried to the little inn.

A small crowd was waiting.

"Here you are," said the landlord, coming out

to meet them. "I tell a few chaps you was coming. I got that mantelshelf all ready."

The landlord's wife called the Death and Glories to come into her kitchen and have a cup of hot tea. Perishing they must be, she thought. They went in with her, leaving the landlord and half a dozen eager fishermen busy round the packing case. Ten minutes later they heard the voice of the owner of the *Cachalot* calling them. They ran out of the kitchen into the inn parlour. At the door they pulled up short.

The room was full of people. Just opposite the door was a wide brick fireplace and over this on the wide mantelshelf was a glass case, the biggest they had ever seen. In the case was the world's whopper, swimming against a pale blue background among green weeds that looked as if they were alive.

"Gee whizz!" said Joe.

"I've been fishing sixty-seven years," said an old man with a white beard, "and I've never caught a fish like that."

"Talk about heathen worshippers," said the landlord cheerfully, looking at the admiring crowd. "No, I don't care who caught it, nor yet what I pay. They'll come from all over England to the Roaring Donkey to take a look at that there old fish."

"Go on," said the owner of the *Cachalot*. "Go on and read what's on the case."

The three boys went nearer. Men, staring at the fish, made room for them. On the glass front of the case, in gold letters, they read the weight of the pike, the date when it was caught and . . .

Pete was reading aloud and suddenly choked. . . .
"Pike . . . 30½ pounds. . . . Caught by . . . why,
it's us." There in gold letters were their own three
names.

The old fisherman with the white beard turned
from looking at the pike to look at the Death and
Glories.

"Are you the boys who caught that fish?"
he asked.

"We didn't exactly. . . . " began Joe.

"Poor lads," said the old man. "Poor lads. . . .
So young and with nothing left to live for."

"Let's go and catch another," said Pete.

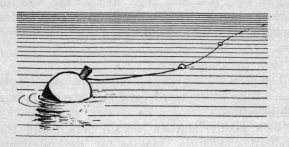

THE
ARTHUR RANSOME
SOCIETY

The Arthur Ransome Society was formed in June 1990 with the aim of celebrating his life and his books, and to encourage both children and adults to take part in adventurous pursuits – especially climbing, sailing and fishing. It also seeks to sponsor research, to spread his ideas in the wider community and to bring together all those who share the values and the spirit that he fostered in all his storytelling.

The Society is based at the Abbot Hall Museum of Lakeland Life and Industry in Kendal, where there is a special room set aside for Ransome: his desk, his favourite books and some of his personal possessions. There are also close links with the Windermere Steamboat Museum at Bowness, where the original *Amazon* has been restored and kept, together with the *Esperance*, thought to be the vessel on which Ransome based Captain Flint's houseboat. The Society keeps in touch with its members through a journal called *Mixed Moss*.

Regional branches of the Society have been formed by members in various parts of the country – Scotland, the Lake District, East Anglia, the Midlands, the South Coast among them – and contacts are maintained with overseas groups such as the Arthur Ransome Club of Japan. Membership fees are modest, and fall into three groups – for those under 18, for single adults, and for whole families. If you are interested in knowing more about the Society, or would like to join it, please write for a membership leaflet to The Secretary, The Arthur Ransome Society, The Abbot Hall Gallery, Kendal, Cumbria LA9 5AL.

SWALLOWS·AND·AMAZONS·FOR·EVER!

Join the RED FOX Reader's Club

The Red Fox Reader's Club is for readers of all ages. All you have to do is ask your local bookseller or librarian for a Red Fox Reader's Club card. As an official Red Fox Reader you only have to borrow or buy eight Red Fox books in order to qualify for your own Red Fox Reader's Clubpack – full of exciting surprises! If you have any difficulty obtaining a Red Fox Reader's Club card please write to: Random House Children's Books Marketing Department, 20 Vauxhall Bridge Road, London SW1V 2SA.

Other great reads *from* **Red Fox**

Further Red Fox titles that you might enjoy reading are listed on the following pages. They are available in bookshops or they can be ordered directly from us.

If you would like to order books, please send this form and the money due to:

ARROW BOOKS, BOOKSERVICE BY POST, PO BOX 29, DOUGLAS, ISLE OF MAN, BRITISH ISLES. Please enclose a cheque or postal order made out to Arrow Books Ltd for the amount due, plus 75p per book for postage and packing to a maximum of £7.50, both for orders within the UK. For customers outside the UK, please allow £1.00 per book.

NAME_____

ADDRESS_____

_____

Please print clearly.

Whilst every effort is made to keep prices low, it is sometimes necessary to increase cover prices at short notice. If you are ordering books by post, to save delay it is advisable to phone to confirm the correct price. The number to ring is THE SALES DEPARTMENT 071 (if outside London) 973 9700.

Other great reads *from Red Fox*

Enter the gripping world of the REDWALL series

A bestselling series based around Redwall Abbey, the home of a community of peace-loving mice. The first book, REDWALL, was nominated for the Carnegie Award.

REDWALL   Brian Jacques

As the mice of Redwall Abbey prepare for a feast, Cluny, the evil one-eyed rat, prepares for battle!

0 09 951200 9   £4.50

MOSSFLOWER   Brian Jacques

The gripping tale of how Redwall Abbey was established through the bravery of the legendary mouse Martin.

0 09 955400 3   £4.50

MATTIMEO   Brian Jacques

Slagar the fox is intent on revenge and plans to bring death and destruction to Redwall, particularly Matthias mouse.

0 09 967540 4   £4.50

MARIEL OF REDWALL   Brian Jacques

The start of the second Redwall trilogy with the adventures of a young mousemaid, Mariel.

0 09 992960 0   £4.50

SALAMANDASTRON   Brian Jacques

Redwall is in trouble! Feragho the Assassin is attacking the fortress of Salamandastron and Dryditch Fever approaches . . .

0 09 914361 5   £4.50

MARTIN THE WARRIOR   Brian Jacques

Badrang the tyrant stoat, has forced captive slaves to build his fortress, but a young mouse, Martin, plots a daring escape.

0 09 928171 6   £4.50

Other great reads from **Red Fox**

Dive into action with Willard Price!

Willard Price is one of the most popular children's authors, with his own style of fast-paced excitement and adventure. His fourteen stories about the two boys Hal and Roger Hunt in their zoo quests for wild animals all contain an enormous amount of fascinating detail, and take the reader all over the world, from one exciting location to the next!

Amazon Adventure
ISBN 0 09 918221 1   £3.50

Underwater Adventure
ISBN 0 09 918231 9   £3.50

Volcano Adventure
ISBN 0 09 918241 6   £3.50

South Sea Adventure
ISBN 0 09 918251 3   £3.50

Arctic Adventure
ISBN 0 09 918321 8   £3.50

Elephant Adventure
ISBN 0 09 918331 5   £3.50

Safari Adventure
ISBN 0 09 918341 2   £3.50

Gorilla Adventure
ISBN 0 09 918351 X   £3.50

Lion Adventure
ISBN 0 09 918361 7   £3.50

African Adventure
ISBN 0 09 918371 4   £3.50

Diving Adventure
ISBN 0 09 918461 3   £3.50

Whale Adventure
ISBN 0 09 918471 0   £3.50

Cannibal Adventure
ISBN 0 09 918481 8   £3.50

Tiger Adventure
ISBN 0 09 918491 5   £3.50

Other great reads 🦊 *from* **Red Fox**

Chocks Away with Biggles!

Squadron-Leader James Bigglesworth – better known to his fans as Biggles – has been thrilling millions of readers all over the world with all his amazing adventures for many years. Now Red Fox are proud to have reissued a collection of some of Captain W. E. Johns' most exciting and fast-paced stories about the flying Ace, in brand-new editions, guaranteed to entertain young and old readers alike.

BIGGLES LEARNS TO FLY
ISBN 0 09 999740 1   £3.50

BIGGLES FLIES EAST
ISBN 0 09 993780 8   £3.50

BIGGLES AND THE RESCUE FLIGHT
ISBN 0 09 993860 X   £3.50

BIGGLES OF THE FIGHTER SQUADRON
ISBN 0 09 993870 7   £3.50

BIGGLES & CO.
ISBN 0 09 993800 6   £3.50

BIGGLES IN SPAIN
ISBN 0 09 913441 1   £3.50

BIGGLES DEFIES THE SWASTIKA
ISBN 0 09 993790 5   £3.50

BIGGLES IN THE ORIENT
ISBN 0 09 913461 6   £3.50

BIGGLES DEFENDS THE DESERT
ISBN 0 09 993840 5   £3.50

BIGGLES FAILS TO RETURN
ISBN 0 09 993850 2   £3.50

Other great reads from **Red Fox**

Share the magic of The Magician's House by William Corlett

There is magic in the air from the first moment the three Constant children, William, Mary and Alice arrive at their uncle's house in the Golden Valley. But it's when they meet the Magician, William Tyler, and hear of the Great Task he has for them that the adventures really begin.

THE STEPS UP THE CHIMNEY

Evil threatens Golden House in its hour of need – and the Magician's animals come to the children's aid – but travelling with a fox brings its own dangers.

ISBN 0 09 985370 1   £2.99

THE DOOR IN THE TREE

William, Mary and Alice find a cruel and vicious sport threatening the peace of Golden Valley on their return to this magical place.

ISBN 0 09 997390 1   £2.99

THE TUNNEL BEHIND THE WATERFALL

Evil creatures mass against the children as they attempt to master time travel.

ISBN 0 09 997910 1   £2.99

THE BRIDGE IN THE CLOUDS

With the Magician seriously ill, it's up to the three children to complete the Great Task alone.

ISBN 0 09 918301 9   £2.99